SKIPJACK MADDOX 1859

THE CREEKSIDE SAGAS

SKIPJACK MADDOX 1859

ED MIDDLETON

Published by Skipjack Holdings LLC

ISBN: 978-1-7330258-2-9

Also by Ed Middleton
Mr. Maddox 1953
Riverboat Bill 1961

Dedicated to Jason and Ava Jane

"Now faith is the substance of things hoped for,
the evidence of things not seen."

HEBREWS 11:1

"When we look back to a moment in the past, it is hard not to read
into it nearly everything that we know is to come after it. We can't
help but see it as something carrying along with itself a future that
we already know about, an awareness that gives us a perspective very
different from that of the participants in that past moment."

WILFRED M. MCCLAY,
THE LAND OF HOPE: AN INVITATION TO THE GREAT AMERICAN STORY

THE CREEKSIDE SAGAS

SKIPJACK MADDOX 1859

CONTENTS

CHAPTER 1

THE FAMILY BUSINESS

Skipjack sat behind his bar eating radishes, greens, corn bread, and beef. He was dreaming between bites about things he wouldn't have spoken out loud. What these visions meant, he didn't know. He was grinding his molars when three men burst through the door. With his hand gently draped on his pistol, he kept chewing and looked them over. Rough, but they weren't river men. He could see that right off.

"You seen 'em? The runaways?"

The man who asked this was swarthy and obviously full of drink. The other two, huddled behind, grinned. All three had their hands inside their coats. Skipjack picked up a chunk of corn bread and stuffed it in his mouth. Didn't respond in any way.

"Have you seen them?"

"Explain yourself."

"You seen the runaways we're after?"

"Them ones that just had steak and potatoes before walking on water? No, I ain't seen 'em. What you boys doing here? Run out of leads?"

"Maddox," the fat one said, "we know they come this way, at least far as the creek and it ain't the first time."

"You accusing me of stealing?"

"No, sir, I just want to know what you know."

"Awful polite, after barging in, ain't you? What I know is this. I run a business here. Nothing gets past me. I'm here. Who you are, I don't know. During open hours, we got food. I got mail for boats going by and I'm eating supper after a long day. Been up since early and I'm tired. What I've seen is nothing compared to you. Get lost."

"Man who hired us don't like jokers."

Skipjack snuffed the candle between his forefinger and thumb. The room fell dark. He cocked his pistol.

"Gentlemen, you got the moon at your back. Follow it home."

They scuffled out. Skipjack, in a loud voice, reminded them that the law didn't shine on trespassers. Then he bolted the door, relit his cigar stub, and threw his scraps into the slop pail he kept for his dog. He had lost his appetite for food and apparently, the dog had lost her appetite for being a watchdog. Skipjack hadn't heard a peep before the scum had washed in.

The moon was full and clear, no ground-hugging fog, so through the window he could see down the lane a good way, where the three men joined a fourth with two leashed dogs. Then they split. Two started into the corn and two toward the creek. Skipjack loaded his ten-gauge, stuck a pistol into his belt, indulged a taste of whiskey, stepped outside, and crunched through river gravel, making as much noise as possible. He was boiling mad, but proud of his nerves, cool as a mountain stream. He even whispered that out loud before he crouched and started stalking.

The men, so involved with dogs—probably not worth a damn— wouldn't have heard him coming if he had been calling hogs. He hesitated exactly where they had branched off and without trying at all, heard them thrashing through corn on the one side and brush and weeds on the other. At first, he only said hello, but that got no response, so then he said, "Hey there," and when that didn't suffice, he fired the ten-gauge into the air. The full moon seemed unaffected. Seemed like everything else took note, even Gracie, his mixed breed mutt, ran up wagging her tail, proud of the rabbit dangling from her mouth. She seemed to be asking for directions. Skipjack reloaded and stroked the dog's head. The world was suddenly quiet. The moon continued to scoot through rolling clouds plump with moist air from the south. He smelled rain and smiled, stroked his dog, who was mouthing her kill.

"Get the hell out of my corn or I'll blast your ass sure as shootin."

He knew they would. They had nothing in the game: trash, busted-down dirt squatters, scratching out whatever for whoever would pay a penny. They cared as much for the man that they were working for as another who might pay them to burn the same man's barn down. They were broken and desperate.

None of the men looked familiar, but banks were foreclosing, and big farms were gobbling up smaller. These men might have owned land only a few months before; made you want to spit or cry. Skipjack unbuckled his belt, slipped it around Gracie's neck, and led her back to the tavern. The whole time she resisted, afraid her master would claim the rabbit.

Before opening the door, Skipjack scanned the corn, which was all he could see in the moonlight, but he knew the vegetable patch, not small either, was there. Next to it ran the creek full of catfish and bass. He took a deep breath and felt rich inside. The still had made money, lots of it, but now this tavern suited him just fine. His wife was young and healthy, thank God, for their boy, Billy, was a handful. He had to admit, though he seldom dwelled on it, that Marcie and Billy were his life's blood.

It amazed him she had said yes those years ago. Skipjack still could not believe it and out of superstition dismissed that thought. He looked up the hill, saw light flickering in a window of their solid frame house only a half mile away, and could feel steady warmth from where he stood. Jessie, his mule, snorted impatiently in the small stall she often shared with Ducky.

Inside, he relit the candle and looked at his old pocket watch. It was exactly four past nine. He would have sworn it was midnight. He smiled at his watch. Everything belonged to somebody, even most folks' time.

He shook his head with gratitude. How Brawl's boy had dragged the child out of the river, he would never know. All he knew was that he and Marcie hadn't had another picnic on the banks of the Ohio River until Billy could swim like a bluegill. Brawl's boy had wanted nothing but had seemed pleased with a dollar and the promise of inheriting a pocket watch. It was a miracle that the stripling had found Billy beneath the roiling springtime torrent. There was no way to repay him adequately, so the dollar and promise of the watch hadn't seemed out of place. He and Marcie would have given the world.

He sat back down. This time he was fortified with his pistol, a shotgun, and the thought of Marcie. He glanced at his watch once again and noticed the moon was going undercover. He fired up what was left of his cigar.

But this time, Gracie barked and growled. Skipjack had to laugh. The back door meant one thing tonight. He took his handgun just in case. Didn't sound like knocking as much as scratching, but he opened the door wide anyway. There was Aleeta in her servant's livery, white collar and apron contrasting with a black starched dress. Her face was pale as moonlight; behind her in the bushes were some folks he could not clearly see.

"The moon is dark as you said it should be," she whispered.

"How many?"

"I heard three, but there are five; one only an infant."

"How long you been on this property?"

"No sooner than the moon went in. Maybe ten minutes at the most."

"What they got for me?"

Aleeta handed up a pouch. Skipjack motioned her inside. At the bar, she accepted a shot of whisky and poured it down neat. He held the pouch like he was weighing it. His hand beside hers on the bar was dark and strong; hers was pale and sleek.

"Catchers following?"

"These ones been hidden two days in our place's smokehouse until minutes ago. No one knows we're here, I'm near to God certain."

Skipjack poured the money out and counted it, then laughed. "That's all they had."

"Seems that's your story over and over."

"Times are tough for all and sundry," she said defiantly.

"You win, Aleeta," Skipjack said as he scooped the money back into the pouch.

"You'll do it then?"

"Give me an hour. I need to poke around. I've had visitors tonight. If you need to keep the baby quiet, help yourself to some whiskey."

Aleeta grabbed his hand and kissed it. Skipjack grabbed his shotgun and, with Gracie, walked the property. When he got back, he lit a lamp in the tavern and turned it down low. Within minutes, they were mid-stream. The river was low and less than a quarter mile wide. The moon cooperated and stayed hidden. No one spoke. The baby threw up on her mother's shoulder. Skipjack said, "Use this," and stuck the money pouch into the woman's hand. The skiff scraped the Indiana shore. A man on the hillside waved a dim lantern.

"Go now!"

The passengers scrambled up the bank. Skipjack rowed about a quarter mile upstream, then allowed the lazy current to slosh him home. When he tied up at the dock, he saw Miss Aleeta fishing off his flatboat. That surprised him a bit.

"What you caught?"

"Nothing, but you're mad about money."

"No, not worth a fidget," he said. "There are dogs out. You better go."

"Mr. Maddox, please, don't forget that I am white and almost free, sir."

"That's a lot of details for a tired man, Miss Aleeta. Goodnight."

Skipjack didn't even harness the mule, just climbed aboard. Gracie and Ducky followed.

Skipjack tossed oats into the feed bin, drew out his knife, and carved five more notches into the locust post beside the door of the small stable that adjoined his house. Quite a few notches now.

Skipjack sponged off in the kitchen. Marcie was already in bed. He needed a bath but was dog tired and thanked God for soap and a wash bowl. He rinsed out his mouth with the stuff she had bought him, then climbed up to the bedroom and slipped beneath the blankets. He draped his arm over her waist and as she sighed and moved back into him, gently held her stomach and breast. Then sleep walked in and just before he went under completely, he saw faces, broken into moonlit bits and pieces, like seeing up close in midnight shadows will do. He wished his passengers well. Next thing he heard was the rooster.

Since every dead man he had ever known had made an appearance, he awakened glad that dreams were dreams; they could have spooked him if he had thought otherwise. Skipjack smelled bacon and coffee as he slipped into his same old clothes. Why such a pretty woman would put up with him, he would never know.

He walked into the spacious kitchen and sure knew why he put up with her. He hugged her before she had even turned around. When she did turn around, he kissed her tenderly, knowing how scratchy his old beard must be, but she kissed him back.

"Honey, where's Billy?" he asked.

"Trying to catch you a catfish for breakfast. He's trying a dough ball this morning."

"Maybe that's what I should've baited with yesterday. Didn't pull anything out last night. "Some nights are like that. All the trotlines empty."

"You were late."

"Nothing to be done about it. Be home regular tonight—I sure hope so."

Skipjack drank coffee and let morning clear his mind.

He remembered the night they met. She had been with another man, a dealer in horses. Skipjack hadn't thought one way or the other about him but recalled thinking she was fine. Something about her sparkled his mind. There had been no longing he could remember, but then a year later, when they were reintroduced, something moved him.

She was a little plump, but he didn't care. There was something about her. Turned out she was pregnant. He couldn't believe it himself when he asked her to marry him. The thought made him smile. Now there was Marcie right in front of him. No way to figure. No way he knew anyhow. Could talk about anything, but often didn't. He figured they knew each other better than anybody ever, yet she was full of surprises and, of course, there were things she should never know about him, but not for lack of trust.

In the morning light, his eyes rolled at the thought of that word. He didn't even know what something so huge meant and so the notion slid off into dust motes and hid. Couldn't tell her everything, he knew that much. Maybe he didn't want to frighten her or maybe he was afraid to look closely at what he was doing. He could not explain half the stuff he did. Like the night before. Why trouble her? There is no big deal in carrying a few folks across the river when it ain't running fast. That's the way he approached it. Just do it. Something says go, you go. Something says stay, you stay. How could you explain that?

"Thought you might want some oats and molasses," she said, as she placed a bowl in front of him.

He nodded and thanked her. If you tried, where would you begin? He was drifting as his spoon slipped into the oats. There was no way to justify the risk, not even to himself. That's why he very seldom took money and also why—besides haste and dark—he almost never remembered the crossing, not even faces.

Skipjack took a big sip of coffee, and thanked Marcie for the jowl bacon and fried eggs she set before him. What could he say? Most folks, if they don't earn and pay their way, don't appreciate anything. Or if they pay too little, they think they got away with something.

This was a different critter altogether. How could you explain slavery? He bit into his bacon.

"You're quiet this morning," Marcie said as she sat down.

"You say Billy's fishing?"

She answered in the affirmative, but he was already distracted, wondering how long he could keep this up and if there was any point in it at all. Where would these folks end up? Were they better off?

"Honey, are you all right?"

"Not quite awake yet, but everything's fine," he replied.

She didn't believe it, but then Billy ran up with the smallest bluegill to ever bite a hook. She fried the morsel in the bacon grease and everyone had a tiny piece. There was a bigger one, of course, that got away. Skipjack made a big deal over his portion and that had pleased everyone.

Skipjack rode to the tavern on Jessie's swaying back. He was grateful there was work to do, and lots of it, but his mind needed rest. The lane he was on crossed the narrowest points of two large farms, and Jessie had made this trip back and forth for years; Skipjack's mind was free to wander.

He had a hard time but tried to love the boy. Skipjack supposed it was because he loved the mother so. He had never been close to many people and had tried to be man of the house when his own father had died suddenly of a summer fever. Skipjack remembered all the wet towels they had wrapped the man in. His mother was carried off a few years later. Some of the churchwomen had been there and all he could recall of that was fussing and worrying about her soul. He was only fifteen when she had passed, but old enough to hold his brother's hand and hug his sister, too. Soon after, his sister had run off with some traveling preacher. Brother had stuck around awhile but had never amounted to much.

Skipjack loved Billy he supposed, but the boy reminded him of Brother, a sweet kid, but almost hollow, like some vital part was missing. Marcie saw the child as a gift from God. Skipjack saw him differently, a gift of raw human nature. All he had ever got out of Marcie was that the attack had happened on her return trip from the mill; she was knocked silly and brutally taken in the back of a wagon by someone she never even saw.

Skipjack's brother, Timothy, had helped some with farm chores and with the still, but about the time Skipjack started hand holding with Marcie, he came to notice Timothy was slipping away. He had always been a talker and a big dreamer, then one day he was gone. Last Skipjack had heard, his brother was a dealer on riverboats. Every time Skipjack looked at Billy, he saw Timothy; couldn't help it to save his soul.

When Skipjack saw Brawl Thurston coming his way hauling lumber, he was glad for the change of thought. He yielded, and Jessie stepped off the road out of the way, even though Brawl was a black man. Brawl was free, and as the morning sun lit his face, he came out with a howdy-do that seemed to come from somewhere special, a place you might want to end up. A free man. Bought his own freedom and now owned a couple slaves, too. He stood in his wagon straight and proud. The boys who were steadying his load looked serious. They weren't much older than Billy. Skipjack waved and smiled top of the morning.

"Mr. Maddox, good morning, sir, and thank you."

Skipjack touched the brim of his hat. Brawl had dignity. Even his boys looked proud. They were apprentice carpenters and boat builders, learning trades against all odds.

The rhythm of the mule's pace some days might have lulled his mood and calmed him, but this day it did not. Skipjack was fouled by the notion that Billy was somehow beyond his reach and his mother's, too. He could see something in the eyes of the black men that he had passed that he couldn't see in Billy's eyes, as hard as he might try.

When they arrived at the tavern, Jessie walked back to her stall, comfortable as always. Skipjack thought about the poster he had seen nailed to a double-trunked pin oak: A. Lincoln vs. Stephen Douglas. Then right above it, the handbill about a reward for three slaves who had been stolen or had run away.

Andy walked over to the stable with a bucket of water and Jessie snorted at him. He was a welcome sight this morning, but little more than two years back, Skipjack had thought he was close to stupid. Skipjack had bought him from Brawl, who had allowed that he was no good at boat building but might be all right for simple stuff like splitting wood or cleaning up. Brawl had sold Andy cheap, and at first, Skipjack was suspicious, but after a while, began to notice that Andy was forever appearing with whatever was needed.

Skipjack thanked him. Andy nodded. Skipjack strolled into his tavern and it smelled clean. That was Andy's work, too. He had bought him for a song. It would be hard to let him go, but a deal was a deal. Three years, that was all. Skipjack had worked Andy's ass off.

The coffee was already brewed. Skipjack poured himself a mug and lit a cigar. Brawl drove a hard bargain: rent not ownership, that's all it was. Andy was worth it; Brawl hadn't been wrong. But no matter how hard he tried, Skipjack could never forget, no matter how close they seemed, that the upper hand was his and that troubled him somehow.

The whole damn deal stunk. Maybe he had more money than Brawl and maybe Brawl had more laborers than he did from time to time, but the whole damn thing made him queasy. Brawl had looked at him across the bar and his eyes hadn't flickered, when he called out his price and said three years.

Andy would be free in a short while, but it still left a bad taste. Then he thought of Aleeta, the white woman—indentured is what they called it. She wouldn't be free for about five more years. The labor situation was flat out confusing.

He walked out to the pig lot, but Andy had beaten him. Fine hogs and shoats well fed. Then there was Andy, over-seeing the vegetable patch, which covered at least three acres. Nobody was slouching, everybody weeding or hoeing, or picking. Must have been near fifteen people, most of them kids, but all working. Skipjack didn't quite know how Andy did it, but he knew it wasn't only the small money he gave him per month. Andy waved. Skipjack raised his hand.

Skipjack believed in bonuses. He didn't have to pay Andy anything, but he did it to keep him loyal. A lot of the slaves around this part of Kentucky worked for their owner most hours but were allowed time to work a vegetable patch or even hire out. In Brawl's case about fifteen years back, he managed to build wagons and boats on the side. Brawl had been smart. The more his owner pressed him for a larger share of the proceeds, the slower he worked. The owner caught on quick and backed off, but what he didn't know was that Brawl was training kids in basic carpentry and had farmed them out a few hours a day. Brawl could build anything and was a great teacher, and he ended up making enough to buy his whole family. Brawl had built Skipjack's skiff and his flatboat. His apprentices were forever patching things at the tavern and then the river men would see them working and hire them to fix things while they were laid up waiting for their turn to unload downriver just above the falls. Skipjack had benefited as well and had provisioned the tavern with fine wines from New Orleans, exotic cigars, and all kinds of stuff in trade that no one would expect to find in such a place.

It was a crazy set-up that somehow worked. Sometimes he paid the river men in cash, sometimes with brandy. Once he traded a brace of roasted ducks for a bolt of fine satin that had pleased Marcie beyond his hopes. His chief cook, Mary Frances, had roasted the birds and they had smelled so good he felt like asking for two bolts, but did not. He had traded whiskey for his two favorite weapons, his Colt and his New Haven Arms .44 Rimfire. Whiskey was always handy for trade. River men could never get enough.

Mary Frances was a large-boned white woman, good with everybody. Bigger than life with a heart as stout as she was.

She walked to work every day, seven days a week. She lived in a small shack with her husband, who had been injured in a logging accident. He was unable to do much more than get out of bed. She had two young kids, none too bright, yet never once had Skipjack heard her complain. She would cuss, but only for effect at appropriate times. Skipjack didn't have to mess with the menu, just asked her what it was and licked his chops.

"What you cooking?" he asked as he stepped into the kitchen.

"Rabbit and chicken stew. For those who want 'em, chicken pieces and pork chops. Got corn bread and greens, too."

"Ain't you the rascal?"

"Not hardly," she said, patting her hip with her knife.

"Take no chances, do you?"

"No pressing need, Skipjack."

Two men drank at the bar and Louis, the bartender, was polishing the bar top with a brick wrapped in a towel soaked with linseed oil. He asked the men drinking, politely, of course, to raise their glasses. As he passed through the bar, Skipjack raised his eyebrows. Louis allowed as how he should have done that the night before. The customers didn't seem worried, so Skipjack winked and slapped the bar. Louis cracked an egg into a shot glass and squeezed in a splash of whiskey, then set it down.

Skipjack nodded and looked out through the open window onto boat after boat moored against the shore. It was early yet. Lunchtime would be a belly buster. He swallowed the concoction in one gulp and tweaked an imaginary waxed mustache just like the real one that Louis wore. Louis smiled and went back to polishing. Skipjack wandered outside to the gallery and surveyed boats upstream and down. He looked at his watch. Nine fifteen. In an hour and a half, this place would be bustling.

Because of loading and unloading schedules downstream six miles in Louisville, a lot of these boats might be laid in for a day or three. It was boon time for Skipjack. Hell, he had a woman who did laundry, a doctor on call, food and drink, and sometimes music.

He walked down toward the water and some fellow walked up to him and slapped him on the back, thanked him for something or the other. Man was so drunk he was unintelligible, but that was not unusual, and didn't bother Skipjack at all.

He stood on the bank and listened to water hiss across pebbles and sand. The river was low. His crops were green, but rain was scarce upstream. Boats were still coming down, but slack water had started stacking them. Skipjack could smell rain in the air that would bust out the beans, squash, and okra, and maybe even open spaces for some new boats with more money to spend. Hell, they had no place to spend it on the river. They might as well spend it here. Better the tavern than downtown, where the prices got fancy and the girls did, too.

"What you thinking, old-timer?"

"Thinking money. What you thinking about?" Skipjack replied.

"Whiskey and the good thing. Hears you got both."

Skipjack winked and pointed.

INDEPENDENCE DAY

Two bands were scheduled for the Fourth, three days hence. One was a jug band. Black boys, except for the fellow who looked to be white, but you couldn't tell the way he played. Mainly they were a vocal group that tooted on jugs and one guy played mandolin. Amazing how they stirred people. Then later, a gang called Lost Creek Ramblers were going to kick up their heels. Both bands were big draws. Skipjack was praying the rain he felt coming would be gone by then.

Turned out to be a fine afternoon and evening, too. It had rained like hell on the third and had got cool enough for a fire, which was unusual, but then on the Fourth, normal returned, meaning scorching hot and so clammy close that everybody was dripping sweat standing around. There was a tent out on the riverbank with red, white, and blue bunting. One of the paddle wheelers had a calliope that shrilled and trilled.

All day long, people ate and drank. Not only boat people; people had arrived in wagons, buggies, and carriages, too. At dusk, the jug band started tooting and the air was filled with light-hearted music and the smell of hickory-smoked pork.

Marcie disliked dense tobacco smoke, so she and Skipjack were on the edge of the lawn seated at a table, ready for fun. After all, the food was good, the beer was fresh, whiskey was flowing, but somehow the crowd was cool toward the music. There seemed to be something in the air like an erratic electrical charge. The players coaxed melodic rhythm out of their jugs while the mandolin rang, and the whole outfit rivaled the calliope that had jangled and puffed all afternoon, but the crowd sagged on the edge of the pine plank dance floor, remote and uninvolved.

Marcie placed her hand on Skipjack's and he nodded, then walked up in front of the band, who kicked up a ruckus and hit a crescendo as he raised both hands and welcomed everybody. Skipjack felt like he had yelled into a cave that possessed a mocking echo. He glanced at Marcie and she kept nodding.

Something wasn't right. This same band had played five years straight. Most were slaves, but at least a couple were free. They were good boys who loved music and loved to make people smile. Something was askew, the crowd was spooked, and Skipjack was damned if he could see what it was. The band was tops and shined and played with clowning, good-natured mischief. Skipjack thought they looked free as birds, but most folks just stood, staring. Then suddenly a white man with crazed eyes jumped in front of the stage, stuck out his tongue, gyrated in some crazy way, and screamed, "Don't forget John Brown!"

The band kept playing. The ones not tooting jugs tried to smile, but their humor was dimmed when this other fellow rushed out of the crowd and screamed, "Wake up fools, lest monkeys take over." He was a big man whose eyes resembled those of a hog. Defiantly, he turned to the band, raised his fists, and demanded that they play "Dixie."

Skipjack jumped forward to confront the men, but then another came out of the crowd and laid him out flat. There was total mayhem after that, but of course, Skipjack didn't know; he was listening to bluebirds.

Only a few wanted to mix it up. Most were retreating. Marcie, moving toward her husband, glanced up and saw Andy and Brawl on the bandstand. She was elbowing forward when she saw one of the torches come down and then an enormous explosion launched a singe across her scalp. Over the creek, a puny blast and a faint scattering of stars.

Seemed like everything froze in the heat. Marcie looked up on the stage and Brawl towered like carved granite. Andy stooped, looked left and right, and both men leveled shotguns. The crowd quieted.

Mary Frances, with a butcher knife held high, raised Skipjack to wobbly feet. He looked around, jaw clenched tight. She stepped back and lowered her butcher knife to the level of her waist. Skipjack thanked her as graciously as possible, and people surrounding the stage chuckled.

"Ain't no point trying to explain how welcome you are if you want to be. I suppose you already know it; however, if you don't yet, I will tell you. You are as welcome as you will allow yourselves to be. We will not tolerate heckling, fighting, knifing, or clubbing," he said, rubbing his head. "You got a need for that, there is no place for you here."

"What them niggers doing armed?" some ragtag screamed out.

Skipjack pulled the Colt from his pocket and walked straight at the man who tried to blend back into the crowd, but the man didn't get far before a huge fellow hoisted him one-handed.

"Skipper, this the boy you stalking?"

Maddox grinned, seeing the levitated specter squirm, but then saw a knife blade slash. Both went down. The big man was cut good, bleeding out and whimpering. The skinny man was dead, neck broken. A crude knife glinted beside his empty hand. People awkwardly stepped back.

Before Maddox had time to think, Mary Frances threw a tablecloth over the dead man, and started wrapping the wounded man's shoulder with strips of apron. Moments later, she led him off to the kitchen.

Skipjack looked back to see Andy standing beside Brawl. He turned and eyeballed the folks who had stuck around and didn't sense trouble. What he saw was how few it had taken to trigger it. He raised both hands in the air and backed slowly. He climbed on the stage and continued.

"We got music, food, whiskey, and fireworks. You want that, you're in. Sure hope you stay."

The crowd was so quiet that when he snapped his fingers, everyone could hear. He looked over his shoulder and the Lost Creek Ramblers took the stage. Andy and Brawl moved to the flanks and Skipjack felt a little better when he saw some men, led by a constable, haul the dead man away. Folks parted as he was removed, wrapped in a blanket. Skipjack felt better still when he hugged his wife. The musicians started to play. The banjo and mandolin trilled his blood. When he looked into Marcie's eyes, he could have forgotten most anything. People started clapping. He couldn't be sure, but he thought she said that she loved him; since he wasn't certain, he said, "Me, too."

The rest of the night was uneventful, except for the rocket that exploded right over the bandstand and showered everyone with sparks. No one was burned—a few slightly singed—but the explosion had messed up a tasty breakdown. Before the fireworks, the Ramblers played "The Star-Spangled Banner" and just when their skinny little singer with the strong voice sang, "O'er the land of the free and the home of the brave," some lout screamed, "Play 'Dixie.'" The man then attempted the chorus, "Look away, look away . . .," but Mary Frances quickly escorted him off the premises.

There was fine music, dancing, and tomfoolery. Platters of good food were scarfed and much booze drunk. Two deckhands from rival boats got into a knife fight down by the river; neither was killed.

Could have been worse. The way things had started off, it all ended up better than Skipjack might have expected. The band closed with "Yankee Doodle."

———————

"Stuck a feather in his cap, called it macaroni," Skipjack garbled to bullfrogs as he and Marcie rolled home. Minutes before, in the tavern's kitchen after all the mess was cleared away, whiskey had been rationed out and tips paid. Then Marcie playfully grabbed him by the ear and steered him to the buggy, which Andy had hitched to Jessie. She believed in bonuses too, but knew that for every one he doled out, he took one as well. She was only considering his health, and besides, she didn't want to hear people were robbing him blind and then have to explain that it was his own self giving it away. She loved the man but had been through that a time or two before.

Marcie held the rifle across her lap. She sipped a brandy, her second of the night, and held the reins loosely as Jack began to sing. She rubbed his thigh until he got the message, which pleased her. His voice was as deep as a bullfrog's, but less melodic. He leaned into her and rested his head on her shoulder. The satchel of money was between their feet and a Colt .44 was in his hand.

She was the only one who called him Jack. Everyone else called him Skipjack, Skipper, or Maddox, but when they were first introduced, he said that he was Jackson Maddox and before the night was over, Jack was his name.

He was a light sleeper but was dozing now as the moon slid through clouds. The evening was balmy, but motion created a slight breeze. The chances of being waylaid were slim to none, at least not until the track crossed River Road and started into the wood. The path there was dark, but only for a minute or so. There were little shacks along the way that the help stayed in. Marcie wasn't worried but was mindful of her rifle and glad Jack was easy to awaken. Jessie broke wind as they crossed the road, then Jack snored. Marcie had to laugh. She thanked her lucky stars.

Maybe that was the secret. The preacher who married them had told her there was a price to be paid for everything. She had accepted his premise. Jack snored as they entered the woods. Tree frogs were chattering rain. This mysterious man whose head was on her shoulder would awaken before they hit the top of the rise. She knew that like money. She was awful glad she had listened to the preacher man.

Jessie needed no whip or guidance and it was a good thing, for the last grade was steep. She strained into it and just before the rise flattened, Jack sat straight, and an owl swooshed across. The thrust from the wings frightened Marcie, though it had happened twenty times before.

"What the hell?" Skipjack exclaimed.

Marcie laughed.

"Wide awake now, are you? Should have seen the bear."

"Aw, nothing out here but groundhogs an' rabbits."

"Show me one and I'll make you breakfast."

Skipjack chuckled.

"Must've dozed. Sorry, I ain't good company."

"I'm not complaining. It was such a peaceful ride."

"Turns out you were right not bringing Billy," Skipjack said.

"Bet he saw enough."

Skipjack put Jessie up, then as he walked back toward the house, passed the girl who had watched Billy.

"Could you see fireworks?" he asked.

"They streaked the whole valley but heard 'em mostly. The boy was scared."

"Thanks, Lacy, for watching Billy," he said, as he pressed some money into her hand.

"Miss Marcie already paid me, Mr. Skipjack."

"I knew you would say that. Thank you. It's a bonus."

"God bless you, sir," she replied.

"He does every day, but please keep it to yourself."

She nodded, and he turned away and walked to the back door. The lamp was still lit in the kitchen and Marcie was at the table. Skipjack was afraid he knew what was coming. He rubbed the knot on his head before he stepped in. He saw the look. She wanted to talk. He was tired and didn't, so walked in with a smile and headed straight for the whiskey. He raised his hand, prepared for a lecture, even before he poured. Marcie didn't say anything at all, which worried him. He sat down opposite her, expecting to hear about violence and riffraff. He was resigned but said nothing. He stared at his drink, then attempted to light a cigar. Finally, she spoke.

"Jack, we need to raise prices."

He had taken a swig of firewater and almost blew fire across the room.

"Raise prices, you say? God, yes, let's do that," he responded, trying to keep his relieved face straight. He had expected a homily about the evils of drink and half felt it was deserved.

"Five cents is too low for a drink, Jack, and you know it."

"Where's Billy?"

"Don't change the subject, Jackson Maddox, or I don't know what I'll do. You know Billy's safe or I wouldn't touch this. I do the books, in case you forget, and it ain't working. We're not losing, but you've got to raise prices. Down in Louisville some torch holes are getting fifteen cents. I guarantee nobody will balk at seven and for fancy, ten. We can't make it at five and I don't plan to lose, do you?" She smiled. He found himself nodding.

"Are you hearing me?"

"Yes, dear, but can we keep it simple?"

"Sure, with your permission, I'll tell Mary Frances tomorrow."

"Easy does it," he said as he raised himself. "Remember, I work the front line."

"Be aware, Jack Maddox, no matter what you do, I work the books."

He nodded and said, "Want to get cozy?"

"You want to agree or think?"

"Agree, I believe."

She grabbed his arm before the last syllable had breezed her ear. She smiled and nodded. Prices were going up.

Next morning after breakfast, she gave him the price list. He knew she was right and hugged her. Billy was still asleep, so she wasn't wearing a stitch. The kiss that followed tempted him to get out of hand. Marcie squirmed free and glowed as she said, "Now, Jack, don't be greedy." He pulled her to him, kissed her neck, and squeezed her ass.

"You're a funny one to be talking about greed, raising our prices by fifty percent across the board."

"Quit exaggerating. Barely raised beer at all. Green is charging too much for his whiskey, I'll tell you that. Maybe you should go back to making your own."

"Damn, you feel good," Skipjack whispered.

"Jack, you scoundrel, you didn't listen to a word, did you?"

"You bet your sweetness I did, sugar. Distracted, I surely am, but please don't blame me for that. I can do sums, thanks to my momma. I can figure this whiskey price going up, but I'll be darned if Green's ain't better and making the stuff is so damned much trouble. Selling him corn is easy. Waiting for whiskey's a bitch and guarding it's worse."

Marcie gave him a kiss to carry around all day, then she said, "Maybe we should have two grades. One easy on the purse and one a bit more civilized."

"Hell, Marcie, why beat a dead horse? We had both behind the bar for a bet; Green outsold three to one. Now why fight that? Sell the man corn, trade for whiskey."

"I never could stand the taste," she said.

Skipjack hugged her again before he walked out the door. Marcie was part Cherokee. He had learned never to argue whiskey. She liked it when she liked it and hated it when she didn't and that was that, end of subject. Skipjack hated to argue, especially when winning was never possible. She won every time and in some crazy way, he loved it. In some way he couldn't figure and seldom tried to, she kept him honest. Maybe it was the uncertainty, or was it certainty? He scratched his head on the way to his mule. She called out that she would try to come down for lunch. Jessie snorted as he turned and waved.

The mule's unhurried gait soothed him. Sunrays sparkled and streaked, spotting his rude avenue through tangles of locusts, wild cherry, maple, and oak. The ground here was loamy, rich, dark, and pitched downhill. The sun was still low and the air full of motes and charged with bird song. Cool for July with a slight breeze, faint but enough to relieve Skipjack from wiping his brow. Jessie stepped so carefully, avoiding buggy and wagon ruts, that one could have read the book of Luke in small print and not missed a word.

A woodpecker rattled the air and some bird no larger than his thumb swelled the morning with joy. What could he say but thanks? And in his own way, Skipjack said thanks. He did this most every morning. Sometimes in winter, he was somewhat gruff, but mostly not. How could he be? Who was he to be so lucky? He licked his lips and still tasted Marcie. He saw light dapple River Road ahead. What else could he say? Raising prices? The night before he feared she might want to shut the deal down. He rubbed the knot on his head. It wasn't all that big. Despite the dead man, he felt like a fish that slipped the hook. Jessie farted, pop-pop-pop, as if to warn everyone before they crossed River Road. She snorted in satisfaction after observing the road was as clear as the day ahead.

All she wore was a harness and lead strap. Jessie knew the way. Marcie said she might be down for lunch and that meant send Jessie home. When they got to the tavern, Skipjack gave Jessie a small bowl of oats with some beer, slapped her ass, and said, "Home." Jessie headed back to Marcie without any hesitation at all. Simple as pie.

STORM CLOUDS

He walked into the tavern and Mary Frances raised a forefinger to her lips and shook her head. Skipjack halfway knew what it meant already. He was right. He walked through the joint out to the gallery and there sat five women dressed black as starched crows, shoes like chunks of coal; some faces were bloated, others pinched. Lethargy left faces as soon as he walked into their midst. They were having tea.

"There he is," a pinched one chirped.

Mary Frances brought Skipjack his regular, a raw egg in a spot of whiskey. He poured it down.

"The devil's potion," Mary Frances said as she walked away.

"God bless you, each and every one," Skipjack said.

The women grimaced. Their minds were settled. His was not. They said nothing, so he didn't either. They eyeballed one another for quite a while. Mary Frances had time to ask when the bacon was coming. He shrugged. The eldest of the group rose to speak. She cleared her throat, but Skipjack spoke first.

"So, you don't like booze and you don't like the killing that comes with it either? If you believe I like it, you're mistaken. Speak your piece."

"You must shut this place," the lady said. "This instant. It must be done."

"Done, simple as pie. Please tell my employees they're out of a job. Better yet, you tell them they have a better one, ladies. Surely, you must have something better to offer, do you?"

"My nephew died here last night, killed at your hands," one of the ladies hissed.

"Why weren't you here to protect him from himself? I never raised a hand."

"A bad man. You are a bad man. Don't heed his tongue, sister."

"May I offer you breakfast, ladies?"

All said no at once.

Skipjack strolled back into the kitchen and nodded at Mary

Frances. Within a few minutes, she had driven them off and didn't even burn one slice of ham. He had to laugh and admit that he wouldn't want to tangle with her. He knew how gentle she was, but she brought out the child in people. She stood well above six foot and her bigness wasn't fat.

"There's something else you need to know," she said. "Your brother's here. On his boat now, but he had some breakfast earlier and ain't changed a bit. Said he'd be back after a while, which I takes to mean lunch. Says he's switching boats, moving up to something fancier."

Skipjack got a funny feeling. He looked nonchalantly at the river but realized there was no hiding from Mary Frances. She saw right through him, always could.

"Still the same?"

"Can't believe he's your brother is all. If there's something right about him, it's disguised. I made the serving girl peel potatoes and served him myself, if you catch what I mean."

"Mostly he's all talk," Skipjack said.

"You call it what you want. When he smiles at the girl, flashing his money and teeth, I could swear I was seeing the devil himself oozing out. I promise you her knees were wobbly and she sure weren't wanting to peel potatoes."

"I'll talk to him."

"Afraid you got a blind spot there, Skipjack. There's no talking. He's all in himself."

"Well, we can't have him messing with help."

"He can't do anything but mess. That's what he does."

Skipjack walked out back. He wanted to see his brother about as much as a bad storm, all smiles and quick laughing, glad-handing and scheming. But there was one rule at the tavern: No one messes with help. Screws up everything. Help gets jealous. Customers feel slighted. Stuff doesn't get done. Couldn't have it. He would talk to him. He greeted some folks strolling up for breakfast, then disappeared into his office to think.

The room was small, dank, and stuffy, barely lit by one tiny window; furnished with a desk, two chairs, and a worn-out sofa, surrounded by stone walls. Nothing to recommend it except that it was out of the flow with a door he could shut. This time of year, without a fire lit, it was damp. He usually got thinking done fast.

Skipjack lit a cigar and paced. He couldn't understand why, but he was especially agitated. Normally he sat while he thought things out. He was almost in a fighting mood and that made no sense. He hadn't seen his brother but twice in five years and nothing all that bad had happened, but Skipjack wasn't in the mood for babysitting and making excuses and he didn't want any questionable card dealing either. The last time he'd seen Brother, he'd had to break up a poker game and run everybody off. They were all cheats, each and every one. They raised voices and made threats and he'd had to throw out the entire bunch with a gun drawn. All except for his brother Timothy, who would not leave; played the brother card, and Skipjack had let him. It bothered him to this day. The more he thought, the madder he got.

Finally, he did sit down, took out a bottle of whiskey and poured a shot. He settled back and took a sip. It was from the best batch he had ever made. Not too much remained. Just wasn't worth the trouble. No point in being greedy. Let Green make a dollar. He might just spend it here. Damn if he didn't several times a year, especially spring and fall. Green would bring a crowd down and nearly take over the joint. Brought his own party for damn sure, sometimes his own musicians, too.

Halfway into thinking about how he was going to deal with Timothy, he'd start thinking about Billy, almost like they were reflections shimmering in ripples side by side. He shook his head, but the image would not disappear. He stood again, puffed his cigar, and paced three steps forward and three steps back. The boy had done nothing and neither had Brother. Nobody was going to mess with the help though. He sure was going to tell Timothy that.

There was a knock. Skipjack put the whiskey back in the drawer. Brawl Thurston called his name. This was unusual, to say the least.

Brawl was free, and they had business dealings, but there was an unspoken rule: free blacks didn't rub peoples' noses in it. It wasn't good for business, not for either party. Skipjack let him in nonetheless, shut the door, and locked it. Brawl was as big as Sampson and looked mad as hell, but neither said anything until the door was shut solid.

"That girl, little Julie, that serves out of the kitchen, is my niece."

"She's a good girl. Honest and good-natured."

"Want to keep her that way," Brawl said.

"What's this about?"

"Your brother offered her more money than he likely has, that's what."

"I need to talk to that son of a bitch," Skipjack said.

"Best do it quick. She's a fine girl."

"Done," Skipjack said. "Sorry, he's always been like that."

"We go way back. I sure hope we go forward," Brawl said.

Brawl walked out and that was that. Skipjack lit a candle, sat down, and started thinking.

How he got into carrying folks across he could hardly remember. It wasn't exactly a conscious decision. Brawl had nothing at all to do with it. In fact, even to this day, he wasn't sure what Brawl knew or didn't know. Skipjack's dealings with Brawl were straight up, and though unusual, were legal, even backed by paperwork. His dealings with the others were something else entirely.

He was half drunk the night it started ten years before, toes in the water and fishing off his raft. He had been thinking about nothing, wasn't even sure there was still bait on the hook. He was sitting there angling, about half afraid to go home. Maybe it was that time of month or whatever, but it seemed like Marcie wasn't treating him right. No matter what he said, it was wrong. So, he was hiding out in his own way with nothing on his mind in particular, when a man walked up with a woman carrying a child. Skipjack had barely noticed. The child burped. Skipjack had chuckled.

"What you all been eating?" he said, being silly.

"Not much, tell the truth, sir," the man replied.

"If I relied on fishing, I wouldn't hardly eat either," Skipjack said.

The man said nothing for so long it got uncomfortable.

"What you want?" Skipjack asked.

"Ride across. We'll pay what we got."

Skipjack looked up and knew they were running. "What happened? Why are you here?"

"We lost our way about two days ago. Heard there was a crossing here near about. We're hungry, been hiding for two days."

"You're laying it all out, ain't you?" Skipjack replied.

"Mister, what can we do?" the woman asked.

"Suppose you could shush and ask for food and not raise your voice." Skipjack stood and said, "Follow me."

In the kitchen, the stew pot was still warm. Fact is, it was hot as he discovered when he lifted the lid and was forced to fling it. He got some bowls and spoons, found some corn muffins, and served the folks. While they were eating, he ducked into his office and took a drink. What was he to do?

They wouldn't tell him much. They were supposed to meet somebody right near this creek, a white woman, but the one who was supposed to lead them had not showed. They had hidden two days until hunger had brought them to Skipjack.

He didn't take their small money. Never even asked how much it was. If he hadn't been drinking, he might not have done it. He was live and let live. He didn't like slavery one little bit, but on the other hand, he could appreciate the bottom line. He had used slaves on his place but had never owned them. Sometimes some of the more industrious ones would work at odd jobs after they had finished their chores and he had paid them—not much—but he had paid cash money.

That's how he met Brawl, who could build anything. Brawl wandered up one evening and pointed out that the original section of porch on Skipjack's house was listing and had promised to fix it free, if materials and tools were supplied. Skipjack had to chuckle at that. About all the man owned was a hammer and saw. Before the job was finished, Skipjack's step-down porch stretched the full front of the house and was built right, but suffice it to say, Brawl had a few more tools. He also had made a couple of friends. Marcie had liked him as much as Skipjack did. Brawl built birdhouses and flower boxes out of scrap lumber without being asked or asking for anything. He ended up in charge of maintenance and new building projects for the house and tavern, as well. The man was sharp. He worked cheaper, better, and harder. At the time, he was still a slave.

But that night on the riverbank, Skipjack wasn't thinking worthiness when he hauled the runaways across. He wasn't thinking too much of anything actually. He found out they were from about fifty miles away and had been walking by night without food or shelter and that a storm had thrown them off schedule. The man offered to row, but Skipjack pulled the oars and was surprised, if not quite frightened, when a dim lantern came out of the trees as their bow scraped bottom on the other side. All ducked down. Skipjack gripped his pistol.

"Come ashore, children, in the name of God Almighty; come ashore," a husky male voice entreated.

The man and woman scrambled off and waded in toward the shore. Skipjack and the man nodded. The woman and child never even looked back. The lantern blinked out and, in darkness, Skipjack stroked back into the lazy current and pointed slightly upstream, headed across. It wasn't until he neared the Kentucky shore that he realized how crazy he had been: hadn't even brought a fishing pole. What was he going to say? I was just out for a row? But no one had been there to ask. He slipped back into the tavern and refreshed himself with a warm bowl of stew.

He never could remember their faces. All he ever saw was fear and a glistening, desperate determination. Most were young men.

———————

Brother in town. Oh, brother.

He glanced at his pocket watch. The damn thing had stopped. He knew it was later than ten to ten. Mary Frances had the time, almost quarter till eleven. She was cranking out food and sweating a downpour. She had Julie and two other girls hopping willy-nilly. She barked out orders only they could understand. When Skipjack held up his watch, she instantly understood and yelled out the time.

"Get that damn thing repaired and quit messing with working folks."

He returned her wink as he cranked his watch. On the gallery out back, it was hot and steamy. Only one table was occupied. Two bearded men were bent forward and talking softly. A calliope tootled downstream and the bushiest bearded man burst out laughing.

"See what I mean, Harshaw, nothing beats experience. Might be the most new-fangled contraption, but still there is a man behind it. Am I right or am I not?"

"His D is sharp, and his A is flat," the other replied as he puffed on his meerschaum.

"So, you can still hear?"

"My ears have outlived my mother's prayers, Burnett. We'll see how well you're tuned when the contest kicks up at sundown."

"He might be your son, Harshaw, but if I don't win her, I'm rooting for him, damn you!"

"He's just getting started. You know how it is."

"Let him tune all afternoon. He's drowning out birds to produce steam skeeters. Have to clench my jaws to listen to the painful mess."

"She ain't pretty, I admit, but at least he ain't wearing a dress and saying, 'Wherefore art thou, Romeo?'"

Skipjack didn't wait around for the point of that gaff to bite and meandered back into the kitchen, made a point of checking his watch as he slid past Mary Frances.

"You're about two minutes slow, Skipjack," she said. "You best be careful."

"You got eyes like an eagle."

"And ears like an owl."

Skipjack let that one lay and walked on through.

He looked up the road and didn't like what he saw drawing near. The face of Jessie the mule was comforting and above it was Marcie's face, but peering over her shoulder was Brother Timothy, with an arm wrapped around Marcie's waist and a smile about as reassuring as a jack o' lantern. Billy was clutching Timothy with one hand and waving the other. Skipjack tried to hide his gut reaction but snorted like a mule.

His brother's grin annoyed. The words that fell from Timothy's lips, when he looked down and spoke, stung like sleet. Skipjack hugged the son of a bitch, though he wouldn't have had he not been clenched first. His lip curled.

"Yo, hey, Big Brother, you're looking stout and fine. Certainly appreciate your hospitality. Been awhile," he said. He lowered Marcie down as the boy slipped off Jessie's stern like a dropping turd—at least that's the way Skipjack saw it.

"Hotter than blazes, ain't it? How you doing? Billy sure is gaining and Marcie, Lord, how did you get so lucky, Big Brother?"

All Skipjack saw was teeth. He stole a glance at Marcie, but she was fussing with Billy's hair. Brother lurched forward and gave him another unwelcome bear hug, squeezed so hard that Skipjack nearly said something, but didn't.

"Something eating you, Jackson? You awful quiet. Boy and I been playing skittles, haven't we, Billy? You play skittles with Daddy, don't you, son?" Timothy rubbed the boy's head. Marcie pressed into Skipjack, who suggested a little lunch might be in order.

"You're the man, Brother. I am along for the ride. Be around a couple of days, if you don't mind too much," he said softly, then made like he would hug all three of them, before adding, "unless I would be in the way."

"You're not in the way, Uncle Timmy," Billy said.

"Sure hope not, son, but of course, not for me to judge."

"Let's eat," Skipjack said. "What you say, Marcie?"

She clutched his arm, squeezing a little harder than he thought she should. He looked her square in the eye. She only nodded. At one of the outdoor tables, as Timothy was impressing Billy with his dexterity handling playing cards, Skipjack asked her, "Everything all right?"

"Far as I can tell, everything's fine. And you?"

Mary Frances stood over them with hands on her hips and announced they better get orders in quick before they had to wait in line. She rubbed Billy's head. The boy was fooling with a deck of old cards Timothy had given him and tried to look annoyed, but when Mary Frances laughed, he grinned from ear to ear. Everybody did, even Timothy.

Mary Frances cast a spell, but so did Andy and Brawl. Skipjack had never thought about it before. He was staring down and it was now Marcie's turn to whisper was he all right. Of course, I am, he tried to imply with a glance.

Throughout lunch, Timothy made it plain that he was well on the way. Money was his game and he had aced the receiving end. His new job was one of the most coveted in the business. He expected to triple the take. He said he wanted to be close to family and that was the reason he chose to stay with them, rather than downtown where accommodations, though elegant, lacked a family touch. He patted Billy's head and grinned. Skipjack noticed that Billy was learning to shuffle, and that Timothy seemed to be on the verge of tears.

"Hard to explain what family means. How could you know, having one? You folks take so much for granted. Lord hold me back," he said, voice quavering and added, "No blame, but you can't know what you have. I am here to tell."

"Here to tell what?" Skipjack asked.

"Brother, are you upset with me? Please, I was only pointing out blessings. Can it be I have been misconstrued?"

"I wouldn't know," Skipjack said.

"Do you know what it's like to go to sleep alone?"

"With your fingers blistered from dealing hot cards, you mean?"

"He doesn't mean anything. Will you two quit acting like boys?"

"Honestly, Marcie, I am only cleaving to sacred truth. You two are blessed lucky."

"Luckier than you could know, Timothy. Jack didn't mean a thing. Now hush."

"I am as calm as my earnest heart will allow," Timothy responded, "but can you not perceive how I covet your situation?"

"We all make choices," Skipjack said.

"What kind of choice is chance encounter?"

"I don't know what you're talking about, Tim."

"What's all the yelling about?"

"You tell 'em, sweetie," Marcie said.

"I'll tell 'em our lunch is here, isn't it, Momma?"

Sure enough, it was. Fried pork, fried fish, beans, okra, corn bread, and cabbage. Mary Frances placed the dishes and laughed as she watched the boy's eyes.

"The way that boy's looking, he'll be bigger than his daddy in a couple of weeks," she said.

"Couple of days," the boy said, digging in.

"That's my boy," Timothy said, as he patted Billy's back.

"Easy, son, we got all afternoon," Skipjack said. "There's no rush."

"Listen to Daddy. Chew each bite," Marcie said.

Marcie tried to juggle moods and keep things smooth, which worked with the boy, but the men kept needling. She had no time to figure what they couldn't let go of. She gave up trying and made sure the boy ate properly.

Down by the river as they strolled after lunch, Marcie realized that it was a good thing that Timothy was staying only a few days.

She tried to ignore him but could see why Jack couldn't. Timothy was in Jack's face, talking too loud and usually about something that he didn't know much about. He posed as an expert on almost every subject. Never asked questions but predicted outcomes and offered judgments. He would do things this way and he would do things that way. Jack was clearly annoyed, lips pressed together, jaw clenched.

Finally, Jack could take no more. Marcie saw fury flash before being suppressed. Timothy was talking about how out of date the tavern was compared to others he had seen. Feeding people was one thing, he was saying, but if you wanted money, gambling was the way. Think big he was saying. What do you want to raise hogs for? Servicing riffraff off flatboats and working men from God knows where. Hell, he was saying, you could build a gambling house and draw folks from up and down.

"Farming's for birds," he said. "Keep up with the times."

"Finished, Little Brother?" Skipjack asked more politely than Marcie had expected. "Why the hell don't you buy us out? You got ideas. You got cash?"

Timothy turned to face him and said, "You inherited this. You got the cash, Brother. I'm simply trying to help you appreciate what you have."

"I have worked this place, Timothy. I can't help my place in the birth order. We might have worked something out. You're the one that run off to strike it rich."

"I had two claims that would have worked out with backing."

"I sent money more than once and never got a thank-you."

"Now, Big Brother, that's not true. I have always been grateful. I just want to see you prosper. You could build a gambling hall that would be a destination."

"It won't hunt," Skipjack said. "Too many churchgoers and the timing's wrong. Besides, what I know about gambling is betting on rain."

"Well, you see, that's where I come in," Timothy said.

Skipjack threw up his hands. Marcie stepped in and said she had to get home. Timothy winked and allowed as how he might go take a nap before the evening card game.

"Roll it over in your mind."

"Roll what over?"

"My proposal, of course."

"If that's a proposal, I'm a cord of firewood," Skipjack said as he waved to Billy, who was down on the riverbank pestering mallards. The boy ran up. Skipjack told him to look after Momma, kissed Marcie on the cheek, and went back inside.

"He's always been like that," Timothy said.

"Really, how do you mean?" Marcie asked.

"Short and gruff, like Daddy."

"That's not the way I see him."

Jessie strolled out of her stall and stopped at the limestone mounting step. First Marcie, then Billy, and finally Timothy climbed on. Jessie paced slowly.

"You don't need the reins, Timothy. This mule knows the way," Marcie said as she spread her elbows and Timothy's hands were replaced by Billy's.

"Maybe we should go fishing tomorrow."

"Show me card tricks, I'll take you this afternoon."

"Tomorrow will be soon enough. Maybe you'll scout likely holes this afternoon."

"Maybe he'll weed the garden instead," Marcie said.

"I'm only here for a couple of days, Marcie."

Marcie clucked, and Jessie started toward River Road.

CHAPTER 2

OH, BROTHER

S kipjack was stirred up and confused. He hid in his office instead of checking on things. Hogs could take care of themselves and the corn would grow no matter what. He slumped and felt such dissatisfaction that it bewildered him.

Often this time of day, he would walk from operation to operation and encourage folks. Vegetables coming along nicely. The docks need shoring up. How big was lunch, Mary Frances?

He had never liked Brother much and had not enjoyed lunch at all. Still, what the dreamer said wasn't all that bad. It wasn't anything past, long gone, or recent, gnawing his guts. Nothing Marcie had said or Billy either. Skipjack closed his eyes and tried to squelch the cacophony, and nearly had, when there was a knock on the door and then some quiet voice inside said *go home.*

"Come in," Skipjack said.

"Hate to trouble you, sir."

It was Andy. Skipjack always allotted time for him, so he attempted to ignore this quiet voice and motioned him in. Andy sat silently, but Skipjack's inner voice was not. Andy's gaze was placid, but Skipjack distinctly heard *go home, now.* Andy was so reliable that he normally could have rambled on about anything at all, but not on this day.

After a short description of a busted pump, Skipjack growled, "Then buy what you need and fix the damn thing."

"I thought you might want to know, sir," Andy said.

"You know this place. Treat me right, I treat you right. Saddle up the mare."

"Yes, sir."

There was no way he knew to replace Andy. The fellow only asked for advice to stay out of trouble. He knew what to do. If Andy would agree to stick around, he might try to keep him on. Trained by Brawl, the man could do most anything.

He gave Andy a few minutes, then walked out back, and mounted up. Told him he would be back. He didn't hurry home. He let the horse stroll. For the life of him, he had no earthly idea what was wrong, or if anything was wrong. He felt nauseated but was in no real hurry to discover why.

When he got home, Skipjack put the mare in the stable with Jessie and then walked into the house. He called out for Marcie but got no reply. He called for Billy as he walked toward the back door. He crossed the yard through Marcie's vegetable patch. As he neared the springhouse, he called Marcie's name again.

"Jack?"

He stooped and ducked into the springhouse. She was sitting on a stone with her feet dangling in the water. She looked puzzled.

"Everything all right?"

"You tell me," he answered.

"They've gone fishing. I felt like cooling off. It's hotter than hell's shingles."

"But everything's all right?"

"Hope so. You reckon not, or you wouldn't be here this hour."

"Something told me come home. How do I explain that?"

"Don't. Sit down and hold my hand."

"You all right?"

"With you here."

Marcie suggested he roll up his trousers and remove his boots, so he could soak his feet.

"What's on your mind, Jack?"

Without hesitation, he said. "Something said get home, so I got home. No reason, I guess."

She rubbed his back and told him she was glad. He took a deep breath, blew it out, and placed his hand on her thigh. She leaned into him and kissed his neck.

"I was wishing you here with all my heart," Marcie said.

"Any particular reason?"

"Not really," she said softly, "but I sure feel a lot better. Lacy's supposed to be here in about an hour to help in the garden. I'll be all right, if you have to get back."

Skipjack said, "Not real fond of Timothy either, are you?"

"Glad something said come home."

"Did he try anything?"

"No."

"Then what is it?"

"I don't know."

There was a snake on one of the rafters and its tail drooped as it adjusted its coils. Marcie sighed.

"In this place are weird crickets I never seen the like of and spiders with legs long enough to jump a mile, but I swear as tame as old Fred is, I'll never get used to him. Seems he only moves once a month, but when he does, I wish he wouldn't."

"Old Fred wouldn't hurt. Let's get out of here and slip upstairs," Skipjack said.

"What if they come back?"

"We'll hear 'em coming. Besides it's our place, ain't it?"

"Just hold me, all right?"

They stood up and Skipjack said, "All right."

As they were strolling back to the house, Timothy and Billy walked into the clearing. They were grinning. Billy was holding up a small catfish. Skipjack felt Marcie's mood sag as Timothy praised Billy's angling.

"Snatched him on the second nibble, like you taught me, Daddy."

"Did Daddy teach you how to clean him, too?" Timothy asked.

"Not yet. I'm not to play with knives."

Skipjack skinned and cleaned the fish while Billy feigned interest in the instruction he was supposed to be receiving. As soon as the fish was filleted, the boy decided he needed a nap like Uncle Timothy. Marcie salted the fish and placed the bowl on a shelf cooled by running water inside the springhouse.

"They'll keep until morning," she said to Jack.

"Me, too," Skipjack said. "Unless I'm lucky."

"Want to get lucky?"

She took his hand and led him back into the springhouse, but after a few kisses, decided that place wouldn't do. With her in the lead, they trotted up the hillside and settled behind a large chestnut tree.

"Remember this spot?" she asked.

"Of course, I do," Skipjack said, while his forefinger traced a gentle radius around her neck.

They were kissing and touching, when suddenly Marcie stiffened. Eyes open, she pushed him away.

"What?"

"Can't you hear? Somebody's coming."

Sure enough, it was Timothy.

"Oh, sorry to bother. Damn, please excuse my intrusion. I wasn't tired after all and started thinking about the old lookout. Do you go often, Brother?"

"Can't say that I do but suit yourself."

"Oh, let's all. It's not far. We can view the whole place."

"You go."

Timothy squatted, looked at the ground, and picked up a stick, then poked among leaves at his feet.

"Listen, we could climb up there together, Big Brother, you and me, or you, me, and Marcie, but by myself, it would not be the same. Come with me," he said, "Let's climb the hill."

Marcie squeezed Jack's hand. Jack hardly knew what to do or say.

"You go. Maybe tomorrow."

"We never know tomorrow." Timothy went back down the hill.

Skipjack stood, shook his head, and Marcie hugged his waist.

"He's not right, Jack."

"Never was," Skipjack said. "He always ruined everything."

Back at the house, they discovered that Timothy had decided to nap after all. When Lacy showed up, Skipjack went back to the tavern. The two women, one brown, one white, waved at him as the mare carried him out of sight. The more he thought about it, the more dangerous this tutoring seemed. That's all they needed, loose talk, but at least Marcie was safe.

Down at the tavern, the afternoon slid like butter across a skillet. Skipjack wasn't needed for anything. When Timothy reappeared and made a point of saying that he hadn't meant to intrude, Skipjack shrugged.

The bar was buzzing, and the gallery tables were full. Timothy and crew were boisterous with their card game in a corner of the dining room. Some lady complained about cigar smoke, but that was ordinary. She was the type who would complain about anything.

When it got close to dark, Skipjack told Mary Frances he was going fishing. He had about as much interest in fishing as digging a latrine. What he wanted was to be alone with Marcie, holding her close, but he hadn't checked his trotlines for a day at least.

He started across with his mutt, Gracie, who stood in the bow studying dappled water with a big grin. Some man from a clump of men drinking on the shore pointed and asked where he was headed.

"To my fishing hole, if it suits you," Skipjack replied and pulled on the oars.

He rowed upstream but aimed toward the Indiana side; could have done it blindfolded, he had done it so often. Gracie was his sentinel. If a boat was stealing downstream, she would bark. She also knew about driftwood, though sometimes was overly cautious in that department.

The twilight moon was a sliver and before he was halfway, the river was leaden, then darker still as a cloudbank covered the moon. Couldn't have planned it better; nosy bastards would steal any damn thing wasn't locked down. He pulled on the oars and smiled, imagining those ones who might think he hauled secret cargo. Truth is, he only ran slaves every now and again, but to keep things interesting, for whoever might be watching, he rowed the river several times a week, good exercise and prudent, but less tiring and a lot easier to buy from fishermen who dropped by most every morning, as in fact Mary Frances usually did. Skipjack claimed his were better.

This night they weren't. They couldn't have been. He was in his spot below Fourteen Mile Creek. Didn't need a lantern to know where. The lines were gone, except one, and all it held was a small turtle not worth messing with.

Skipjack smelled smoke curling across the water. Before the moon ducked back in, he spotted something faintly pink on the shore a couple hundred yards downstream, then he saw the faint glow of a fire. He drifted quietly, then slid into the sand and listened. He had his pistol cocked.

"Told you to set the hook, rattle brain. Never said nothing about pulling up fish. That means drop anchor, in case you're listening."

"You ate some, didn't you?"

"Cleaned 'em, too. Where you from, farm boy?"

"Leave him alone. Turned out all right, Damon. Sure beats fishing supper."

"We're about out of whiskey and tomorrow's a long haul. I say a couple of us trade some across the way for booze."

"Sit tight. You drink anymore, you won't be worth shooting. We'll take the rest over in the morning and sell 'em to the big cook. They fine now hanging off the stern."

"They got women over yonder?"

"Now don't you start. Where'd I get this crew anyway? Whiskey, women. You want whiskey and women? Just wait till we drop off them rifles down in Louisville. Just a few more hours. Payday!"

"I'm still thirsty."

"Yeah, and I'm still captain. I'll buy breakfast when we sell fish, but ain't crossing over tonight. City slicker, you can't set no hook, but you ain't half bad on that guitar. Play the damn thing and redeem yourself."

"I'm thirsty, too."

"So sweet of you to tell me, lamb chop. Now, play."

The man wasn't bad. Skipjack didn't recognize the style but liked it. The men started laughing and one broke into song, but the others told him to hush. The moon was smudged, and the men were up the bank behind a big rock, so he backed off the sand and slid down to their flatboat hunkered into shore.

Sure enough, there was an anchor line off the stern and attached to the same cleat were his trotlines. He cut them loose and knotted them to his own cleat; considered cutting the anchor line, but that would have been sheer stupid meanness, because the flatboat was lashed to the shore.

A vengeful urge would have been as far as this foolishness would have gone, but Skipjack was stirred and the guitar player inspiring. Before he had landed a reason why, he was aboard the flatboat and found a candle as if magic had guided his hand. He lit it, then instantly blew it out, as some undeniable internal voice demanded *leave here now.*

Skipjack, bewildered and chilled to the bone, heeded the message and slipped furtively aboard his skiff, then rowed away with firm strokes. He was nearly halfway across when the moon hid completely and about that time, he heard a ruckus. A powerful flame pulsed against the Indiana shore. He heard a few pops that sounded like fireworks. He hauled in his fish and removed them from their hooks. The current was doing his work for him; all he had to do now was drift. Across the river, the entire hillside flickered, and deep shadows dancing between dark trees were amazing.

He steered into the creek and tied off. With Gracie proud beside him, he carried the bucket of fish through stragglers outside and presented them to Mary Frances, who whistled for one of her girls.

"What's going on across the river?"

"Damned if I know. Brother still here?"

"Ruling the roost."

"Any trouble?"

"Besides him, not yet." Mary Frances turned away.

"Anything I need to know?"

"Nothing you don't already."

Skipjack went to the bar and ordered a whiskey. From where he was leaning, the gallery tables were in plain view, and through the few folks milling around, he could see silhouettes gesturing as a diminishing glow slid along the Indiana shore. He couldn't hear much, but apparently, some of the folks outside could. He could hear nearby laughter interspersed with far-off sounds like shrill angry crows.

He walked back outside, sat on a bench beneath a window that opened onto the dining room near the poker game. He didn't know exactly why, but he sat and listened.

He wasn't a gambler. Banter interested him not at all. Brother's voice had a false cheerful edge. The rest of the four or five voices meant nothing to him. He heard Timothy call for another round. Skipjack shook his head, knowing that the man almost never drank. That was one thing about him. Brother knew his limit. He could drink a beer. Skipjack heard him order one, then he heard a bunch of raucous laughter. Suddenly, Mary Frances called in such a way that he would have walked through the wall if he could have.

Brother was grinning from ear to ear when Skipjack stepped into the room. The rest of the gamblers seemed to be studying cards. Julie, Brawl Thurston's niece, stood behind Mary Frances, whose face was scarlet.

"It's late, Skipjack. I was fooling."

"Your ass," Mary Frances said.

"There's no need for a knife, Mary Frances. Clean up the kitchen.

I'll take care of this."

He looked Mary Frances square in the eye and nodded, then looked at Timothy and said, "Play out your hand, then we're going to talk."

Timothy grinned. One guy folded, and then another. Mary Frances and the young woman went back to the kitchen.

Timothy flashed an even bigger smile. The two seated men squinted at their hands. The two who had folded walked out.

"Gentlemen. We're closing this shop."

"Brother, that ain't right. I invited. They got whiskey and the game is young."

Skipjack said nothing. He cleared his throat.

"Hit me twice," said one of the fellows.

"Ain't right. You want these men to think this is a set-up?"

"Don't much care. You heard the man; hit him twice."

Skipjack walked into the kitchen. Mary Frances was hugging Julie and shaking with rage. He put his hand on her shoulder.

"This girl ain't his to put in the pot or to paw else I quit."

Skipjack raised his forefinger to his lips and motioned with his head toward the game. He asked Julie if she was all right. She nodded.

"She's too damn young for devilment and you know it."

"I'll talk to him."

"You'll do it quick, too, or my sharp-tongued friend will get there first. I ain't kidding. Twice in one day? I'll serve him for lunch before he knows he's cooked."

"I broke up the game, Mary Frances. I'll send 'em home. Close it up."

"Me and this child might be home tomorrow, too."

"Now, don't you say that. You know you will be here like always."

"He's your brother. You take care of him."

"I'll talk to him."

"You got to do better than that. Come, girl."

Skipjack knew there was no point in discussion. Julie turned and waved. Mary Frances dragged her out and he bolted the door.

Brother and his buddies had started another hand. He told them to finish and started blowing out candles.

Mary Frances had a new hiding place for the late-night cash. Skipjack didn't even know where. He looked at the crocks lining the shelves. It could be anywhere. He got the main cashbox out of the little safe in his office and laid it on the desk. He sat, bowed his head, and prayed in a loud whisper.

"Lord, please help. Please, in all your mercy look on my situation with Timothy, for I am surely at a loss where to begin."

There was a loud knock. He reached for his pistol and then said, "In Christ's name, amen. Who's there?"

"Who do you think?"

The door was too thick to shoot through and almost too thick to hear through. He repeated his question and this time recognized Timothy's voice.

"Thought you wanted to go home."

Skipjack looked him over and liked him less for having done so, nodded and said, "I did. Let's hitch the mare. Still remember how?"

"What's eating you, Brother? You need to relax," Timothy said as he followed Skipjack from lock to lock. He offered to carry the cashbox, but Skipjack told him he was used to it. Timothy jawed about how the place was a gold mine but didn't lift a finger to help harness. He did stroke the horse's neck as Skipjack shut the gate.

As the buggy rolled away from the tavern, everything Skipjack had planned to say seemed to float off his forehead. It was such a peculiar sensation that he looked at his brother in disbelief. The moonlight, though dim, was clear enough to see Timothy's eyes, but he could read nothing in them. Brother grinned like he was on a joyful hayride.

"It's good to be back. I've missed the place," he said.

The mare knew the way; Skipjack shut both eyes and nodded. It wasn't really a headache, but whatever gripped him was worse. His mind felt blinded. He found himself clenching, as a quiet voice asked *is this right?*

"Is something troubling you?"

Skipjack slumped forward, chin on chest and cleared his throat. After a deep breath, he took a swallow of whiskey and reached in his pocket for a cigar. Scratched right above his ear and the back of his neck and still felt like he itched everywhere at once and that scratching—no matter where—didn't do a bit of good. He took another deep breath and tried to ignore Timothy's questions: "Are you all right? You don't seem yourself. You know you ought to cut back on whiskey. Smoking will kill you. I've seen it. A glass of wine is all right, but rotgut will do just that, rot your gut."

Skipjack lit his cigar.

"There is something bothering me, Timothy. You."

"Surely, you're joking. The crew I brought spent more than the whole place. How can you be upset?"

"Do you understand I could give a damn?"

"Of course, I understand. Ain't that what I been trying to say? I got hundreds of sharps eager to beat me and I'm willing to share. Hell, I made five hundred clear. Think about it. Cut me in; I cut you in. What you think?"

"I don't care about the money."

"Everybody cares or else they're dead."

"Then maybe I'm dead and don't need it. That's not what I'm driving at, Timothy."

"You ain't driving at all. The mare's doing the work. You sitting there, killing yourself with tobacco and whiskey."

"Laugh, Little Brother, but I'll tell you something and you listen. You touch one more girl in the tavern and I'll shoot you."

"What are you talking about? Shoot your brother for liking candy? Hell, Mary Frances is probably doing worse. I'll tell you that much. You ain't been around like I have. A tease, a squeeze—who does it hurt?"

Skipjack closed his eyes and reminded himself that it was only about another quarter mile. He drew on his cigar.

"All right, you're mad about this morning, but think about it.

I offered her more than you pay in a month. The way you run this place is crazy. You could make these people decent money."

"You call it decent?"

"All money's decent if it's yours. You don't know that, shouldn't sit at the head of the table."

"You're an interesting man, Timothy, very worldly. You must find me dull."

"No, Brother. I can't afford to think that way. To circulate in my realm, I have to be open-minded. Please, don't blame yourself. But my explorations of this great land have stretched my mind. I have learned that there is more than one way. Customs change place to place and time to time. If you don't learn that, you won't last long."

"No argument there, but will you agree not all things change in the same way at the same pace?"

"Now Jackson, New Orleans is quite different from Comanche territory, which is far different than here. That much is obvious."

"Then when you are in Cincinnati, you don't expect New Orleans's fare, do you?"

"I don't see your point."

"If you don't, you're blind. Keep your hands and your money off my girls. We might get along."

"Tell me you don't get a taste now and again. Come on, who you talking to?"

"You, I'm afraid. Understand why or not, hands off the girls or I'll kill you."

"Jesus Christ! You sound like you mean it. Hey, I'm your brother."

"If I were you, I would watch Mary Frances, too."

Skipjack clucked and slapped the reins on the mare's back.

TRESPASS

He put up the mare and the buggy, but right before turning in, climbed the hill and sat on his favorite old stump. From there, he had a view. He had a bottle hidden and he snatched it out. Before taking a swallow, he lit his cigar stub. Then surprised himself, put the bottle back and threw his cigar into the bushes. He sat a few minutes and watched the stars.

Too upset to take a drink or enjoy a smoke. Tried to slow his breathing. Loosened his belt. When he placed his pistol on the ground, he thought about the moneybox he had stashed beneath straw in the stall. He picked the pistol back up. It was no use. Maybe he could relax when Brother was gone. He cinched up his trousers and started back.

Some instinct told him to slip into the brush. He did, listened with all his might, and heard nothing except tree frogs and night birds, doves and owls. After a few moments, he sensed a scuffling sound too clumsy for any four-legged animal unless it was wounded. He couldn't tell if it was coming up or down, so he stood stock-still in shadow. Whatever it was stopped and was suddenly so quiet Skipjack was afraid to cock his pistol. Besides owls and doves, other birds tweeted and warbled back and forth. Between their calls was silence deep as space between stars. Somebody said, "Cigar."

Skipjack cocked his pistol, hoping some critter would camouflage its strong click. Shuffling sounds resumed, coming down. He backed a few stealthy paces off the path.

"Lives right below this hill," someone whispered.

"How did you smell the cigar?"

"Let the man do his job, Woosley. He'll find where they hid."

"Turned off here."

"They don't go down to Maddox?"

"Didn't say that. They turn toward the creek here."

"What we do?" the scratchy whisperer asked.

"Want to follow their trail, we turn here."

"But that's steep, almost straight down."

"Not too bad, if you're strong, but at night, it's an extra two dollars."

"Wait just a minute, you four-flushing half-breed, we done settled on a price hooked to results."

"Climb down then. They gone that way. Ain't sure where cigar smoker's gone."

"What you talking about?"

"Cigar still warm. He is up here."

"Why didn't you say that before?"

"Said you want runaways. You want to know everything, pay the price."

"We ain't going tonight. You think he's up here?" the voice whispered.

"Can't say. Might run home or maybe behind tree."

"That's enough then. Let's get back."

Skipjack heard them scrabble back up the hill and exhaled when he heard someone laugh.

"Get up front and lead. Earn your keep. Cram your laughter."

"Want to come back in light?"

"Just lead."

"Yes, sir. You're the boss man."

Skipjack did not even try to take a glimpse. As they got further away, it became more difficult to hold his ground, but that's what he did. What if one stayed? Long after he could hear nothing of them, he took a step toward the path. Then another and another, until he was heading toward home. About halfway, he heard something coming up. He jumped into the undergrowth. Gracie sniffed him out and jumped all over him. Somebody was still coming, so he wasn't eager for attention.

"Brother, where are you?"

Skipjack stepped onto the path with his pistol cocked. The dog ran toward Timothy.

"I'm here. What's the problem?"

Timothy pulled up close, so close that Skipjack could see his teeth.

"I wanted to say I was sorry."

"I'm tired, Tim. Why don't we talk in the morning?"

"Seriously, I am remorseful. I have been on boats too long. You have girls come into the joint, don't you?"

"You haven't seen them, you're blind."

"Well, you know what I mean then. You get used to that sort, you expect it."

"Maybe that's the trouble."

"I didn't mean any upset. Swear I want to be your partner and your brother, too."

"If you want to run girls, Tim, work a city. People expect more and pay more. After you took off, when what they call the gold rush crew was coming, hell, there were so many people throwing money around it was impossible to keep whores out. I don't have to try now. Lot of things have changed. We're not the first stop anymore. Some stop upriver. Some don't stop at all. The railroad's gonna take a lot of the produce we used to get and the roads they're building already haul a bunch. Hell, River Road was nothing but dirt lane last year. Now they're building a highway leading up into Oldham and Trimble counties. All these things are taking business. You want my opinion? If you want to run a gambling house with girls, get your ass in town. I'll end raising pigs and selling eggs side of the road."

Skipjack stopped and put his finger to his lips. He grabbed Gracie and urged her into shadows. Timothy followed.

"Are you armed?"

"Only this," Timothy whispered, pulling a derringer out of his coat pocket.

"Keep your mouth shut and stay out of the way."

Several deer crossed the path. Gracie could barely contain herself. A moon sliver sailed clear of clouds and faint light filtered down.

"Sort of jumpy, aren't you?"

"With good reason. We'll talk in the morning."

But in the morning, Skipjack smelled bacon, while Timothy counted sheep. Marcie was wrapped up in a winter robe though it was warm. Skipjack wanted to talk. He didn't want to whisper, but things he wanted to say he couldn't. Marcie was quiet. Their eyes met over and over, but she must have felt the same. They ate breakfast in silence. He clutched her hand before he left, then kissed her and told her he would be back for lunch. She looked puzzled and he confused her further when he told her he would need a small bucket of lard. He winked when he said that, and she squinted when she heard. Skipjack kissed her and nodded. Told her he would take Jessie, so that they could have the buggy and mare.

About halfway, a man stepped onto the trail and slowly waved both hands over his head. Skipjack cocked his pistol and continued. As he drew closer, he could see that the man was likely part Indian.

He pulled Jessie up and without revealing his weapon asked what the man wanted.

"Just talk, boss."

"Then say your piece. You're trespassing."

"I can help."

Skipjack spurred the mule and trotted past.

"Follow then," he yelled across his shoulder. Damned if he was going to be ambushed in his own woods. He crossed River Road and when he looked didn't see the man, so he slowed Jessie. He uncocked his pistol and was enjoying watching three buzzards swoop across blue morning sky when something told him to look back. The man was standing on the edge of the cornfield with arms outstretched. Skipjack cocked his pistol in plain sight and rode straight toward him.

"All right, what you want with me?"

"Last night I was there."

Skipjack pointed the Colt square at his heart, but his eyes were sweeping the corn.

"What you want?"

"To talk."

"Who's with you?"

"Alone."

"Over there on that rise underneath the walnut. I ain't talking here."

He remained mounted on Jessie. When the man trotted up, he kept the gun resting on Jessie's neck.

"I don't take kindly to trespass."

The man nodded and said, "I didn't want to, but they paid me to track. We come over the new road, then up the hill and down to behind where you was."

"You knew I was there?"

The man nodded.

"Why didn't you tell them?"

"They not good people. They treat me bad. Call me half-breed and try to cheat me out of money. Did it for money, not insults."

"So, how do you plan to help me?"

"Easy," the man's eyes glinted. "Give me money; I take them off track."

"What track you talking?"

The man looked off before he spoke.

"Ones they tracking come through and then over the rocks toward the creek. I could take them somewhere else. They won't know."

"I don't want nobody on my property, understand?"

"They give me five dollars. You give me five, they won't be back."

"Until they give you six. Why should I believe a word coming out of your mouth?"

The man pulled a small cross out of his shirt and dangled it.

"What's your name and where you from?"

"Jess Block from Red River near Lexington."

"Those men. They're from Lexington?"

Block nodded.

Skipjack took out his wallet and gave the man five dollars.

"Go home. If I catch you around here, I'll shoot you. Walk wherever you want, but not here."

The man snatched the money and nodded. As Skipjack watched him lope across the field out to River Road, he wanted to laugh. When the man started skipping, he did laugh. He knew he had been had but hoped the man might skip back to wherever and stay.

Down at the tavern there was nothing unusual happening. He paid some bills. Later there were a few river men drunk at the bar arguing the slavery issue. They were loud and, as far as Skipjack could see, had no dog in the hunt; unless they got real lucky in a poker game, none of them would ever own any.

Mary Frances was at war as usual. She was hollering orders as fast as she could, and ingredients were being chopped, diced, sliced, and spread out to her satisfaction. She surprised him when she winked.

"Everything all right?" he asked.

"Dandy," she replied.

He walked around and inspected, spent some time in the office thinking, then went home, but took it slow. In fact, he detoured and traipsed up River Road to where a road gang was building a bridge over the creek. He watched them lay limestone block into place for about an hour, which means he actually saw two being set. "These will be here forever." He must have heard that said ten times. The old bridge, part stone and wood, which he had ridden across moments before, seemed with its warps and creaks to question that premise, but he kept his mouth shut.

When he arrived home, Marcie was scrubbing clothes. She was more than happy to be interrupted. Timothy and Billy were off fishing again. Jack and Marcie slipped inside like teenagers. In their own bed, they proceeded as adults. Time was of the essence and they got there. Laughing and chuckling, they held each other, delighted in the sweat that ran between them. They had stolen a moment and wasn't it grand. She kissed him deeply and meant it. He kissed back, and they held tight and gazed at one another.

"I have two questions to ask you, my dear Marcie."

"What might they be?"

Skipjack knew he was wrong but couldn't help it when he asked, "What's for lunch and do you have a lard pail ready for me?"

Marcie stuck out her tongue and shook her head.

"I was kidding, sweetheart."

"The answers are soup, yes, and no, you weren't kidding."

"Now don't be mad."

"Who could be mad at you?"

"I'm not so good at saying stuff, am I?"

"I don't like to argue, Jack."

"What kind of soup?"

"It has more vegetables than frogs. How about that?"

"Sounds good," Jack said.

"What you want with the lard?"

"Keep the boy off the hill and trust me on the rest. Nothing to worry about."

Skipjack carried the lard up to the point where the Indian had claimed folks went. One look at the ground told him it was a lie. There were no tracks going down. Why would anyone climb down what was almost a cliff when they could walk another thirty yards through the woods and take a gentle path to the creek. It was bogus—simply a way of making the job look more dangerous and worth bigger pay.

He walked a deer path that would cross the steep one. On that narrow ledge, he grinned before he slopped out the lard onto the stones right below his feet. As he watched, the bucket load started its slow, sloppy descent. They would be slippery rocks for sure. He strolled back home for lunch.

The next afternoon he wandered uphill and sure enough could see results. On the first ledge, he could see where fingers had lost grip. There was nobody dead at the bottom, but Skipjack was near certain the scoundrel would not be back. He saw something glinting in the slanting afternoon sun. At first, he thought it was an insect caught in a web.

VARMINTS

Time for Timothy to go. He had worn out the patience of everyone except for Billy, who was fascinated with card tricks. Unfortunately, the *Sonata Queen* was not to leave until late Friday morning. She was scheduled to race the *Cincinnati Belle* to St. Louis. The *Sonata Queen*, a newer boat, was the heavy favorite among those interested. Timothy pestered everyone with bragging and swaggering. Although he kept his hands off the girls at the tavern, he ordered people around like he owned the joint.

A river pilot Skipjack had never met confided that the new plans for the tavern dining area were most appealing. The man volunteered that Timothy was a visionary. The pilot said he could "keep a secret" and winked. Skipjack winked back. Just a small thing, but a little later that same evening, Louis, the bartender, took him aside and wanted to know if a Mr. Bancroft was planning to open a combination brothel and gaming house behind the vegetable garden.

"Mr. Bancroft?"

"Yes, sir, he's been here every night playing cards with your brother. He's a big tipper."

Skipjack closed his eyes before he asked, "Does he tip before or after he pays?"

"No, sir, your brother buys. Bancroft only tips. Your brother feels sorry for him I suppose. Seems the gentleman can't get enough of losing. Might run a decent dollhouse, but he ain't a card player. Your brother's taken him under his wing and has him on his tab."

"May I see it?" Skipjack asked.

"Yes, sir, but there's two of 'em."

"Two?"

"One is official, and the other is the one he is going to give to Mr. Bancroft. The official one has the family discount; the one he will show is all premium pricing."

"Let me have those things and no more discounts, understand? I don't care what my brother says."

"What if he fires me?"

"He can't, but I will if you don't do what I say."

Skipjack went to the office and wished there was some way to copy the damn tabs and send them to owners of all saloons Brother might frequent. He fumed and decided to ride back uphill to confront him. When he was about halfway, he no longer wanted to beat him, but was bound and determined to call him out.

He put Jessie in the stable. The mare and buggy were gone. Skipjack walked into the house. There was nobody home. It wasn't close to dark and he wasn't expected, so he wasn't so much worried as curious. When the sun started blinking through the tree line, part of him wanted to remount Jessie and go looking. About a half hour later, he heard the buggy rattling. He tried to look as natural as possible, but when it burst into sight, he could see something was wrong. For one thing, Marcie was switching the mare and Billy was clutching her arm with both hands. Skipjack hurried out to greet them. Marcie looked at him and said, "Please." She jumped from the buggy and ran to the house.

"Billy, what's wrong?" Skipjack said.

"Momma's crying," the boy said and then ran after his mother. Skipjack calmly unhitched the mare and put everything away properly. He stepped into the house quietly and climbed the stairs. The bedroom door was shut. He didn't notice Billy, who was in dark hallway shadows at his feet. Skipjack tapped lightly. There was no response, so he tapped again. Billy startled him when he tugged his trousers.

Skipjack looked and could see the boy shaking his head. The boy took his hand and led Skipjack down to the porch but seemed to want to lead further. Skipjack resisted.

"Is Momma all right?"

The boy nodded, obviously troubled.

"She was crying," he said.

"What do you know?"

The boy tugged his hand and Skipjack followed to a shrub where the road turned.

"I was swimming and when I walked up, I heard Uncle Tim say how it was a wonder how much I looked like you."

"That's all?"

"That's all I heard. She wrapped me in this towel. When we left, she made him scoot over. She was shaking. I was beside. He put his hand on my knee and squeezed. I never saw Momma cry before, did you?"

"Anything else?"

"He said he was family; squeezed my leg, then jumped out and said something I shouldn't. He looked mad. He walked off toward the tavern."

"He's leaving, son. Let's go see Momma."

"I don't like to see her cry."

"I don't either."

When they entered the house, Marcie was at the kitchen table with a drink poured for Jack and one for her. Before any words were said, she hugged Billy and hustled him off to his room. She was gone for a lot longer than Skipjack expected, so he peeked in the door. She pointed to the kitchen. After a few minutes, she joined him.

"What happened?"

"Nothing happened," she whispered, holding her forefinger to her lips.

"Why were you crying?"

"Hard to say."

"Did he . . .?"

"Didn't touch me. Only things he said. He brought up the night it happened. About how it must have been. How big you were to take me."

"Lord God," Skipjack exclaimed.

"He said folks thought you crazy."

"Well, how would they know? I never ever told."

"Well, I was showing, and of course, it didn't take genius to count."

"Never doubted from the first."

"He said that. Said when I was a girl, you swore to make me yours."

"That's bull. You didn't live here when you were a girl."

"Jack, way he talks, I swear he can make you believe anything. Said Billy looked like you and he does someway and then he grinned. All of a sudden felt dirty and sick. Never have known what happened that night."

"You don't think—?"

"That it was . . .? Oh, Jack, please! I can't think anything. I thought that awfulness was long gone."

"It is long gone."

"Not tonight."

"Don't worry; he's not staying. He can sleep on the riverbank for all I care. I'm running him off."

"Please stay here. I don't feel good."

"Me neither, but Tim has stirred up more trouble than I can stomach. Promise I won't be gone an hour. Lock the door and put the shotgun beside the bed. If he comes in, shoot him."

"Jack, don't do anything crazy."

"Marcie, he's been stealing. I already knew that, but this is it."

"Stealing, how?"

Skipjack told her about Bancroft. Marcie's eyes narrowed. Her lips drew thin.

"I'm going with you, Jack."

"Honey, you stay with Billy."

"I'll kill him myself. Messing with receipts?"

"Marcie, stay here."

Billy opened his door and announced he was hungry. Skipjack suggested Marcie throw some food together. She laughed and suggested he take the buggy and bring something back, so that's what he said he'd do.

The mare was lathered when Skipjack arrived. He had one of the kids hold her and instructed another child to fetch a bucket of water. Skipjack had his pistol tucked in his belt.

The rat had slipped off moments before. Louis—not having the receipts in front of him—had mistakenly overcharged Timothy, who had then insisted on seeing the bill. When he learned that Skipjack had both copies, Tim suddenly changed his tune and persuaded Bancroft to not only give him a lift to the *Sonata Queen*, but after promising him dinner and libations, had convinced him to pony up the lion's share. Louis said Timothy had promised the man that it would pay.

He hadn't been able to decide between chicken, roast pork, or catfish, so Skipjack returned home with all three, plus roasted vegetables and corn bread. Marcie was sitting on the porch when he pulled up. She walked down the steps carrying a rifle. Skipjack had to smile.

"Mary Frances sent this home, too. Wouldn't tell me what it was; said it was for you."

"I smell it. Coffee cake with cinnamon."

"Damn, that woman does love me."

"Don't get puffed. She sent it home to me."

"Yeah, but sent it with me, which means she trusts me."

"What happened?" Marcie asked, obviously relieved by Jack's good humor.

"He's gone and damned if he didn't sucker some other chisler into footing the bill and giving him a ride out. I didn't even see him, and we made out because he overpaid."

Marcie started laughing. She couldn't figure how. Skipjack told her, and she doubled over and said it served 'em right.

"Louis ain't all there, falling for that," he said.

"Timothy's slick, Jack. Something about him could make a soul believe morning was midnight. I swear it's true. Tell Louis no special deals no time for anybody ever. I don't think he's so dishonest, just simple."

When the two of them sat by candlelight at the table, Skipjack discovered how hungry he was, and Marcie discovered she had almost no appetite at all. She picked at vegetables and nibbled a chicken leg. He ate an entire catfish and gobbled roast pork.

"Amazing how much appetite chasing down a man you want to kill can leave."

"Amazes me how one man can kill appetite entirely."

"He is not welcome anymore long as I breathe."

"He'll be back, smooth as he is. Before we're looking. That's how he is. We have to guard against him, that's all."

"Maybe so. Billy lost his appetite, too?"

"No, I fried him eggs. Wasn't sure when you'd be back."

Skipjack took a bite of pork and nodded. He felt an unexplainable urge to find something good in Timothy.

"He sure took a shine to Billy though, didn't he?"

"The boy to him as well, but Timothy spoiled the shine. Billy's reached the age where he needs a man. You never have liked him all that much I know, but—"

"Shhh, whisper, sweetheart. Walls have ears. Let me speak for myself, please," Skipjack said.

He looked down at his empty plate and rubbed his brow with all ten fingers. Without looking up, he said, "I have had trouble." He raised his hand although Marcie was not about to speak. "Tonight, the boy showed something. I thought about it most of the way back. I felt love from him, Marcie, for the first time. He took my hand and led me away so as to spare feelings when he tried to tell what he heard."

"What did he hear? I mean, what did he say?"

"Is there a difference? Told me Tim said he resembled me. Is that what Billy heard?"

"Yes, I suppose. Tim was talking awful. I don't even know what he said from what I thought I heard."

Skipjack took Marcie's hand.

"Marcie, I saw something in Billy I was afraid was missing."

"You're shaking, Jack. You all right?"

Skipjack nodded. His face was no more than an inch above his plate. Tears were pushing through slammed-shut eyelids. Part of him wanted to shout and swear; part of him wanted to pray.

"Dear God, please bless this house and all folks in it. Save us from evil and may we somehow serve your purpose. Thank you for the dear hand holding mine and for the young boy in the next room. Sorry for praying so late in the meal. In Christ's name, I ask this. Amen."

Marcie had never heard a prayer quite like this before. She thought of Jack as a good man but had never expected to hear him pray.

"Are you all right? Tell me you're all right."

He nodded without looking and said, "I'm all right." He squeezed her hands tenderly. "Honey, ain't every day you set out to shoot your brother, miss the chance, and discover your boy might have some backbone and heart, and that your wife is solid as rock. How can I not be thankful? Besides that, he's gone, praise God."

"Where did you learn to pray, Jack Maddox?"

"There weren't no learning."

"Jack, let's lock the doors and go to bed."

"I thought they were locked."

"Double check. I'll be upstairs waiting."

"You might say I need a bath, Marcie."

"You might say the same about me."

Skipjack lit a cigar and walked out onto the porch, slipped out of his boots, trousers, and shirt. He peeled down completely, spread his arms, and bowed his head. Under his breath, he said, "I meant every doggone word. Please believe me." He stubbed his cigar, scooped his clothes, and climbed the stairs to bed. Venus shone in the bedroom window. In dim light, he tumbled his clothes on the chair and then pulled the curtains. He crawled in, half expecting snores, but was pleasantly surprised by an embrace and nibbling kisses.

"My goodness," he whispered.

"Oh, Jack," she answered. "Keep your goodness to yourself."

CHAPTER 3

A FINE-FITTING SUIT

N ext morning, as he walked into the bar, Skipjack was surprised to see what at first appeared to be a finely appointed gentleman. From the back, Skipjack noticed the fellow was draped in a suit of fine quality gray material. A dark stain on the collar appeared to be wet. At first, he didn't think much about it. He declined Louis's offer of a shot of whiskey and egg and allowed as how he needed one of Mary Frances's sit-down breakfasts. He asked Louis if there was anything he needed to know. Before Louis could speak, the stranger turned to face him.

"Hell yes, there's some news," he said. "Two steamboats rolled out of downtown about three hours ago and one of 'em had a boiler blow. I heard at least ten was killed. They was in a race."

Skipjack looked closely. Something didn't look right. The fellow was drunk. That wasn't strange, but there was strangeness in how clothes hung, sleeves too long, and stains on the knees of his trousers didn't bone up right. His face wasn't shaved, hands rough. Even a fine pink handkerchief could not distract from the fact: this man did not fit the suit.

"What you looking at, mister? I got money good as you."

"Hold on, friend," Skipjack replied. "I never said a word. What boat was it?"

The stranger smiled like he was possessed of arcane knowledge.

"The new one they call *Sonata*. I seen it. Just when they took off, it happened. I've worked them boilers. They can be tricky, let me tell. Poured it on hard too soon. That's what it was, sure as gravy."

The man's eyes were glinty and his hair unkempt. There were coin-sized stains down the coat front. The rough boots the man wore didn't square. Skipjack smiled as he noticed the man's glass near empty. He patted the bar and laid money down.

"Give the man another of what he's having."

"You won't drink with me?" the man said gruffly.

"Well, now that you mention, I will, sir. Thank you. My tonic, Louis, if you please." Skipjack nodded at Louis, who was not looking comfortable. "By your comportment, sir, I would propose that you are an investor, either that or a first-class passenger."

The man looked down, then up to the ceiling, and his eyes twinkled when they settled on Skipjack. He grabbed what remained of his drink and polished it off, then snatched up the other almost before Louis had set it down. He scowled at Louis, then smiled at Skipjack, who picked up his drink and held it like a chalice. Without drinking, he said, "Can you see colors swirl in morning sunlight? Reminds one of sunset somehow and evening's rest, don't you agree? I can surmise you are well acquainted with finer things. You are an investor. I got that part right, didn't I?"

"Yes, you are correct. But an investor in the one that didn't blow, tell the truth. Now that new one surely blew a pipe. She didn't sink, least while I was there, but the screaming was awful, here to tell."

Skipjack downed his and ordered another round. The stranger insisted on paying and fumbled in his pockets until he found the one with money.

"Oh, Louis," he said, "make it a double. For God's sake, man, it's a brand-new day. Hell's fire, make her a double double. I'm buying. Heed what I say."

Louis lined them up and the stranger poured one down and then another. Skipjack took a sip and smiled.

"What brings you upriver, my friend?" he asked.

The man looked at him fierily and said, "Investments."

"What kind?"

"Ain't free to talk. Don't want to show your hand, you know?" He grabbed up his drink, looked over his shoulder at Louis, and slapped the bar. "Look sharp and set us up again."

"What you think about this reach? Think there's money?"

The man shook his head and looked mournful. When he spoke, it almost seemed rehearsed.

"Mister, I see you are a man of quality, even though your style don't speak to that. I'll tell you what I think. Move. That's what I think. Ten years ago, when the gold rush bunch was coming west, this place could have been a gold mine. Look at it now, a heap of shacks and one stone building on a sleepy bend. Hell, all the money's in town and the railroad's gonna haul that away. But there is hope, if somebody got hold this place and done something with it. But the owner of this place I hear is a deadhead."

About this time, Andy walked in. Skipjack scowled and waved him off. Andy's eyebrows raised; Skipjack's lowered.

"What's a nigger doing in here?"

"They wander in time to time," Skipjack said. "By the way, I thought you said you were from Cincinnati?"

"No, I ain't ever said."

"Well, you said you come upriver looking."

"Sir, that's a fact, I did say that," the man said. "What I didn't say was where I was coming from, as you obviously know Cincinnati is upstream."

"True enough," Skipjack said. "You sound like you might be from Mississippi Delta country, my friend."

"Never you mind, stranger, where I'm from. I come hunting prospects."

"I ain't doubting, for goodness sakes. So, you're heading to Cincinnati where you're based?"

"Most likely, though lately, Memphis has been home."

"That's something. You sure get around. Of course, that's the way of business, I understand."

"Yep," the man said. "It is that way."

"Give us another round, Louis," Skipjack said. "By the way, you think this place might have a future? Maybe the two of us could talk over breakfast. I'm working an appetite."

"Nope, not necessary," the stranger said.

"I know I'm small," Skipjack said, "but I work hard and got money saved."

The man's eyes lit. "Sure, money, but what you need is control. I got control. Do you? Without control, you ain't got nothing. Are you connected? Don't even answer. I know the answer already or you wouldn't be here drinking. I am connected and will own this river and you will know my name."

"You going to buy the entire river?"

"No. I didn't say that."

"If I am wrong, Louis, give the man a shot of the best brandy this joint has to offer." He winked when he said it, and to Skipjack's relief, Louis reached for the cheap.

"Damn, I could have sworn I heard you say."

"Whatever," the man muttered as he poured down the brandy. "I'll tell you this, there's folks better wake quick or mud will be slippery beneath their feet. Powerful folks in this world called kingmakers and they don't calls them that for nothing. Average folk get by, while those folks take what they want when they want. Mark my words. Nothing stands in their way, so nothing stops 'em."

The man excused himself and stiff legged out to the latrine. His fine clothing flapped, but there was no breeze. Louis leaned across the bar.

"That ain't his suit. That's Mr. Bancroft's suit."

Skipjack nodded and said, "Tell Andy to send for the sheriff. Then come right back, but first, pour my drinks off and set another round for him."

The man staggered back in just as Louis was leaving.

"Hell is everybody? Place is asleep. Now downtown is different. Suppose you seldom get there, but this is lugubrious. Where are the womens?"

Skipjack shrugged and pointed to the man's fresh drink.

"I got to ask you something confidential," the man slurred. "Do you know the owner of this joint? I got business with him and hear he is a lazy son of a bitch don't work a lick and goes fishing every night. You know if that's true?"

"Well, I've heard he fishes and don't spend time here. Heard he sets across about dark. Some says he heads upstream, then again, some says down."

"Same as I heard, farmer. Lazy son of a bitch. He inherited, I hear. You got me?"

"Think so," Skipjack said.

"I worked all my life to get mine, hear me? Inherited, my ass. Don't respect a man who gets booty for nothing. Did you buy your land?"

"No," Skipjack said. "It was Daddy's, but I've worked all my life."

"Seem all right," he allowed. "Maybe you're different, but most who get it that way think they're better than Aunt Louise."

"You think I think I'm better than you? Louis, bring us a brandy. I'll show you I ain't."

"Mister, suppose I might be getting close to full. Standing right now is a pretty fair trick," said the stranger with a conspiratorial leer.

"You won't drink with me?" Skipjack asked. "Who needs a place to stand, when there's a place to stretch and rest your bones out back? You said you got business with the owner here. Take some advice; you better get sharp, you hear?"

"Sharp enough. Won't see me coming," the man said with a grin.

"Or going either, I'd bet."

"Neither one, own the joint 'fore he sees me. Slick and sharp as a folding razor."

The stranger clutched the brandy snifter but missed his mouth and bloodshot eyes rolled as he slid to his knees. Skipjack nodded, and Louis called for Andy. The stranger was locked in the corncrib before he even snored.

"Poor man has probably been up all night," Skipjack said. "Did you get word to the sheriff?"

"Already sent word to the store. Sheriff'll be here shortly," Andy replied.

"Take good care of him. Strip him down and bring his clothes and stuff to the office, if you wouldn't mind. Better put some water in the corncrib with him. Be careful; he's bad news. Take this pistol. Louis, you help. Keep the gun on him. He's bound to have a knife or two at least. If you have to, shoot him. I'll say I done it."

Andy said, "I'll do it, sir, but what I was fixing to tell you earlier, I caught a lowdown stealing chickens. I whacked him across the head. He'd already killed a few."

"When was that?"

"Just before sunup. It wasn't hard, man has a broken arm. Got him tied up by the hog lot in the shade."

"Awfully considerate. Why don't you strip him down and drop him in the corncrib, too?"

Skipjack ate breakfast. Nobody disturbed him while he was doing that. Mary Frances stood guard, and no one could get through her. As soon as he had chewed the last bite, Mary Frances informed him that the buggy the corncrib stranger had driven smelled to high heaven.

"You know something?"

"How long we been together? That ain't his buggy."

Skipjack sat at the desk while his stomach churned. Why did he want to bother about what kind of rig the imposter rode in on? He took a slug of coffee. Damn, his brother had worn him out. Glad he was gone, he sighed just before there was a tapping on his door. Skipjack placed his hand atop the pistol grip and asked who was there.

It was Billy. Mary Frances loomed right behind him.

"What is it?"

"Your son wants to talk to you, if I'm not mistaken."

The boy nodded rapidly.

"Well, what is it? Can you tell me?" Skipjack replied while looking at Mary Frances.

"Uncle Timothy's come back and told me to get lost and then yelled at Momma."

"Back? What did he say?"

"Don't yell at me, Daddy. Please don't yell. He told me to get lost and I don't know what, I just ran," the boy said and broke down crying.

"Son of a bitch."

"Please, Daddy, don't yell."

Mary Frances held the boy. Skipjack's eyes looked wild. The boy trembled. She stroked his head.

"That was up at the house?"

The boy nodded, and Skipjack took off running. He waved as he passed the corncrib and then jumped off a crate up onto Jessie's back and off they went at a swift trot. There was nothing he wouldn't put past his brother. That son of a bitch would screw an earthworm or an angel with equal relish.

He didn't think much as Jessie pulled the hill. She was old, so he didn't dig in the heels, but at the top, when he saw the quarter top-buggy and mare were gone, he flat out blew his stack. He yelled for Marcie and when he got no answer, his blood ran cold. He searched the place; discovered his brother's valise was gone and noticed that Marcie's snuffbox was not on the kitchen table. The last observation comforted him temporarily.

He jumped back on Jessie, apologized, and headed downtown. He figured his odds were better than fifty-fifty. No way would the man risk the Cincinnati road. Probably come for his bag. Skipjack calmed himself as best he could. Though fearing the worst, he assured himself he would encounter Marcie on her return.

He was right. In less than a mile, he thanked God when he was sure it was her coming his way. He jumped off Jessie and ran to the buggy.

"Where you been?"

Marcie shook her head and Skipjack realized he better shut up. He tied Jessie to the buggy and sat on the seat beside his wife. He said nothing till she handed him the reins.

"He made you drive him someplace?"

Marcie nodded her head and asked, "Where's Billy?"

"With Mary Frances. Billy's who told me. He's a good boy," Skipjack murmured.

"Hope so," she said.

They proceeded slowly, Jessie tethered behind. Skipjack knew better than to start speculating, so he studied the air between the mare's chestnut colored ears and from time to time glanced at the clear blue sky. Through her skirt, Marcie's thigh felt like stone.

"He came to get me. He is a good boy to do that."

Marcie nodded. Skipjack noticed her fingers were clenched, but he fought the urge to speak.

"Why is he so hateful?" she whispered.

Skipjack clucked, encouraging the mare to pull the hill.

"He didn't lay a hand on me or Billy, either, but you would have sworn he'd as soon slice us to pieces the way he yelled. I told Billy to run. Didn't have to say it even, just gave him a look. I never saw anything like it. Timothy's gone crazy!"

"Where did he have you take him?"

"He wanted to go all the way to town, but then he saw some dandies right before Goose Creek. He jumped out while we were still moving. Grinned, snatched his stuff, and hopped into their buggy, then blew me a kiss. Can you believe it—a bunch of dandies?"

"Which way they head?"

"Honey, I don't know. I turned around, sick to my stomach. Billy's all right?"

"Unless Mary Frances has changed, he is. Did Timothy say anything at all?"

"Didn't say much. Was the way he said the things he said. That man is all the way gone. I just wanted him away. I would have done anything, and he knew it. He said nothing on the way to town, except for how it was a nice day, then smiled when he said he appreciated the lift."

"Let's go get Billy."

Marcie nodded.

"Excuse me, honey. Please stop, I have to relieve myself."

Skipjack pulled over beneath a mulberry tree. Marcie climbed down. A redwing blackbird squirted deep red juice on the seat. Then another flopped right on her blouse. She stepped back aboard, and they rolled off.

"What's that on your hand?" Marcie asked.

"Mulberry juice I wiped off the seat cushion. Forgive me."

"What have I got to forgive you for?"

"Stopping under a mulberry tree, I suppose. Damn bird got your blouse, too."

Marcie looked blank. She brushed reddish juice off her shoulder.

"Jack, his dealing hand. He kept it in his pocket most of the time, but when he snatched his bag, his hand looked like it was gnawed on by a hog. It was purple, blue and—"

"What?"

"Your hand reminded me. His looked chewed on; dark holes like teeth make. His thumb was purple."

"Brother's in deep."

"Deep into Sheol! Gone devil-dog crazy."

"He won't be back."

"I don't know, Jack. He could do anything."

"I got a jerk locked up in the corncrib who might shed some light."

Marcie placed her hand on his shoulder as Skipjack clucked at the mare.

"Let's get Billy like you said."

"I'd feel a lot better if you stay down here till we can go home together."

"I would, too."

"When did he come back?"

"You hadn't been gone ten minutes."

"Just walked in?"

"Didn't even look. Stormed straight to Billy's room, came out with his valise, and threw it on the front porch; poured coffee with the wrong hand now I think. Everything about him was wrong. Snarled, what was I looking at? I said nothing. He paced around and when Billy walked in, he actually growled, and then said he was kidding. Billy ran to his room. Timothy went back out to the porch, then yelled hitch the buggy. Believe me, I did it, no question."

Skipjack and Marcie were approaching the tavern; some kids walked forward to tether the mare. A child carrying a bucket of water strained under its weight.

"Where was Billy in all of this?"

"When I came back into the kitchen after hitching, Timothy was cussing Billy. I gave Billy a look and that's all it took; out the door. He knew one or the other of us was going to kill him."

The tallest kid grabbed the halter. Skipjack handed him a coin. Skipjack and Marcie walked straight into the kitchen and sure enough, Billy had been made useful. He was washing pots and pans until he saw them and ran up to embrace his mother. Mary Frances strolled over.

"He's a worker. He ain't no shirker," she said.

Billy ran back to pots and pans and scrubbed fitfully.

"We call him Willy here," Mary Frances said without looking back.

Marcie and Skipjack slipped into the office. Clothing was stacked on two chairs. On the top of the fancy suit was a razor knife. The other pile was crowned with a crude, very sharp, wooden-handled knife. There was a pile of money on the desk and some scraps of paper. One of the notes was unintelligible; one that could be made out said, "the river flows and flows." The third was a bill of sale. Scarf Bros., but it was only the top fragment.

"Just stay beside me a minute," Marcie said from the sofa.

Skipjack sat down. He pulled her to him, but she seemed to be holding back.

"Honey, I don't know what to do. You tell me, all right?"

"Jack, Tim's a monster. Believe me, he's much worse than we thought."

He breathed in deeply, concentrated on the doorknob and held her. He loved to comfort her but felt the need to look in on the vermin confined in the corncrib.

"Why don't you stretch out? I'll lock the door," he whispered.

"You would leave me? What if Billy comes?"

"Something tells me to get out to the corncrib."

"Well, let's go."

"Marcie, they're naked. Two naked men."

"Oh, good, I get to test my morals."

CORNCRIB CONFESSIONS

As they neared the corncrib, they saw the sheriff dismounting. The prisoners rattled the slatted door.

"What you got?" the sheriff asked.

"One sure-thing chicken thief and, if I'm not mistaken, a murderer for hire."

"Well then, let's have a look-see," the lawman said, as he adjusted his belt and drew his pistol. "They ain't armed?"

Assured they were not, the sheriff nodded, and Andy sprung the latch. The two men climbed out gasping, too hot and thirsty to worry about nakedness.

"Better bring these boys water. They both look dry. It is hot, ain't it?"

Marcie took one look and then shooed away the children who were gathering. Andy reappeared in a few moments with a pail and a dipper and placed it at the naked men's feet, but neither drank.

"Ain't you boys thirsty? A drink might help tell your stories. Start with you, scout; what's your tall tale?"

The man looked down. The drunk fellow grinned and reached for the dipper.

"Did I tell you to have a drink, Slasher?"

The hand retracted and covered privates.

"I recognize you, Slasher. Do you recognize me?"

Slasher shook his head. The other prisoner fiddled with his splint.

"I reckon you got to know each other pretty well in there with all them cobs. Tell me, halfwit, what you know about Slasher?"

The man said nothing.

"Know enough to keep your mouth shut, don't you? Good boy. You might do fine in jail. What about you, Slasher? Know something I need to hear?"

Slasher shook his head. The sheriff allowed as how he had been out riding the county all day and that he was hungry, thirsty, and in need of a breather. He smiled when he said this. He instructed Andy to lock the men back in the corncrib.

"Come on, Skipjack, you owe me one. What's Mary Frances got cooking? I could use a drink while you tell me what you know about these characters."

The sheriff was as thirsty as he was hungry. He poured down beer and some whiskey before gobbling a chicken and a plate of greens. He was not a small man. The offering did not seem to fill him up.

"Wish I didn't have to travel so far, or I would sample more, but I have to be mindful of my steed."

Skipjack filled the sheriff in and showed him the stuff in the office. Mary Frances suggested the buggy would be a fine place to look for clues. The sheriff asked for another beer and agreed. Within a few minutes, there was enough proof to haul in Slasher for theft. Bancroft's signature was on a ripped bill of sale found wadded beneath a cushion. It matched the piece out of Slasher's coat pocket.

Slasher was still too ornery to talk straight, so they gave him a spot of whiskey. He grinned at the man with the splint as he chugged.

"You're on top of your game, Slasher," sheriff said.

The poor man was so stupefied that he nodded and grinned. The sheriff took the other guy aside about thirty yards. No one could hear what was said. After a few minutes, the sheriff marched him back and thrust him in the corncrib and walked off with the staggering Slasher. It was shameful looking. They ended up sitting down on the tailgate of a wagon, but it didn't look like they were talking at all.

The sheriff waved Skipjack over.

"Do you realize," the sheriff said, "that this critter has eluded me for two years? I tell you, Skipjack, this boy is so shifty, he is darn near invisible. You looking at him, but then you'd swear you weren't, isn't that true?"

Skipjack nodded. The poor man squirmed.

"See how pale and I ain't talking about privates. I'm sure he shares space with cave spiders and rats; comes out at night on tiptoe. Used to lift wallets like floating feathers, but the Slash has taken to drink and lost his touch. Hold out your hands steady, boy."

The man didn't respond. The sheriff grinned and cocked his pistol. The hands stretched out and trembled.

"This poor fellow needs another drink; don't you think so? Look how he's shaking."

Nobody spoke until Andy walked up with a bottle of brandy. The sheriff thanked him.

"Memphis, is it, Slasher?" the sheriff asked, uncorking the bottle and admiring its contents. "I believe you offered as how you were looking to buy this establishment, said you had backers, big bucks behind you? Would you like a wee nip, little Slasher?"

Slasher stared at his hands, which were still extended and trembling. His eyes were dim, and he did not respond. The sheriff fired his pistol into the air.

"I'm talking to you, Slash. Would you like a drink?"

Slasher covered his ears and gritted what was left of his teeth. The sheriff handed him the bottle and cocked his pistol. Slasher clutched it and poured some down. He looked pleadingly at Skipjack.

"Skipjack, I got this man dead to rights for one murder from a year ago. He's been hiding with guttersnipes down in Memphis. Wonder what brought him back. Do I have to ask you where you got the suit and the fancy ride, Slasher? Take another drink while you ponder."

The man desperately slugged a gob full. Skipjack hated to watch, so he glanced toward the corncrib, saw Andy was there still, but no one else. Skipjack didn't want to be either. Slasher tilted the bottle and sloshed down some more.

"That should be enough, Slasher. Consider it kindness I'm cutting you off. Going to book you for murder sure thing, but that was a full year ago. You sneaky devil; ear to ear makes two smiles. What brought you back from Memphis, Slasher? Want another drink? What the heck? Probably your last. I sure would love to know how you got away that night." He paused. "Will you look, Skipjack? Here come my boys with the wagon to haul these two. You ain't slipping this time, slick. But before you go down, would you like to tell me where you were holed last night and where you got the suit? You tell me that and maybe I'll let you keep the bottle for the ride with your corncob pal."

Slasher shook his head, so the sheriff stood, pointed the gun right at the man's head, and instructed him to hand the bottle to Skipjack. Slasher shook his head, clutched the bottle like it was a baby. Skipjack swallowed involuntarily.

"You the owner?" Slasher croaked, squinting through watery slits.

Skipjack nodded. The man inhaled, hissing through his rotted teeth. "You never said so, farmer. You're a damn liar."

"You been had, Slasher," the sheriff said. "Somebody's going to have a big time and you're not. How's that make you feel? You want that bottle, might want to talk about what happened."

The man said nothing.

"Tell me what happened after you stole the buggy and disposed of the body of the man whose throat you opened to night air."

Slasher took another drink, glared at Skipjack, and hugged the bottle.

"Do you like to be laughed at, Slasher?"

"Didn't dispose nobody."

"Did you purchase the buggy with hard-earned cash and happen to inherit a bloody suit? You're better than that, I'll grant you. Your trick is clean, Slasher."

"Maybe somebody forced him, sheriff," Skipjack said.

"I hadn't figured that. Maybe I've been too hard on him. Have a drink. There's still a chance."

The man rolled his eyes; he fumbled the brandy and poured what he could into his mouth. He opened his eyes as far as he could and nodded.

The sheriff fired his pistol again. The man grimaced.

"Who was this man?" the sheriff asked. "Did he give you the suit? Did he give you the buggy?"

Slasher waved his hand and chuckled. His chin fell on his sunken chest. When he said no, no, no, his voice rasped like a wounded crow's.

"Drunk . . . but remember better than you know. I didn't do no killing. Seen it though. Man who done it said this fellow tried to rob him; showed me how his hand was bloody. Asked would I run him out. Offered me half the dead man's roll. Upfront money and I said let's go. He peeled the man and dumped him in the creek. I didn't even help. Didn't ask; he just give me the suit."

Slasher fell silent and when he drank some more brandy, the sheriff cocked his pistol. Deputies were walking over. The sheriff waved them off and winked at Skipjack.

"I drop him off. Supposed to pick him up. Didn't forget neither. Yeah, drunk, but truth is, pretty sure I was next."

"You ought to be a good judge of your peers."

"Well, thank you, sheriff. Known my share, heaven knows. Look here. Before he threw him in the crick, he cut off the balls like cutting a hog. It was dim light, but still that made me think. When he commenced talking about taking over this tavern and how would I like to be his right hand, I 'bout forget what I seen him do. Part wanted to believe, and part couldn't. Was not myself someway."

Slasher dropped the bottle and then jerked awake. Skipjack rescued the bottle before much had spilled and handed it back.

"Thanks, farmer," he said and sagged. "Was supposed to fetch him after a short spell near the top of that hill." He pointed up toward Skipjack's house. "But I come into drinking." Slasher chuckled and winked. "Come to think, man he wanted cut was you, farmer. Now ain't that funny?"

"Not real funny," Skipjack said. "You said you have backers?"

"He was the backer; said he was going to own this river. Stood him up, 'cause I was jittered."

"Can you tell what this man looks like?"

"Sheriff, close as I can. He looked like Satan—dressed in dove gray with a tongue of silver, I swear. It's just I had second thoughts. God help me."

Both men steadied Slasher as they walked him back. He became violent when one of the deputies tried to take the brandy.

"Let him keep it," the sheriff barked. "Okay with you?"

Skipjack nodded and said, "It's got to be Timothy."

Sheriff laid his heavy hand on Skipjack's shoulder. "This man is a consummate liar. He eats and breathes lies."

"Might be so, but I believe him."

"No hard feelings then?" the sheriff asked. "I do, too, mostly."

———

Willy, as he was now known to the staff in the kitchen, wanted to continue snapping beans and washing dishes, so Skipjack and Marcie sat outside sipping cool drinks and watching the river flow. There was a front blowing from the north and the breeze was cool. Both were thankful for clouds, which hid the bright sun time to time.

"Always something to see on water," Skipjack said.

"I don't feel like cooking tonight."

"Maybe Billy can fix us something."

"Exactly my thought."

Skipjack raised his eyebrows.

"I'll go place an order with him. You need a break."

"I'm sure you're right," Skipjack said as he raised his glass.

"I'll take care of that, too." She stood and winked.

Skipjack yawned and slouched back in his chair. He saw a fish leap, arc, and splash. A dark shape slashed from the sky—a golden eagle—then a flash of water and a glinting fish, pierced by talons, was airborne. Skipjack smiled and admired the lifting strength of the bird, which loosed that fish, dove again to snatch another. This time the eagle lifted and angled upstream toward the cottonwoods on Twelve Mile Island. The eagle still looked large as it settled. A flatboat slid downstream and a sternwheeler trailing black smoke steamed upstream. Skipjack stretched and yawned again. Marcie was right. He needed to relax.

She brought them both whiskeys with sprigs of mint. He accepted his gratefully.

"I had a talk with Louis. There will be no more family discounts."

"Not even for me?"

"Nope," she said. "Once you make exceptions, you open the door to trouble. We need none of that."

"How are Billy's dinner preparations coming?"

"You'll be satisfied."

Billy walked out proudly and stood before them rubbing his hands on his apron.

"Honey glaze or whiskey sauce with walnut bits?"

"Get out of here," Skipjack said laughing.

"I'm serious. Which one?"

Skipjack and Marcie looked at one another. She nodded.

"I'll bet you favor honey glaze," Skipjack ventured. "If so, that will do nicely."

The boy nodded and started back to the kitchen. He turned and announced it shouldn't be long.

"I like this."

"Keep your fingers crossed, Jack. He's only a boy."

"Yeah, maybe, but I'm getting ideas I hope you like."

"When you gonna cut me in?"

"I'll tell you when I get 'em better, like maybe on the ride home or maybe later when we stretch out. They're only pecking the shell now. They ain't hatched."

"Maybe I have some for you."

As they ascended the hill, sunset flickered through weaving branches. The buggy jounced and squeaked.

Skipjack knew he'd left the tavern in good hands. Mary Frances knew where to stash the cash and Andy was standing guard. Skipjack felt free to smell the honey-glazed pork and, as it turned out, the honey-glazed new potatoes. There was okra, beans, and squash with some bacon and poke greens, but in these dishes, not even a hint of honey glaze. The corn bread, on the other hand, was full of molasses; that had mollified Billy, plus Mary Frances had let him stir it in.

"When do you turn twelve, son?"

"Right before Christmas."

"There's some things I need to show you."

"Like what?"

"Want to go fishing on the river in the morning?"

"Where the big ones are?"

"Sometimes they are, and I want to teach you to shoot, too. Think you can do that?"

"Jack, no point in pushing things."

"No doubt you're right, Marcie. Why don't you come along fishing in the morning? We'll talk about it. I don't want to push for damn sure."

"If you weren't a young man, Billy, believe I'd be inclined to call you Honey Glaze. The meal you fixed was delicious."

"I didn't do it all. Mary Frances helped pretty much. I did do the potatoes by myself, except for taking 'em out of the oven. She wouldn't let me do that, but she showed me how to poke with a fork to see they're done. She's nice."

"She's a big-hearted woman."

"Can I work with her again, Momma?"

"If you make food like this, I'll vote for it," Skipjack said. Marcie nodded.

The three of them sat on the porch and enjoyed the cool breeze and the lightning bugs. Billy caught one and was intrigued by the intermittent soft yellow glow.

"I wish I could do that. How do they do that, Daddy?"

"Well, son, I can't tell you how, but I can tell you why."

"How come you can't tell me how?"

"Because it's one of life's mysteries I haven't solved. In short, I don't know the how. I do know why. Would you like to know why?"

"I guess so."

"They're looking for treasure."

"Looking for treasure?"

"Sure, all God's creatures are looking for treasure one way or other. See how they seem to swoop and dance, first here, then there. They're busy all night making nighttime interesting. Why, that's a treasure in and of itself, won't you agree?"

Billy opened his hand and watched as the lightning bug crawled to the tip of his forefinger and flew away.

"Go find your treasure, little friend. See, he's looking."

"And dancing."

"Time for you to dance off to bed," Marcie said. "You're bound to be tired working in that kitchen."

"Not all that tired," Billy said with a yawn. "But if you promise to help Dad solve the mystery, I'll say that I am."

"I promise we'll try. Come on, Honey Glaze."

"That's what Daddy said he was gonna call me."

"No, I didn't," Skipjack said. "I said I would call you that if you were a girl, but you are a young man. Give me a hug before Momma tucks you in."

"Thought you didn't like hugs."

Skipjack pulled the boy to him and rubbed the back of his head.

"You're scratchy," Billy said, but was laughing. "Still want to go fishing?"

"Sure do. Try to talk your Momma into going."

The boy nodded and waved. Skipjack found himself wanting a glass of whiskey, but didn't feel like stirring, so he sat there and watched the fireflies' sparkling. A few minutes later, Marcie walked out with a taste of whiskey and a glass of wine.

"Damn, you read my mind."

"Part of the job."

"Thanks."

"You were good with Billy."

"He was good to me. Running all the way down to tell me."

"I'm proud, too. You had me worried, though, with the mystery-of-life stuff."

"Not sure what you mean."

"He's only a boy. I was afraid you might tell him things that might confuse him."

"Never occurred to me. I was only thinking about the magic of nature."

"He is young."

"Might be young, but he does need to learn to shoot. I don't mean kill, necessarily."

"Then why shoot? I don't like it."

"We'll shoot targets. I don't like the idea of him not knowing guns. Feel the need to teach. Hope to God he never needs to use one."

"Amen to that."

"Would be a whole lot better if you went with us in the morning. I'm going to take most of the next few days off. Seems like we should stick close until we know what's going on, don't you think?"

"Suppose so, but I got Lacy coming here early afternoon."

"You know better, but I bet Billy'll be bored by late morning unless we have a boatload of fish. Even so, we'll get you back."

"Let's lock it up. There's something I want to tell you but feel the need to tell you upstairs."

"Billy says I'm scratchy."

"Maybe I'll like that. Finish and come on up."

By the time he hit the top stair, he could hear light snoring. He slipped in beside her and tucked the sheet beneath his chin. Her breathing was slow and easy. He thanked God for that.

In the middle of the night, he got up to pee. He skipped past the chamber pot and went out to the porch. It was the first cool night in weeks. He raised his arms as his bladder drained and allowed coolness to encircle him. There was no good thing to be done about Tim. Skipjack knew that full well. He looked in on Billy, who was so quiet Skipjack touched him to make sure he was there.

Later as a faint glow filled the window, Jack rolled toward Marcie. He put his thigh over hers.

"I believe I forgot to tell you something," she whispered.

CORN BREAD AND HONEY

They decided to have the leftovers of Billy's meal for breakfast, except Billy who wanted only corn bread and honey. When Marcie returned from the springhouse, she was puzzled.

"Did you fellas slip out and raid the food?"

Skipjack and Billy both shook their heads.

"Well, somebody did. Looks like we're all eating corn bread and honey, 'cause that's all that's left. Eggs, bacon, everything's gone."

"Damn. I got to put a damn lock on the springhouse, too."

"Who you think did it, Dad?"

"I hate to think. You notice anything besides missing food?"

"No, the door was shut and latched."

Skipjack went to see if he could spot anything else. He made Billy stay with Marcie. Jessie and the mare were fine. Gracie padded over and tried to lick his hand. Her brown eyes turned curious when Skipjack growled.

"Worthless mutt."

She followed right at his heels as he walked to the springhouse. Nothing stood out. It was a cool dew-misted morning. Birds were celebrating sunrise. Everything looked fine. Inside the springhouse, Old Fred slouched on his favorite rafter. Skipjack asked him if he had seen anything peculiar. Fred flicked his tongue. Skipjack closed the door. He needed a good stout hasp and a first-rate lock. It burned him up. Billy was on the porch eating. Skipjack shrugged when he walked past him. Marcie was seated at the kitchen table with a mug of coffee.

"I hardly know what to think. Everything looks all right. Besides a good lock, we got to get a new watchdog. Gracie ain't worth a hoot."

"Don't be too hard on Gracie. Maybe she knew whoever it was. You think of that?"

"Just did as you were saying, and Timothy never did like corn bread either, especially with molasses. He always hated molasses. But I have a hard time believing that he would show around here."

"Jack, I don't know; the man is a hellhound, believe me, please."

"I hate to call for the sheriff again."

"Jack, not only this. I'm thinking next."

Instead of going straight to the tavern they stopped at the little store in the fork of River Road and asked Miss Metcalf to please tell the deputy when he checked in to tell the sheriff Maddox needed to see him.

"Some trouble?" she asked.

Folks knew to not give Miss Metcalf too much information unless they wanted it spread countywide, so Skipjack asked her politely to please just do as he had asked. Miss Metcalf chewed on that like a slice of sour apple.

As luck would have it, Brawl Thurston was passing by hauling a full wagonload of lumber.

"Damn, you got your work cut out. Just unloading that will take to dinner."

"Nah. You should see the crew they got up there. I'm only a splinter.

The place we're building's as big as ten houses and barn all in one. Gonna have ten chimneys and three different staircases. It's railroad money."

Skipjack shook his head and said, "Damn, I was hoping to persuade you to secure my springhouse with a hasp and lock tougher than the county jail."

"When you need it?"

"I wish I'd had it last night."

"Be done before dark."

"Don't want to put you out."

"You do me right, I do you right. Maybe I call on you sometime."

"You call on me anytime."

"I'll be there this evening."

"Thank you. I'll be there."

"That worked out well, wouldn't you say?" Marcie and Billy both nodded.

"We still going fishing?" Billy asked.

"That's the plan and so far, so good. You know, wouldn't it be nice if there was some kind of lantern that would light up when the wrong foot set down on a property?"

"How would the lamp know?"

"Billy, I haven't got that far, but the more I think, that wouldn't make much difference. Good folks wouldn't mind, the others would. But no point worrying. The springhouse is going to have a lock tonight."

"Maybe the stable should, too," Marcie said.

"Damn, you sure are right again. This craziness has got to stop."

At the tavern, Andy greeted them and while Billy and Marcie were distracted by a runaway piglet, Andy whispered a disturbing bit of yesterday's news in Skipjack's ear, but now all was business as usual. No surprises this morning. The corncrib was only a corncrib. Everything was running smoothly. Skipjack told Andy he was going fishing and if the sheriff came by, to say he'd be back before lunchtime and that everything was on the house.

Thornton Green was having his breakfast outside. He was seated by himself devouring beefsteak and what looked to be a half dozen eggs. Mary Frances had tipped them off to the fact that he was there, so Marcie and Billy had scurried to the office to cut a check for whiskey money.

Skipjack walked up and greeted him. Green stood. Once again, Skipjack was amazed at how large the man was. Even his moustache would have been comfortable on a buffalo. His eyes were small but were friendly, jovial companions.

"Ain't this a fine morning? Cool for a change and look at the fog lifting. I'm telling you, it's special, ain't it? Won't you join me?"

Skipjack held up his hand and told him he was taking the wife and son fishing. He said Marcie would be right out with the money for the last delivery. Green said he wasn't worried; he had come for the priceless view.

"Say," Skipjack said quietly, "Andy told me you saw Brother yesterday. I assume it was River Road. You said he looked beat up?"

"Pretty damn sure it was him. Was our side of Beargrass Creek. Walking with one hand over his face like he was shielding eyes from sun. Thing is the sun went in and he still kept the hand up. I called his name. He waved me on and looked away. Hand he waved looked bloody."

"Was he carrying anything?"

"Not that I recall. Seems like he stuffed his hands in his pockets; shuffling like he was drunk. It was strange, that's all. I never saw Timothy drunk. Something wasn't right. He waved me off, so I kept on rolling."

"Damn, I can't figure," Skipjack said.

"You think he'd come here something was wrong," Green said.

Marcie and Billy walked up. Marcie smiled graciously and handed Thornton Green an envelope. Green spread pleasantries all around. She was beautiful. Billy was growing like a tree. He wished good luck fishing, while waving off flies that had decided he was finished eating, and he was urged by Skipjack and Marcie to prove them wrong.

He sat down deliberately and wished good takings once again.

Green stood waving a napkin as they shoved off. The fog mostly lifted, only spritely wisps and small puffy traces attempted to cling. Once Skipjack rowed out of the shadow of cottonwood trees anchoring the bank, sunrays struck full force. He put his back into it and was soon quite sure they would be home before noon. The breeze, which cooled them the night before, had stopped and now the weather decided to come from the south. Most likely, it would be a scorcher.

He knew a place about a mile upstream on the Kentucky side. Below a slight bend, fish of all kinds seemed to like to feed. He suggested that Marcie and Billy bait and troll as he rowed. They had minnows and worms. Skipjack suggested minnows, but Billy wanted to try a worm. He said he had a feeling and damned if he wasn't right. He hooked a largemouth bass less than a minute after throwing the wiggly dangler in. He wore the fish out and Marcie scooped him up and dropped him in the bucket.

Skipjack kept rowing. He took a close look at Marcie, hoping she wouldn't notice.

"What's the matter?' she asked.

"You seem quiet all a sudden."

When she noticed that Billy was excited angling for the next fish, she asked where the two bar tabs were that Timothy had made Louis write up. Skipjack told her they were stashed under his paperweight and gave her a funny look.

"Who else has a key to the office besides Mary Frances?"

"Nobody but you and me."

"Somebody does, Jack. I looked everywhere. They're gone."

"It's a basic lock. A skeleton key can open it."

"We better change that one and all the rest."

"Why didn't you tell me back there?"

"Didn't want to spoil our fishing."

"Catch a fish then; we'll deal with it later."

"Yes, sir," she said as a fish broke the water and did its damnedest to escape, but soon was scooped up, too—a fine crappie that looked a bit crowded in the bucket beside the largemouth. Skipjack's arms were tired. It must have rained upstream; the current was running. He dropped the hook.

"Well, this might be a good spot," he ventured.

Marcie gave him a smile.

"Well, it might be; has been so far."

But it wasn't. They sat there for about fifteen minutes while Skipjack smoked a cigar, then moved upstream. They had scarcely gone a hundred yards, when Billy shouted he had one and did. The fish was the catch of the day, about a five-pound catfish. Skipjack put on gloves before he hauled it in.

"They'll fin you awful," Skipjack said, as he dropped the fish into the crowded bucket. He scooped up some water to keep all three fish submerged. He was ready to quit and to his surprise, Billy said he was hungry. The sun was climbing and there was no objection from Marcie.

After bragging rights, the biggest decision was which fish to cook. Skipjack stayed mum. Mary Frances suggested that she fry the catfish.

The sheriff, God bless him, showed up in time for lunch. Marcie walked with Billy while the two men talked. Before long, Mary Frances laid out food. The potatoes were honey glazed. Billy informed the sheriff he had dreamed up that recipe. Sheriff only nodded, but Billy nudged his mother and whispered, "See, he's eating them all."

The filets were delicious. The sheriff complimented Billy on his catch. After lunch, the two men went into the office, sat down, and lit cigars.

"Skipjack, this business is part of a bigger problem. The slavery thing tearing us apart. Everybody feels like a victim. Poor white man, hell, any and all, figure they needs to get their share. Figure everybody else is. Your brother—think about him. I bet most pockets he empties are beneficiaries some way."

"Might be. Found out anything?"

"Bancroft was living in St. Louis, but he was from Mississippi. His people were cotton brokers. He was educated at the University of Virginia. He owned a bank there."

"How do you know that so fast?"

"Found some slick who knew him. That's how we get most everything. Anyway, the man was different. He was a man's man, you know?"

"Not sure I do."

"That boy was gonna die anyway. He was pushing luck."

"Not sure I'm following."

"Your brother knew what Bancroft preferred and used it."

"You saying my brother is—?"

"No, I'm saying I believe he knew Bancroft was. It's only a guess, but a good one. We found his body tangled in Beargrass Creek. It weren't pretty."

"Were his nuts cut like Slasher said?"

"Yeah and shot through the gut with a small bore and cut across the neck."

"You think Slasher cut him and my brother shot him?"

"No, Slasher didn't cut him. It was messy. I questioned Slasher at the jail and he pretty much stuck to his story. Said he heard a loud pop. He was camped under the bridge drinking. Went to have a look and heard your brother saying let me go. Claimed he walked up while your brother was stripping Bancroft's clothes. Slasher hadn't been drunk, good bet Brother would be dead.

"Without surprise, Slasher is nothing. I guess your brother sized him up and offered him the suit and then offered money. As far I can figure the rest of what Slasher told is true about driving him out here and all. It was a money thing."

"You think Timothy hired him to kill me?"

"He wouldn't talk about that. Said memory failed."

Skipjack told the sheriff what Thornton Green had seen.

"Walking back, huh? Strange. Sounds like he got rolled himself."

"Yeah and before that when Marcie drove him down there, she

noticed that his dealing hand looked mangled. I need to tell you, last night somebody got into our springhouse and stole food."

"You think it might be him?"

"Hard to say. Not a good feeling though. Marcie's upset."

"Try not to leave her alone. He don't seem predictable. Slasher was telling truth when he said he was scared. Scared's a hard thing for Slasher to admit."

"You don't think it's unusual for Timothy to come back this way?"

"Skipjack, for one thing we don't know he did. And no, it's not unusual. He knows this area and if he was rolled, he's broke, and if his hand is all messed up, he can't play cards. He's in a pickle. But on top of that, I suspect the man's lost his mind. Think about it: he was fixed, chief dealer on *Sonata Queen*. If he's gone crazy, he could find plenty of like-minded company around here. You been up the creek lately?"

"Nothing takes me up there, but I've seen some crews come down that make me not want to."

"Nothing but thieves. It started out shanty boat squatters, but it's bred into something worse. Hell, none work. They live stealing. It's where the likes of Slasher settle when booze gets 'em. They all claims they're fishermen. Funny thing, they're always eating chicken, pork, or beef. We find livestock slaughtered in the field. Just enough butchered off for a couple of roasts. They raid boats sometime, too. Only a week or so ago, they set a flatboat on fire upstream from here after robbing some poor gentlemen at gunpoint. They're an awful bunch. Could be your brother slipped in with them. Nobody wants to go down there anymore."

"I'm changing all the locks."

"We'll do our best to catch him. Just keep sharp."

"It's hard to believe, ain't it?"

"Skipjack, I hate to say, I never did like him."

"I tried to."

CHAPTER 4

GHOST RIDING UPHILL ON A MULE

They started with a 20-gauge bird gun. Billy was excited but also frightened. Skipjack understood. He put a moldy sack of oats on top a fence post in the pasture and showed the boy how to hold and aim. Billy struggled to grip the stock tight against his shoulder. The whole business was wobbly, the barrel heavy.

Skipjack was a good shot. He pulled a coin out of his pocket, gave it to the boy, and said throw it straight up. When the boy flung it, there was an explosion and the coin was gone.

"Where did it go?" the boy asked, still cupping his ears.

"Hard to say. Doubt if you'll ever find it. See the trick is to point your gun where you're looking. That's the main thing there is. If you follow that, most everything else takes care. Don't let your hands fight your eye. Let me show you something."

He put the gun down against a fence rail and took a dollar out of his pocket. He asked Billy to watch where he put it. He reminded the boy that it could be his. That got his attention.

"See how you perked up. Now close your eyes and finger point right at the post it's on."

"You're missing by a mile. Son, look and see and feel where you are; take your time. Now close your eyes and point your finger. Don't hurry, just do it and keep your eyes shut and do it."

"Am I doing better?"

"You are at that. Want to know why?"

"I think so."

"You saw it before you closed your eyes. You knew it was there and you wanted it, didn't you?"

"Yes."

"Well, that's enough for today, all right. You learned plenty already."

"But I want to shoot the gun."

"I don't think so. Let's check on Momma and Lacy, what do you say?"

"I still want to shoot."

"You ain't scared?"

"Not so much as I want to shoot."

"You gonna shoot that old bag on the fence post?"

"You're gonna help me, aren't you?"

"A little bit maybe," Skipjack said as he handed Billy the shotgun.

It was a double-barreled shotgun and both barrels were loaded. The boy grimaced and jerked the trigger, and probably killed some butterflies and bees. His eyes had been clamped shut. He opened them and shook his head.

"I guess I missed," he said.

"Yeah, but take another shot and this one counts. It was loud, wasn't it? Did the kick hurt you?"

"I don't know. I guess it's loud."

"Steady down. Sight right down the barrel and gently touch the other trigger behind the first one. Real easy, there, let your finger touch soft, seeing what you're gonna hit, breathe easy now, and squeeze."

Blam! The oat bag blew fifteen feet, shredded.

"You tumbled that varmint. Good shot."

"What?"

"I said you bagged him. Good shot. Let's go check on Momma. That was good."

Billy started to hand Skipjack the shotgun.

"No, boy, that's yours. Carry it pointed down. I might ask to borrow it time to time."

"Not sure I want it."

"You will."

———

There was mumbling when they walked onto the porch.

"That's Lacy. Momma's learning her to read."

"Can you read as good?"

"Better than her, I bet, but I know not to tell."

"Not anybody ever, remember? What she teaching her to read from?"

"The Bible, what else?"

"Let's us sit quiet. What do you say?"

"I'm thirsty."

"I could use a drink myself, son, but let's sit tight."

"E-nun-ci-ate, Lacy. Pro-nounce each sing-gle syll-a-ble. E-nun-ci-ate. Try once again, please."

"Yes, ma'am."

"Start slow, not fast. Go easy. You know it already, Lacy."

Skipjack nodded at Billy and lit a cigar. Marcie's voice was soothing.

"Now faith is the substance of things helped—"

"Lacy, please, you know this already by heart. You don't even have to read. You believe it, too."

"Yes, ma'am. I'll try once again. 'Now faith is the substance of things hoped for, the evidence of things not seen.'"

"God bless you, Lacy, you got it. I'm so proud of you."

"Should I try to go on?"

"No, not this evening. My menfolk will be here soon."

Skipjack nudged Billy and scuffled his feet as he stood.

He clomped toward the door and opened it wide and heard Marcie say thanks as the back door shut softly.

"How was the shooting?"

"I hit something finally, but Dad hit a penny on the first try."

"Did not."

"You did too," Billy insisted.

"That's the first you saw; bet I missed that shot a thousand times before I hit it."

"Oh."

"After a while, you might get lucky, too."

"I hate to fire up the stove, Jack. It's hotter than blazes."

"Then don't. Why don't I ride down and get some food from Mary Frances?"

"Brawl's coming, remember?"

"He knows what to do. Boy, load your shotgun and look after Mother."

On the way down, Skipjack met Brawl and asked him if he wanted food from the tavern. Brawl shook his head.

"I heard something," he said.

"What you hear?"

"Some of the hod carriers talk too much. I overheard your brother's living up creek. Later, talking to Thornton Green, he told me he saw him. Well, then some of the off-loading boys was talking about a fella sounded a bit uppity, all beat up in clothes a little too fancy for a creek rat."

"Did you hear where?"

"No, all I heard was what I said. The rest was crazy."

"What's crazy?"

"Said they was worshiping the earthly Jesus and that your brother was a found son and that this society lady he was shacked with was an anointed witch. Now, you make sense of that." Brawl finished with a laugh.

"No sense to it, Brawl."

"No offense, but some white boys we get down that way talk no sense."

"Strange times, my friend."

"Thought I'd tell, in case you could figure. I brought extra locks and hasps, if you want."

"I do indeed. Ask Marcie. I'll be right back."

Down at the tavern, everything was smooth. The crowd was slow and steady. Skipjack ordered food and a whiskey from Louis at the bar. He walked out back. A burly sort waved him over. Skipjack couldn't place him but walked up to the table anyway.

"Understand you're the owner," the man said as his bushy eyebrows wriggled up and down.

"Feels like it sometimes."

"Will you settle this argument?"

"I ain't in the arguing mood," Skipjack replied and smiled at the two men looking up. The skinny one grinned ear to ear but said nothing.

"No pirates here about, is there? Snaggletooth says there is."

"Depends what you call a pirate, Mister. There's thieves and stone-cold killers, but they ain't only here. They're all over."

"None on this creek though. He says they are."

"Maybe he knows something."

"Only what I heard. Only what I heard."

Skipjack looked out over the river's surface; orange, blues, purples, and reds. A heron croaked and lifted off the riverbank. He couldn't figure why these two were asking about anything.

"Van Nutt here says there's something called the pirate's code," the burly man said.

"There must be, but I wouldn't know."

"I don't believe in pirates here. They're on the ocean."

"They're here. They're here," the skinny man named Van Nutt said.

"They got a plan. They got a plan. Sure thing."

The man's Adam's apple bobbed up and down. He nodded emphatically and looked like a scarecrow with a skimp of leftover flesh. Skipjack decided to play along.

"What's this plan you're talking about?"

"Don't know exactly; can't say for sure."

Skipjack winked at the big man, nodding at the smaller. "You ain't one of 'em, is you?"

"Heavens no! Heavens no, I hear things," he said and stared at Skipjack with defiant, troubled eyes.

"Well, how do you hear things, my friend?"

"I'm a trapper, a fisher. Got traps and lines in all the cricks. Plenty on this crick, plenty."

"Explain yourself. How you hear things?"

Skipjack signaled for another round.

"I trap and catch. I'm quiet. I'm in. I'm out. Most never see me. Those do think I'm silly. It's all right. I tell you, it's all right. See things they don't. Hear things they don't."

"The man can trap," the big fellow said. "He's got instincts; can't fish worth a crap."

Drinks arrived, and Skipjack sat. The skinny man explained he slid up and down creek like a leaf.

"Even whispers sounds like shouting. Hear things, I tell you, and know where deep shadows are. Know where to go and where not."

"He's been doing it for years. He knows his business. I buy his pelts."

"How come I've never seen you before, Van Nutt?"

"Been here many times, many times. Just never been noticed before."

"If I buy a steak dinner, will you let me ride one night?"

"No sir. Draw the line. Don't eat steak. Don't touch it."

"Well, what you like to eat?"

"Catfish. Catfish with greens, corn bread, and molasses."

"Will you take me?"

"Can't smoke. Can't talk without say so and got to stay down."

"That's fair. It sounds interesting. When?"

"Go every night. This crick tomorrow about three o'clock of the morning."

"Where can we meet?"

"New bridge. Half past two. New bridge."

The big man allowed he didn't mind a taste of steak, so Skipjack made sure both men were taken care of. He urged them not to tell.

"I'm quiet. Real quiet," Van Nutt whispered.

"He's good," the brawny man said. "Pleasure to meet you, Skipjack."

"You got to keep quiet, real quiet. Spots are secret, real secret."

Skipjack raised a forefinger to his lips, smiled, and nodded.

———

Skipjack reached the top of his hill and could see Billy and Marcie seated. Both stood; Marcie's rifle dangled from her left hand, Billy's shotgun was pointed down.

He handed Marcie the basket of food, then inspected the spring-house. The new set-up was definitely sturdy. Brawl was tangling with a locust post at the stable. It was wobbly.

"No point in putting a lock on if some fool can push it over. I cut you another one about two foot longer. Got some rocks from the creek to wedge it in with. She'll be tight as soon as I get this one out."

"You know, Brawl, we need to change the locks down at the tavern."

"Missus was telling me. I'll do that tomorrow evening. Things is strange, ain't they?"

"You let me know if I can help you with something, Brawl."

"Well, there is something, Skipjack. There is indeed. Two things or maybe three come to think."

Skipjack laughed, thinking about how their association had started.

"I ain't talking tools. You know that. Listen, what you going to do with Andy?"

"Keep him on, if you don't want him back. That is, if he'll stay."

"It's not exactly that. I don't want him back and I want him to get ahead even more. Presently I got another young man, this one full of anger. Got him for a song and I've worked a bit of sense into him."

"What you trying to tell me, Brawl?"

"Well," Brawl said, "not enough sense yet, but he's real good with stonework, which seems to calm him."

"Stonework?"

"Yes, sir, the boy can build a walkway, a wall, or even carve a likeness with a chisel if he's got good rock. He knows rock. I don't know how. Anyhow, he's no good with wood yet. Wood's too quick and tries his patience and he tries mine, too, frankly. I would be willing to bet you could use him around here and down at the tavern to make stuff."

"What kind of stuff?"

"Who needs a dirt path up to a house? Your flowers need edging and a stone border, too. Did I mention that this young man can make anything grow twice as tall and bushy as previously imagined? I see that I didn't. Well, he can. Tavern needs work, too. You need steps down to the river. They're mud ruts now. Think about all the dirt you'll keep out. Don't tell me now, because I'm busy and you're hungry. You think about it. He's cheap and good. You'll both benefit."

"We'll talk about it, if you'll help me with Andy."

"You won't go wrong."

"Not yet."

"There is a third thing."

"Come out with it, Brawl."

"This girl I got is too smart. I need to learn her to read and do figures. Can you help?"

"Not officially."

"How 'bout between us?"

"Most likely can make a difference."

"Maybe we speak soon? I need to finish before dark."

"No doubt you will. We'll settle up, too."

"You know I ain't worried about that. Go eat your supper."

INTRUDERS

Skipjack couldn't relax. Night sounds that usually lulled irritated. Cicadas rattled nerves. A glass of whiskey did no good. Tree frogs chattered loud and if it would shut them up, he would have shouted. Marcie molded her hands to his shoulders and he flinched. She started kneading his tight neck muscles. Skipjack wanted to convey these ministrations felt good, but they didn't, so said thank you, wishing he was underwater where all swayed quiet and cool.

"You're holding your breath. Breathe easy, honey, just breathe easy."

He nodded and tried a couple of deep breaths. He felt like he needed to check on the tavern. He dared not say that to Marcie, who would urge him to do just that. He didn't want to leave her alone.

"You're not breathing."

"Am I dead?"

"No, but you're working on it. We're all right tonight."

"Be a lot better if Brother was behind bars."

"Don't you think the sheriff is looking?"

"Don't know, but I bet he's where the sheriff ain't too eager to go. He as much as said so."

"Don't you dare think about a one-man army."

"Not tonight, but those folks got to be rooted out."

When Marcie went to use the privy, Skipjack stood guard. He decided he would ask Andy to watch the house the following night.

Around midnight, he gave up on sleep. He snuck out of the house, locked the back door behind him, then walked uphill. Skipjack sat on a rock right off the path and watched the house by the light of a pale moon. He lit a cigar. His mind kept churning. He had never discussed the rape with anyone. If Marcie had, she had never told him.

One evening before Billy's birth, she had unloaded reluctantly, and once started, her words become a stampede of crazy awful thoughts. Her voice, hypnotically soft as she revealed what she could remember, grew strident until she began to talk faster and faster, fingers clenched. Tangled word scraps raced off her tongue, yet Marcie's face appeared almost calm. He reached out and coaxed her to him.

After that conversation days before the wedding, they had never talked about the rape; by mutual consent it became "that night," an experience to be forever left behind.

As Skipjack sat there, something told him to get back to the house. He walked quickly down the hill, cradling his rifle, fumbling with the new keys. He opened the door, slipped in, locked it, and threw the bolt. Still carrying his pistol and rifle, he tiptoed upstairs. The bedroom was lit by a candle and Marcie sat straight with the sheet drawn around her. She looked at him and shook her head. Skipjack laid the rifle on the floor and the pistol on the table beside the candle. He lowered himself onto the edge of the bed, looked into Marcie's eyes, and placed his hand on her knee. She reached down and covered his with hers, eyes steady on him.

"You never told Timothy, did you?"

"Marcie, I've never told anyone. Have you?"

"No. What would have been the point? So, you never told anyone ever?"

"Never."

"Oh, my God, Jack! It's got to be him. When did you know?"

"Just now, uphill. My mind kept churning: 'How did he know? He looks like you, just like you. How did he know?' Something real quiet said go to Marcie. Makes me feel blind stupid."

"Jack, don't be hard. That night is past where it should've stayed."

"Damn hard, but it's got to be."

"Jack, promise you won't do anything."

"Pray I won't."

"There's no proving. There's only three that know. Please, don't make worse what already is."

"He's got to go down."

"I don't want to lose you, Jack."

"You're not going to lose me."

Marcie bowed her head. Skipjack leaned closer until foreheads touched.

"He was right about one thing. We are lucky ones."

"Hard to say now, but I believe you're right."

"Believe it," Marcie whispered.

They held each other through the night. Morning birds were already tentatively singing, and a light rain started tip-tapping on the leaves when Marcie and Jack began to doze.

"Tree frogs weren't lying. It's starting to shower," Skipjack whispered.

"We need it. Feel the breeze. If I weren't so sleepy, I would walk out and stand in it."

"Right there with you."

"Love you, Jack Maddox, with all my heart."

Skipjack nuzzled, nodded, and snored. Marcie tried to dream-sculpt shifting wall patterns, then closed her eyes and focused on trilling birds dodging raindrops.

There was no sign of a break in. That was the first thing Mary Frances told them when they rolled up in the buggy with Gracie and Ducky riding shotgun and Jessie plodding behind. After three hours of sleep, Skipjack and Marcie were already frayed. Billy had awakened them, saying he was starving to death. Not wanting to leave them alone or to dawdle either, Skipjack hauled every living thing down to the tavern. Billy, of course, saw it as an adventure. Marcie saw an ordeal. Skipjack saw precaution.

They were greeted by Andy, who ran beside them pointing at Mary Frances, who glared out the open back door. She looked heftier than usual and the effect was augmented by the butcher knife that crossed her chest.

"Nothing's gone," Andy said, when they climbed out of the buggy.

"Horse feathers, Andy," Mary Frances yelled. "They made off with my burgoo and I don't know how much whiskey. Damn place is all tore up."

Skipjack asked Marcie and Billy to stay outside with Andy, but they followed him anyway and he said nothing. The bar was near stripped. Only a couple of bottles were left half-empty on the bar. There was a turd behind the bar and another in one of the chairs beside a table with a glass half-full of urine and a doused cigar butt. Some of the furniture was overturned, and a couple of chairs were smashed to pieces. One of the best paintings was punched through the middle and smeared with blood.

"Get the boy out of here, Marcie," Skipjack said.

Marcie nodded and pointed to the floor beneath the ruined painting. She took Billy by the shoulder and steered him toward the door.

"There's a woman involved in this," Marcie said as she walked out. Mary Frances nodded and motioned with her head at one of the stones of the wall. There was a handprint. Mary Frances put her hand over it, but not on it.

"Too tall for a child, too small for a man," she whispered as she made an ugly face. She crooked her finger and Skipjack followed her into the kitchen. The kitchen had a faint handprint smear on the wall beside the back door. On the other side of the doorjamb, there was the partial print of a much larger hand. Skipjack looked closely. His lips curled. A crude sideways cross was carved into the limestone. The part that hadn't absorbed blood was still white and dusty. On the floor was a puddle and about waist high was a damp stain that meandered down.

"I don't believe this," Skipjack said. Mary Frances nodded and crooked her forefinger again. He followed.

"Wait till you see my pantry."

He followed her into chaos of busted crocks and flour dusting white walls dripping molasses, buzzing wasps and flies. Ants crawled on the overturned main table. Almost all of the shelving was pulled off the walls and jars of jams, jelly, and honey lay broken on the floor.

"What about the money?" Skipjack asked.

"Something told me to take it home."

"Well, thank you for that, but we can't open."

"I put out a sign already. Skipjack, our flatboat is gone."

"You're kidding me. What about the skiff?"

"Must've overlooked it. Still tied where you left her. I'm afraid you need to see the office."

Skipjack sagged, and this time led the way. The room smelled of sour musty smoke. The last of the final batch of fine whiskey was gone; bottle empty on the desk. His desk chair was destroyed in the corner. All of Marcie's files were wet and smoldered in the middle of the stone floor. The air was so pungent you could barely breathe. Desk drawers were turned upside down and his office pistol was gone. Skipjack took the deep breath that had eluded him for the last twelve hours. After he exhaled, he looked Mary Frances in the eyes.

"You still on board?"

"You know I am."

"I wanted breakfast, but I guess we best clean this son of a bitch."

"They forgot the bacon and we got fresh eggs. I was waiting for you to get started. I was about to send Andy. I'll make breakfast."

"Deal. Mary Frances, be sure to make food for everybody that's helping. This here is dirty work, no lic. Who could do such a thing?"

"The devil."

"Can we do without Andy? I want him to watch the house and yours, too. I'll have him riding Jessie up and down the road."

"Skipjack, these are weasels. They work night. They ain't going to show their face today."

"You think not?"

"Go be with Marcie. Let me fix some food."

"I'm not sure I can eat. Can you?"

"You don't eat, they win."

Skipjack shook his head, then closed his eyes and nodded.

"Afterward, make a list of what we need. Also, send Andy for the sheriff."

"You're slow this morning, Skipjack. I already have. Bet you got enough booze stashed in the old still house to last a day."

"Maybe so, unless they stole that, too."

"Only us ever had a key to that, remember?"

"That's right; it wasn't on the extra set, was it?"

"Only you and me and Marcie's got keys. I don't know about no extra set."

"It has to be my brother."

Mary Frances nodded.

"Now you talking. I tell you it was the devil himself."

————

Tough to deny customers, but there was no way to serve them. Some boat hands who came up to eat and drink offered to help. Brawl heard about the trouble and he showed with the stone man and the young woman he had referred to the evening before. Mary Frances took charge and Andy was her lieutenant. Skipjack took him aside and asked why he had said that nothing was taken. Andy told him Mary Frances had shouted at him to go see if any of the stock was missing. It wasn't. Andy hadn't yet been inside. Satisfied, Skipjack thanked him and thumped him on the back.

"I believe that chicken thief had something to do with this," Andy offered.

"Why you say that?"

"Feel it. I don't know why."

After eating, they loaded whiskey out of the still house into a wagon and drove it up to the back door. Andy and Skipjack off-loaded the booze and the same wagon was loaded with trash. Billy was busy with a broom in the pantry and Marcie was straightening up the office as best she could. Brawl was replacing locks. The young man was working with Louis to clean up the bar. The place was a beehive and Skipjack made sure all the workers got food and beer.

When the sheriff showed about suppertime, the place was near functioning. At least the bar was open, which suited the sheriff. Mary Frances fried him some catfish. The bar was jovial with workers drinking free beer.

"So, who you think done it, Skipjack?" the sheriff asked.

"No break-in. It had to be Brother."

"Now, now, let's not jump to conclusions. Did he have keys?"

"Not rightfully, but the spare set is missing."

The sheriff nodded, squinted, and leaned into Skipjack.

"I see you got Brawl doing locks. Will he have a set when he finishes?"

"You accusing Brawl Thurston of this?"

"No, no, Skipjack," the sheriff said, holding up his hand. "I ain't, but I'm asking a simple question. Will he or won't he?"

"I don't know," Skipjack replied. "Let me ask you a simple question. Have you found out where Brother is?"

"Not yet, but we're looking."

"Where? Down on the creek? Have you looked there?"

"Skipjack, we got about forty men for this entire county. We would have to surrender everything else to lawlessness to go down there and then still be outnumbered. I ain't even sure he's there. I've heard stuff, but usually we try to catch those folks on their way out or their way back. Need a militia to get 'em out. You can't walk door to door. There ain't no doors: there's tents, wagons with roofs, flatboats with siding and tarps. I don't have enough men or jail space to arrest them. If he's down there, God help him."

"God help him. That sure is a funny way to put it. What's happening with Slasher and the other prisoner? You turn them out?"

"Slasher's dead. He hung his self." The sheriff winked. "Or else was persuaded to."

"Why did you wink?"

"Did I? Slasher's gone to his reward and the other's gone, too. He made his bail; can you imagine that? A chicken thief making bail?" The sheriff shook with silent laughter.

"Can you?" Skipjack asked.

"Not hardly. He must have friends."

"Were they cellmates?"

The sheriff seemed to ponder. His forefinger and thumb troubled his jaw. He nodded.

"Come to think of it, they was and another fellow, sort of a small fry in for disturbing the peace."

"I suppose he's gone, too."

"Hardly more than a child—drunk in a public place and pissing in the street. My jail's too small for the likes of that."

"Was his fine paid, too?"

"You know, I can't recall."

"Can't or won't?"

"Now, Skipjack, you have a right to be burned, but please realize, I wasn't even in the courtroom. Can't keep track of everything. Do the best I can; that's all."

Skipjack was so angry it was an effort to be civil.

"Skipjack, let it play. He'll mess up again."

"Hell's bells, sheriff. He murdered a man. He's robbed my house and my business. What you waiting for, a massacre?"

"We don't know sure who done this. Slasher's dead, so there ain't a witness to Bancroft. I can't drag a man in with nothing."

"So, you're telling me you ain't looking?"

"No, I didn't say that. We're looking, but I can't just drag him in. It's an unfortunate thing. He was the last one seen with Bancroft. I can see what you're thinking but can't arrest him for your thoughts. I may believe he did it myself, but the law's got my hands tied here."

"So, what are you gonna do?"

"Keep my ear to the ground. Somebody will talk."

———

When Skipjack entered his office, he pushed the door open and knocked a young black woman to the floor. She sat in a spreading pool of soapy water rearranging her dress. She eyed him warily.

"Damn, I'm sorry," Skipjack said and rushed over to her. "Are you hurt?" He extended his hand. She shook her head. He extended his hand further. She took it and he pulled her up. Just as he was about to ask where Marcie was, she crawled out from under the desk.

"Julie, you all right?"

"Yes, ma'am, I was caught off balance. Didn't fall hard."

"Didn't see you. I'm sorry."

"No way can anybody see through a solid oak door."

"That's why you don't bust in like a bull," Marcie said.

Both Skipjack and Julie looked down at their feet, but when they looked at each other, both smiled. Skipjack explained why he was so steamed.

"Sheriff is no help at all."

Julie went back to scrubbing the door. The place still smelled like smoke. Brawl walked in with his toolbox and the new boy for Skipjack's consideration. His name was Tom Thurston. When Marcie asked if this was his son, Brawl nodded in such a way that she knew he wasn't.

"Skipjack, you can't just wash this off. You got to seal it in. Shellac is the only thing will do it. Every inch of the place or else it will smell like scorch forever. I'm telling you soap and water won't cut it."

"You mean we're wasting our time?"

"No, ma'am, you ain't wasting time, but it won't finish the job. You got to use shellac. Smoke can't get through."

"Brawl, are these locks safe?" Skipjack asked.

"No lock's more than a temporary confusion. I got keys to all your locks, but so does anybody else who wants them. Nothing's safe."

"Why do you put them in then?" Julie asked.

Everyone smiled when they looked at her. Julie shrugged.

"Holds them off a little while," Brawl answered. "This is the last one."

Skipjack studied the wiry young man assisting Brawl. Thin as he was, his shoulders and forearms would have fit a man much thicker. The young man caught him sizing him up and turned his back to Skipjack, who suddenly had a fine idea.

"Son, I would like to ask you a question."

The young man reached into the toolbox and handed Brawl an awl but gave no indication he had heard anything. Skipjack smiled and tried again.

"I hear you're good with stone?"

"Yes, sir."

Brawl nudged with his elbow. "Turn and face the man, Tom. Speak up now."

Tom turned and faced Skipjack. He looked him dead in the eye. "Yes, sir, I like stone."

"I need some improvements at the house. Steps, a path, borders around the flowerbeds, for starters. Can you start first thing tomorrow?"

Brawl looked at Tom and nodded.

"Yes, sir. Do you know what you want?"

"Not really. Maybe you will have some ideas."

A quick faint smile flashed across his face. Skipjack noticed that Julie was scrubbing harder than before.

"How about seven? We'll figure a starting point and come up with a plan."

"I'll be there, sir."

"Brawl, can I take Tom to show him what you and I were talking about with the path to the river? Can you spare him?"

"Sure."

"I'll meet you out front, sir," Tom said.

Skipjack studied him; realized the young man didn't want to walk through the bar and the outdoor tables.

"Tom, follow me."

Tom shrugged at Julie, who scrubbed furiously, and then he followed Skipjack.

"Julie, we have all day. Don't wear out that brush," Marcie said.

"You need shellac," Brawl said as he pried the new lock into place.

UNDERCOVER

Skipjack had it all arranged. Andy would watch the house from two thirty in the morning until dawn. Tom Thurston was to show up at seven to discuss the flowerbed borders and the new pathway to the porch. He was to start that day. The house would be watched. Skipjack was free to go on his foray with the skinny trapper and there would be activity all day at the house. Bone tired as he was, he felt good about that.

Knowing that Andy was going to be perched on the hill with a loaded rifle almost led him to think he didn't have to tell Marcie about his planned jaunt, but after dinner, he thought better.

When he told her that he was going out with the trapper, a stern look settled on her face. Marcie didn't say anything until she had ushered Billy into his room. The boy was dead tired, so she reappeared in a couple of minutes, but the same hard expression was fixed solid. Skipjack knew he should have kept his mouth shut. She grabbed his drink without even asking and topped it off, poured a glass of wine, and sat beside him.

"I knew you were going to do something reckless."

"I ain't done nothing yet."

"Jack, what will you accomplish by going back up that creek?"

"Damned if I know."

"Are you planning to talk things over or shoot him? Neither one's right."

"Marcie, I plan to look around, that's all."

"I don't like this, Jack."

"Andy's watching the house. I won't be gone three hours."

"To hell with Andy's watch; I'm thinking about you. Don't you know that?"

"I got to get a feel of it," Skipjack said.

"What do you think you're going to get a feel for?"

"I don't know yet, honey. I'll tell you in the morning."

"Morning comes quickly. Bottoms up." She drained her glass.

"A fine proposal." Skipjack winked.

"Maybe in the morning and why don't you think about that?"

Her chair scraped across the floor as she pushed away from the table and as she ascended the stair, Skipjack fought the urge to get in the last word and succeeded. He took his drink out onto the porch and lit a cigar. In less than a minute, she joined him, closed the door gently, then rubbed his neck and kissed the top of his head.

"He's crazy, Jack."

"I'm not. I'm going to have a look around."

"Look around right now."

———

"At least take the rifle," Marcie said when it was time. He agreed. Andy was already uphill. She followed Skipjack out to the stable and then fetched the key he had forgotten so they could open the gate.

Jessie turned toward the tavern at the bottom of the hill. Skipjack said, "Haw." Jessie corrected and aimed toward the bridge. The mule's hooves clopped and softened silence intermittently broken by birdcalls. A cloudy sky made the moonlight faint. Skipjack had no idea if the skinny man would be there or not.

He tied Jessie in shadow beside the bridge. Van Nutt was already there. Skipjack climbed into the canoe and they set out.

"I can paddle, too."

"No need. Keep down. If I tell you 'cover up,' you cover up."

"Are you baiting or taking?"

"Little of both, little of both. Stick with me. Know what you want."

Skipjack started to light a cigar. The man told him to put it away, tossed him a small blanket, and told him to get down and duck under it when told.

"Now?"

"Not now. Not now. Up a few stretches. Know what you need."

"How you know?" Skipjack whispered.

"Just know. Get down and under. Now."

"Now?"

Skipjack saw nothing but pale green smooth water. Heard nothing but the soft steady swoosh of the paddle. He kneeled down anyway, pulled the blanket over his head, but kept a peephole open. The skinny man started humming what sounded like a gospel tune. Skipjack drew the pistol out of his belt and felt the cool steel of the trigger.

"False alarm, false alarm."

"What was it?"

"Shush."

Skipjack was a bit annoyed. He cradled the rifle across his lap and held the pistol in his hand. He began to wonder if Marcie wasn't right. He was tired; heart beating fast for nothing he could see. A muskrat dodged off and ducked beneath the bank. All he saw was flat open water.

Suddenly the canoe veered and nudged into the mud. In the blink of an eye, there was the sound of chain rattling, a flash of silver, and a thump in the boat. A few seconds later, there was a splash and once again, they were headed upstream. This same process was repeated several times.

"Git down! Git down."

Skipjack kneeled and pulled the blanket over his head. The canoe scraped against a gravel bank and branches tugged at the blanket that covered him. He heard what sounded like rhythmic splashing coming toward them. He was more curious than alarmed; still his finger wrapped the trigger.

"Hello, Trapper, say something fer yerself. What you hidin' from?"

"Hiding? Hiding? Ain't hiding, no sir, not hiding."

"Hum us a tune then."

To Skipjack's surprise, the skinny man did just that; caught a slow and mournful tune and hummed with all his might.

Oars scooped the water, and somebody said that's enough fun. Van Nutt started hitting high notes and the canoe seemed to tremble with them. Skipjack saw a large rowboat slide past.

"Leave the poor fool alone. You might be next. Row, you bastards."

Trapper and Skipjack laid in for a few minutes and neither said anything. The skinny man pushed off and they continued upstream.

"Where they from?" Skipjack whispered.

"Be showing shortly. Be calm, real calm. No shooting; armed to the teeth."

"How many are there?"

"Don't know. Don't know. Sprang up like mushrooms. Shhh!"

Skipjack ducked down and heard voices coming closer. The canoe dodged under some branches and Van Nutt baited a trap and tossed it in. He hummed as he reentered the middle of the stream and eased into song with a voice whiney enough to irritate mosquitoes.

"The Lord is my shepherd, I shall not want. He maketh me lie down by still waters . . ."

His pitch was so piercing, Skipjack had to suppress a chuckle when a gruff voice in the approaching vessel proclaimed, "God have mercy! The man's killing catfish. Swear to God."

Trapper paddled harder and sang ever more forcefully.

"I swear he's a menace to Mother Nature, not to mention high society. Why a man could clear a whorehouse with a voice such as his'n."

"Curly, I would rather not inquire about what you know of society," a familiar voice said calmly.

A raspy female voice scoffed, "That he knows about other places, I can personally attest."

A chill stung Skipjack's entire body. He inhaled through his teeth, turned his head, and tried to see the speakers, but all he could see was a tangle of shadow. He knew Timothy's voice like he knew his own.

The woman sounded like many fallen bawds he had suffered. The syrupy curl of Brother's voice entwined with the exaggerated elegant slash of the woman's made Skipjack want to retch.

"Shhh. Stay down, almost there. Almost there."

The blanket stunk; smelled like dirty wet dog with a sprinkle of skunk. It was coarse wool and scratchy, but that wasn't all that was bothering him. Skipjack was dripping sweat. Creepy crawly itch that had nibbled the back of his neck now claimed his entire body. He couldn't tell if the parts that actually itched had somehow convinced other parts or not, but Skipjack's skin crawled head to toe. His peephole provided small consolation.

"Sit tight, sit tight," the skinny man barely whispered. "Keep looking to the right, to your right."

"Can't I sit up?"

"Wouldn't advise that."

Skipjack laid low and peered at a flatboat with a cabin that looked like a tornado had dumped it on the deck, torn it apart a few spins, and then squished it together again. On the shore, a fire was burning. Behind that was a wagon with a patchwork tent. There was a silver candelabra on the drop gate of the wagon. Several candles were lit and since there was no breeze, flames held steady. What looked like shadow with a long white beard approached the fire and fiddled with a skewered shape that made flame jets dance. The sizzling hunk wasn't large so Skipjack assumed it was a piglet. A woman walked up behind the man and slapped him on the head.

"Lucky she didn't blow, you drunken fool."

"Tend yer beans, daughter. Mind who yer callin' fool."

First one dog and then five or six others charged down the creek bank, snarling. Trapper opened his windpipe and within one spine-tingling stanza, the dogs were persuaded to circle glowing coals where they covered their ears with paws and whimpered, but that did not stop the skinny man. In his quiet metallic way, he ascended to a note past Skipjack's range and all the dogs howled at once as if being troubled by specters.

A nice flatboat was decked out with a cabin made of woods as colorful as Joseph's coat. The craft was sturdy looking with a white board next to a red, then a blue one beside that caught Skipjack's attention. On one plank, there was a red and green sunray shape and beneath that, a stick man painted in reddish brown. Skipjack remembered well the day that plank had been painted. He had been there. The cabin was much larger now, but the board with a stick man was painted by Billy two years past.

A huge man sat on the bow of this flatboat and didn't budge as they passed. There were several more rafts with slopped-together cabins and there were some lean-tos sagging on shore.

The small peephole made it difficult to judge distance or to figure anything, but seemed like the mess amounted to about seven or eight floaters and five or six tent-like structures. Several cramped minutes later, Van Nutt ducked into the bank. Something thumped out and in an instant, something splashed back in.

"You can get up now."

"Damn, how many are there?" Skipjack whispered.

"More than she looks. Sleep like quail."

The creek was overhung with branches, so the only light came from faint flickers reflecting off water and pale leaves. Nestled underneath, Trapper busied himself baiting. He had no time to talk until he had finished. Skipjack lit his cigar, but Trapper made him put it out.

When Van Nutt turned the canoe back downstream, he rolled a cigarette and lit it. He told Skipjack to smoke if he wanted. Skipjack was almost too tired to ask why.

"They're smarter than you think. Know things. Smart."

"They know cigar smoke?"

"Why take chances? Why?"

There was almost no current for the lack of rain, so Trapper paddled vigorously. Once again, Skipjack offered to help.

"No paddle."

He enjoyed most of the cigar, and then Trapper again told him to duck. He took a full pull of cool morning air and reluctantly pulled the scratchy stench over his head. As they passed the encampment again, a stronger stench filled his nostrils, but only for an instant, then wood smoke blurred it. For that instant though, Skipjack was nearly happy for his blanket, for rank putrefaction had attacked and was something he feared might not wash off.

"You can smoke again, if you want."

Skipjack sat up and stretched; bridge in sight and dawn-lit eastern sky back-lit spaces between leaves. He could almost taste fall. He inhaled deeply, then lit his cigar stub.

"What was that smell?"

"Anything you can think of."

"God Almighty!"

"He needs to come calling. Ain't been there in a long while."

"You ever seen them coming back?"

"Be here shortly. Don't see what they bring back. I'm only a fool, a grinning fool."

"You're no fool."

"Gotta be. Gotta be. They kill you. Get off. Get out. Saw what you saw. Forget about me."

The man faded into what remained of darkness and Skipjack slipped uphill. His rifle and pistol, instead of providing comfort, made him feel conspicuous. He stroked Jessie's jaw and nuzzled her neck before climbing on and heading home.

"Mr. Maddox. Mr. Maddox, where is your key?"

Skipjack opened eyes onto Andy's earnest face and smiled. Jessie's soothing, sure-footed gait had lulled him into the sleep he had sorely needed. The air was crisp, and first light flickered in Andy's eyes.

"Damn, I nodded. See anything?"

"Just you coming up the hill like a ghost on a mule."

YOU'RE KIDDING ME

Skipjack threw kindling into the firebox and lit the stove. No sooner had he started grinding coffee beans than Marcie walked in.

"You're dead on your feet, honey. Lie down a minute and I'll join you if you want."

He nodded, scuffled upstairs, and after removing his shoes, fell across the bed. He awakened for a moment as Marcie rubbed his shoulders, then Skipjack sank like a stone. When he awakened, birds were squabbling outside the window and he could hear voices. He peered out and saw Marcie pointing at her flowerbed and Tom Thurston nodding. He slid into moccasins and stumbled downstairs for coffee and a cigar. Though he felt like a dark cloud, he attempted to appear breezy as he dashed to the outhouse with what he hoped was an invigorating smile. Once the outhouse door was latched, the night's visions haunted him. There was no way to describe such befouled strangeness. Skipjack was troubled by that because Marcie would want to know everything.

"Thank you, God, for cigars," he said softly.

His pass back to the house did not go unnoticed, so he attempted a broad grin. Threw some clothes on, then with a mug of coffee in hand, pretended to be in control, which fooled nobody. Marcie laughed aloud, and Tom turned away. Skipjack knew he was beat. He sat on a stump and slurped coffee. Such a night, what a day.

"What did you see?" Marcie whispered.

"More than enough. We'll talk later."

On the porch, a large yellow butterfly skipped flower to flower, then landed on Skipjack's arm and feasted. He wondered if it was salt or water or both it was after. The first hummingbird he had seen all season dashed close to inspect his nose, then whirred off to dip nectar.

Skipjack was groggy and stumped. A fly landed on the lip of his coffee mug and walked halfway round before being whisked. Skipjack realized he felt more annoyed than threatened. He knew one thing sure. He wanted his brother and the rest of the lowlifes uprooted. They were squatters, right on the southern tip of a finger of his property and some were probably on Mason's land. The ones on the creek were on a navigable waterway. Not much could be done legally. The sheriff would be no help. Mason was an old man and his son was a drunk.

He yawned and stretched. Marcie stepped up behind him and kissed his stubbly cheek.

"Tom wants to know if he can use the skiff."

"What's he want it for?" Skipjack answered, welcoming the diversion.

"He says there's a dry bed about a quarter mile where he can dig enough stone to edge the flowerbeds."

"He can't haul enough rock in the skiff."

"He said Brawl's got something he can tow it in."

"Fine with me if he's got it back by tonight down at the tavern."

"You all right?"

"Perplexed, you might say. Brother's at the hellhole they've thrown together. I heard his voice. Honey, we got to get rid of that bunch and God help me, I want to shoot the son of a bitch right between the eyes."

"Not this morning, Jack."

"No."

"Trust me, our time will come."

"How?"

"I don't know. Don't be hasty."

"At a loss what to do, Marcie. Hate to admit it."

"Then don't. Simply say you don't yet have the answer."

"Well, I can say that easy."

"Say it."

"I don't have the answer yet."

"Now you're talking. We're on our way."

"Where did I find you?"

"Don't you remember? I found you."

"Never told me that."

"Wasn't necessary."

Skipjack laughed to himself, skin tingling, not knowing what to believe. He stared through treetops and took a slug of coffee and relit his cigar. In a smoky reverie, his brother Timothy was already comfortably six feet under, holding a deck of marked cards.

"Thanks for telling me now," he replied, relishing her smile and his daydream of Timothy in peaceful repose.

"Anything else you might need?"

"What about young Tom? Doesn't he need a ride to the skiff?"

"Billy's riding him down on Jessie," she said, responding to his raised eyebrows with an alluring smile.

"You don't say?"

"Only if you have strength, sweetheart."

"So, you say you chose me?" Skipjack asked as he stood and took Marcie's elbow.

"I did say that, didn't I?"

———

Afterward, as they curled together slippery with sweet moisture, Marcie pressed Jack's hand against her breast. When she sighed, he sighed with her.

"Lord, I needed that."

"You still feel like killing?"

"Not so much."

"Jack, where they're camped, they can't stay if they want to. A flood will wash them out."

"Hell, Marcie, we don't flood in August. It's dry as bone."

"We need rain. You just said."

"So?"

"Mark my words. They won't be there long."

"You know something I don't?"

"Lots of things."

"You can't bring a gully washer, can you?"

"To keep you from getting killed, maybe, but Jack, I've got news."

Skipjack yawned and kneaded Marcie's breast. Her hand stroked his gently.

"Does my breast feel a little larger?"

"Maybe so; seems like."

She turned her head back to search his expression, but his eyes were closed. She smiled and chuckled silently.

"What?"

"Jack, I suspect we're having a baby."

Skipjack's eyelids squinted open and his brow knitted. Suddenly he was wide-eyed, and his mouth dropped open. He roughly jerked up onto one elbow.

"Easy, you want to tear my hair out?"

"You're kidding me."

Marcie muffled her laughter into the pillow. Skipjack stroked her flank. He squeezed her buttocks and then stroked some more.

"After all this time? You're kidding, aren't you?"

"Yes, Jack, I'm kidding you. I think we're going to have a baby."

"Yahoo. Yahoo. Damn, my goodness gracious."

"Now calm yourself. Pretty sure, we'll know right soon."

"Damn, honey. We need to build another room."

Marcie started laughing out loud. She opened her arms and Jack leaned into them. He started asking lots of questions that made her laugh and cry. She was pleased he was pleased, even though he was acting silly as a child himself. She held him close and when he asked why she was crying, she shook her head and buried her face into his neck.

"It'll be all right. Don't cry, sweetheart," Skipjack said.

Marcie nodded.

"Don't get yourself killed, Jack. I need you."

"What's all the yahoo about?" Billy cried out as he bounded up the stairs. Marcie pulled the sheet over them, looked at Skipjack and shook her head, as Billy stomped into the room.

"Why are you sleeping? Are you crying, Momma?"

"We were thinking about a good breakfast, honey. That's all."

"Mary Frances fed me corn bread and molasses. Besides, I ain't hungry, 'cause afterward some dead man floated up. He was naked, too, and cut up just awful."

Marcie sat up and patted the bed beside her. Billy sat, and she stroked his head.

"You saw what?" she asked.

"I was the first one that did. He was almost underneath the skiff. I saw him first. Andy pulled him out. His head was almost off. He was a bloody mess between his legs."

Marcie hugged the boy. The boy nodded and grinned tightly.

"It was real ugly, but I wasn't scared. Tom couldn't look. Andy sent for the sheriff. Told me to get home quick."

Marcie put her free hand on Jack's knee and squeezed.

"I know what you're thinking. Sit tight. Trust me, please."

Sheriff Ballard Winston agreed the thing was done nearly identical to Bancroft but explained again that the only so-called witness to that had been such lowlife that his word was as worthless when he was alive as the memory of his recounting was now he was dead. Skipjack was disgusted. About the only useful thing the sheriff did was haul corpses. Skipjack told him he was certain Brother was back at the creek and that the stolen flatboat was, too. The sheriff told him he already knew and was waiting for the right time to move. Skipjack calmly asked when he thought that might be. Winston replied it was a matter of grave seriousness that he was not going to jeopardize with talk until the investigation was complete. He said he wanted all his ducks in a row.

When the sheriff left, Skipjack found Andy and asked him to meet him in the office as soon as he finished mending the fence around the hog lot. He walked into the bar and carelessly slapped the bar top before he thought to catch the drift of what was being bandied about there. Louis walked up with a glass of bourbon.

"Skip the egg."

Louis tilted his head slightly toward three men squabbling at a table. Without looking, Skipjack knew he would be better off in the kitchen. He started that way.

"Ask Skipjack. Just ask him. No? I'll ask then. Skipper, what you think about this abolition stuff? This fool don't respect a man's right to property. How would you react if he took away your lawful property, Skipjack? Tell the man how you would feel."

Skipjack, dead sure he was too tired for this confab, waved his hand, smiled, and tried to keep moving toward the kitchen, but the loudmouth stood and insisted that he answer, so he did.

"Grainger, I appreciate your business and as you point out, this is a lawful enterprise. I would not appreciate anyone attempting to take it."

"Hear me, Tom Harold, I told you so. He's dead agin it."

The third man at the table pushed the loud man down into his seat and fixed his eyes on Skipjack. The other two men seethed one to another.

Skipjack continued. "I don't own any; do you, Grainger? Why are you boys so stoked this morning? Let me ask one."

"Ask away."

"What if I owned you?"

"That's different, 'cause you don't."

"What if I cut you off and put you out for being a nuisance? Like you say, it is private property."

"You in league with this scum?"

"No, you are, Grainger. You're drinking with him. Hold it down or I'll put you out."

"We got a right to be here, Maddox."

"No, sir, you don't, I do. The tavern's my property, gentlemen. Calm down or I'm putting you out."

CHAPTER 5

THE MAN CAN'T MAKE A MISTAKE

Mary Frances was teaching Julie Thurston how to filet catfish without getting finned. Mary Frances skinned them alive and they wriggled something awful. The knives used were sharp as razors with points like needles. It was a crude and delicate operation all at once. When she saw Skipjack, she grabbed the fish from the girl.

"Like this," she said and before Julie had quit shrugging, the fish was filleted. Mary Frances crooked her finger and Skipjack followed her outside. She looked over her shoulder, then led him down toward the river.

"There were two fellas out here when Andy dragged the floater out. They were off a St. Louis boat. I heard them whispering they had seen the same in Cincinnati. I don't think they were canoodling. They were whispering and nodding behind their hands. One of them looked real worried. He kept saying, 'I know, I know. There's most certainly something afoot.'"

"Were they that way?"

"How do I know what they were? They weren't deckhands. They had clean nails."

"How's the new girl working out?"

"Slow like the rest at first, but I'll whip her into line."

"Keep listening close. We got to stick together."

"You know who, plain as day," Mary Frances said over her shoulder.

The cool breeze tasted of autumn and then with a wind twist, was summer again. Surrounding him now was moisture from the south. Skipjack walked down the dirt path to the river and realized Brawl's limestone steps would eliminate slop. Always something. Inch it forward was all he knew.

Wind was rolling the river and drift seemed to hover, barely moving, slow current no match for the breeze. He turned, then looked back, wondering how the bank might look if the tavern weren't there at all. Easy to do. Only some stone walls, tables, benches, a one-story building and folks wandering around. Then he remembered Marcie's words and thrilled to the marrow. He had to shut his eyes before fantasy enchanted. How big did the place need to be? He didn't want to fall into bigger is better. Things were working fine just as they were.

As he was walking up the riverbank, a well-dressed fellow hailed and asked if it was always so picturesque in this part of the world. Skipjack, still thinking about Marcie's news, stretched the truth a bit and said the weather was perfect every day. The finely dressed lady hanging on the gent's arm purred, "Thomas Floyd, isn't that what I just finished saying?" With twinkling eyes, she asked Skipjack if Jim Porter, the giant, still ran people to and from town.

"No, ma'am. Jim Porter passed last April, but if you need to get to town, we can arrange."

"Honey, he was big as Goliath," she said to her gentleman friend. "Wasn't he, Mr. Maddox?"

"I ain't sure 'bout that, but Jim was near eight feet," Skipjack responded. "Unlike Goliath, he was kind and his best friend wasn't tall as you are in those fine boots."

Her eyes flashed as she curtsied ever so slightly. Skipjack strolled on. Maybe, if it was a boy, he would name him James, but if it was a girl, he was thinking Esther. He was happy to be happy. It seemed like forever since he had been so pleased. He liked the way his knees felt as he sprang up the incline. He decided then and there, as he looked down, that a wrought iron handrail would go well with limestone steps.

Skipjack hadn't been seated at his desk more than a minute when there was knocking on his door.

"What do you want, Andy? Sit down." Skipjack pointed to a chair.

"I'll stand," Andy replied.

"What you want?"

"Sir?"

"You have become a valuable part of this operation. I won't hide that fact. I'd like you to stay on. What do you want?"

"My contract's up in three weeks."

"Yes, that is so. Would you stay?"

"That is hard to say, sir. I need to talk to Mr. Brawl."

"And talk to yourself, Andy. Don't forget yourself," Skipjack said and winked.

Andy's entire body seemed to stiffen.

"Scary, ain't it, Andy? What if I tell you to slop the hogs?"

"I'd do it, sir."

"And do it right and probably rather do that than talk, but listen and listen close. You don't want to be doing that forever, and besides, I ain't going to be here forever. Neither is Brawl."

"Yes, sir."

"I know you can help me. You have proved that. I believe I can help you, if you will stay."

"Things been good here. But I gotta think."

"Want to ask you two questions, Andy. Is that all right?"

Andy looked down.

"Do you like to work here, and do you yearn for a better place to live?"

"Mr. Maddox, I would do anything for you, but I don't know how to answer."

Skipjack jumped out of his chair, walked over to the door, and locked it.

"Okay, you play that way. I won't condemn. You're mine three weeks, understand, so I'll drive that point home. Son, you are no more than thirty years old, am I right? You don't have a wife or kids. Don't have nothing to call your own."

Skipjack sat behind his desk, opened a drawer, pulled out a bottle of whiskey, pulled the cork, and took a swig. He slammed the thing down and glared at Andy.

"Stand up straight. Look me in the eye. I am your master for three more weeks."

"Yes, sir."

"You gonna run off?"

"No, sir."

"I would."

"You would?" Andy asked, looking up, eyes twinkling like he knew something unexpected was coming. "You would run off?"

"Look at me, son. I'm going to tell God's truth. Did you ever hear of Moses? Did you ever hear of David? Did you ever dream of deliverance? If you haven't, you're one rare bird. If I was you, faced with what you're faced with, I would want to run and hide. You don't?"

"No, sir, I didn't say that."

"Never said you did. But you have learned to please, haven't you?"

Andy grinned and shook his head.

"Andy, go fetch me two glasses from the bar and some ice if the iceman ain't forgot."

"Yes, sir."

Andy left, and Skipjack bowed his head and asked for guidance. He relocked the door. He had no idea what he was going to say next and paced the room that still smelled of scorch and soap. He sat at his desk and rubbed his forehead. He took a deep breath. There was a knock.

"Come in," he yelled.

The door rattled, but he stayed put. After a couple of thunks, he stood and said, "What you want?"

"I want in."

Skipjack unlocked, and Andy walked in with a glass full of ice and a glass full of water.

"I didn't want water, Andy. Did I say water?"

"I guess not, sir."

"Will you sit down, please?

"If you say so."

"Will you please hear me? Fix us both a drink now."

"I don't drink, sir."

"Hell you don't. You're lying. I can't help if you lie."

"Mr. Maddox—"

"Don't tell me what you think I want to hear. How can I help?"

"Well, sir, how you want your drink?"

"I want half the water and half the ice. Mix 'em and put the glasses here on the desk, and then pull up and sit down. Standing makes me nervous."

Andy did as he was told but perched on the front of the chair as if he might spring at the drop of a pin. Skipjack pretended not to notice and poured whiskey into both glasses. He picked up one and pointed at the other. Andy picked it up hesitantly. Skipjack took a sip; Andy did not.

"Ice is precious, Andy. Be thankful. Don't waste. Drink your drink, man."

Andy took a big slug and shuddered a little. A fleeting smile flickered on his face.

"Some of Green's finest."

"Yes, sir."

"Listen. I don't want to be hard. Sit and relax a bit. The door is shut. I just want to talk."

"Yes, sir," Andy said and scooted back. Skipjack offered him a cigar.

"No thank you, sir. I don't smoke; that's the truth."

"Can you read and do sums?"

"Yes, sir. No point in lying to a good man."

"What makes you think I am a good man, Andy?"

"I've seen things. Brawl and his Lucy have backed 'em up."

"They're the ones taught you to read and do sums, ain't they?"

"Yes, sir."

Skipjack dismissed his reply with a wave, relit his cigar, and peered down its barrel. Puffs of smoke encircled his head. Andy shrugged and took a sip.

"Why you think they taught you, Andy?"

"Because I was like their son, I guess."

"Son? Like a son?" Skipjack mumbled. "Listen, Andy, you have been blessed as a favored son. Do you understand that? You have been offered the key to freedom. You hold it in your hand."

"I still need to talk to Brawl."

"I suppose you do, Andy, but did you ever think about having a talk with yourself? I mean, did you ever sit down and ask what *you* wanted?"

Andy closed his eyes. Skipjack sucked his cigar and admired the whisky's golden hue. He had no idea what to say next. He was waiting for Andy to give a clue. Skipjack sat and waited, somehow knowing that a chink of light was bound to break through.

Several minutes passed.

"What do you . . .?"

"That's not it, Andy, and you know it."

"Yes, sir."

"Okay. Finish your drink. Take a few hours off. Probably got a headache about now."

"Must be a mind reader, sir."

"You're the one reading minds, but one you're leaving out."

"Yes, sir," Andy said, looking relieved as he finished his drink.

"Do you understand what I'm saying?"

"I'm not so sure."

"Then promise you'll dig around what you're not so sure about, Andy. Do you hear?"

"Yes, sir, I believe I hear."

"Come see me tomorrow after lunch. Go fishing or take a walk."

Andy pulled the door. Skipjack sagged back into his chair.

The first shot Billy got lucky, square hit the log, but missed the coin clean.

"Try not to blink, son," Skipjack said. "Reload."

The boy fumbled with the bolt, ejected the spent shell and reloaded.

"Kind of a small target, ain't it?"

"Suppose it is, at that. Why not aim at the log itself this time?"

"That's easy," the boy said.

"With your eyes shut?"

"No way," Billy said. "Not with them shut."

"That's what I've been telling you, but sight in on it, then close and shoot."

"I can't do that. It won't work. I gotta see it if I'm to hit it."

"Try it," Skipjack said. "Just try it one time."

"All right, but you're not gonna like it."

The boy took dead aim, steadied himself on the branch, then closed his eyes and fired. There was a soft thud as the slug dug into dirt well beyond the target.

"What did I hit?"

"Nothing you wanted. Now listen to me. These bullets ain't cheap and that's the least of it. Most times, you get one chance. You got to be steady and see clear. Think you might do better with an eye open?"

The boy nodded. He reloaded without being told. He took careful aim, then he stretched out of his crouch and took a deep breath.

"My breathing's jerky, and it makes me shake."

"Breathe out. No need to shake."

"Just the log, right?"

"Yeah, forget the coin is there, but you might want to aim right beneath as an aiming point."

The rifle fired and the coin as well as the tree bark beneath were replaced by raw wood.

"I hit it."

"Yes, you did at that. Just you remember; breathe easy and see your target clear. Give me that rifle. That's enough for one day."

"I only shot a couple of times."

"That's enough."

———

Back on the porch, Billy and Skipjack could hear voices inside. One said, "Once again." The other said, "I don't know."

"Never ever will either unless you try, so try, Lacy. I'll bet you teach me something soon."

"Let me go slow."

"Just go."

"'Then Peter said, Silver and gold have I none; but such as I have give I thee...'"

A wagon rolling up the hill drowned the rest of it out. It was Brawl. The whole outfit jangled like Christmas. Billy lit up when he saw Brawl's big broad grin and jumped off the porch.

"Ho, Bill. Hey, Mr. Maddox. Just dropped by to see Tom's work. Are you satisfied?"

"Brawl, truth is, I ain't looked. Fact is the one that needs satisfying is inside teaching Lacy."

"That's a good thing your missus is doing. My sweet Lucy has gone near blind. It breaks my heart but, except for reading, she can do most anything a sighted woman can. Even chops wood when I ain't looking. Hard to believe. We no older than you are."

"Damn shame," Skipjack said. "But otherwise?"

"Fit as a fiddle. However, I do believe there is a young 'un coming. How you take that?" Brawl said with an infectious grin.

"How'd you know that already?" Skipjack asked.

Brawl puzzled, smiled, and crinkled his eyes. He climbed down off his wagon, turned, and shrugged.

"I ain't kidding, Brawl. How did you find out so quick?"

Billy looked at what looked like giants to him and asked, "Find what out? What little one you all talking about?"

Brawl and Skipjack smiled and shook their heads. Brawl started chuckling, then so did Skipjack. Both nodded at once as they stepped toward each other and hugged.

"What's going on?" Billy asked.

"You, too?" Brawl asked.

"So I was told."

"Well, praise the Lord for late summer fruit."

"Damn it, Brawl, you sure got that right. Can you believe?"

"I guess I better. Another mouth to feed."

"What other mouth?"

Both men started laughing and their laughter glowed golden and tinged Billy's confusion with joy.

"What mouth? Won't you tell?"

"Let's go see Tom's work. We'll talk to Momma. She's better at explaining."

"She's better at lots of things, you ask me," Billy said, said scuffing the grass.

"No doubt, but think she can shoot better than you?"

"Maybe."

"And maybe not. I couldn't shoot as well as you at your age."

"You couldn't? You swear?"

"We ain't supposed to swear, Billy, but no I could not. You are a natural."

"What's that mean?"

"Mean's you hit the bull's-eye. I had to shoot a thousand times. You got something. Do me a favor and put that rifle up, okay? Then come out. We'll check on Tom's work."

CONSTERNATION

After Billy trudged off with the heavy rifle and bag of ammunition, Brawl and Skipjack strolled into the backyard where the wagon stood that had hauled creek stone up from the riverbank. The mule was still in harness. There were two kids, a girl and a younger boy, lifting rocks off the tailgate and dragging, rolling, and stacking. Brawl touched Skipjack's sleeve; both stopped and observed.

Tom was digging a shallow trench with a spade. It was obvious that he had a plan. The line he had scored did not conform to the configuration of the previous bed. String stretched between stout twigs up to the back door of the house and intersected with string that led to the privy, and another led toward the springhouse. Both men smiled and nodded.

Tom glanced over his shoulder and harshly yelled at the boy that he was due a thrashing. The children looked frightened. The boy wrenched the stone up onto the stack of middle-sized rocks. There was a large stack of small stones and a smaller stack of large stock. The last stones being unloaded were middle sized.

The two kids scurried back to the wagon. Brawl shook his head and without moving an inch, called out, "How's everything going, Tom?"

"Fine, fine enough, except these ones are slow as molasses."

"Time to quit now," Brawl said.

"I ain't laid any stone."

"Have you noticed the hour? I know these children have, and boy, what is that mule doing hitched? He did his part. That wagon has a break. That mule should be free. What you thinking? That ain't your mule. That's my mule."

Tom stabbed his spade but did not turn or glare.

"Stack your tools, Tom, let's go."

"It ain't squared off no more. See that?"

Brawl and the children holding his legs nodded. Tom laid his shovels and picks beside a tree.

"Tom, you come over here," Brawl said.

As Tom walked over, it was obvious how young he was. Swagger gave away his age. No more than eighteen; trying to appear a whole lot older and aided by stature, but not by his movements, which were unnaturally forceful. For the first time, Skipjack realized what Brawl had meant about anger and it saddened him. For a fleeting moment, he wanted him gone far away, gone in some way he couldn't have explained. Brawl told the boy to take 'em home.

The kids on the tailgate were grinning when Tom scrunched off. They waved. Billy walked out with Gracie at his heels. He yelled, but Tom did not turn around. Gracie barked, then sat and licked her chops.

Skipjack said, "Can we talk for a minute out on the porch, you and me?"

"Course we can."

"Billy, tell your mother we need two drinks on the porch right now."

The two men settled into the chairs and bathed in leaf-splintered light. Minutes later, Marcie appeared with two glasses, whiskey, and a small pitcher of water. Both men thanked her as she placed the small tray on the table.

"You want some water in yours?" Skipjack asked.

"Don't want it, necessarily, but yes, suppose I should."

Skipjack poured the water in and the mixture swirled amber and gold. Brawl loaded his pipe. Skipjack lit a cigar. Neither spoke. Skipjack sighed and took a drink from his glass. Brawl did the same.

"All right, I'm stumped," Skipjack admitted. "Andy's got me up a tree. Can't figure how to approach the man."

"I don't doubt what's understandable."

"Well, Brawl, I sure hope you understand, because I don't."

Brawl took a deep drink and finished off most of the contents. With hand gestures, Skipjack offered to replenish and Brawl accepted.

"I know what I want but don't know what he wants and don't want to put words in his mouth."

"Good thing you don't, but somebody might have to help him find words."

"Ain't so sure I'm following, Brawl."

"I'm guilty as you. Let me say that first." Brawl fired his pipe and a cloud of sweet smoke mingled with the tang of Skipjack's cigar.

"Guilty of what? We both tried to do right."

"True enough," Brawl said as he accepted his freshened drink. "That's true enough, but think about it: We always told him what to do and when. And he done it. Then we commenced to tell him he was a good man."

"You never told him to do nothing wrong, did you? I know I didn't."

"No, Skipjack. I always told him to do the right thing. But it was always my right thing."

"The right thing's the right thing, I figure," Skipjack said.

"But how do you learn what the right thing is?" Brawl said. "I mean you personally."

"Well, you try stuff. Sometimes it works and sometimes not. You figure from there."

Brawl started chuckling, drew on his pipe, and stared with amusement at Skipjack.

"Did you ever make a mistake?" Brawl asked.

"Hell, yeah, make 'em every day. Sometimes the same ones."

Brawl started laughing.

"What's so damn funny?" Skipjack asked.

"What if you couldn't?"

"Couldn't what?"

"Make mistakes."

"Nothing would get done, that's what. If I had to make everything perfect, I couldn't put my boots on."

"Does Andy make mistakes?"

"No, he's near perfect. You trained him right."

"That's why I'm saying I'm guilty as you are. The man can't make a mistake."

"What are you saying? That he's perfect?"

"No, I'm saying what you know and why you want him, but that's exactly why he don't know what he wants. The man thinks, but he don't think for himself. He thinks for you. He thinks for me. Can't think for himself. Andy don't know how to listen up to himself outside you or me."

Skipjack drizzled whiskey into both glasses and chewed his cigar. Gracie sauntered up and he stroked her head. She smiled and nuzzled.

"Also think about this: What if he had and I didn't like the way things proceeded and had given him hellfire and a whipping? Told him to do it my way or he wouldn't get supper. I did more than once. He's got a mind all right, but I never encouraged him using it."

"Your Lucy taught him to read."

"So he could take instructions and read the Bible. Weren't all bad, I admit. But he's afraid of mistakes. Mostly my fault I fear."

"What we gonna do? He's a good man and I need him to stay. You know I'll treat him right."

Brawl scowled.

"How do you treat a man right, Skipjack? I ain't no authority apparently, so tell me what *you* mean by treating him right?"

"You know me, Brawl."

"Well enough to know you ain't got the answer to my question. Think about it. We'll talk in a few days," Brawl said as he stood to leave.

At supper, Billy was enthusiastic about Tom Thurston's strength.

"He can split a rock from just looking."

"Bet you he used a chisel and mallet, too," Skipjack said.

"Well, sure, but he just seemed to tap; seemed they broke more with eyes than anything."

"He's been taught where to strike, honey," Marcie said.

The three of them sat on the porch and watched clouds roll. The air had a touch of cool. A damp coolness—welcome in late August—suggested rain. The fireflies were thinning. All three of them were unusually quiet.

"How does Tom know where to put the string lines he puts out for flower beds? He don't even seem to be looking," Billy said.

"Doesn't seem to be," Marcie said.

"Whatever. He doesn't seem to even look," Billy restated and then yawned.

"You moved some rock today, didn't you, boy?" Skipjack asked.

"Some. He wouldn't let me move much. He made the little ones. He wasn't so nice to them."

"Marcie, this young man can shoot."

"Wonder where he comes by that? But my boy is tired. I'm going to tuck him in so he can be steady tomorrow."

Billy didn't protest and allowed himself to be led to bed. Skipjack sat on the porch and felt the temperature drop ten degrees in five minutes. There was a rumble of thunder to the south. A storm was coming. Hot and cool were mixing it up and would soon collide. Something about Tom disturbed Skipjack. He could see no immediate threat, but there was something puzzling he couldn't figure that bothered him.

When Marcie returned, he asked her what she thought of the young man. She shrugged.

"He seems to know what he's doing," she said.

"He's not forceful toward you?" Skipjack asked.

"Heavens, no."

"Something about that boy tightens my stomach."

"That's coming from somewhere I don't see. He bosses the kids, that's all. I think he's okay. Remember what I told you this morning?" Marcie smiled.

Skipjack nodded. He reached out his hand and she clasped it.

"I can't believe this," he said.

"You're not troubled, are you?"

"I hardly know what to feel. But troubled ain't part."

"Are you pleased?"

"That and sort of scared to death."

"Me too, but we can do it."

"I know that we can do it, but God almighty better help too or else . . ."

"He will, Jack, and guess what? I believe it's going to rain."

"What's rain have to do with babies?"

"Jack, my breasts are swollen. You promised to care for me, am I correct?"

"Once," Skipjack said.

"Think I need assistance, sweetheart."

As he stood, Skipjack said, "I'll do what I can."

As they climbed the stairs, Marcie was laughing softly as wind tossed treetops side to side, and rain pitter-pattered. A storm threatened. There was a hum in the wind and a whistling, too.

"We better snuggle in, sweetheart," Marcie said.

After wonderful exertions, they found themselves softly breathing, pressed close, listening to rainfall and distant thunder.

In gray first light, Skipjack fought the urge to piss, but the steady dripping urged him downstairs and he peed off the porch. The downfall was steady. Thinking of Marcie's sweet warmth, he ascended the stairs and crawled back in bed. He knew he should get up, but caressed Marcie instead. He dozed and then slept.

When he awakened, it was raining cats and dogs. He grinned and hugged his woman, who pushed back into him. There was no way to sleep, but no desire to leave the bed either, so he smelled Marcie's hair and tried to alleviate the pain in her breasts. She didn't seem to mind and next time he opened his eyes, the storm was torrential.

Even though their house was situated on a hillside and there was no danger of flooding, the deluge created rivulets that sluiced down and pooled around the stone foundation of the house. The limestone slab at the back door was like the stern of an anchored flatboat; water splashed against and over, sprinkling Skipjack's toes as he surveyed the situation.

"You said it was going to rain, didn't you?"

"That's not all I said," Marcie replied.

"The ground can't hold it."

"You remember that part. I said, 'might as well be landing on stone.'"

Skipjack grinned and was about to turn to Marcie, but in the roar of the pounding torrent, she had slipped up behind him and squeezed him around the waist.

"I need you, Jack. Just trust the Lord."

"This'll bring out the rats though," Skipjack said.

"If it doesn't drown them first."

"Lord, I hope. If this keeps up, we'll need a boat to get to the privy."

"Keeps like this, there might not be a privy."

"I'll build the next one out of rock," Skipjack said.

"Always looking ahead, aren't you?"

"Where would you have me look?"

"I believe you know the answer to that, dear husband."

"That's why I build the next of stone."

The downpour kept pace with increasingly aggressive thunder and redoubled its efforts and roared. Water poured off the roof in solid sheets. Skipjack slipped out to feed Jessie and the mare and was drenched with his first step. Water swirled around the animals' feet, though they were calm and seemed glad to see him. Skipjack was barefoot, and the straw was cool and slippery. A bolt of lightning exploded overhead, and he jumped a foot into the air, then slipped and fell, spilling oats, but when he stood, he felt a twinge in his back and stretched to pop it free. He limped to the privy in wind-tossed rain. The privy was a mess. One end of the pit was full and overflowing; the other wasn't far behind. He took his seat and didn't know quite what to pray for. If the storm continued, no telling what other problems would develop, but on the other hand, if she kept coming down, she might wash out the creek. With that thought, he smiled, and a slow growling rumble muffled pounding rain.

The door opened, and Marcie ducked in, hair plastered to her head and whatever garment she had wrapped herself in clung like gossamer. She shook and smiled.

"Watch your step, sweetheart," he said.

"Lord Almighty," Marcie replied.

"Here, this is high ground temporarily; take this one," he said pointing to his seat.

Marcie made a face and nodded as Skipjack stood.

"This is awful," Marcie said.

"Yeah, that it is and we're on a damn hill," Skipjack said with a wink.

"I had nothing to do with it. It felt like rain, that's all."

"Keep up the good work, mother," Skipjack said as he stepped through a wall of water.

A few minutes later, Marcie was heating rain on the stove and admonishing him for tracking through the house. Skipjack claimed his feet were rinsed clean.

"Not clean enough."

She made him sit down while she dragged out a shallow copper tub and set it in the middle of the kitchen floor. Skipjack poured himself a glass of whiskey and offered one to Marcie, but she declined. She poured herself a glass of port.

"Alcohol is alcohol," Skipjack said as he lit a cigar.

"So they say," Marcie said as she fed a log to the stove. "Damn, there's a chill in the air."

"Yep, there sure is and we're under roof and snug, thank God. I guarantee that creek is boiling now."

Marcie nodded and noticed for the first time that Skipjack had his pistol beside him on the table. She said nothing and stirred coals.

"Wouldn't it be nice to have hot water whenever you wanted?"

"I been working on that," Skipjack said.

"How far have you got?"

"Not far enough."

"Get busy, honey; I'm chilled."

"We could go back upstairs for a minute."

Marcie took a slug of wine and snorted.

"We're taking a bath. You might think about shaving, too. I'm raw all over."

"Whoops."

"Don't get me wrong, honey. Just a suggestion."

Before Skipjack could respond, Billy walked in rubbing sleep out of his eyes and announced in an annoyed voice that there was water dripping on his bed. The whiny tone of his voice and his slouch stirred Skipjack to respond harshly.

"Did you move the damn bed?"

As soon as the words left his mouth, Marcie spun around. Skipjack apologized. Billy shook his head, genuinely confused.

"Please, son, help me move the bed."

"The bed ain't that big," Billy said.

"No, but you are and it's your bed, understand? Maybe we'll find the leak, too. Will you help?"

"But I gotta go first."

"Well, then go."

The boy looked to his mother and she opened the door. The rain was steady and determined. The boy wasn't.

"Maybe I'll use the nighttime pot," he said, as he ducked back into his room. A few minutes later, he came back out.

"There ought to be a way to have the outhouse in the house," Billy said.

Skipjack and Marcie chuckled.

"I'm serious," he said.

"Jack, add that to your 'work on' list," Marcie said.

"That inside pot ain't right somehow," Billy said.

"Isn't," Marcie said.

"Isn't right."

"Well, let's move the bed, son," Skipjack said.

"I just did."

"Thank you," Skipjack said.

FLOTSAM

Andy appeared mid-afternoon on the front porch, wringing his hat, which seemed ridiculous. He was completely soaked head to toe. Skipjack looked into the earnest expression on the young man's face and invited him to stand by the fire, but Andy shook his head and motioned Skipjack out onto the porch.

"The river rose, sir. Tavern's dry, but creek's rised up over the river. I saw some of the queerest things and I thought you should know what I seen, sir."

Now Skipjack had seen many creek runs, where swift run-out dammed up and then stacked until it toppled over into the river current's swirl. But Skipjack's brow furrowed when he heard the edge in Andy's voice.

"What was it you saw, Andy?"

"Well, first off, the creek is way up as you would expect. Almost up to the tavern. Within a few foot anyway, and things was running through them big cottonwoods, tree trunks, dead animals, trash, and stuff. I wouldn't have troubled you for that. Mary Frances said that was normal, but whoever heard of this believes in Noah. Have you ever seen such rain, sir?"

"Andy, calm yourself and tell me what you saw that drove you here."

"Yes, sir," Andy said. He took a deep breath and tried to calm himself. "I saw wagons and boats with tents and dead cows mixed with barrels of whiskey. I saw what might have been our old flatboat, and I saw a man riding in a coffin waving at a near naked woman who was ugly as sin and if she hadn't held up a cross and bent over uglier, I might not be here. I swear lightning crashed nearby and some drowned dead men glowed green like they were asleep on the waters and I had to come tell you what I seen. A lot of it sideways, some was upside down."

"Did you see anything peculiar?" Skipjack asked.

"Ain't that enough?"

Skipjack burst out laughing and ushered Andy in and halfway wrestled him through the door. Andy stood by the stove on which slices of ham now crackled.

"Dead men sleeping in the raging creek and one of 'em jolly in a coffin?"

"No, sir. He weren't just floating and I ain't saying it was a coffin. I'm saying it sure looked like one. It was all black and was tied to a rope that was hooked to the raft the particular woman rode. Four or five men with poles or paddles were pushing and paddling, but they probably could have done as good as the dead men, rolling and turning. They was cussing and shouting, though you could hardly hear through the storm, but the creek had 'em sure and then the fall down grabbed 'em and dropped 'em in the river. They flashed past in a minute, fearful as devils, and I barely go to church. I thought you should know, sir."

"So, they're heading downstream now in your best judgment?"

With an indignant look, Andy said, "There's no way they could head otherwise."

"Well, then, they ain't devils."

"Never did say they were."

"No, you didn't and thanks for telling. They are worse, 'cause they could change what they are. They are trash; thank God the creek washed them out."

"You're not laughing at me, sir?"

"Not laughing at you. I'm laughing about them rolling downstream; hope they roll past New Orleans. You say some were dead?"

"Some didn't look too lively."

"Could you see the coffin clear?"

Andy looked away. Marcie walked in and offered him some tea.

"Could you make him out, Andy?" Skipjack asked.

"He might have been your brother, sir. I never saw him with beard and top hat before."

"Then what leads you to think it was him?"

"Can't say, something hard to describe."

"Think so, though?"

"God is my witness, I do."

"Stay and have some food, Andy. I'll take you back."

"Thank you, sir. I've been thinking about what you offered."

"So have I, Andy, we'll talk later."

———

On the way downhill, they swayed in silence. Rain was now gentle, at times a mist. Both stared ahead.

"Your Miss Marcie sure can cook."

"Glad you could share with us, Andy."

Marcie had sat Andy opposite Skipjack. He had been the first to be served. Marcie said the blessing, and all had nodded. The corn fritters were crisp and delicious, but only Billy mentioned that fact. So was yeast bread and the ham and succotash; they ate mostly in silence. Andy had nodded at the end of the meal and thanked Marcie in a muffled voice. They all had felt awkward somehow.

Skipjack clucked at the mare for something to do. As they approached River Road, Andy suggested that he could walk from there, but Skipjack allowed that he had to check things.

"So, what have you thought about?"

"Not enough, I guess, but I have been thinking."

"What?"

"Well, I've been thinking about good cooking and how nice that could be."

"Does that take you somewhere?"

"It might, sir."

"Say no more, Andy. I don't know why, but that seems like a good start."

"I'm working, sir."

"Take your time," Skipjack said softly. "You have almost three weeks."

"I should talk to Brawl, don't you think?"

"That's up to you."

———

Skipjack spent an hour in his office before he entered the kitchen. Mary Frances said business was lousy. She sent Andy for next morning's firewood, nodded at Skipjack, and they stepped outside. She shushed him before a questioning word had left his mouth.

"Had them in the whiskey house two days; Aleeta brought them. Didn't know what else to do. Louis is going to have to get some whiskey out tomorrow sometime. They can't stay there."

"How many?"

"Three: a man, a stout boy, and a woman."

"Jesus."

"You sure got that right. The river's running."

"I got to get Andy out of here," Skipjack said under his breath.

"Only two at the bar; I can handle them," Mary Frances said.

"Let me see what the water's doing. Close the place down."

Skipjack stumbled, then slipped on his way down to the river's edge. He cursed under his breath and made up his mind for certain that he was having stone steps laid. He could see that the creek was once again flat, but the river was swift. A white sycamore log skimmed past. Damn, too old for this, but he could tell by the slow drag against the riverbank that it was possible. Sure wanted to be in bed instead, then he made up his mind.

Back in the kitchen, Mary Frances informed him the bar was shut. Louis walked in, hung his apron, and acted like he wanted to fix a snack, but Mary Frances ran him off by promising a double helping of cobbler next day. Andy stacked wood in the log bin until Skipjack asked him to stop and do him a favor.

"What's that, sir?"

"Go watch the house a couple hours. I'll get you a gun out of the office."

"I'll run him up."

"Good. I'll take you home later, Andy," Skipjack said.

"Shut her down, Andy," Mary Frances said.

Skipjack unlocked the office with his new key and got Andy a Sharps rifle, still slick with oil, and his grandfather's pistol that hadn't been fired in years.

"If I were you, I would favor the rifle," Skipjack said as the buggy rolled off.

The skiff was near swamped, loaded with enough rainwater to make Skipjack curse. He should have considered that before he sent Andy off. There was nothing to do except wade aboard and bail. He thought about getting a runaway out of the whiskey house to help, then dismissed that thought as being risky. It wasn't completely dark.

Skipjack bailed bucket after bucket over the side and still stood in six to eight inches of water. When he took a breather, he looked to the west and saw a bank of clouds slowly rolling upriver and since prayer seemed to be working, he tried another and prayed the bailing would go faster.

He put his back into it again, and again scooped and heaved, scooped and heaved. There had to be a better way. At least the river wasn't rising; in fact, seemed like it had dropped several inches.

If only a man could harness that current and make it power some kind of siphon.

Nothing to do now but bail. Skipjack decided to dream about that sore-backed scheme later. He scooped and heaved. Finally, his bucket was scraping ribs and water was barely above his ankles. Something told him there were eyes fixed on his back. He damned himself for not carrying his pistol, dropped his bucket without looking around.

Listened with all his might but did not turn at first. When he did, he moved slowly. He searched the shore and saw nothing unusual, which spooked nearly as much as if he had. Shook his head, took a deep breath, and exhaled. Figured his nerves were raw with the brother business and bailed a couple buckets, then walked up to the tavern and armed himself.

Skipjack didn't walk straight to the whiskey house. Instead, he meandered over to the creek and then back to the skiff. Hated to admit it, but his stomach was queasy. His instincts were usually right on the money. Something didn't feel right; he couldn't put his finger on it but was glad the pistol was crammed in his belt and the double-barreled shotgun was in the crook of his arm. The clouds spit light rain. He liked that; didn't much like being soaked but guessed nobody else would either.

He circled the tavern and ended at the whiskey house. He turned the heavy key in the lock and it snapped. He swung the door and said, "Come out. It's time."

No sound came back, so he said it again. Third time, he added, "Don't be afraid," and realized how ridiculous that must sound. "Come now, I'll take you. Be quick. Come. No talk."

Shapes stood slowly and followed Skipjack into drizzle. He jammed the lock shut and motioned. Silent as ghosts, they slunk quickly to the side of the tavern and stuck near the wall. Before traipsing to the river, Skipjack satisfied himself that no one was around.

"Come," he whispered.

The big man tried to hand him a pouch.

"Later. Come quick."

Afraid of the dark swirling water, the woman balked. The man lifted her into the skiff. Her fear was palpable, but at least she was quiet. The young man hopped aboard, then the older one.

Skipjack propped his shotgun into a notch he had hacked out for this purpose. He cast off and dug into the current. The downstream flow out of the creek tugged more fiercely than he had suspected. He rowed into that mess with all his might, knowing that if he could get past the creek, he could hit slack water. His plan was to stay out of the channel until he was far enough upstream to turn and slide down on the diagonal, then land on the opposite shore above the tavern. He was hoping for strength to make it back across, but as he dug into the creek run-out, knew he had to test the river. He slid out further from shore and sure enough, the current eased, and they started to make progress.

Skipjack ducked into some slack water to take a breather. The older man offered to row. Skipjack asked him if he knew how. It was now so dark, he couldn't see the man's face. The man said he could.

The skiff was set up with two sets of oarlocks. He had two extra oars on brackets. He set the man up.

"Think we can work together?"

"Sure do. Yes, sir, better than hunkering."

Skipjack gave the young man a bucket and asked him to bail. He told the woman she could sit up, too. They set out again and the older man was good. They were in rhythm after a few strokes, while the bailing bucket tickled the ribs of the skiff. The woman started humming a song and since drizzle had turned to noisy rain, Skipjack didn't ask her to stop.

He knew this stretch like the back of his hand. In tandem, the men rowed; the bucket scooped less and less; the woman's mournful tune, warm and hopeful somehow, helped counter clammy dampness.

"This is far enough," Skipjack said, as he checked his bearings. "Let's turn out now, let the current do a little work. Keep her pointed upstream till I give word."

A stiff breeze began to blow upriver and it helped to offset the downstream tug of churning water. Skipjack instructed them to watch for drift. There was big stuff floating down he didn't want to tangle with. They were the only boat; seemed everybody else was snugged in. Occasionally small stuff thumped the side, but they threaded their way to the midpoint of the river without mishap.

"Now, sit tight, keep low, and I'll do the rest." Skipjack let the river and coaxing oars point them to the landing point. The woman stopped humming and when Skipjack looked over his shoulder, he could see her hugging her man. The young fellow was still watching for drift and even though there was no need, seeing as how they were well positioned and drifting, Skipjack said nothing.

Totally dark now and he could barely make out ghostly shapes of treetops as they swooped closer to the Indiana shore. He rowed very little most of the way and then poured it on until he was in dead water close. He drifted a few yards, then nosed in, stepped off, and dragged the bow up a small gravel beach.

"Here we are. Step easy, step lively. Come on."

First the stout boy and then the man and woman climbed out. The man held out the small pouch. Skipjack pushed it away. The man offered again.

"Ain't gonna take it. You need it. No one here tonight, apparently. Can't say I blame 'em. There's a church that direction." Skipjack pointed at the hillside that, from where they were, looked like a thicket-infested mountain. "Climb straight up. Not as steep as it looks. Just be careful. When you hit the road, follow it that way," he said pointing again. "They'll feed you and you'll be all right."

"Thank you, sir," the man said. The woman and young fellow both nodded. "Maybe I can do something for you someday, sir. If I can, I swear I will."

"You got plenty to worry about. Forget me. You could shove me off, if you will."

Next thing there was a slight push, then his passengers who had looked spectral on the shore faded into the hillside, and Skipjack drifted into inky black. In terms of drift and such, this was where it got dicey. This pass, he was asking for a rising moon, but it was dark as pitch.

The tavern was downstream, so he wasn't fighting current so much as working it, but if he miscalculated and overshot, then another upstream battle would ensue.

There were riverboats lit up on the Kentucky shore, but that didn't help. They came and went all the time. Then he saw a faint glow from what he knew was the tavern's kitchen. Right on the money. He headed upstream in anticipation of the run-out from the creek. When he hit that water, he used its thrust to slide the skiff home.

Skipjack knocked on the door of the kitchen and Mary Frances let him in. Although it was warm, he was soaked and immediately moved next to the stove that Mary Frances had stoked. She handed him a glass of water and a bottle of whiskey. She was frying up ham. Neither spoke until he had slugged a little of both liquids. Skipjack noticed that Mary Frances had a glass of what looked to be brandy.

"I never seen you so wet," she said, obviously amused.

"Yeah, well, I suppose this dousing might somewhat please Marcie."

"I wouldn't bet. Women in the family way are known to be particular."

"So she told you. Now, what do you think? Can you believe it?"

"I wonder what you will believe, crawling and stooping to scoop a two-year-old."

"Ain't there yet," Skipjack said right before tilting the bottle and taking a gulp. "Man, this is smooth." His eyes bulged, and he coughed a few times before attempting to light his sodden stogie.

"Why don't you get a fresh one? That thing's wet as you are. You want some eggs?"

"Naw, ham'll do, thank you. I believe I will get a fresh one. That's a mean river."

"Had me worried, sure enough," Mary Frances said. "Worried something might run you down."

"Got lucky—no boats. Dodged drift, but one hell of a current."

After finishing the fried ham, Skipjack fired a fresh cigar and noticed Mary Frances was looking at him funny. He watched her sip from her glass. Her eyes seemed to be twinkling.

"What?" he asked. "What you looking at?"

"You, you old codger. What you doing this mischief for?"

"What mischief you talking about, Mary Frances?"

"Making babies for one; stealing folks across river for another. I can't figure."

Skipjack chuckled.

"The first part's easy. That's nature. Now the second part, I ain't sure I know."

"Oh, sure you do. It ain't money. We both know that."

"How do you know it ain't about money?"

"You never take money."

"It ain't about money."

"Then what you stealing across for? I want to hear you say it out loud."

"Hell if I know, woman. Call it stealing? How you steal what can't be owned? Answer that."

"Don't have to. I ain't involved," Mary Frances said.

"Not involved, my ass," Skipjack exclaimed. "You been involved since that first night you caught me and this batch you hid out your own damn self. Why?"

"What was I supposed to do? Turn them away? Tell Aleeta no thanks?"

"Well, I wasn't here. Why didn't you?"

"I knew you wouldn't like it."

"That's your reason?"

"Why do you do it?" Mary Frances asked again.

"I don't know the why of anything. What if I didn't?"

"Make you feel good?"

"Right now feel frog cold and tuckered. How you feel? Why didn't you turn me in the first night? Tell me that."

"Wouldn't have set right; thought you might have some reason."

"See what I mean? Your reason for not was based on something you still got questions about. My reasons for doing are maybe the same mysterious thing."

"Glad you're back safe."

"Marcie's probably worried sick. She don't know a thing. We best be heading on."

"Why haven't you told her?"

"Would worry her to death."

As they walked toward the buggy in a gauzy mist, Mary Frances was relieved to see that Skipjack had his pistol. He handed her the shotgun he was carrying.

"What's this for?" she asked.

"For shooting varmints. If you see one, shoot."

"You suspect something?"

"Been jumpy since I bailed the skiff. Like somebody's out there."

"Likely nerves but felt that way when I pulled up. I keep a sharp knife handy."

"You see anything?" Skipjack asked as he gently tapped the mare with the reins.

"No but expected I might."

"I'd feel a lot better if my brother were dealt with, that's for damn sure."

"Skipjack, it hasn't always been like this."

"Agreed. Still, you see something strange, shoot."

Skipjack clucked, and the mare broke into a trot.

NERVES

Time he got home, Skipjack was chilly, and Marcie was hot; anxiety transformed to anger. Mary Frances hadn't told her anything about what he was doing. The sight of Andy trudging uphill with a rifle hadn't eased Marcie's mind one little bit. Billy had wanted to load up a shotgun and go with him, but she had made him stay put.

She allowed him to load his shotgun but made him stay in the house with her.

When Skipjack walked in, she searched his face, which revealed nothing.

"What have you been doing? You're clammy as a wet rag."

Skipjack claimed he was taking care of some things, bailing out the skiff and other stuff that needed tending. Marcie wasn't pleased.

"What are you trying to do, kill yourself? There's a chill in this night air."

Skipjack took a slug of whiskey and tried to let her blow off steam, still planning to run Andy back down to his cabin behind the tavern, but she was so stirred he was afraid to say.

"I'm going to stroll uphill and check Andy. I'll be right back."

Marcie busied herself at the stove and didn't turn. Skipjack slipped over and wrapped his arms around her, hoping this would soften her mood, but instead, she stiffened.

"I worry about you. Don't you know?"

"Ain't nothing to worry about now. I'm back."

"How long does it take to bail a skiff?"

"Did other things, too."

"What other things?" she asked, wiggling free. "I don't want you getting killed."

"Ain't anybody getting killed."

"Jack, give me a minute. Go check on Andy."

"Yes, ma'am. That's what I'll do."

As he climbed the hill, his stomach knotted. Everybody was on edge. Mary Frances, Marcie. Hell, he was. He called Andy's name a couple of times before he got an answer. Andy was edgy, too; hadn't seen or heard anything in particular.

"Just a feeling."

Andy offered to stay the night, said he could sleep in the hayloft above the stable. Skipjack invited Andy in to dry and Marcie made him a cup of hot tea. Skipjack poured himself a glass of whiskey and offered some to Andy. Andy pointed to his cup and declined.

Marcie placed a plate of corn bread on the table and both men took a chunk.

"Andy's offered to stay the night," Skipjack said.

"Where's he going to sleep?"

"The loft."

"I'll get some bedding and a lantern."

"I'll be all right, Miss Marcie."

"I'm sure you will, and Mr. Jack is going to wash, or he'll be sleeping with you. What you get into, honey? You smell like a hard day's work."

Skipjack was glad she was smiling.

"Hell, I might even shave," he said.

"No might about it," Marcie said. "I'll strop the razor and shave you myself."

———

Before the shave, Marcie left Skipjack alone to his ablutions; a believer in the therapeutic benefits of soap and water, she went upstairs to change the sheets. She didn't make a big deal about it but carried Skipjack's pistol with her. Once in the bedroom, she walked over to the window and peered into the yard. She saw nothing before drawing the curtains and lighting a candle. She knew Skipjack was uneasy, could smell the sourness on him, and hoped his cleanup would wash that away. She tried to ignore a voice whispering *not that easy* and laid the pistol on the table.

Marcie was convinced there was no other woman and was certain it wasn't some dreadful vice. She loved and trusted the man she had married, but he was holding something back and that troubled. She was upset about Timothy herself, but somehow felt something more was disturbing Jack, but what? She decided to ask him while giving him a shave. She chuckled, imagining his shifting eyes.

After she lathered him, Marcie stood back and smiled. She looked into the clear blue eyes that seemed to float above a puffy cloud.

She had planned to go slow and dribble out questions until she shaved his throat and then she would get to the point. What the hell were you doing for the last two and a half hours? But as she looked at him, the anger drained out of her.

"What's so funny?"

"You are. You know you might look good with a snow-white beard."

"You be careful with that razor and I might live long enough to show you a real one."

"What were you doing down there?" she asked as she slid the razor down his cheek.

"I told you. I was bailing the skiff."

"What else?"

"Marcie, I was mainly just thinking."

"What's wrong with thinking here?"

"Ouch! I think you got my chin."

"So I did. Sorry. What were you thinking?"

"Can we talk about this after? That damn razor makes me nervous."

Marcie laughed. "What am I going to do with you, Jack Maddox?"

"Honor and obey me, I hope."

"You've got to earn that, Skipper."

"I'll do my best if you don't bleed me to death."

"Don't be such a baby. It's just a nick."

"You know, Marcie, we should add on another room. I was thinking we could stuff the walls with straw. I bet you that would make it cozier. Maybe put a fireplace in there as well. How's that sound to you?"

"You weren't scouting out your brother, were you?"

"Hell, no. So, you don't think we need another room?"

"Maybe. Don't talk for a minute, Jack. It's hard to do close work when you're talking."

"Yes, ma'am, you're the boss. I'm quiet as a bloody mouse."

"Hold still, too, and quit your smiling."

"Hard not to smile when I'm looking at you, but I'll try."

"Close your eyes."

"Hard to do that, too, you holding that razor."

"A clear conscience has nothing to fear."

Skipjack winked and closed his eyes. Marcie worked gently around his lips.

"We want this area nice and smooth, honey, so be real still."

Skipjack didn't make a sound.

CHAPTER 6

LET US SPEAK LIKE CIVILIZED MEN

He awakened at dawn, stretched luxuriously and, to his surprise, found himself alone in the bed. He smelled coffee as he descended the stairs. Marcie was seated at the table. There was a steaming cup waiting for him at his usual place.

"You're up early. Everything all right?"

She nodded. "Woke up and couldn't get back to sleep."

"Wasn't snoring again, was I?"

"No, you were purring like a kitten."

"You sound jealous," Skipjack said as he sat and patted her hand.

"I am. You dropped off right afterward and stayed dropped off. I tossed and turned most all night; seemed every little sound had a story to tell. I knew the doors were locked, but I swear one time I could have sworn someone was on the stairs."

"The night I walked from the hill was that way," Skipjack said, and as soon as he spoke, he wished he hadn't.

Marcie looked down and shook her head. Skipjack grimaced.

"Didn't mean to bring that up, honey. I'm sorry."

"How can you bring something that won't go away? Why did that monster settle here?"

"I don't know. Hoping they washed over the falls."

"Don't think so."

"You know something?"

"No, but I feel something. You know how some folks crowd and smile? That's the feeling. I fear he's coming back, Jack, and soon; like he's already here. Part of me wishes he was, so I could tear his eyes out. Forgive me, Lord, but that's how I feel."

Skipjack stiffened, reached, and covered Marcie's hand.

"Jack, I need to practice shooting, too."

"I got an idea," Skipjack said. "Let's have a picnic. We'll row up the creek. Fish a little bit. Then we'll have a shooting match. What do you think?"

"You'll win. I'm rusty and Billy's a beginner."

"You might surprise yourself. We'll shoot with pistols, rifles, and shotguns. We'll make it fun."

"Truthfully, I'm not feeling fun."

"Understand that, but will you?"

"What about the tavern?"

"Mary Frances and Andy can handle the tavern for another day and Tom will be here, so the house will be safe. I'll show you where they were. Seeing it washed clean might make us feel better."

"Assuming it is. What if they're back?"

"They won't be back. Not yet anyway."

"But what if they are?"

"We'll go to plan B."

"And what might that be?"

"Oh, I'm sure you'll think of something," Skipjack said, grateful for a smile.

"Well, first I'm going to make us a big breakfast. Mary Frances can handle lunch."

"Thought we were gonna fish. Ain't you bringing a skillet?"

"Sure will, but the moon might be wrong. They might not bite."

Skipjack dug in with the oars. Today the river was running faster than the creek, though both were considerably slower than the night before. He knew heading up the creek was a gamble. He didn't expect trouble, or he never would have suggested this outing. He was glad to have the rifle and the shotgun along, however, and his pistol was on the bench beside him.

Billy had two lines in the water and Marcie was knitting. The air was clear and fresh. The breeze was out of the north and it pushed cottony clouds through clear blue. The midmorning sun's warmth was welcome between Skipjack's shoulder blades. He rowed slowly and steadily, savoring the fine day.

He hoped this wasn't one of his bull-headed mistakes. The creek had been up about eight feet; debris on tree trunks and junk in branches told the tale. The deluge had created a torrent that had roiled the creek course and taken everything not rooted or wedged for a wild ride. Skipjack was reasonably certain that the encampment he had seen and smelled was flushed out completely. He saw a goat carcass entangled in an uprooted rotten cottonwood, but since no one else did, kept that information to himself. Billy was intent on fishing and Marcie was coaxing yarn into neat rows. He stroked at a comfortable pace.

Why did he feel it was so important to do this, to come to this spot? Was he trying to prove something? Hell, they could have had a shooting match at home. There was no point coming up the creek except for the hard fact that he owned this idle land. Sort of like a dog pissing on a bush, he was marking territory.

Billy hooked a fish. A smallmouth bass that ran until plum out of wiggle room, then broke the surface and the line all at once. Billy made a disgusted face, but before Skipjack or Marcie could say a thing, his other rig bowed and this time, he managed to land the fish. The same damn fish. They could tell by the line dangling.

"Damn, I never did see that before," Skipjack said.

"I caught him twice," Billy said triumphantly as he struggled to remove the hook.

"Want some help?" Marcie asked.

"No, I got him, Momma," he said. "Don't mess with me, Mr. Fish." He tossed him into the bucket.

"That's a fine smallmouth," Skipjack said.

"He didn't know to quit when he was ahead," Marcie said.

"Maybe so, but I don't quit either," Billy said as he threaded another hook on the line the fish had snapped.

Marcie smiled at Skipjack, who kept stroking the water. How did I get so lucky?

"Why do you think Andy wouldn't have breakfast?" she asked.

"Said he had to check on the tavern," Skipjack grunted.

"Honey, take a break. For goodness sake, this is a picnic, not a job."

Skipjack lifted the oars and closed his eyes.

"Ain't that funny? I forgot."

"Relax. Shouldn't your daddy relax, Billy?"

"He ought to catch some fish. That's what I think."

Skipjack gently guided the skiff under the low white branches of a sycamore that arched across the creek. Wonder it still stands. The tree's gnarly roots, bigger than legs, explained its apparent levitation. He was grateful for a bit of pale shade.

"It's like a tent in here," Billy exclaimed and as he said it, another fish bit and hit hard. It bent the pole. Bent it until the tip touched water and then dipped under. Billy worked the tugging fish, tried to convince him to change his mind. Billy's intensity became curiosity as the skiff seemed to follow the line back out into the stream.

"He's pulling us, you all."

"Let him pull," Skipjack said, "but ask him if he would consider pulling upstream for a while."

"He heard you. Look he's doing it."

"Seems he's changed his mind," Marcie said. It was true; the skiff slowly nudged straight out into the mild current of the creek, then turned downstream.

"Damn him," Skipjack said. "He's working against us."

"I'll turn him around, Dad," Billy said flashing a smile.

In a moment, the three of them were laughing as the fish turned in a slow wide arc and began to tow the skiff upstream. Whenever the fish slowed, Billy gave a little jerk on the line and the fish would respond with a spirited tug.

"Whatever you're doing, keep doing it."

"I am. I am," Billy responded, barely able to contain his mirth.

The water was still muddy from the previous day's downpour, so when Skipjack stood and looked where the line met the surface, he did not expect to see anything, but he thought he did and what he saw was bright red and teasing the ripples. No way! A red fish? He knew it had to be a black channel cat. Nothing else in this water had that kind of strength.

"Give that bad boy another jerk, Billy," Skipjack said.

The fish zigged, zagged, then lit across the creek into a shoal consisting of small stones and coarse sand in water no more than six to eight inches deep, then retired there. He was through. The fish was at least six feet. His wide-eyeballed head was huge: a big broad channel cat caught up somehow in a red shirt that he had slipped into like he was trying to impress his brethren.

Billy was laughing. Skipjack and Marcie were tickled as well, but then Skipjack stepped out of the skiff, took his knife, slashed the shirt off the fish, and cut Billy's line. He nudged the cat and it swooshed its tail and disappeared.

"Why did you do that?"

Skipjack didn't answer at first. He reeled in what turned out to be a clothesline festooned with several other shirts, some dungarees, and assorted female apparel. He winked at Marcie.

"Billy, that fish has had enough to do with our kind as it is," Marcie said.

"That was my fish. I caught him."

"Yeah and I owe both you and your fish for hauling us about a dozen stretches, but Billy, your momma's right. Besides, that fish wouldn't be good. Get that big, the meat's too strong. Good job though. We treated him right. Maybe you'll catch him again and take another ride."

Billy pouted for a few minutes until Skipjack told him that the fish was absolutely the biggest catfish he had ever seen caught on the creek, that he was bound to be the granddaddy of all the fish, the king cat.

"Besides that, who but you can ever lay claim to catching a giant fish wearing a red shirt?"

"Nobody, I guess."

"I wouldn't tell just anybody, unless your momma and I are there to swear to it."

"Can we tell Mary Frances and Tom Thurston?"

"We'll tell first chance."

As they neared the site where the "vermin," as Skipjack called them, had camped, more human stuff festooned weighted branches. Something tan that looked like it might once have been a tent draped over a low-hanging limb of a water maple, oddly marking the flood's crest. Pieces of cloth, planks, and a bottomless bucket ornamented unlikely junctures.

A strong odor of decaying flesh seeped from a partially butchered calf wedged in the crotch of a sycamore. Skipjack stroked harder. Billy held his nose. Marcie squinted and shook her head. Half a canoe lay crushed beneath a toppled dead locust. What remained of a raft was busted upside down on the hillside.

The site itself was empty except for a pig, spread-eagled and nailed to a tree next to what had been a fire pit surrounded by creek stone. There were ropes hanging from the trunks of trees that were perhaps hastily cut mooring lines.

"Look there's a dog over there," Billy said, pointing at an unfortunate bloated thing. The dog had been tied to a tree and the flood had slung the rope over a limb. The dog's rear paws just barely touched the muddy ground.

"This place makes me queasy, Jack," Marcie said.

"What's that?" Billy asked, as he pointed to what, at first glance, Skipjack had taken to be a tree stump stripped of bark. But the more he looked, he realized there was a crude leering face carved and beneath that two cone-shaped female breasts. There was a waist, a gouged-out belly button, and then a realistically carved erect penis and, beneath that, an open slit. Skipjack shuddered.

"Do you see what I'm seeing?"

He looked at her. She nodded and was already shielding Billy's eyes with her hand.

"Well, what is it? Why can't I look?"

"Why don't we use it as target practice? Don't want that on this property."

"Let's move on, Jack. I mean right now! This place is fouled."

Marcie's tone was such that Skipjack took a half dozen strokes before he looked at her. She was holding Billy's head as she pointed downstream.

"Plan B," was all she said.

Skipjack nodded. As he looked past them into the campground, he saw wobbled tent stakes driven into bare muddy ground. Light flickered on a plank still attached somehow to a blackthorn locust. He strained to make out the red letters on it. *Meke . . . inharet tha . . . erth . . . Jc.* He kept that to himself and angrily rowed. *What the hell was I thinking?* He saw a brook streaming out of mossy limestone on the hillside beside the decimated camp. As he passed the point where this tiny stream entered the creek, something told him Brother would be back. He asked one simple question: *How can I welcome him?*

Plan B went better. Mary Frances made a wry face at the smallmouth and two bluegill that Billy presented her and asked if any fish got away. The three of them had laughed uproariously.

"Okay, you got to let me in on the joke. There ain't anything funny about this measly bait. You all laughing like you beat the devil."

"I hit the bull's-eye twice, but Daddy won mostly."

"Good for you, Willy," Mary Frances said as she relieved him of his fish and tossed them into the sink. "Just glad to see you all looking happy."

"No, we had a good day, Mary Frances," Marcie said reassuringly. "But there have been strange goings-on and it looks like it'll take more than one storm to flush them out."

"Some still there?"

"I saw a pig nailed to a tree and a dog with a fat belly hanging from a limb," Billy exclaimed.

Mary Frances reached for the child's shoulder and pulled him to her. She said nothing and looked Skipjack dead in the eye. Then her brow furrowed.

"You wouldn't believe," Skipjack said.

After a moment, Mary Frances said, "So where did you shoot?"

"On the beach just upriver."

"Wanted to take us over to Twelve Mile Island," Marcie said, "but I didn't want this man to wear himself out."

"Smart thinking. Believe you might need him," Mary Frances said with a wink.

"Why don't Willy and I make a snack out of this bait?"

"That ain't bait," Billy protested. "They's fish."

"Isn't bait; they are fish, Billy," Marcie interjected.

"Do you want to help or not?" Mary Frances asked as she squeezed the boy. "About time you learned to clean fish."

"I don't like that part."

"Then I guess you don't want to help?"

"Yes, ma'am, I do."

"Then get your apron on. You two pilgrims look like you could use a drink. I'll send Louis out."

Skipjack and Marcie sipped their drinks in one of the shady spots at a table on the gallery. Two men a few tables over slugged down whiskey and puffed cigars. The mid-afternoon sunlight sparkled on small windswept waves that traveled upriver. All seemed peaceful until the man with his back to them stood and swore.

"Damnation is your dwelling place. Poisoned by Lincoln; I might as well drink with the devil. Listen to what you're espousing and be well aware to whom you are speaking. Damn your hide!"

Both Marcie and Skipjack bristled.

"That ain't no way to talk to a friend, Rawls, and you know it. Sit yourself back down and let's speak like civilized men. There are ladies present."

"You'll hide behind anything, you son of a bitch!" the big man said gesturing toward Skipjack and Marcie. "How the hell would you know the woman doesn't agree?"

"Calm down, Rawls; it's been a long day."

When the big man turned to face Skipjack and Marcie, several things struck them at once. First, his eyes flared red and glistened above a bulbous nose set in a wide face that seemed to join a trunk with no neck. Second, his chest, broad beneath rather weak-looking shoulders, was no good match for a massive belly, which was distended in such a way that it nearly concealed the fact that the gentleman's trousers were carelessly buttoned. Third, this glaring, tottering mass, stood in tiny slippers embroidered with gold thread. Despite the absurdity of his conformation, the man was truly menacing. Skipjack placed his hand over Marcie's.

"If I call a catfish horse or better yet a monkey a man and dress him in finery, would it make him so?" the big man slurred, rolling his eyes before fixing them on Marcie and then boring into Skipjack. "Why answer such foolish speculation? I understand your dilemma, but my former friend clearly does not, you see?"

The other man waved his hands back and forth above his drink, shaking his head, grinning in a pained manner, and stared heavenward. At the table beyond, Skipjack admired the gracious way Julie seated a finely dressed young couple. The lady was as pale as Julie was dark. Her gentleman's eyes were fixed on hers and both seemed oblivious to everything but each other. Skipjack was grateful for that.

"I'm a reasonable man, as I am sure that you are," the big man continued. "I vouchsafe you would agree that no amount of sugar-coating will turn a sour apple into a sweet, nor can a splash of water and some holy scripture sanctify a baboon, even if that baboon should learn to speak and ape God's truth. Is this not so apparent that I risk foolhardiness stating it? Why, even the little lady understands."

Skipjack gripped Marcie's hand a little tighter. The man grinned, exposing pearly teeth. His tablemate was looking down and shaking his head. Julie's dark eyes were intent as she attempted to take an order from the young couple who looked agitated. Suddenly the clear blue sky reminded Skipjack of shattered glass.

"So, what's your point, friend?" he asked the man.

Marcie squeezed his hand and he nodded but did not take his eyes off the big man's face.

"My point is," the big man said most deliberately, "you will be called upon to decide."

"Decide what, stranger?"

"Perhaps I am amiss. Perhaps the likes of you can remain asleep in the drowse of backwater turpitude. But you best not, my friend, lest you be awakened by a sudden intrusion of nightmarish proportions. Do you not understand? There are those would have you bed down with animals. There are those infected by this Lincoln and his ilk who would attempt to destroy our sacred way of life and anoint chattel with holy purpose, attempt to breathe souls into beasts, and turn the descendants of these beasts into begotten progeny."

"What on earth are you talking about?" Marcie asked.

"Sir, sit yourself down and hold your tongue," Skipjack said calmly.

"Fools. *Fools!* Who are you to tell me, Ralston Belton Zanzinger III, to stifle astute prognostication?"

"We are the proprietors of this establishment, sir," Skipjack said. "Please, sit and share your opinions quietly with your companion if he will have them."

"Oh, proprietor, stranger to me, if I had known you as such, my tongue would not have been less emboldened, but let me assure you, my companion, as you herald him, will amply enjoy the fruit of my prophecy as will you all."

"Well put. Sit down."

"Are you an abolitionist, sir, or worse, a theiving collaborator in the freeing of these pernicious demons?"

Skipjack stood. The big man minced toward him with a grin that seemed to drip grease. His eyes were watery, and his lips fluttered with indignation.

"Will you not answer me, sir?"

Skipjack pointed toward the kitchen and Marcie went there. The young couple sat aghast.

"You will leave now. What you may owe, the house will cover, but leave now, sir."

"You are what they say, aren't you, Maddox?" the big man sneered.

"If they say I will kill a poisonous snake, they tell no lie."

"You run 'em, don't you?"

"You run your mouth, don't you, hoghead?" Skipjack raised his pistol.

The young couple slinked away, nearly colliding with Mary Frances who was slipping up with a meat cleaver in one hand and a long knife in the other. Andy followed with a shotgun cocked and a great big grin.

"Fine place you keep," the big man said.

"Not too bad," Skipjack replied.

"Sorry to despoil your illusions. Perhaps we shall take our leave."

"Good plan," Skipjack said. "And you can stuff your 'perhaps' right up your—"

"Shush!" Mary Frances said. "Step like you ain't wearing pitter-patter or you won't be needing shoes."

Andy stepped in behind with the double-barrel leveled and the four of them walked slowly around the side of the building. There was no talk. A group of four patrons seemed to float out of the bar. Skipjack smiled and nodded. The gents were squiring downtown girls with prissy airs. Skipjack saw nothing but more trouble. He slid into the bar, then back to the office where he found Marcie and Billy nibbling fish morsels.

"Who was that man?" Marcie asked.

"How would I know?"

"Sure you don't? He seemed cocksure about you."

"Honey, I've never seen him before and hope to never see him again."

"I'll support that, sweetheart. But what did he mean? What they say?"

"Lord knows, Marcie. People say all kinds of things."

"He seemed awful certain."

Mary Frances filled the doorway and folded her arms across her chest.

"So do lots of folks. That's usually the hell of it, ain't it, Mary Frances."

"I got no time for philosophy. I'm cooking, unless you got other swine needs to be shown the trail."

"He wasn't too much trouble, was he?"

"No, almost had us convinced hitting the road was his idea. But I wanted to ask you something 'fore I get back."

"Ask away."

"Did you notice what he was riding in?"

"No, we come off river, remember?"

Mary Frances raised her cleaver and knife and tapped them flat side on the top of her head.

"He was riding in the dead man's rig, same horse and everything. Sort of gave me shivers."

"You sure—Bancroft's rig?"

"Yes, sir. What you make of that?"

As they drove up the hill, Skipjack said, "That is queer, ain't it?"

"I'll shoot 'em right between the eyes they try anything," said Billy who cradled his shotgun across his lap.

"You're not shooting anything tonight, you're cleaning up and changing clothes. You're starting to smell like a working man," Marcie said.

"Shoots like one, too," Skipjack said.

Billy raised his shotgun to his shoulder and pointed it into the thicket that lined the trail.

"Think I see something I can shoot right now," Billy said excitedly.

"What you see?"

"Not sure."

"Never shoot unless you are, you hear me, boy? What you see?"

"Looked like a man ducking behind a tree," he said as he swiveled, keeping the barrel leveled.

"Just keep a sharp eye and don't joke."

"I ain't joking. I saw something move."

"Hold your fire. We're almost there," Skipjack said.

"I'm sick of this, Jack."

"Don't that make two? I want to settle this thing."

"How?"

"I've got an idea, maybe."

———

Truth is, he had lots of ideas—too many and none good. Later that evening, Skipjack and Marcie sat on the porch and discussed the news that Brawl had brought them when he had come to collect Tom.

Brawl had climbed off his wagon and, after admiring the flowerbed stonework, which Tom had completed, the four of them carefully walked between twine lines that designated the various paths. The curving one from the turnaround in front of the stable up to the house made Brawl smile. He had told Tom to pack it up and then asked Marcie and Skipjack if he could speak with them privately.

A hod carrier had told Brawl that the "bad creek bunch" were having some hard times settling in downriver off Beargrass Creek.

This young fellow was too stupid and drink-addled to know better than to talk about such things. Brawl figured it was the fact that he paid the man daily and in full that rendered him so loquacious.

The young man confided that what he called the devil lady was unhappy downtown and was planning to move back to her old haunt on the creek. Skipjack's heart sank. He had hoped with all his heart that his intuition was wrong.

"You believe this man?" Skipjack asked.

"He's too simple to lie and why would he?"

"Damn. We got to do something."

"Somebody best. That boy tells me your brother is their newfound king."

"He knows Brother?"

"Boy's an outlier. I doubt he really knows him, but the way he described, it's Timothy all right. He's taken up with the devil woman. Hell, they can't practice thieving downtown like they can out here. You know that. Too many folks and there ain't as much open water."

"I can't figure out what to do about this damn mess," Skipjack said later as he and Marcie sat on the porch.

"Thought you said you might have an idea."

"Hell, they flicker like fireflies and I need something steady I can see. Seems everything is shifting and turning strange. You ever hear old-timers talk about the 1812 quakes and how the Mississippi ran backwards for a time? Some of 'em swore they felt it coming for weeks before and animals turned skittish and went off their feed. Well, that's about the way I feel."

Marcie gently touched the back of Skipjack's hand.

"We'll get through this, believe me."

While Marcie freshened his drink, Skipjack stared into trees that lined the drive and wished leaves would fall so he could see straight through. Earlier, when Billy had thought he had seen someone, Skipjack was near certain he had as well, but for the sake of safety and calm, had kept it to himself. A kind of nausea—more than fear—tightened his gut.

One of his ideas was to plant a keg of black powder in their fire pit and try to fuse it in such a way that it would shred all at once. That was a pipe dream and he knew it. He thought of poisoning the brook they drank out of. But he came to realize that he needed something a lot more certain. If he didn't cut the head off the snake, namely Timothy and the woman, he was simply stirring the cauldron.

A screech owl's shriek knifed through loam-scented night air. When he and Marcie had first married, he teased her when she found the sound frightening. Tonight, if he could have, he would have lit the place brighter than blazing sun. Instead, he sat under a moon that was a sliver slicing wisps. When Marcie handed him his drink, he was grateful for her steady gaze.

"How you feeling, sugar?" he asked.

"Sort of hard to say, Jack. Part of me is real excited and hopeful. Part of me is watchful and anxious. I try not to pay much mind to the second part, but it's hard."

"I hear you. Half a mind to dump this place and head west. Feel like everything's soiled, even wish the leaves would fall so I could see."

"You saw something earlier, didn't you?"

"Did you?"

"I'm not sure. Something red ducking behind a stump?"

"Wasn't a catfish, was it?"

"Maybe it was at that." Marcie chuckled. "It looked more like a skirt this time."

"You're kidding?"

"My eyes might have been playing tricks. I saw a red swirl like a full skirt could make and then nothing but tree trunks and leaves."

"I didn't see red, just a shape. Would have spotted red, don't you think?"

"People notice different things."

"Suppose so. I know we got to do something, but damned if I can figure what. Could you make an earthquake swallow them?"

"If it would work better than the flood has, I would."

"Well, think about it," Skipjack said with a smile.

The owl screeched deep in the woods. Gracie padded onto the porch expecting to be loved, but before she could settle, they both shooed her.

"Dear God, what has that dog got into?"

"I ain't sure, but if she don't stay clear, might be her last supper."

"Now, let's don't take it out on Gracie."

"I know, but enough is enough."

"Jack, be careful lest we become just as awful."

"Hard not to."

"It wasn't always this way. Remember? Lord knows these people might destroy their own selves. We might not have to do anything."

"I love the sound of that. I wish I could believe."

"Why don't we hold hands and try?"

Skipjack extended his forefinger, but soon Marcie's fingers entwined. A cool breeze sluiced through the nearest trees at the edge of the woods and swirled over and past. Then the night was as still as it had been before.

PRE-DAWN STROLL: EARTH DEFILED

There was no reason to get out of bed. He hadn't heard anything, but knew when his eyes opened, they were open for good. He dressed so quietly that Marcie didn't stir. Didn't bother with coffee. He lit a cigar, stuck his pistol into his belt, grabbed his rifle, and after locking the door, stepped into the backyard. There was no moon at all now. He took a few steps and tripped over one of Tom Thurston's stakes, recovered his balance, and cursed under his breath, then started walking uphill by memory more than light, stopping every few paces and listening. All he heard was night.

When he reached his log, he turned, sat, and stared over the faint blank shape he knew was the roof. He smoked, then reached down for the bottle that he kept there, but all he felt was leaves at first. When he found it, he pulled out the cork, but before raising it to his lips smelled the contents. His nostrils instinctively shut, but not before a whiff of something noxious closed his eyes. He brought the bottle close but could barely see his hand. In a fit of anger, he threw the bottle aside.

God help us. What is that smell? Threw the cork down and sniffed his fingers. There was a dead smell of decay and rot, reminiscent of how Gracie had smelled on the porch. Skipjack wiped his fingers in the dew. He smoked his cigar with the wrong hand and listened to the ringing between his ears, so angry he sat still as solid rock. Then he sighed, and it seemed all emotion drained, and when he yawned, was replaced with an odd sort of peace. The North Star caught his eye and he found the big dipper with almost as much wonder as he had as a child. Lord, a baby is right now knocking, wanting to enter this world. Will you please help us, please? I can't stand this no more. Take charge. Send angels. Just please help.

Skipjack immediately sank into a reverie of how to destroy this vermin. After a few minutes, he realized he might as well have been dreaming. All he was doing was staging assaults on the camp where they had been, playing out imaginary scenarios. He and Andy, Brawl, and Mary Frances opening fire from the ridge—nonsense and he knew it.

But then an inkling spurred him to walk the ridge that snaked along above the creek. As the crow flies, it was only a mile to where their camp had been. The sun would rise soon. The eastern sky was filling with cool morning light. He stood and looked down at his house. He started up to the ridge and as he walked, felt a sense of purpose though he did not know what that purpose was.

He was on an overgrown logging trail, but the undergrowth was not dense and before long, he was looking down from a large limestone boulder onto what was left of the campsite a hundred feet below. The first spears of light glinted on the horizon, and as he stood there, Skipjack could make out the fire pit.

Although Skipjack had a good imagination, he was usually focused on practical things and not inclined to see figures in clouds or discern patterns in branches or rock formations, but as he stared down, what he saw made him uneasy. The earth all around the pit was dark, almost black. A few small new plants were trying to re-establish themselves already. He wished them well. God knows the soil was fertile enough to grow anything. He wanted the whole creek bottom to be blanketed with luxuriant green. He wanted the stench to be covered and erased as if it never had been.

The carved stump from this angle was only that: a stump. Even the faint shadow it cast on the ground was nothing more than shadow, but still, something about the area seemed unnatural and menacing. Skipjack began to discern what made him want to avert his eyes.

Morning sun cleared the ridge and warmed his face. He squinted, and shadow further darkened ground around the rock-girded fire pit. Those stones suddenly looked like broken teeth surrounding a gaping maw with some short unkempt beard. Then alerted by other darkening within splashes of soft sunlight, he noticed smaller stones spaced several feet from the pit itself. All at once, his mind linked them up and he blinked and lurched back from the edge. As he did, a loosened rock tumbled over, bounced down the steep incline, and came to rest at the tip of the beard and instantly disappeared. Skipjack shuddered, then rubbed his eyes and looked again. The leering, taunting face was there no longer. Not wanting to witness what he had just seen, almost against his own will, he forced himself to squint. He wanted to see simple rocks and the plain shadows they cast, but he also wanted to figure out how his eyes had been fooled. Now, try as he might, all he saw was tramped-down earth skimmed with dark silt, the oval fire pit and a scattering of random stones.

Within minutes, sunbeams through breeze-fluttered foliage suffused every surface with inviting warmth. Wisps of moisture rose from dew-laden leaves and were visible floating off the forest floor. Several does stepped into a small clearing across the creek, hesitated, then agreed to drink. Skipjack rubbed his brow, then shielded his eyes with the hand that still reeked of the god-awful stench. He stared down once again. Two squirrels chased each other, taking turns in a game of hunter and hunted. Finally, one scurried up top of the carved stump and barked out a clattering victory chant until the other could no longer feign disinterest and scrambled to dislodge him. Soon they were down and off again, willy-nilly, zigging and zagging until, bored with the ground, they sought out treetops.

The woodpecker rapping and the blue jay voicing concerns should have reassured Skipjack that this was familiar territory. The mallards swimming into a large pool of golden sunlit water on the creek seemed to be trying to convince his mind that all had been a waking nightmare, now swallowed and replaced by honest-to-God daylight. Still, as he studied, try as he might, he could no longer guess what optical tricks had conspired to deceive his vision; the twisted visage hung in his mind. Yes, he could see the deer drink and hear birds and the busy cluck-clucking squirrels. Knew they were real but could not quite convince himself that the other thing was not.

Walking back, he could not shake perplexity or escape the feeling he was being observed. He saw no evidence to support this notion and wasn't frightened; however, his eyes flickered over and through every space they could probe or pierce. In spite of his rifle and pistol, he felt more like the hunted than the hunter, but only once did he stop and look back over his shoulder. He walked briskly until he got to his log and savored sweet hickory smoke fluffing out of the chimney. After a brief search, Skipjack found his whiskey bottle in the weeds. He bent down and examined it without touching. Most of the contents had splattered the foliage and some had poured onto the ground. He could still detect the sharp sweet smell of sour mash. Stooping closer and not breathing, he saw what appeared to be old coagulating blood and retched.

As he rinsed his hands in the spillover sluice of the springhouse, Marcie appeared in the doorway. He had planned to keep the whole thing to himself, but when he looked into her inquiring gaze, he knew he could not.

So, he explained his predawn walk. Skipjack even told her about the face. Marcie's expression seemed to tighten, but her reaction was hard to read.

"Don't you want some soap?"

"Do you think I'm losing my mind?"

"I think you're crazy walking around in the dark."

"You didn't answer me."

"You lost your mind a long time ago," she replied with a slight smile.

"Well, I swear I believe its old blood in that bottle and I did see a face clear as hell."

"I bet it was blood. Look what they did down at the tavern. I don't know about the other."

"I can't explain, but I can still see it. For an instant, it was real as fire; then, nothing there but flood silt and rocks."

Before entering the kitchen, Marcie turned and placed her hands on Skipjack's shoulders, leaned forward, and kissed him on the forehead. The block of stone that served as the backdoor step allowed her to look down into his upturned face.

"Don't let 'em drive you to something foolish. That's what they try. Can't you see?"

"We don't want to live looking over our shoulder all the time."

"True, but we don't need them to force our hand."

CHAPTER 7

DARK AS IT IS, NONE OF IT'S GOOD

acon was sizzling, and Skipjack was on his second cup when Billy padded in, rubbing sleep from his eyes. He sat and cradled his chin in his hand. Gracie barked outside, announcing the arrival of Tom Thurston. Skipjack thought it a little odd that the boy's face did not change a jot.

"Your buddy's here," Skipjack said.

The boy stared down at the table and didn't respond. Marcie turned from the stove and then walked over, wiping her hands on her apron before placing her palm on the boy's forehead. Billy shook like the touch annoyed him. Skipjack and Marcie looked at one another with puzzled expressions.

"What?" Billy drawled sleepily.

"Cat got your tongue?" Marcie asked as Skipjack winked approvingly.

"I had a bad dream is all. Can people row boats up roads without water on 'em?"

"Not hardly." Skipjack laughed.

"Whose roads, honey?" Marcie asked gently.

"This road, our road. I seen 'em row straight into this room howling like wind."

"There's no way, son," Skipjack said.

"What were they like, Billy?" Marcie asked.

"It was Uncle Tim with long fingernails screeching and they wouldn't stop rowing. They were bleeding and blood dripping down on everything. Uncle Tim was just himself, holding cards, saying everyone should sit down and catch fish. There were fishhooks hanging all around. Hands yanked and tried to make me open my mouth. A big boot pushed me down and I couldn't open my mouth for anything, not even to yell. I woke up right when they were all bloody teeth laughing."

"It was a nightmare, son," Skipjack said. "We all have 'em sometimes."

"Why? Who needs to be scared to death when they're sleeping?"

Both Marcie and Skipjack laughed gently, but Billy didn't think it was funny.

"We're not laughing at you, Billy."

Billy looked at his mother for a few seconds before he spoke.

"Does Uncle Timothy scare you to death, Momma?"

Marcie drew in her breath and glanced at Skipjack before she spoke.

"Not as long as two strong men are mindful, I'm not."

"He's a bad man, isn't he? He tried to hurt you, too."

"You know what he did," Marcie said as she turned to the stove.

"Besides making your mother cry, has he hurt you in any way, Billy?"

"Not really. He squeezed me hard when he kissed me goodnight and that hurt."

"When was that?" Skipjack asked, trying to sound calm.

"When he was staying in my room. He whispered me stories about talking trees that walked around the forest at night with lots of branches waving around everywhere who talked softly so that no one could hear. Then I got scared and asked him to light the candle. He told me to hush and said he would protect me, then he hugged me so hard his scratchy face scared me."

"Anything else?"

"After I told him he hurt, he kissed me on my cheek and then my belly. Seemed like he was crying. He told me not to be scared 'cause he'd be here."

"You know what to do if you see him again, don't you?" Skipjack said gravely.

"Run and come get you, right?"

"Right. You do that, unless your mother's in danger, then get your gun and shoot him. Shoot the son of a bitch. Aim for his chest and blast him. You hear me?"

Billy nodded slowly, face revealing shock from these words so harsh as if he expected his mother to admonish Skipjack, but she said nothing, and Skipjack asked him once more if he had clearly heard.

"Billy hears you, Jack. Your father's right. We don't want Tim around here ever, no matter what."

"He always seemed nice. Did something happen?"

"God knows," Skipjack said. "We can't, but Uncle Tim ain't welcome. No point wasting time figuring. He's worse than I could tell."

After breakfast, Billy loaded his shotgun and slid it under his bed. Skipjack didn't see him do it but would have approved. Marcie wouldn't have, but she was discussing the front walk with Tom. She wanted a little more curve. Skipjack agreed that would be nice, but actually was thinking he wanted a thirty-foot wall around the entire property. He had half a mind to call on the sheriff. He decided to put that off until he had something new to tell and that thought sent his mind restlessly glancing through growth at the edges of the clearing. Marcie and Billy would be safe with Tom there, so he decided to take Jessie down to the tavern.

Has to be some way out of this. He said it aloud a split second after he mounted, but solutions were no more forthcoming than Jessie was as they slowly plodded the familiar path. Skipjack was armed, and if he had seen anything in the woods, he might well have disregarded his advice to Billy about identifying the target before he fired. If he hadn't been agitated, the ride would have been peaceful. Can't deny what I saw. What am I gonna tell the sheriff? I had a vision?

It was near time to harvest corn. He tried to allow that slight comfort to lead him into other seasonal everyday pursuits, but it didn't work. At the tavern, Andy grabbed Jessie's halter and told Skipjack that Mary Frances was about ready to send for him.

"You been thinking, Andy?"

"Yes, sir, thinking closer most every day," he replied with a smile that seemed to have a life bigger than its owner.

"Now, Andy, who is she? That ain't your everyday smile."

"Oh, Mr. Maddox, you know this is my smile, sure thing."

"Well, it looks good on you. Whatever you're thinking, keep thinking."

Mary Frances handed Skipjack the envelope before their eyes had even met. "Found it in the crack of the door when I come. You can guess who from," she said as she turned back to her stove. He couldn't. His name, scrawled on the front in brown ink, was in an unfamiliar hand. He stuffed it in his pocket and looked out the window. A distinguished-looking gentleman reading a newspaper caught his eye.

"Who's that man out there? Do you know, Mary Frances?"

"All I know is the gentleman is hungry enough for two. He's already had one meal."

"Seems like I've seen him before, but I can't place him."

"When he sat down, a couple of men seemed to change their minds about ordering and when I came back out, they'd left without paying for the coffee they drunk. I saw the funny looks they give him, but I don't know why. He just sat down and opened his paper. He never said anything that I heard."

Perhaps because the office was closed up so much of the time, there was a stale mustiness still lurking. Mid-morning in this season, the sunlight darted through leafy tree branches and glanced through the narrow window onto his desktop. Skipjack was only vaguely aware of the musk, but to mute it, he unconsciously opened the drawer of his desk, lifted out a flask of whiskey, uncorked it, and swallowed a shot, then fumbled the letter and tore it open. As he unfolded coarse paper, his eyes perused the same unfamiliar penmanship that had adorned the envelope. He placed the missive in sunlight, squinted, and read.

We must talk, Brother.

I have a buyer a legitimate buyer who can make our dreams come true you can make out and so can I. This is not to be disregarded. Times have changed & the old way is gone. A new wind is blowing. There really is no choice. Live or die. Fold or call.

I urge you to meet me in the back bar of Langly's tavern down on the wharf tonight at thirty minutes past ten. This man is not slow old money & he is eager. I fear that this is the only chance you have to meet him. He is very powerful & private. This is your chance. Understand no foolishness. I am powerful too.

We are watching. Believe your brother, this is your best chance. You will not be disappointed.

T. Maddox

CASSIUS CLAY

Skipjack puzzled through the thing twice before the crudely lettered message sank in, twisted his innards, and brought something vile to his throat. His first reaction was to crumple or shred the paper, but he fought this, and involuntarily, his chin sank. For a brief moment, he saw Timothy as a child swinging on a rope before flinging through air, waving arms and legs, reveling in propulsion.

He refolded the letter and this time, slipped it inside his shirt. He was about to take another slug of whiskey, but then corked the bottle. Louis must have felt him coming because there was a drink at his place when he got there. Louis simply nodded and perused the tables.

"Everything all right?"

"So far, so good," Louis said quietly as he polished the bar top with a rag.

"You heard some grumbling?" Skipjack asked.

Leaning forward and talking behind a cupped hand, Louis replied that he had heard a little worse than that. Four men had walked through the bar; two had been through earlier, but Louis had never seen the others before. They walked over to the back door and one of the men had said, "That's the son of a bitch, sure as God's holy fire."

Skipjack looked out and saw a clump of suits caging a man with his back to the burly trunk of a cottonwood down near the water.

"Go see if you can find Andy. Something about this don't look right."

Skipjack tucked his pistol under his left arm to keep it temporarily out of sight. He cocked it as he strolled toward the group. He stopped about ten feet away. The only one who had noticed him come up was the man with his back to the tree. Their eyes met briefly. The man was steadily looking from side to side. Skipjack wasn't sure what he saw in those eyes but didn't see fear.

"Gentlemen," Skipjack said deliberately. "Gentlemen, you will back away from the man slowly and turn so I can see you."

The man on the left jumped back and Skipjack saw the man stuff a pistol into his belt. The other three turned slowly.

"Put the weapons away, gentlemen, and there will be no trouble."

"Who in hell are you?" asked the tallest of the four.

Skipjack, with his pistol flat across his chest, stepped forward and stared into uncertain expressions. He told the one against the tree to put up his blade.

"I sure as hell mean it. Everybody put 'em up now."

Although they were all well dressed, at least as old as he was, Skipjack was reminded of awkward boys as they grumbled, shuffled, and tucked.

"I run this establishment and I got to tell you there is at least one rifle backing me up. You see, I don't shine to those who harass paying guests and, by the way, two of you scoundrels owe me for coffee. Don't much like folks that don't pay, but I don't want money; I want you gone. Go back to your boats or if you come by land, give a wide berth to the building as you head to the stable. Now get moving before I change my mind."

"What about him?" the big man asked.

"Not your problem. As long as he's here, he's mine. I warn you, my patience is stretched."

The men started slowly walking down the riverbank. The farther they walked, the bolder they became, until finally, when they turned, all Skipjack could do was laugh. He winked at the gentleman who had brandished the long knife. The man peeled himself off the tree and seemed to settle about two inches lower.

"Thanks for your help, Mr. Maddox. Could have been a mess. Thank you and I mean that." The man stepped forward, hand extended.

"Don't believe we've met. How do you know me?" Skipjack asked as he shook the man's hand.

"I'm Cassius Clay, sir, and I've known of your operation for years. I've been here several times, but never, praise God, in such need."

"Fine knife you got. Still against four armed men . . ."

"They caught me daydreaming. They're cowards. You backed them down and I thank you. But I must admit, you had me worried."

"Afraid I'd miss?"

"No sir, afraid you might not discriminate."

"Mr. Clay, I believe I left one on the bar, and if you'll join me, there is one for you."

They had a drink at the bar and then another while smoking cigars in the office where they could talk freely. Neither man was overly effusive, but it would have been obvious to anyone that these two men had something to share.

"So, you hold that this Lincoln might win the presidency? That's hard to believe."

"What other hope is there?"

"Hope, Mr. Clay, is a fine thing and, confidentially, I pray he does, but people are stubborn when it comes to change, even changing bad things that work against them. But you're right, this slavery business is tearing our world apart. There is nothing but pestilence in it."

Clay drew on his cigar, then raised his hand.

"My hope is in men like you who think and ask questions. Mr. Maddox, I see fire—a reasoning fire—behind your eyes. You have saved my life, most likely, but you acted without having to think."

"I saw cowardly trash, Mr. Clay. I didn't hear anyone cry thief. There was no excuse for what I saw. Why were they so determined to drag you off?"

"The paper I published, the *True American*. A lot of the old guard want my hide stretched and nailed to a barn. Their day is past. Slavery is dead. It's a matter of exactly when and precisely how that is accomplished. Do you own slaves, sir?"

"I ain't big on slavery, Mr. Clay. I got one, who about runs the place blindfolded and he's due to be free in a few weeks. It's a long story. I bought him from a freedman under the condition that I would let him go at a certain time, and I want the man to stay on for wages. But what's your point?"

"Your man's got a job, right? If all slaves were freed at once, do you realize what that would do? Starvation is one thing near certain. No place to live. I could go on and on. The curse of this abomination will tear this nation into shreds barring divine intervention. It is my opinion that Lincoln is the one with vision that can perhaps forestall and maybe even prevent tragedy."

"What are his chances?"

"Not good, but he's the best we've got."

"It'll take more than one man to stop what we're facing, I fear," Skipjack said.

"What choice do we have though? Any course will breed conflict. A man can't defy natural law without consequence. Allow slavery to continue and it will rend the fabric of society. Abolish it in one stroke, and that will do the same. Strikes at the very heart, as corrupt as that argument has become, of the property rights issue. You can't have democracy without property rights. You can't have democracy with slavery. Forget the wretched slaves for a moment and think of the whites who have to compete with them; and don't forget those who one day will have to make do without."

Mary Frances banged on the door. Skipjack knew it was her with the first thump. She announced that the sheriff was at the bar and wanted to have a word with him.

"I got to talk to the sheriff about some lawless ones, Mr. Clay," Skipjack said with a smile. Clay drained his glass and stood to leave.

"Not the ones after me?" he asked.

"No, sir, others, as bad or maybe worse. Just plain evil for no damn reason I know of. Wish I had a bead on 'em and a cannon big as the world."

"I've got a cannon," Cassius Clay said.

"I'll bear that in mind," Skipjack said as he put his hand into the small of Clay's back and steered him to the door.

"I appreciate your hospitality, Mr. Maddox. I'll stay out of your way while you speak with your sheriff, but I wonder, sir, if you might have someone you could send for my luggage off the *Nancy Jane*. I don't fancy traveling another bend with those scoundrels. Can you help me?"

"Will you pay the man good money?"

"Yes, sir," Clay replied.

"My man Andy will help you, but you got to do the talking; they won't give him your belongings unless you're with him. When is your packet scheduled to leave?"

"In the morning."

"He'll take care of you. Have a drink and I'll put you with him."

———

Skipjack could feel in his bones that something was happening to make things look different and it wasn't booze. This Cassius Clay fellow who swaggered in front of him troubled his gaze with too many details: the slick shine of dark hair, the broadness of his shoulders, his thrust of jaw when he surveyed the room as he entered the bar. The sheriff inhaled and smiled, his usual gesture, but Skipjack saw soft, fawning weakness. He knew he didn't want to hear what the man had to say before the sheriff flapped his lips. Skipjack noticed deep creases that defined hanging jowls and the glittering eyes above. As the sheriff walked to the bar, Skipjack became aware of the paunch that strained olive green suspenders. He motioned to Louis and sent for Andy before he returned his eyes to the sheriff's glass, which was empty.

"Are you having another, sheriff?"

"Thanks for offering, Louis," the sheriff drawled, grinning at the bartender before he hiked up his britches. He turned to Skipjack. "You know, I always enjoy dropping in. You got a gold mine, you hear me? Those poor souls scheming out to the Comstock Lode and what have you, if they only knew what you sit on, they might try to set down some roots, hear me?"

Skipjack decided to keep his cards close. He had planned to tell the sheriff everything: about the letter, the man in the woods, the blood or whatever it was in his whiskey bottle but decided to let the sheriff do the talking. He noted that the man smelled sour and that he had a lot of hair trying to grow out of his ears. Down the bar he saw Andy and Mr. Clay nodding.

"So, what've you found out?" he asked.

"More than I am at liberty to discuss. Except for this; there has been another murder down on the wharf and we been watching your brother and we're sure he ain't done it. My sources tell me your brother and company might be moving back this way soon, but they been quiet of late. I ain't sure yet that he's our man. In my opinion, Bancroft and the other one might have been killed by someone else. I know you don't like to hear it, but we can't bring in Timothy unless we got something more than we got. All we got now is suspicion."

"So why are you here, except the price of whiskey?"

"Now look here. We go back a long ways. I was checking on you to see if you have anything. I'm overtaxed as it is, can't do this without help."

Skipjack nodded enough for Andy to notice, and he saw Clay and Andy move toward the door a few seconds later.

"No, can't say I've heard much of anything, sheriff."

The sheriff's brow knitted ever so slightly before he closed his eyes for a moment.

"Unusual," the sheriff muttered. "Don't you think you would be the natural one to turn to?"

"Timothy and I have never been close."

"Yeah, maybe so, maybe not," the sheriff said. "Let me ask you something straight out. Fruit don't fall too far from the tree, right? If your brother is a thief like you say, how do I know you're what you say?"

"What are you driving at?"

"There's no reason you would be fixing to sell, is there?"

"What the hell you talking about?"

"Let's say I hear things. All kinds of things."

"Keep hard looks to yourself, sheriff. What are you talking about?"

"I've heard two things and maybe we should go to your office before I tell you what they are."

"Not necessary. Speak your mind." Skipjack surveyed the nearly empty room.

"All right," the sheriff said. "I hear there's an offer on this place that you're likely to take, because of the second thing I heard." He opened his eyes wide.

"What?"

"That you been running niggers," he whispered, then pulled back a bit and waited for a reaction.

Skipjack smiled and said, "Yeah, I run 'em all over the place. I bet one tied up your horse before you made it to the bar. I ain't selling, sheriff. Who told you that?"

"I got sources," the sheriff said as he polished off his drink.

"So, you ain't telling?"

"Nothing to tell, same as you."

The man dug around in the deep pockets of his trousers with eyes full of concentration as if searching for the proper combination of coins to pay his bill. Skipjack fought the urge to laugh but said nothing until it was obvious the pocket was empty and then told the sheriff that drinks were on the house. The sheriff blubbered something about how he was eager to get a move on as soon as he could figure out how. As they walked out of the bar, Skipjack noticed the sheriff's waddle for the very first time. Skipjack walked with him to the stable's side door and pitied the poor horse whose job was to carry the man.

Skipjack went back to the bar and slapped it hard. Louis scurried up and seemed to smile a little more than was necessary. Skipjack pointed with his finger and a glass of whiskey was in front of him. He glanced up at Louis's fluttering eyelashes and the entreating pale blue eyes they were designed to shutter before he returned his gaze to the bar top—oiled and slick over burns, drink rings, and carved initials.

"Are you all right, sir?"

"Who's asking, Louis? You or them?"

"Sir, I have no earthly idea what you're talking about."

"Quite all right, Louis; carry on. Tell me though, who else drinks for free?"

"Sir?"

Skipjack scowled and meant it. He instructed Louis to have Mary Frances bring him a plate of food. Louis skipped off like it was the last day of school, and Skipjack took the deepest breath he had taken in weeks. Langly's. Got to get to the bottom of this.

He wasn't a gambling man like his brother, but he felt like the dice had already left the cup. He could feel chance bouncing across worn green felt. As he slumped into his brand-new office chair, he realized there wasn't much he could do. He had to be alert, that's all. He decided to ask Andy to guard the house while he was off to Langly's. Then after picking at his lunch, he leaned back in his chair and closed his eyes.

When he awakened a couple of hours later, he stretched and studied the iridescent wings of a fly that appeared to be wading in gravy on his plate. Skipjack lit a cigar and blew smoke over the fly, but the fly was unperturbed. Thoughts of Timothy occupied his mind. He was trying to fathom some good reason to meet with him other than shooting him. Try as he might, he could not, but had no real desire to kill him either; simply wanted him gone. The gravy fly was joined by another and then both decided to sample some applesauce. Skipjack did not interrupt their feast. He realized that he felt more respect for the flies than his own brother. That insight did not bother him. He hated messes and to kill the man would be messy. The reality of sitting across the table from the maggot disgusted him, but something told him he had to. He felt in his gut that somebody was protecting Timothy from the law. Brother had always been a braggart; maybe he could goad him into showing his hand. He was damn sure the sheriff knew more than he revealed.

Skipjack wanted to keep the meeting a secret, but knew he had to tell Marcie. Andy would stand guard and maybe Brawl. He was about to go looking for Andy when he recognized his knock at the door. As Andy entered, Skipjack became aware of the graceful strength in his bearing. He was almost ashamed to admit to himself that the first impression he had formed of the man had tainted his perception for as long as he had known him. Even now, after he knew he wanted Andy to stay and knew how much he depended on him, Skipjack was surprised by the calm clarity of Andy's expression and the power projected. Andy was definitely coming into his own. Skipjack found himself praying that Andy was figuring that out himself or better yet, already knew.

"Mr. Clay wants me to run him into town. We already got his stuff off the *Nancy Jane*. I told him I had to check with you. He said he'd pay."

"Thanks for checking. Turns out I need you up at the house tonight. Guard duty and I want you to send for Brawl. I want him up there if he'll do it. I'll pay Brawl his going rate and I'll pay you the same, but don't tell Brawl that. Where's Clay?"

"Mr. Clay's at the bar, sir."

"Tell Mr. Clay I want to talk to him. Send him back here and then track down Brawl. Find out if he can be at the house at eight o'clock sharp. Tell him I think it's important."

When they were alone, Skipjack asked Clay, "Can you wait until evening about eight? Or let me put it another way; I want to ask you as a favor to ride in with me to a place called Langly's where I am to meet an unsavory character who happens to be my brother, Timothy. I want you to be my witness and to cover my back if I need it. I hate to ask, but I can't spare Andy."

"I'll be pleased to help if I can. What're we facing, if you don't mind?"

"Damned if I know. Some say it's the devil himself. I think my brother's lost his mind. He's bad to the bone and in with a rotten bunch of thieves. But he says he wants to buy this joint and claims to have big money behind him. Tell the truth, I have no idea if he does or doesn't or what he wants from this meeting. He might want to put a knife in my ribs or a bullet in my head, so I won't blame you if you make other arrangements to get to town."

"Is this place for sale?"

"Hell no, but somebody's trying to run me off. I'm damn sure it's him, but like the way he plays cards, you never can catch him. There's a couple murders I think he's done, but no proof. Here, let me show you his note that was stuck in the door this morning."

Clay's eyes narrowed as he read the thing, then tilted his head as he passed the note back.

"Don't sound right, does it?" Skipjack said.

"Hell no, that's a flat-out threat. You got your family covered? I sure don't like that 'we are watching' bit."

"The house will be guarded front and rear, I assure you."

"We head out at eight?"

"First, to the house as soon as I hear back from Andy. We'll leave from there right after supper. You got any weapons beside your knife?"

Clay nodded.

"Appreciate your help, Mr. Clay."

"Don't mention it, sir. Seems like you might be in a tight spot."

"Might be," Skipjack said.

RENDEZVOUS

There was no point in trying to calm Marcie. She wouldn't have it. She did her best to be civil to Mr. Clay. Skipjack felt like a damned fool. Billy kept glancing like he was supposed to do something, and Marcie kept asking why. Why? And if she said it once, she said it fifty times.

"Why the devil do you have to go there? What for anyway?"

"Now, honey, please don't carry on."

"Carry on, my behind! You stupid excuse for a husband; no excuse missing what's basic."

"Excuse me, Mr. Clay," Skipjack said.

"What the hell you think you're going to do?"

"Honey, Clay is as good a back-up as was ever born."

"Jack, you know Timothy's not right."

Skipjack swallowed before he replied. Clay nodded, and Billy coughed like something was troubling his throat. Marcie's eyes burned into Skipjack's and did not waver.

"I know that almost as well as you do," he said quietly. "That's exactly why I have to go. There is no backing away from this sort of thing; if I could, I would."

"You can't run off the devil, God help me for saying so, but you can't, Jack."

"Momma, Daddy's trying to help," Billy said before Marcie's eyes returned his to his plate.

"Marcie, please hear me. Andy, Brawl and Tom are going to be watching the place. Mr. Clay and I will be all right."

"You and me will be watching, too, Momma," Billy exclaimed.

"That's right," Skipjack said. "Everybody's going to be looked after."

Marcie clenched her jaw and shook her head.

"Jack, the man's like smoke, don't you know? You can't keep him in; you can't keep him out."

"Might be able to douse his fire though."

"You're going to kill him?"

"I ain't there yet, honey, so I don't know."

———————

On the way to town, the mare felt frisky. The road was hardpan and horrible, but the mare attacked potholes and ruts like she was concerned with comfort as well as speed. The two men leaned back into cushioning and shared points of view. They were armed and well provisioned.

Skipjack passed the bottle to Clay and asked him if he believed 'this Lincoln fellow,' as he called him, had a real chance. Clay said he was one of the shrewdest politicians he had ever met.

"So, you know him?"

"Well enough to think that if anyone can solve the problem, he would be the one."

"Maybe so," Skipjack replied.

"Earlier you implied it should end," Clay said as he passed the bottle back.

"Pardon me, Mr. Clay, if I seem guarded. It's from years of habit. I run a public house. I'm not accustomed to speaking out, but the main question that defies me at every turn is how. Can you tell me how to solve the riddle?"

"I used to think so."

Clay shook his head. They rode in silence past a cornfield. Several minutes passed before a monotony of corn stalks ended in a stand of trees. They pulled onto a short bridge that crossed over Goose Creek about a hundred yards before it fed into the river.

"I love sycamore trees," Clay said. "I never tire of the mix of tan and white bark."

Skipjack didn't answer, but then he said, "The next creek is where the first murder my brother did took place—banker fellow by the name of Bancroft. Cold-blooded murder."

"How do you know it was him? Was there a witness?"

"Was a witness. He was murdered in the jail."

"Your brother?"

"Not likely, but see, my brother's fallen in with this bunch that until recently were shacked up on my creek about a mile from the house. I can't believe I didn't know they were there: a gang of cutthroats run by some fallen woman. They steal everything they can lay ahold of on water or land. Folks used to call 'em pirates, but I call them trash. Anyway, I saw their camp and there was a mess of 'em. The sheriff's afraid of 'em, or worse."

"What do you mean, 'or worse'?"

"I don't know, maybe I'm impatient, but I don't trust the man. You know how hard it is for some sons of bitches to turn down look-the-other-way money? God knows what they haul in off the river, but you know some of it's worth plenty. They got to be selling somewhere. No doubt, they leave a trail of stolen stuff and bloody bodies. They steal and hunt down slaves, too. The only son of a gun the bastards won't kill is a running slave. Sheriff claims he's working on a plan to bring in my brother and the lot, then he says he don't have the manpower, then he says he lacks proof, especially now his witness is dead and both of the witness's cellmates have been released by a judge. But the deal's bigger than just a killing and the sheriff's bound to know. Hell, I've been broken into twice myself. The sheriff smiles and urges patience. The whole thing stinks to high heaven."

"Why're we meeting with your brother? All you can do is run them off or kill them."

"Don't know, to tell the truth. I appreciate you coming."

"Sure they aren't planning to bushwhack us?"

ED MIDDLETON

"Not at all. That's why I asked you to join me." Skipjack passed the whiskey and winked.

Clay accepted and nodded.

"So, if we happen to make Langly's, where we going to keep the buggy safe and what role do I play? Give me a clue."

"What kind of clue did your friends hand me this afternoon? What part did you ask me to play? You'll know what to do."

Both men stared straight ahead over the mare's withers and at the sun going down between her ears.

"Don't misunderstand. I'm with you," Clay said. "I just need to know, am I in the foreground or background and what are our signals and what is our story?"

"You be my lawyer. But all you do is listen."

"What's to discuss?"

"Nothing. Keep a sharp eye. They're up to something. Tell you straight: neither Marcie nor I can take much more, and if I have to, I will kill the son of a bitch."

"So, what you want?"

"Keep your wits and hand near your knife. Let me do talk. Tell him you're my lawyer. Won't know. He ain't been around for years."

"What am I called, assuming no one recognizes me?"

"How does Clay Mason suit?"

"Guess that'll work, but you think he's at Langly's?"

"Don't you? You saw the letter."

"You say he's crazy and fallen with a band of thugs. He would fit, since the whole wharf teems with lowlife. A good man could easily bleed out the last minutes of his life before he sees law worthy of the name. Still, it doesn't seem like a good idea for your brother to show his face there or anywhere right now, you think?"

"Honestly, Clay, don't know. I can't tell you half. Slick. That's about all I can say. If anybody can slip in and out undetected, it would be him. He can pull the wool over anybody's eyes and make them believe black is white. I've seen men beg him to play another hand and then another after swearing he was a cheat. There's something

I can't explain. I'm hoping to smoke out intentions and, like you say, drive him off. I'm tired of locking up and looking every step. Don't know how to put it better: something I got to do."

"You got to go with that."

They were heading west, and it was a relief when the sun's setting made squinting unnecessary, but now as crimson-bellied clouds smeared the horizon, both men became aware of deepening shadow. They weren't alone on the road, but there were stretches where undergrowth would provide good cover. A haze of wood smoke from cook fires and stench from smoldering garbage pits stung their eyes.

"Bet you don't come often."

"There was a time. Air is foul in summer, chock full of fevers, and winter, smoke's thick as fog. Makes you think evening at mid-morning. Rain makes you dirty and snow turns black. I wouldn't live here no matter what money."

"This is the murder creek? What's this creek called?" Clay asked as they rattled across the wooden bridge, gingerly weaving a path to avoid busted planks.

"Beargrass, and I hear that Brother and company have made their camp somewhere up there. That's what I'm told. Don't know firsthand." Skipjack swatted a mosquito. "Damn, the son of a bitch got me," he said as he saw blood on the palm of his hand.

"They thick, aren't they?"

"Wouldn't live down here for anything."

"What's that?"

"What's what?"

"Slow down," Clay whispered. "Something just ducked behind the piling of the bridge." He cocked his pistol. Skipjack pulled his out as well. They approached the end of the bridge, both warily aiming in the direction that Clay indicated, but when they rolled past the piling, they looked over their shoulders and there was nothing but dusty poke greens with dark green leaves and clusters of purple berries.

"I swear I saw a man's head."

"I bet you did. Keep an eye out behind; I'll try to do better up ahead."

Skipjack gently prodded the mare and she snorted as she picked up her pace. They began to pass tumbledown shacks. Many looked like they had washed up in high water and settled. Urchins clothed in dust chased around and if they were a bit older, raggedy tatters. From a stoop below a dark doorway, a pale teenage girl—skeletal and furtive—scolded, fierce blue eyes retreating to glare. Both men were surprised when the bony fist covering her lips opened and appeared to wave. Skipjack pulled back on the reins and halted the mare.

"I got to give that child something; looks like she's starving."

But the young girl spoke harshly to her charges, and within seconds, the door was shut behind them. Skipjack and Clay were left looking at a patch of dirt and an empty stoop.

"Best move on," Skipjack said and clucked to the mare.

"The best place to ambush somebody would be between those two creeks. There's a lot of dead space there and the best time to do it would be between now and daylight. What're you going to do if he doesn't show?"

"Cuss the bastard and head home."

"By yourself?"

"Hadn't thought. Figure he'll show, don't you?"

"No, something tells me he won't. Seems like he would prefer to negotiate in dark with odds stacked."

"I can't leave Marcie and Billy alone."

"I'll ride out, if you'll put me up. Had a belly full of public."

"We'll cross that bridge when we get there. Appreciate your offer, but I believe he'll show."

"Up to you."

SEMAPHORES

They sat in the corner at the back barroom at Langly's. As Skipjack was checking his pocket, a woman in a greasy apron tried to give them menus. Her heft blocked their view. Skipjack snapped his watch shut and ordered whiskey. Clay ordered the same. Both men peered past and around her as she made her way through the crowd toward the bar. The room was so smoky that the entrance was a blur and so noisy a pistol shot might have been mistaken for a slamming door. Langly's was three operations in one. The ground floor, where they were seated, had two bars. The second floor was for dining and even featured white tablecloths. The third floor was a brothel with at least a dozen small rooms and a parlor for introductions.

"See anybody you recognize?"

"Not by name," Skipjack replied. "Don't worry about your stuff. I've known Abe Flexner for years. He's reliable. He liveries for the good hotels."

"I'm not worried about him," Clay replied, "but don't you think that the deputy out in front of the livery was a bit odd? What did he say? Something about how the sheriff told him to tell you that he was looking for your brother, that they were making inquiries. Doesn't that strike you as peculiar?"

"I was thinking about being on time, so I paid no mind."

"Why would he say that unless the sheriff knew you were coming?"

"That is peculiar, I suppose," Skipjack said.

"Unless you insist I don't, I'm riding back. What time is it now?"

"He's only ten minutes late. That's not unusual."

Skipjack sipped whiskey and lit a cigar. Each time someone passed through the entrance, he scanned the smoke-shrouded room. After a few minutes, he stood and looked around. He leaned down, cupped his hand near Clay's ear, and then the two of them approached the bar. The bartender was as burly as a stevedore, head bald and shiny. His eyes, when he finally focused on Skipjack, were limpid and clear. He didn't know anything. No message, no nothing. They went out to the reservation stand, where the lady ran her finger down a column in her book and shrugged. The two men looked at each other. Skipjack looked alarmed and Clay squeezed his elbow.

They did not run but walked swiftly to Flexner's. The two blocks on Main Street were a crisscross tangle of all kinds of folk, most off riverboats. The fancy ones appeared disinterested and self-absorbed, then there were others with darting eyes, who seemed very interested indeed. The street also had a share of stumbling drunks, solitary and in unyielding groups, apparently oblivious to everything. Clay and Skipjack cut through all that without incident. They turned the corner at Seventh and Main. Clay caught up to Skipjack and put his hand on his shoulder.

"Dark here. Walk in the middle of the street."

They turned left on Market and as they approached the livery, the glow from two lanterns eased Clay's concerns. The deputy was still slouched against the building and nodded as they entered. Flexner was gone for the night and his man had not yet unhitched the mare, so they were back out on Market in moments. As they passed the entrance, Clay noticed the deputy was gone. Skipjack saw nothing but road ahead. He tilted the bottle and stung his mare with taut reins.

"Sure you want this?"

"Fair is fair," Clay replied.

"Damn it all then. Hang on!"

Skipjack aimed down the middle of the street, and as if his determination were infectious, the mare needed no urging. In fact, drag of the brake probably kept them from tipping as they turned onto Fifth Street down to Main.

"Better surface and more direct," Skipjack shouted above rattles and creaks. Clay held on.

Out on River Road, Skipjack slowed.

"Guess we better pace ourselves. Think he planned this?"

Clay leaned over and said, "Looking that way."

"Like you said, the best spots are between Beargrass and Goose Creeks, but then the cornfield beyond wouldn't be bad either, would it?"

"Friend, dark as it is, none of it's good."

"Hell, the road up to the house ain't a picnic," Skipjack stated wryly.

Clay slid two shells into a shotgun, snapped it shut, and passed it to Skipjack. The half-moon cast smoky light on the ramshackle hovels on the edge of town.

"Hard to believe people live like that."

"Most don't long," Skipjack said.

"This bridge is where I saw the man," Clay said as he loaded the other shotgun and held it pointed at the sky.

"You know poor light works both ways?"

"But they can hear, and I can't see twenty feet, can you?"

"I see a cloud that's about ready to cover the moon," Skipjack said as he reined in a tad.

Clay lowered his shotgun and nodded.

"Don't shoot the mare and I think we'll be fine."

Right before they hit the bridge, Skipjack slapped the reins and the buggy lurched as the mare burst into a bright trot. Both men leveled their shotguns as they clattered across. The moon broke free and dappled the gentle slope of the road. Clay turned back and kept the shotgun pointed low. He saw no one. The bridge was empty and just as he was about to face forward again, a light flickered in the treetops. It flashed so briefly he almost doubted he'd seen it. But it wasn't reflection and wasn't a star. He touched Skipjack's elbow.

He whispered, "I saw a light blink up in a tree."

"Not fishermen?"

"No, that high." Clay gestured with his hand up forty degrees.

"Damn. I believe I'll walk the mare a minute. Pass me that whiskey, if you please," Skipjack said as he relit his cigar.

"Where you think they're going to hit us?"

"No idea. But I need to rest the mare a bit. We might need her soon, don't you know?" Skipjack took a deep slug of whiskey, then turned and looked at Clay before he added, "Marcie and Billy are guarded. My brother wants me dead; dead or bought out. I can't figure how killing them would solve what he's after."

"You said he was crazy."

"So what's there to do? I've got to play close to the rulebook. Believe me, I got a reason to shoot, but nothing I could prove in a court of law."

"Well, I'll be your witness, if he tries something tonight."

"God knows I appreciate it," Skipjack said as he clucked to the mare.

They saw no more signals. When they crossed over the bridge, Goose Creek was silver moonlight. Clay studied treetops but saw nothing. They clattered past a thick stand of saplings and entered a section of road bordered by corn. To Skipjack, this last stretch was the most likely spot for attack, and he sped up and gripped his pistol.

He figured they would jump out, wrestle the mare into the ditch, go about their murder, and hide their bloody business as best they could. This monotonous stretch had never seemed so vibrant to him. Like everything else this long day, he saw the side of the road in detail: moonlight shimmered leaves quite distinctly from yellow to dark blue-green. Skipjack found himself attempting to decipher faint shadows of stones and ruts as if they were calligraphy. He glanced at Clay, who nodded, and Skipjack wondered if Clay understood what was being revealed as corn stalks danced.

"Do you hear something, Skipjack?"

"Keep a sharp eye. This might be a good spot."

Something crawled up his spine. Skipjack suffered tiny talons and heard a sibilant voice: *You are mine.* Skipjack swallowed or tried to swallow the metallic taste in his mouth, but it would not go down. *You are mine.*

Skipjack shuddered.

"You all right?"

"If you say so. Do I look like I have cooties?" he asked grimly.

"Not cooties. How about heebie-jeebies?"

"From head to toe and no lie there. Listen here, if something happens, will you check after—"

"I saw another flash! Back there. No doubt at all. They're signaling for certain."

"Seem to be awful careless."

"Maybe they don't figure you have eyes in the back of your head."

Skipjack pulled up the mare and came to a complete stop. A wagon of some kind was coming their way. Clay turned, looked back, and listened intently.

"Don't think anything's coming behind."

"Believe I know who this is," Skipjack said softly. "Think we're all right here."

Skipjack could make out the profile of Thornton Green and his huge white horse and squeaky old wagon. He hailed him and to his relief, the rig slowed. Green's deep voice answered, and Skipjack urged the mare forward. Both halted.

"I see you're armed," Green said, half raising a rifle and a sidearm. "Heard a couple of gunshots, sounded like a rifle, when I was leaving the tavern. Couldn't be sure, but it sounded like it was coming from your place. Went to your road. Didn't hear anything, but tell the truth, I didn't much relish riding up through the woods by myself. Is that where you're heading?"

"Sure is."

"Want me to come?"

"Suit yourself. I got to get up there," Skipjack said, slapping the reins.

"Let me turn this rig around and I'll be right . . ."

Skipjack knew he would come but didn't wait. The mare stretched out in a go-for-broke run.

Clay felt and heard fury building in the man and feared they might be headed for a trap but kept his mouth shut and his shotgun ready. No more looking for signals. He did glance back once to see if he could spot Green. He couldn't. Darkness swallowed everything.

"He's right behind," Skipjack said.

The road descended on a long gentle curve and the mare was stretched out. Clay just held on.

"Damn him to hell! How could I be so blind? You said all along. God help us."

Clay turned away from Skipjack's earnest face, busied himself with inspecting an upcoming dense thicket. He was both surprised and relieved as the buggy slowed, and Skipjack hoarsely confided that he didn't want to announce their arrival. The mare was blowing hard, but between breaths, the men could hear the jangle of Green's harness and the clop-clop of the big gelding's hooves. Clay cleared his throat, took a deep breath, but it would be an untruth to say he relaxed. They waited at the bottom of Skipjack's hill until Green pulled up. As soon as he did, they slowly rolled forward.

Even with the moon now free of clouds, this part of the hill was dark as pitch. Because of the privacy it provided, Skipjack had never cleared this lower stretch. Silently, he cursed himself. The mare needed no guidance, so both his hands were free. As they rounded the slight bend, moonlight began to reveal the wooded area he had thinned. There was less cover, and as they climbed the last stretch curving toward the house, the pasture was suffused with light. Skipjack doubted anyone would attack on this stretch. Right before they crested the hill, he shouted, "Yo! Hey, it's me, Skipjack. Yo, it's me."

"Come on home," Brawl bellowed. "Come on with you."

As they approached the house, a warm glow filled the kitchen and Marcie stood on the porch beside Brawl holding a pulsing lantern. She held a rifle. Billy appeared with his shotgun. A moment later, Andy and Tom walked around the side of the house.

"Praise God," Skipjack whispered as he jumped off the wagon.

Marcie ran to the yard to greet him. After they hugged, she shook her head.

"I thought they'd killed you," she whispered. "Thank God you're safe."

Skipjack laughed and with his free hand automatically reached out for Gracie to hold her down. Gracie always jumped on him whenever he and Marcie hugged, but Skipjack found himself reaching into nothing but air.

"Where's Gracie?"

"Jack, we had some visitors."

"Gracie tore into the woods and was raising hell with somebody right over there," Brawl said, pointing at the edge of the woods. "Gracie yowled and then went quiet. I heard thrashing and running. Fired a couple of shots, but don't believe I hit anything."

"That must've been what I heard," Thornton Green said.

"Can we go look for Gracie now?" Billy asked.

"No," Marcie said. "When it's light. Everybody inside; I got coffee and bacon, and I'm going to scramble eggs."

"I'm going to have a stiff drink of whiskey before I touch a bite. Thank you, Brawl. Thank you, Andy and Tom," Skipjack said. He nodded at Clay and Green.

"What about me?" Billy asked.

"Thank you, son," he said as he watched Brawl put his hand on the boy's shoulder. Skipjack gently squeezed Marcie's hand.

"Was he good help, Brawl?"

"Sure was; all I could do to keep him from hunting them down his self. Don't believe he's scared of anything."

"He better be scared of me," Marcie said. "You will stay out of those woods, do you hear me, young soldier?"

"Yes, ma'am."

"Good. Now, please everybody, come inside before it all gets cold."

———

Skipjack's eyes popped open about four and would not close. No noise had awakened him that he could name. Marcie snuggled back into him as he attempted to swing his legs onto the floor. He was thirsty and had to piss. Scratching his scalp, he made his way down the stairs and remembered that Clay was on the pallet in Billy's room. Brawl and Tom had followed Thornton Green home. Skipjack assumed they had made it. As his foot adjusted to the uneven plank floor, he reached out for the familiar wall and instead touched a man's shoulder.

"Skipjack, there's someone outside. I think in the stable," Clay whispered.

"Get your rifle," Skipjack said.

"Already got it."

"I'll go out the back. Lock the door behind me. I won't light the lantern till I get there. Get out on the porch, back me up."

Naked as the day he was born, Skipjack slipped through wet grass. He carried matches and his pistol. As he approached the stable, he heard nothing but night sounds. He looked back and saw Clay's silhouette, then with his next stride, smashed his big toe into one of Tom Thurston's stones. He moaned as hot pain seared his leg. He limped slowly forward.

The lock on the gate was firmly clasped. He climbed the fence. Inside the stable, Jessie snorted and stomped. The chain was secure, lock fastened. Jessie snorted again and pawed the ground, then Skipjack heard a pitiful sound like a child's moan; it seemed to come from inside. He kept a spare key under the seat of the buggy. He fetched it, then took the lantern down off the hook and lit the wick.

He dragged the chain through the handles on the doors and swung them open. Shadows danced as he crossed the dirt floor. The mare stuck her head out to be stroked and then Skipjack walked over to Jessie's stall. He frowned as Jessie stomped again and snorted as he held the lantern high and looked in. Jessie was standing at the back wall and—at her feet—Gracie lay snuggled in the straw. He opened the stall and walked over to her. Her brown and white coat looked to be smeared with mud. She whimpered and attempted to raise her head. He knelt down and gently stroked behind her ear.

Skipjack got a horse blanket and bundled her. Gracie was too weak to resist, though not too weak to complain. He carried her to the fence, called for Clay, lifted her over, and told Clay to hurry her into the kitchen. After giving Jessie and the mare a handful of oats, he relocked the stable, then hobbled back to the house. The lamp was lit when he reached the kitchen. Marcie was whispering in Gracie's ear and gently removing dried blood with a damp cloth.

"Looks like she was stabbed," Clay said.

"And hit in the head with a hammer," Marcie added and looked up at Skipjack with a pained expression that turned to annoyance. "Better put clothes on, husband, before you catch cold."

Skipjack chuckled as he limped across the floor. "Stove in my toe on flowerbed rock. Better than a hole in the head."

"Man alive! That will be black as coal," Clay said.

"Let me see that," Marcie said. "Damn it, honey, you broke your toe."

"Don't everybody stare at once," Skipjack said with a grin. "Let me get some trousers on."

"Jack, sit down. I'll get your clothes. Mr. Clay, please keep the dog in the center of the table."

As Marcie climbed stairs, Skipjack pointed at the cabinet. Clay opened it and grabbed the whiskey bottle.

"You are a mind reader," Skipjack said.

"Best tonic there is."

"Might slip a little to Gracie."

"Gracie's partial to beer, Jack, and you know it," Marcie said as she handed him his shirt and pants.

While Skipjack and Clay steadied the dog, Marcie cleaned her and then began to stitch the scalp wound. Both men winced as she shoved the needle through the flesh and pulled the thread.

"You big babies amaze me; troubled by a needle and thread. Hold still, Gracie. This won't take long."

"You think she'll make it?" Clay asked.

"Maybe; she was knocked silly more than anything. Don't think the knife wound did too much. Looks like it bounced off her shoulder. Lot of blood, but I don't think mortal."

Gracie whimpered as Billy shuffled into the room. When he spotted the dog up on the kitchen table, his jaw dropped, and his eyes opened wide.

"Momma, what are you doing?"

"Everything's going to be all right, Billy."

"Don't worry, son. She's not making breakfast."

"And won't either, if you don't watch your trouble-making tongue. She's been hurt, Billy, but I believe she'll mend."

"What they do?"

Skipjack clasped the boy's shoulder and held him away from the table.

"They conked her and cut her, but she run 'em off. Just think about that."

"They deserve to die," the boy said between clenched teeth.

"Don't worry, son. They'll get what they deserve," Clay said.

"I'm going to make damn sure," Billy insisted.

"That's no way to talk. You're not to say damn in this house, young man."

"But I mean it, Momma!"

"I mean it, too," Marcie said, drawing the needle one last time and closing the stitch. "Jack, fetch this poor dog some broth and a beer. Make it two beers. I'm discovering a thirst. Billy, spread out the blanket in the corner. Mr. Clay, help me lay this dog down easy."

———

"Beer's gone flat, I believe," Skipjack said as he placed a pitcher full on the table.

"I don't care, and I know Gracie won't," Marcie replied. "Mix some beer and broth into a bowl and pour me out a glass."

"Think she'll drink?"

"I don't know what else to do, Jack."

Skipjack handed Marcie the concoction. She placed it beside Gracie's muzzle and then gently lifted the dog's head, so she could sniff and lap. The dog took a few slurps. Marcie laid Gracie's head back down.

"She's got the idea now. Life is good. Let's let her rest."

Marcie took the glass of cool beer that Skipjack held out to her and slumped into a kitchen chair. She closed her eyes and sighed. Billy sat beside Gracie, gently stroked her, and told her she was going to be all right.

"Jack, we're gonna have to put a stop to this. What do you think they're after?"

"Honey, I can't say."

"They're trying to run you folks off."

"I believe it's more than that, Mr. Clay," Marcie said.

Both Skipjack and Clay waited for her to continue, but she hesitated.

"Just a feeling I'd as soon not talk about," she replied and nodded toward Billy who was still seated on the floor stroking Gracie.

"They're thieves. That's what they are," Skipjack said.

"Skipjack, this bunch can't be all that sharp. There've been no major river pirates on this water for fifty years."

"Brother's not stupid."

"You said yourself he's lost his mind. I'll bet he's in with others worse off than he is. Might be worth a try to peek into their operation. We're in the dark. What we need is information."

Skipjack took a swallow of whiskey and said, "I'll talk to Brawl this morning. I want to talk to Green."

"Maddox, I've a proposal to make. I have several speeches to compose, which I had intended to complete on my river passage, but I could as easily complete them here. If you want my help, you've got it. All I need is table, lamp, and chair. I could stay on a few days."

Skipjack looked at Marcie. He shook Clay's hand. The deal was done.

CHAPTER 8

JUSTICE IS BLIND

As soon as dawn lightened windows, Clay and Skipjack walked to the edge of the thicket where Brawl said intruders had been. They hoped to find something that would clarify things.

"I got to clear this out," Skipjack said as he pushed through undergrowth with his boots. "Damn, this toe hurts."

Once they were through the perimeter weed growth and into the woods, everything opened considerably. Within minutes, they found a place where the forest floor was tussled and a tree trunk raw where bark was blown off. Skipjack stuck part of his forefinger into a splintery bullet hole. He nodded at Clay, who pointed and said, "Look down there."

Skipjack sidestepped toward Clay and followed his finger. What he saw looked like a bundle of clothes in a heap, but then he saw what might be an arm and hair on what might be a head.

"Don't assume anything," he whispered. Clay nodded, and they separated by several paces before closing in. Skipjack could see right off that the man had been shot. There was a knife in the leaves beside an outstretched hand. The shoulder was a bloody mess. The man looked to be asleep. Clay nudged him with his boot. The man didn't move, but when he probed again, the man moaned softly, and his eyelids fluttered. Skipjack knelt beside him in an instant and then grimaced and clenched his teeth as toe pain erupted. Clay picked up the knife.

"Bet he's the one that cut your dog," he said.

"Who the hell are you?" Skipjack demanded as he rolled the man half over. The man guttered in his throat.

"Who the hell are you?"

"He's not talking, Skipjack. Look at the ground. He's about dead."

"He'll be dead for sure if he don't talk."

"Alive he might help."

Skipjack closed his eyes.

"Sure seems like a lot of trouble to carry him up to the house."

"We can bring the wagon down, and then we only have to drag him to the edge."

"Well, this son of a bitch ain't getting past the porch. Damn, he smells worse than a slop bucket."

"He is ripe. Look at those shoes though. Those are a gentleman's shoes."

"Yeah and look at his damn shirt where it ain't bloody. That's fine stuff there. I bet he's proud of his cuff links too. Lion's heads. Wonder what other treasures he's got on board?"

———

There was no gentle way to drag the wounded man through the woods. They wrestled him through the tangle at the edge and then hoisted him into the wagon. He was pale as paper. Slowly they bounced and jostled up the hill.

"The way the ground was rustled, there were at least four."

"Yeah, but we only got one and he ain't much more than a towheaded kid."

"Bet there were more behind your house. I would venture they were planning to burn you out."

"That shoulder's all torn up. Lucky if this one lives an hour. What you think might make him talk?"

"If you have some brandy, we might try that," Clay replied.

"Marcie's fond of brandy. We got some. Damn, this hill is ragged."

"You better stop, Skipjack. His legs are dangling. He's about lurched out."

"Ain't trying to escape, is he?"

"Don't think so," Clay said. "Believe he's sliding."

"We didn't shut the tailgate?"

"You were in a hurry."

"So I was."

"Well, set the brake and give me a hand. He's not as light as he looks."

The two men coaxed the next-to-corpse weight back onto the wagon bed and shut the gate. Morning sun filled their faces as they ascended the slope. Near the summit, Skipjack clucked encouragement to Jessie and to their relief, they spotted Brawl and Tom Thurston headed up the drive.

Brawl took one look at the man as Clay and Skipjack lifted him out of the wagon. "That's the fella I was telling you about."

The young fellow was dead before they laid him in the grass. A fly busied itself in the man's nostril. Instinctively, Skipjack shooed the fly. When another landed in the blood on the man's shoulder, Skipjack stood and shook his head.

"I guess I hit something after all," Brawl said quietly.

Everyone nodded.

"This one is dead. No light in him. Let's cover him up."

"We better look through his pockets first," Clay said.

"Look then," Skipjack replied. "I've had enough."

"We need to send for the sheriff."

"We'll do that, Marcie," Skipjack said, "but wouldn't surprise me if sheriff already knew."

"Pockets are empty. I say we bury him and save some trouble. Bet some would love to ask Brawl why he shot him. Best keep them in the dark. What do you think?"

"Jack, we never play loose with the law."

"Honey, I can't prove it, but I think the law is playing a little loose with us."

———

Brawl drove Tom down to the tavern, then Tom rowed the skiff back up the creek near the house and helped Skipjack and Clay load the body into the boat. Tom got to work setting stone, while they rowed to where the camp had been and buried him. They dug out the fire pit, then tossed the man in, covered him with dirt, tamped it down, and shoveled ashes and cinders over their effort.

"These people are strange, aren't they?" Clay inclined his head at the carved stump.

"Foul as the breath of hell."

"So, you say they're coming back?"

"That's what I hear."

"Might not be all bad," Clay said as he studied the hillside. "The ridge is high and steep; lots of cover up there, too."

"Damn it! I want the bastards out of here."

"They're not going unless they're forced. Look, let's assume the sheriff is in on it. What would be his cut? Say he's convinced he'll be part owner in the gambling den your brother dreams of building and believes that because he's already being compensated for looking the other way while your brother operates his gang."

"I'm listening."

"What if we can taunt that sheriff into staging a raid on this scum at their camp down on Beargrass Creek?"

"He'll never. The man's a coward and a crook."

"Pardon me for saying, but you're too close. You have no

perspective. Listen, I have no doubt he's a coward. Most crooks are, but hear me, if we are right and the man is covering, there is a reason, and that reason is greed. Correct?"

"I can figure no other."

"Well then, it would make sense that he would want to try to obscure that, would it not?"

"So, you're saying we somehow pressure him?"

"Here's what I'm driving at. We threaten to go over his head. We challenge his courage and sense of duty and pressure the man to commit to stomp out this pestilence. Of course, we both suspect that he won't; in fact, we both know he will hem and haw about needing time to look into it and plan things. That's when we pour it on and act like we're ready to strike ourselves. We push him until he has to set a time to move on these thugs or else we're going over his head."

"You figure he'll tell my brother and Timothy will move?"

"Don't you know? Otherwise, he'll have to act."

"All sheriff's good for is hauling corpses and collecting taxes."

"About the same thing."

"So what's your plan?" Skipjack asked.

"Let's hunt down the sheriff, tell him about the intruders. Tell him we know where they are, and we're poised to destroy them with or without him, and that we're going to tell the mayor, and that we've already sent feelers to the governor. These cutthroats are committing crimes against interstate commerce. They are damaging merchants north and south. He'll be afraid not to listen. And you better believe, if we're right, he sure doesn't want a light to shine on what his part has been. I would bet he will see a necessity to act rather quickly."

"But not tonight?"

"No, not tonight, but soon enough, far enough out for us to devise the plan that will smash their operation from the top down."

"What you mean?"

"Skipjack," Clay said as he pointed to the ridge, "a handful of men with blasting powder and a few rifles could make a mess out of whoever was below. You think about how you'd feel if we were being attacked from there."

"We'd be dead ducks."

"Think about it. To get away, we would have to turn our backs to a firestorm. We can make the creek bank ugly, too."

"What are you saying?"

"Look across. You could hide a wagon in the growth. The trees are like a fortress wall. Hell, that one giant sycamore could shield three. Swear, I believe six good men could cut a platoon to ribbons."

"This is my fight, Clay. Tell me where I'm gonna find six good men."

"I grant you can't order anybody, but I'll bet you solid gold your man Andy would help. He knows the bastards would cut his throat in a minute if they thought they couldn't sell him and everyone else he might love. Brawl Thurston, now he's a solid man. He and Mr. Green know they are next if this bunch gets a firm hold. They don't want these folks. That young one, Tom, is spoiling for a fight. I can see it in his eyes."

"All right, maybe so. But that's only five. I can't advertise."

"Don't forget me. I'm on board, and I'll bet, if we present this properly, we'll attract a few others."

Skipjack eyeballed the thicket across the creek, then studied the thrust of the ridge. His gaze settled on the obscenely carved stump; he shook his head and grimaced.

"You think we can bluff the sheriff into making him believe we're ready to make a move and then they're going to slip back even closer? That makes no sense. Why would they do that?"

"You said yourself your brother's not sane. In his mind, this land is his. There's something else he craves. He burns to drive you from this land. Wants to haunt as much as he wants to kill. Think about it; they could have ambushed us any number of ways. He could have killed you anytime with a well-placed shot from the woods or a knife. Seems to me, the man's possessed by hatred. To drive you to bedlam is what he wants. He covets everything that is yours."

"How do you know these things?"

"I don't know anything, but I suspect I'm right. Why was he luring you to town? What's at your house that you're keeping from him? If your place hadn't been guarded, if your dog hadn't kicked up a ruckus, and if Brawl hadn't hit this boy, what do you think might have happened? He wants you broken and destroyed. God only knows what else he's lusting to do."

"Hard to take in," Skipjack said as he sagged against a stout sapling. "Jesus, I swear what you're saying all makes crazy sense, but can you understand how difficult this is?"

"Some hatreds burn with complexity impossible to fathom. All we can do is beg help. Evil defies logic. We search for reason and cure; evil smirks, then attacks and devours."

"So sickening, I could puke."

"Well, then, before it gets worse, let's stop it."

"I'll get Marcie and Billy down to the tavern, then we'll have a bite and go find the sheriff."

"You do have some powder, don't you, Skipjack?"

"Yeah."

"In a couple of days, we'll have a cannon."

Everyone was edgy. Mary Frances was the coolest of the lot. Off to the side, she told Skipjack there were two runaways in the storage house she had fed on the sly for two days, and she hadn't known what to tell about passage. Morning before, there was a dagger in the front door pinning a note scrawled in an illegible hand, and the only decipherable word had been "kill." But all Mary Frances needed was assurance that Skipjack was still in the fight. When he asked her to look after Marcie and Billy, trepidation grew into a sense of duty.

"I'll do anything you want, and you know that," she said, "but you got to take those folks across. Can't hide folks forever."

"Just watch Marcie and Billy. I'll take these ones this evening, so help me God. But I've got to go see the sheriff now."

"No need to explain. Marcie and Willy, they'll be safe."

Skipjack walked back to the office. When he entered, Marcie was going through the books and had Billy practicing penmanship.

"Be back in a couple of hours, honey. Please keep the door locked."

"We'll be all right," Marcie said.

"It's hot in here," Billy said.

"You're right, son. Stay put. Take care of Mother. If anybody tries to force their way, aim that shotgun and fire. Lock the door and keep it locked. I'll be back soon."

"Jack, we'll be all right," Marcie said as she crossed the room and hugged him. "This can't last forever. Have faith."

"I've got to trust my instincts."

"It's daylight. They want darkness."

Marcie kissed Skipjack in a way that made Billy turn his head. Skipjack reached all the way around her and patted her stomach.

SOMETIMES IT IS AND SOMETIMES IT ISN'T

Skipjack fetched Clay out of the bar. Clay swilled down the last of his tea and asked for pickled eggs. Within minutes, they were on River Road headed to town. The mare seemed especially frisky. Skipjack supposed she might be relishing a slight hint of fall.

Before they had covered two miles, they encountered the sheriff, accompanied by two plump deputies on nags that by comparison, rendered the sheriff's mount majestic. Both Skipjack and Clay knew horseflesh and were not fooled. The sheriff's bulk seemed to weigh down the spine of the animal he bestrode and when, upon mutual agreement, the parties steered their beasts beneath a willow, any observer could have seen that poor horse regained stature as soon as the sheriff hit ground with an audible thud. Skipjack hitched reins to the locked brake and slowly stepped down.

"We were looking to find you," Skipjack said.

Standing as tall as possible, the sheriff grinned and nodded at Clay. "Maddox, I'm not at all certain who *we* is."

Skipjack couldn't help but notice a gold watch chain stretched across the sheriff's middle. The lawman plucked a gold-plated watch out of his waistcoat and studied its face, as if he had somewhere much more important to be. Clay kept his eyes on the deputies who were as expressionless as sacks. He watched them closely nonetheless from beneath hooded lids. Sheriff grinned quickly as he snapped his watch shut and asked all of a sudden, "What is it you want?"

His abruptness took Skipjack aback. He compared who he thought he had known with the man now before him. Was this man, almost childishly swollen with pride, even the same man? The sheriff's flesh spilled out over his collar. Pudgy wrists were adorned with garish cuff links. His soiled coat draped over a bulging belly girthed with a belt that strained. Even the wedding band on his finger was submerged. The sheriff's eyes glinted.

"What is it you want?"

"How do you know I want anything at all?"

"It is my business to know things, Skipjack. That is why I am elected year after year. For starters, why don't you tell who your companion is?"

"Mr. Clay," said Skipjack, "please meet Mr. Ballard Winston, our duly elected sheriff."

The two men nodded slightly. The frond-filtered sunlight washed their faces with a pale green pall. The sheriff's glance left Clay and seemed to focus inward. Looking down he said, "So, what do you have to report this time There is bound to be a body somewhere. I heard you were attacked."

"How you know that, I wouldn't know. But if you're here to haul off a body, where is your wagon?"

"Never said I wanted to haul. Simply asked what you had to report."

"You have a funny way of putting things, Sheriff. But there ain't no body to be hauled. How did you come to hear we were attacked? And I might ask, since it seems you are aware of so much, would you happen to know who might be responsible?"

"What are you implying, old friend?" the sheriff asked.

"I ain't implying. Do you know who followed me from town last night? Would you have any idea who attempted to attack my home?"

"I know what you're thinking and don't blame you," the sheriff replied. "But I'll tell you, I hear things. Some you can bank; most you can't. I know you were attacked and I have heard rumors about who, but it don't add up. My job—in my view—is to ask what you think."

Dark clouds squelched the sun as a strong breeze rustled willow fronds and teased with whistling sounds. Skipjack chuckled first, then laughed out loud. He looked at Clay, sighed, and looked hard at the sheriff.

"Do you hear that thunder rumbling off to the south, sheriff? The breeze on my back tells me storm's coming. Temperature's dropping. We're due one, so if you like, we can discuss this matter at the tavern or to keep it brief, I will tell you right now and you can take your chances out on the road. I do have ideas, but don't feel like getting drenched. What will it be? The long or the short? Your call."

"Keep it short," the sheriff said and nodded.

"First time I ever saw you pass a free meal but have it your way. I know who done it as well as you. I won't be asking for help no more, you understand? Those that done these things will soon burn in hell. We know where they're holed up. Put that word out and see what it gets you."

"Skipjack, you can't take the law into your own hands. Things take time."

"What law are you talking about?" Skipjack replied over his shoulder as he climbed into the buggy and loosed the reins. "You have an electioneering meeting, I suppose, so don't be late. Nice timepiece, by the way. Keep up the good work; you might get buried with it."

"Don't you dare threaten me."

"What would be the point, sheriff? You're digging the hole your damn self. Won't be me pushing you in. You got friends down on Beargrass to thank for that. Might ask them how long you've got to get affairs together. Might be prudent to inquire, because the look on your face tells me you don't like surprise."

Skipjack steered the mare through fronds and up onto the road as Clay nudged him in the ribs.

"You sure loosed a bee up his ass. You haven't seemed quite yourself, but if I had to judge, I would rule you're returning to form."

Skipjack stared straight ahead. He heard the clip-clop of the sheriff's steed hurrying up behind.

"Believe the sheriff might want some lunch after all."

"Skipjack, don't be rash," the sheriff cried out.

Skipjack turned slowly toward the sheriff who rode alongside.

"What is it you're saying?"

"Please, we go back. Don't put us at odds."

"At odds with whom, Ballard Winston?"

The sheriff's face tightened.

"Are you getting hungry, sheriff?"

"We need to talk."

"You know where I'm headed."

———

While Skipjack checked on Marcie and Billy, the sheriff settled in at the gallery table furthest from the building. He had insisted on it though there were several open tables. The sheriff planted himself as if he planned to take root. Mary Frances stared over his shoulder and tried to absorb calmness from the river as the sheriff ordered whiskey and Clay requested tea.

"He's pushing me, Mr. Clay. Do you understand? I want to help, but he is an impatient man."

"Sheriff Winston, how is it you wish to help?"

"I'm not sure I understand your interest in this matter, sir."

Clay smiled and said, "Neither do I. But why not answer?"

"Mr. Clay, I will tell you frankly, my resources are stretched thin and about all we can do is keep records of the transgressions and transactions in this county. The idea of preventing or settling every family squabble is more or less out of the question. What Skipjack Maddox wants me to unravel is more tangled than briar. Where do you fit? I've lived here all my life and don't understand it."

"Somebody's trying to run Skipjack off or worse, to kill him. You know that much, don't you?"

"He'll swear it's his brother and might be right. But so what? Say his brother is all the trouble he says; what am I supposed to do? I got no proof. Clay, there's something happening makes enforcing law seem nearly ridiculous. You tell me whose law am I supposed to enforce?"

"What are you talking about? Most law is pretty clear."

"Sometimes it is and sometimes it isn't. Much depends on who is pulling the levers."

"The law is plain on matters of trespass and attempted murder."

"That may be true, but even that depends on who's sitting in judgment. You take stealing slaves, for instance, and slipping them across the river and out of state. There's a law against that and you know it."

"I am well aware of the Dred Scott decision, sheriff, and I respect property rights."

The sheriff blinked and leaned back in his chair.

"Maybe I misread you. There's some around these parts that are, shall I say, selective in their definition of what constitutes property rights."

The sheriff leaned forward, mashing his chin folds into the palm of his hand, and grinned. Mary Frances placed their chosen libations between them. The sheriff continued to stare as Clay stirred sugar into his tea. The sky was darkening, and insistent breezes jostled the trees. Clay took note of the sudden fierce churn of the river before returning his gaze to the sheriff's squinted eyes.

"Are you insinuating that I am in some way violating—"

"Mr. Clay, please rest your mind on that score. I intend no disrespect. However, I would say, you have chosen a rather odd companion; that is, if you wish to avoid controversy. May I ask how long and how well have you been acquainted with Jackson Maddox? By your demeanor, I surmise that it's not a long-time association. I'm not so sure that I could advise that it should be. Don't get me wrong. Skipjack is an interesting man. He has his own way of looking at the world. As a man of law, you understand that I don't take sides, but I can't always give a nod of approval."

"What sides are you referring to, sheriff? The plainer you explain, the murkier you become. Are you accusing Skipjack of law breaking?"

"Heavens no, Mr. Clay. When I make accusations, they are supported with evidence. That's something Maddox seems eager to ask me to ignore. My point is simply this: there are those who have lodged complaints against Maddox for some time—of course, not founded on indisputable fact—that implicate him in all manner of mischief, including promoting prostitution, crooked gaming, and the illegal transport of Negroes. I have exercised restraint in pursuit of charges against our friend for the exact same reason I hesitate to clamp down on his brother. One word sums it up, Mr. Clay: proof. But I can assure you enough money and pressure can combine to produce an abundance of facts to support most anything. Truth is what we're after here, is it not? Proof buttressed with fact. Of course, it is and we both well know it."

First one lone raindrop spattered on the tabletop and then it seemed like buckets were emptied from atop the towering cottonwood trees. The sheriff did not abandon his whiskey glass, but Clay left his tea untasted on the table. Before they had gained the shelter of the barroom, the table had been blown over. To Clay, the wave crests on the river looked like roving teeth. The sheriff pounded him on the back and cried out, "Lord, have mercy!"

Across the room, suddenly dark as dusk, Clay discerned Skipjack speaking into the bartender's ear. The room trembled with the sky's rumble. Skipjack pointed and winked. The sheriff placed his hand on Clay's back and steered him toward the table Skipjack had indicated. Clay decided to keep his mouth shut, however, it would have been impossible to converse. Thunder boomed and wind whistled. Rain drove into the building. Mary Frances offered Clay more tea, but Clay, pointing at the sheriff's glass, signaled for whiskey. In a few moments, Skipjack delivered the drinks himself.

"Now, that is unusual," he said, pointing at dancing chunks of hail. "We seldom see that stuff this time of year. Normally a springtime thing, wouldn't you say?"

"Just in time to smash young tender plants," Clay replied.

"It'll pass," Skipjack drawled. "They're small anyhow. Sheriff, what you got?"

The sheriff studied Skipjack and swished whiskey around his mouth before he squinted, leaned forward, and answered.

"Skipjack, don't be a hot-headed fool. What I hear or don't ain't going to change the fact that some folks' days are numbered. Everything's changing. Bandits are already attacking railroads. You got to look ahead. I guarantee the folks you're worried about won't hang together more than a season. What's the harm in letting time work?"

"Easy to say when you ain't the target. Are you suggesting I go about like none of this happened? For God's sake, sheriff, they've broken in; they've attacked my house. You know who. What is your angle? Can you tell me?"

"As I have tried to convey to Mr. Clay, I am constrained by lack of solid proof. All that fills my ear is hearsay. Some say, for example, that you run slaves. What would you say if I brought charges?"

"I'd say you're a damn liar."

"What if I told you that a couple of so-and-so's had sworn on Bibles that it was God's truth and that I had to take you in?"

Skipjack shook his head, then took a sip.

"Sheriff, are you going to help me run these people off or not? Yes or no?"

"You don't get it do you? If I listened to everybody who had a grudge, I would be running around like a chicken with its head cut off. You got no proof who done these things, and all I got is your feelings and lowdown whispers. None of it adds up. I can't act on that."

"You know what these people are. They don't work. They're lowlife thieves and worse."

"Skipjack, you have accurately described what many say about you and a sizable portion of your clientele. Do you think based on that I should shut you down? The law is plain on that point. You are innocent until you are proven guilty."

"I run a legitimate business here."

"Can you prove it?" The sheriff scowled.

"We've got records. We keep books."

"Do you think books would satisfy the folks that want you gone?"

"So, you won't help us? Say it out loud. I dare you."

"I can't jump to conclusions. Justice is blind."

As the mare pulled the buggy up the hill, Billy pretended he was a bear, and everyone was amused, but the sight of Tom Thurston's body sprawled across the front porch steps ended laughter. Once they discovered he wasn't dead, but that in fact, was barely wounded, relief and anger replaced concern. A bullet had grazed his head. Tom was knocked silly and in a daze; that was all. Once Skipjack understood that Tom was all right, his resolution focused.

Billy sat beside his friend. Skipjack and Clay stood on the porch and whispered. Marcie tended to Tom with a cool compress and wrung bloody water into a bowl. She knew something harsh was coming. She tried to mask her emotions when she asked Billy for a glass of drinking water. When he stood up, nodded and whispered, "Don't worry, Momma," Marcie knew she had failed to conceal her fears.

"We have to go into town and check out their camp," Clay said.

"Tomorrow night. Let's give the sheriff one last chance," Skipjack replied.

"What sense does that make? Do you trust the sheriff?"

"It's not the sheriff. I need to go down to the tavern and check on something."

Clay's exasperation tangled even more. He paused and reflected before asking, "So you expect me to guard the family while you're down at the tavern?"

"Clay, trust me, this ain't play. I'll send Andy up. You won't be alone."

"There's no alone to it, Skipjack. I don't understand."

"Trust me. I can't explain. You look after Marcie and Billy, and you might be surprised what I will do for you."

"Maddox, I want nothing but truth."

"I won't be but an hour or two."

Clay shook his head as Billy strolled onto the porch and announced that Tom was awake and sipping tea. Skipjack stared through treetops at clouds hiding the moon.

"I'll be counting on you and back before you know," Skipjack said before he strolled to the stable. He rode off bareback on Jessie. Clay laid his hand on Billy's shoulder.

"Why does he think he has to be going?" Billy asked.

"He'll be back," Clay said, "but I have no idea."

"He does this all the time. Momma says she don't know what to do about it."

There were times when his mind was as empty as space between stars. This was one of those times. Shadows shrugged by the moon softened his mood. Anger was present but not raging. It was steady as he rocked downhill on Jessie's strong back. Resolve was in his pulse. His breathing was calm. His eyes were clear and cold as new ice.

First things first. Had to get these folks across river. It was as much for his own welfare as theirs. He didn't need to be caught hiding runaways. Brother would have to wait. Skipjack felt in his bones that the sheriff was in with Timothy somehow and was perhaps almost as dangerous.

Two drunks at the bar were in a heated discussion. Skipjack motioned to Louis and told him to go home, slipped him some cash, told him to find Andy and send him up to the house. In the kitchen, Mary Frances was scrubbing the last pots. It had been a slow night and the rest of the help had been allowed to leave.

"Those pots can wait. Just get home yourself. Be careful."

"You still got money in the bar cashbox."

"I'll take care of it. You go home now," he said, raising his hand and nodding slightly. She stripped off her apron. "I'll start locking up," she said.

In the barroom, Skipjack found the gents behind the bar. In Louis's absence, they had decided to help themselves. One, named Oliver, was demonstrating to his rapt companion, Mr. Fishbone, how to top off a tumbler of Scotch whiskey without it losing cohesion on the rim of the glass. They showed no interest in Skipjack until he was standing beside them apparently sharing their interest in this enterprise. Fishbone peered at Skipjack and leered.

"Oliver has quite the steady hand, wouldn't you say?"

"Don't jostle, Fishbone, or you'll ruin it. This isn't a card trick. It requires concentration."

"He's a master, he is," Fishbone murmured. "Watch him. I dare say he won't spill a drop."

"I doubt that he will," Skipjack whispered as he pulled the hammer back on his pistol. "You're stealing my whiskey. Now both stand away."

Oliver lowered the bottle slowly to the bar. Fishbone froze at the touch of cold metal on the nape of his neck.

"Now, slowly walk out from behind my bar and we will avoid ill consequences. Does that sound agreeable, gentlemen?"

Both nodded and moved past quickly enough that Skipjack had to be careful not to trip over his own feet.

"Now, if you gentlemen will seat yourselves, there is a slight chance I will reward your cooperation. In other words, allow you to partake quickly of the drinks that you have poured; that is, of course, if you are inclined to pay."

Both men sat and vigorously agreed. Skipjack stepped back behind the bar and smiled.

"All you have to do now is show the money."

Both men reached for their wallets. Oliver seemed to be blushing. The one called Fishbone appeared near to a trembling faint.

"I told him it wasn't proper, not even here," he stammered.

"Was that before or after you stepped behind the bar, Mr. Fishbone? Perhaps you would like to pay for everything? Show me the money."

"If you want to know the entire truth," Oliver began, but his oily cockiness drove Skipjack to one conclusion.

"Get out."

"We'll pay. It would be dishonorable not to do so," Fishbone simpered.

"I don't want money. Go and don't look back."

After locking the door, Skipjack carried the cashbox to his office, removed some cash, and stuffed it in his pocket. He lit a cigar, then stuffed some cartridges into his shirt pocket, then took his rifle down off the gun rack. It was already loaded. He took a deep breath and shook his head. He locked up and headed toward the whiskey house. Usually he first walked around, but not tonight. Something told him to get this done now.

The half-moon was bright enough that his shadow loomed on the door as he shoved the key into the lock. He wished for a fleeting moment that a shadow could do this night's work, shouldered the door open, and said, "It's time. Let's go."

The runaways walked out into moonlight and the young man shaded his eyes like it was midday. The young woman was stroking the head of an infant.

"If you believe in prayer, it would be wise to pray for clouds. Now listen to me: no talking, stay close. When we get to the water, climb in the boat and stay low. If we see anybody, don't say anything. I do the talking. You're with me. Understand?"

Both nodded.

"Stay close," Skipjack whispered and through shadow, they meandered as directly as possible down to the skiff. The young man climbed aboard first, lifted his wife and child in after him and settled them down gently on the planks, then remained standing and looked up and down river.

"You sit down, too, damn it, and stay down."

A side-wheeler was headed downstream. There was nothing else moving on the water, so he shoved off, laid his rifle down, and dug in with the oars. Just as he left the dead water close to shore, to his relief, a large cloud slid over the moon. Skipjack pulled, hoping to be out in the middle before being bathed with light once again.

The nearest boats moored on the bank were at least a hundred yards downstream. One of them had a calliope wheezing out some ditty that Skipjack prayed he never would be subjected to again. He grunted and pulled, grunted and pulled. There was almost no current. He thanked his lucky stars and pulled, pulled, aimed upstream, and pulled some more.

In his mind, he rehearsed how he would tell them about climbing the steep bank and the road they would follow to the safe house. There was no way there would be anybody to meet them on the other side when they landed. These folks had been hidden for two days.

So, scramble up what looked like a mountain, then take a road to a church in the dark, where they would find food, clothing, and shelter. He imagined the looks of incredulousness. He could scarcely believe it himself. As far as he knew, folks left his skiff and disappeared. He only knew that they never came back.

He was above the landing point about two hundred yards when the current did some work and allowed his back a rest. The silhouette of a flatboat tied to the bank caught his eye; it was only a dark shape under a canopy of trees. The moonlight at that same instant illuminated the skiff. Skipjack quietly rowed. A lantern suddenly glowed on the flatboat. Skipjack could see the shadow cast onto the flatboat's canvas tent better than he could see the man doing the casting, but Skipjack heard him plain enough.

"Virgil, Virgil, is you blind? Over here. Where you think you're heading?"

Skipjack kept rowing steadily downstream.

"I know I ain't seeing spooks. Virgil, is you deaf on top of blind?"

Skipjack kept rowing and heard discord from rudely awakened men inside the tent. He laughed out loud as he heard the man vehemently insist he had seen what he'd seen. He continued to call out for Virgil, until a tight knot of irritated loud grumbling drowned him out. Skipjack nosed in, and within seconds, one oar thrust put them on shore.

Like a cat, the man sprang to the sand, then lifted his wife and child. Skipjack stepped ashore, pulled money from his pocket and pressed it into the man's hand. The man looked stunned, as if Skipjack had handed him a poisonous snake. Then just as the man looked like he might recover from this shock, a match flared, and a lantern faintly glowed about fifty feet up the steep hill.

"This way and hurry," a hoarse voice said.

The baby started to whimper, and the woman touched Skipjack's shoulder as he turned away.

"Shove me off."

The man pushed so hard Skipjack nearly fell on his face. He allowed the current to haul him downstream while he relit his cigar and then leisurely rowed home, wondering if the man thought to slip the money into his pocket. A large fish jumped and nearly cleared the boat, but instead landed on Skipjack's foot and thrashed on the planks; a beautiful largemouth bass that would make a fine breakfast. What a story that would be. He chuckled and realized it was a story he could never tell. He reached with both hands, snared, and hoisted the fish who fought him every inch of the journey until dropped overboard. Skipjack hated doing it.

SCOUT

As he was securing the skiff, a strangely familiar voice seemed to come out of the coarse bark of a cottonwood tree.

"Fishing with a rifle, sure thing, sure thing. Never seen that, no way. I ain't a talking fish, so don't shoot, don't shoot."

The icicle that Skipjack's spine had become melted and a slow chuckle grew in his chest. He drew his pistol out of his belt just in case. He leveled it and turned slowly toward the voice.

"Trapper?"

"Yes, yes, that's me, Van Nutt, the trapper, yes sir."

"Who you hiding from?"

"Ain't hiding, no sir. Truth is I was keeping an eye on goings-on. Not hiding, laying low, real low."

"Well, come out here where I can see you. Makes me nervous talking to a tree."

Quick as a fox, Trapper was out in the moonlit space between them. He held his hands in front of him like he was pushing against glass. His eyes were steady, feral beads.

"I seen 'em. Yes, sir, passed 'em going up. Yes, sir, I seen 'em."

"You've seen who, Trapper?"

Trapper leaned in and stepped close, cupping his hands around his mouth. His foul breath and the message it conveyed made Skipjack clench teeth.

"They're back, back. I seen 'em. Same as before. Same place."

Skipjack took a step to the side and lowered the pistol. Van Nutt's stare was fixed.

"I appreciate you telling me this, Trapper. How did you know you would find me here?"

"I didn't, no way, no sir, but I got ears, don't I?" he replied, pointing at both sides of his head. "Was drifting past. They was building a fire. Two talking about you; your skiff gone. 'This our chance, our chance,' one say. This scratchy lady voice say, 'No good now. Listen to me: you're blinded by brother blood. Harvest fruit when the moon is right.' I drifted, real quiet, real quiet. They got louder and cursed and hollered. They plotting to kill you, plain as day, Mr. Maddox. Yes, sir."

"Why're you telling me this? You're taking a chance, you know that?"

"Them ones ain't no good. Soon stab as eat. No damn good, that's what."

"So, you'll help get them out of here?"

"No choice, no choice. They're poison, poison, yes, sir."

"Can you ride up to the house with me? It's a ways."

"You aiming to clean 'em out tonight?"

"Sure want to, but no, I guess not."

"Listen here, listen here. You need a plan, you hear? A plan or you stir 'em."

Skipjack may as well have been staring into a bucket of ink. All he saw was a faint reflection of himself peering back, looking stupid. He was not used to this. There was tension in his jaws. He became aware of dry lips, which he moistened. There was nausea in his belly.

"How bad you want 'em out of here, Trapper?"

"Bad enough, bad enough to help. Kill me same as you."

"How about right down here tomorrow at five?"

"Why here, why here? Too public. Public has eyes."

"All right, my place. Can you get there at five?"

Trapper nodded and backed up.

"Better duck down. Duck down now. Coming down the creek. Down."

They both crouched low behind the cottonwood tree and pressed tight into the bark. At first, Skipjack heard nothing but his own breathing, then he heard the dip of oars.

"Son of a bitch slipped back," a man hoarsely whispered.

"I told you no talk. Now shut your damned trap and pull out off shore. Head upstream."

As oars dug and under cover of splashing water, Skipjack asked, "Any more coming down?"

"Don't sound like it. Nope, don't think there is."

They stayed hunkered for a couple of minutes. When a cloud covered the moon, they stood.

"I'll see you tomorrow at five."

Trapper nodded and nodded again. Skipjack walked up to the tavern, locked himself inside, and poured a stiff drink. His rage was nearly out of control. With effort, he tamped it down, poured the whiskey back into the bottle. Reconsidered, poured half into the glass once again, and swallowed. It tasted so fine that he poured out the other half for the slow ride home.

———

Shadows lay on the path like pieces of a puzzle, but Jessie stepped confidently. Skipjack trusted her implicitly. If not for Marcie and what they shared, he might have welcomed a bullet to the head. There was no fear within him. He was as calm as the beast he bestrode; one hand cradled the rifle, the other balanced his glass of whiskey. On the way uphill to the house, he barely stiffened when he thought he detected a mechanical click off to his right. Jessie hadn't flinched, so he hadn't either. He rocked with the muscles that carried him home.

Andy greeted him and offered to put Jessie up. Skipjack suggested that Andy ride Jessie home. Andy allowed that he would just as soon bed down in the loft.

"All right then, you stay the night here. How is Tom doing?"

"Brawl come up and got him. He's mad as a hornet. Wants to talk to you."

Skipjack rubbed his brow and stepped onto the porch. From his chair in the shadows, Clay asked him how it went. Without responding, Skipjack walked into the house where Marcie was seated at the table, chin perched in her hand. Her eyes followed his every move as he closed in on the cabinet that contained the whiskey. He noticed she had a full tumbler of wine in her hand. He armed himself with this knowledge as he poured. She said nothing as he raised the taste to his lips. Clay scraped his chair on the front porch. Skipjack looked quickly at Marcie. She stood. He put his drink down.

"Please, God, let's just go to bed."

Clay walked into the room.

"Let's talk in the morning," she whispered.

"Morning comes quickly, Mr. Clay," Skipjack murmured as he followed Marcie up the stairs.

"What the hell are you thinking?" Marcie hissed as soon as she shut the bedroom door.

Skipjack unbuttoned his shirt and found no answer forthcoming. He sat on the bed's edge and worried with his boots.

"Damn your ass! You can't treat me like this. You will talk to me. Do you hear?"

"What is it you want?"

"You run off. I don't know where . . ."

"Yes, you do. I went down to the tavern and you know it. Look, I don't feel so good myself. Dog tired."

"How can you do this?'

"Marcie, I believe you said you wanted to talk tomorrow. I'm too tired to think tonight." He tugged his legs out of his trousers. "If you would hold me, I would appreciate that, but I can't talk."

"You mean you won't."

"I mean both. Please, I need you now, like you sometimes need me. I swear I'm near dead tired. Believe me." He crushed into the pillow. "Like you said, we'll talk in the morning."

He heaved his chest and arched his back, stretched out weary legs, wiggled his toes, then exhaled. He reminded himself to breathe in, realizing it was not a given. He heard the rustle of Marcie's disrobing. The lamp dimmed, was extinguished. Her hand found his shoulder.

CHAPTER 9

HARD TO SHOOT SNAPPIN' BEANS

A father, a father.

Skipjack descended wobbly stairs; each straining creak clenched teeth. The entire house would awaken, he knew it. He managed to make coffee without interruption, but just as he was pouring out a cup, Clay appeared.

"Let's check them out."

"Go up the ridge?"

Skipjack nodded and pointed at the coffeepot. After a quick cup, the two men were climbing the path. Within a few minutes, they were crouched, looking down on the ragtag encampment. There was only one flatboat now and a skiff. There was a wagon with a tent on it and several crude lean-to shelters. An emaciated horse stood tethered to a hackberry sapling, head down, slumbering in mist off the creek. Smoldering smoke trickled from the fire pit. Even though it appeared the smoke clung to the ground, Skipjack and Clay, nearly one hundred feet up above the camp, grimaced involuntarily at fetid ripeness.

What at first looked like piles of rags turned into human shapes slumbering. They counted five or six sprawled on the ground, though it was hard to tell. One man, then another, sat up in the skiff, then lay back down. The breeze climbed the cliff and the stench of raw excrement accompanied putrid smoke. Skipjack gagged and glanced at Clay whose grin was scrunched to destroy sense of smell. Skipjack motioned toward home with his rifle. They didn't speak for at least two hundred yards.

"I need a damn bath after that."

"Dear God," Clay said.

"Please let's keep details to ourselves."

"There's no way to describe it anyway. My God, those people are hell."

"They're out of here," Skipjack said. "Tonight."

"We don't want to be rash. Do you have a plan?"

"No, but we'll have one. You said yourself that the strategic advantage is from those rocks. We get four or five shooters and some blasting sticks; those bastards won't have a chance. I can't live like this, hear me?"

"I understand that, but do you have the men?"

"Believe so. Hell, the two of us could mess them up pretty good throwing rocks down on 'em."

"You're fooling."

"Clay, trust me a couple hours. I haven't even had breakfast yet. I guarantee Brawl will help and Green, and most likely Tom, and Trapper is on board, I'm pretty sure. There are lots of folks tired of this foolishness."

"So, you just want to attack them?"

"No other way. You can't deal with them otherwise. They're crazy."

"But you need a plan," Clay insisted, egging Skipjack on.

"I want them gone," Skipjack said. "The plan will be in place, I assure you."

They walked through misty ridge light in silence until the smell of ham frying wafted uphill to greet them.

"I never thought I wanted to smell anything ever again," Clay said.

———

Ham, eggs, wheat bread, and strong coffee.

When Clay wandered off to the outhouse, Marcie clutched Skipjack and held him close.

"Please forgive my nastiness. I hate this, and you know I love you."

"Better is coming, sure as God. Just trust. I'm doing the best I can."

"I don't want to be left alone, Jack."

"Then you got to help."

"How can I do that if I don't know where you are?"

"That's where trust comes in; plenty of time later for knowing."

"What are you going to do?"

"Drive them out tonight," Skipjack said.

"How?"

"I don't know."

Gracie, who had been slumbering in the corner, began to growl, then scrambled to her feet, trotted to the front door, and barked like the devil was on the threshold.

"Looks like she's feeling better," Skipjack said as he picked up his pistol and strolled to the window. "It's Brawl and Tom. I'll be right back."

Skipjack had never seen Brawl angrier. As he walked toward the wagon, he also noticed Brawl's sheer bulk, which dwarfed Tom Thurston. Tom's head was still bandaged and for once, he looked like the child-man he actually was. All Tom's cockiness seemed diminished by the focused fury Brawl contained. Tom nodded and smiled; Brawl did not. A rifle was cradled in his arm and his eyes were inscrutable slits.

"We got lucky last night, Brawl, but we can't rely on luck no more."

Brawl tilted his head, which raised his rifle barrel a discernable amount, but he did not reply. Skipjack could not be certain Brawl had even heard. A blue jay's shrill carved otherwise peaceful morning air. Tom grinned awkwardly and lankily shifted. The big old workhorse swished his tail. Out of the corner of his eye, Skipjack saw Clay approaching slowly but decided that his best move was silence, so he took a deep breath and waited for Brawl to speak. Clay stopped beside him and nodded. Brawl's mouth tightened, and he dipped forward so slightly he did not disturb a bead of sweat.

"This boy was nearly murdered yesterday. This here's got to stop."

"I couldn't agree more. Will you help me run 'em off tonight?"

"If we got a fighting chance, I will."

"I think we have better than a fighting chance," Skipjack said.

Brawl looked down and clenched his jaw. "These are evil people, Skipjack."

"We all know that. I believe Green will help, don't you?"

"I suppose, and I can get some folks in the trades, perhaps. They've been stealing us blind off building sites. But we got to get organized. Have you talked to Mr. Green?"

"No, but I will. They're camped at the base of a cliff up yonder. We got the high ground and I believe by the end of the day, we'll have the low ground as well. They got a flatboat, a raft, and a skiff. On the shore, they got a wagon and a couple of tents. If we can pepper them with gunfire from above, I believe I got a man who can take out their boats. But I ain't got it all figured out yet. Can you head back here around five o'clock this evening? I'll talk to Green. I know in my gut he'll help."

Brawl nodded and took a deep breath. He motioned for Tom to climb down off the wagon.

"I'll see what I can do. Meanwhile, why don't you let this boy have a look at the rocks up above this campsite?"

Skipjack nodded.

"Stay low, Tom, and don't try nothing by yourself. You do have some powder, don't you, Mr. Skipjack?" Brawl asked with a twinkle in his eye. He almost sounded amused. "I'll be here at five sharp. See what we come up with."

"Hitting tonight, Brawl," Skipjack called out.

Over his shoulder Brawl responded, "Don't doubt one bit. Can a wagon get close on that ridge?"

"Yours can't. My small rig with Jessie hauling can."

Brawl raised his rifle over his head and continued down the hill.

Clay kept his mouth shut. He had a cannon on the way from outside of Frankfort. He crossed his fingers and in his own way, prayed.

————

When the cannon was delivered, Clay and Skipjack weren't there. They were down at the tavern talking to Mary Frances.

Marcie heard a wagon creaking. Two black men ambled to the door. They asked for Master Clay and when told that he was not around, whispered that they had come to make a delivery at Mr. Clay's request. A crate not too much larger than a small pig, but which seemed quite heavy, was lifted out of the wagon and soon was joined on the ground by two other crates. Marcie found the crates interesting only for the heft that lifting them seemed to require. She thanked the men and offered them water for their efforts. Billy and Tom, busy setting rock in the springhouse path, hadn't even noticed the delivery.

The sun was now straight overhead. Marcie clasped her stomach and though nothing was kicking, noticed something moving. The three stacked crates stood raw on the grass. Marcie realized she knew next to nothing of what was going on. She leaned against the doorjamb, mopped her head, and said, "Please?" out loud in spite of herself.

————

Mary Frances chewed into Skipjack first, who winked at Clay, and then she lit into Clay as well. The two men grinned like naughty boys, but she shook her head and motioned them outdoors away from Lacy who was helping in the kitchen.

"Now hear me close, you rotten no-good bastards. There ain't no one here keeping this game on track but me, and I am more than tired.

I got my own troubles to sort out. I hears this and that, and I been down here without one soul to help me sort out what's what. I hear all kinds of tarnation. Will somebody please tell me what might be going on? I have stood for you, Skipjack; I believe it might be your turn to stand by me."

Skipjack raised his hand and smiled at Clay.

"Don't you dare get cute. I ain't kidding. I've been wading through you know what. I'm so mad I could spit."

"Mary Frances, I've been wading, too. Ain't real happy myself—about ready to kill my own brother before he poisons or destroys everything."

"About time you lay him out, I say," Mary Frances responded fiercely. "If you're in on this," she added, nodding at Clay, "I think I like you better."

"I'm on board," Clay said.

"Well, what damn board are we on, Skipjack? What kind of whoop-de-do am I supposed to play? Do I cut throats or serve rabbit stew? Do I call him Sheriff Winston or His Highness? He's been here every other day; walking around bowing and nodding to folks and admiring the view. What the hell is going on?"

"He's been here?" Skipjack asked.

"A damn sight more than you. I'm standing in dark every day," she said. "I want to help y'all, Skipjack, but clue me in, hear?" Mary Frances's eyes, near shut, brimmed with tears.

Skipjack touched her shoulder. Mary Frances wiped her cheeks with the back of her wrist. She shook her head slowly.

"No sweet talk. Shoot straight."

Skipjack leaned forward and whispered, "Let Lacy handle supper. Come to the house with Andy at five."

"That girl can't handle supper all by herself," Mary Frances objected.

"You want to know what's going on? Make sure she does," Skipjack said as he slipped a few crumpled bills into Mary Frances's free hand.

"Something's telling me to head to town now, Clay."

Before they reached River Road, Skipjack had changed his mind. As he was explaining his convoluted reasoning, Brawl turned in and headed toward them. He pulled up and his big chestnut workhorses stomped and snorted. Brawl was smiling broadly.

"We got some recruits. They don't know it yet, but we got 'em. Down at the new waterworks, these same crooks been robbing blind. The contractors are mad as hell. There was a guard beat bloody the night before last and all they stole was chisels and awls."

"What are you telling me, Brawl?"

"I'm telling you about twenty ornery dagos is on our side. Without stone tools, they can't work. They gonna help us for sure. Got one coming to have a look."

"How they going to help?"

"Tom's a good boy, but these Italians are mad as hell. We can drop rock on those fools like raindrops."

"I don't understand."

"Skipjack, if Tom wrote a song, these boys can make an opera. Are you listening?"

When Skipjack and Clay arrived with Brawl following, Marcie and Billy sat on the porch snapping beans. Marcie's rifle and Billy's double-barrel shotgun were propped against the wall behind them. Marcie's greeting was a joyous steady gaze. Billy seemed to shrink, until Skipjack asked where Tom was. Then with a pained expression, the boy blurted that Tom had snuck up the hill. Brawl clucked his tongue and shook his head.

"She's making me snap old beans I don't want to eat."

Skipjack nodded at Marcie and smiled.

"That's no way to talk to your mother, boy. You finish what you've started. You hear me? Not another word."

The boy nodded and then pointed. "Yes, sir, but what's in them crates over there, Mr. Clay?"

"Those crates, Billy," Marcie said.

Clay beamed. "Folks, we have a cannon."

"Lord have mercy," Brawl whispered.

"Kind of small, ain't it?" Skipjack said.

"Believe me, it will command attention. Let me show you. You got a pry bar?"

"Yeah, but I don't like the idea of Tom up there alone. We'll check that rig out in a bit."

The three men set out around the house.

"Bill, you guard your mother. It's important. You mind her but do what you have to do."

"Yes, sir," Billy said with a nod. "Can I stop snapping beans? It's hard to shoot snappin' beans."

"That's up to Mother. Be right back, Marcie."

"Someone's coming up, honey," Marcie said.

A broad-shouldered, short, bow-legged man was ascending the hill. The way his arms were churning, almost seemed that he was swimming. He had an infectious grin on his sweat-glistened face. He waved the last few paces and then was before them, dark eyes flashing, both hands raised in a questioning accent to his smile.

"Brawl, we go now to this place we want to see?"

"Paolo, that is Skipjack and Mr. Clay. Skipjack, Paolo is the stone-carver boss man from the waterworks. He will be quiet. I know how to talk to him."

Skipjack led the way past the springhouse and up the path. As they entered the woods, there was little talk. When they hugged the ridge that trailed the creek, conversation died and gave way to gesture. The greenery was still thick, and though birds were free with scrawling calls, the men were conscious of each audible step. Their feet settled lightly, but if not, the miscreant's eye was met with glare. All but Paolo were carrying firearms, but when they reached the ridge overlooking the encampment, Clay nodded, and Paolo used his knife as a questioning pointer. Tom Thurston appeared from behind a huge poplar tree and startled them. Skipjack held two fingers to his lips. Tom did the same, then signified that there were eyes and ears down below.

Brawl pointed to Tom, then pointed at Paolo, who grinned. Both men eyed each other, then keeping low and hidden by undergrowth, surveyed striated limestone boulders, some as large as small cabins, that composed a staggered cliff face. They moved so deliberately that not one small stone was dislodged. After a few minutes, they rejoined the group and their sweaty faces nodded in agreement.

Clay located the spot for his cannon; a flat rock wedged between two stout saplings with a sight line to the skiff floating languorously in the sluggish creek. One shot could sink it.

Skipjack noticed four or five buckets mounded with stones. He looked questioningly at Tom and then shrugged. Tom pointed to Brawl who grinned ear to ear.

"Trust me," Brawl whispered, no louder than the leaf-rustling breeze. Skipjack shrugged.

The sounds from below were intermittent: snatches of raucous laughter, the crack of an ax splitting a log, a few notes from a screechy fiddle, but nothing they heard or saw rivaled the smell of putrid rot. It was not possible to believe that any prize could be worth squatting in that dank mosquito-infested foulness; yet there they were, sounding almost merry. Skipjack signaled, his men turned and slipped back down ridge.

Tired of beans, Billy snatched up his shotgun and started drawing beads on every odd splotch that broke through the woods. Marcie, absorbed with private rhythms, was snapping beans, almost completely lost within mindless harmonies and unaware of Billy's gun barrel chasing a mockingbird's swoop until he swung under her nose and said, "Boom! Gotcha!"

Awakened from reverie, she looked into Billy's startled eyes, realizing her guardian was only a boy and said, "Put that gun up where it belongs. Don't fool with that thing ever again. That's no toy."

"Daddy said I was to protect you."

"You do as I say," Marcie said, more with glance than voice, which though sharp, was steady and calm. "Put it up. I'll be all right and if you don't do as I say, you won't be, understand?"

The boy nodded.

"This is our secret. Don't tell your dad and I won't either. Never point a gun unless you aim to kill. Now go feed Gracie. Go!"

Billy looked down, his shotgun pointed safely away.

"You know better, Billy, especially now. Feed Gracie then come back out here."

Marcie took a deep breath and exhaled. She cupped her swelling breast and stared down the dusty lane. She prayed for peace, then hung her head as tears filled her eyes and slid down her cheeks. The boy called Gracie. The dog barked. She decided that the rest of the beans could rot. Just to put these extras back in the springhouse required a damned key. She surprised herself when she thought that and was even more disconcerted as she attempted to open the door with both hands full, realizing she had left her rifle leaning against the house. This time she blew out her breath and called Billy. Before he answered, she managed to apologize to the Lord for taking his name in vain. Jangled and juggling too many thoughts, she slammed the bowls on the table. Billy walked in belting his pants, eyes wide.

"What's the matter?" he asked.

Marcie started crying and pointed at the front door.

"Don't ask questions; just get my rifle off the porch. Thank you."

Billy gave a stern look that seemed to project into manhood. He nodded, but then consternation softened into confusion that erased worry lines that for an instant had aged him.

"Please, young man, just do it," she said gently, and the boy grinned, eager to please.

"Somebody's coming downhill, Momma. I hear 'em," he said in an edgy whisper.

Marcie looked out the back door and saw her husband and the rest of the men.

"It's your dad, Billy. It's all right; just get in here."

The air had become so close that clothing clung. Marcie wished she could strip naked and summon a breeze. Instead, knowing men would be thirsty, she grabbed up a pitcher and her bowl of beans and the blasted key, headed out to the springhouse for some cool beer. Skipjack took the key with a wink. Clay grabbed the bowl. Skipjack popped the lock and took the bowl from Clay, handed Marcie the key, and reached out for the pitcher.

"Let me do this, honey," he said. "Go sit and rest."

"I'll get down glasses for the men."

"And I'll break out that bottle of wine you've been saving," he replied.

"Are you sure that's wise, Jack?"

"Hell no, not sure of one thing except it's likely a long night. Hotter than Hades and we might as well be comfortable. You might send Billy out with the other pitcher, come to think."

———

Beer and wine helped at first. The men discussed plans of attack, but only in the vaguest terms. Clay, for example, wanted to blast the skiff with his cannon. Brawl smiled and said he could concoct some special nail kegs. The stone carver waved his arms and, with Brawl's help, made it clear that he could blast a few large boulders down onto the camp.

All of them looked at Skipjack as they tossed ideas, but although he wanted to engage, he somehow couldn't share their enthusiasm.

First, he thought it was because Marcie and Billy were listening, then thought it might be the heat. The sky was darkening, and he could hear thunder far to the south. You could cut the air with a knife. Suddenly, he snapped into focus. He knew two things: he wanted a strong drink of whiskey and he needed to be alone.

Brawl could sometimes read Skipjack like a book. This was one of those times.

"Why don't all of us load into my wagon and let this family have a moment to themselves. What you say, Skipjack? We'll meet back at five like we planned."

"Amen, Brawl," Marcie said softly.

Skipjack nodded. "Clay, perhaps you could stop by the tavern and have Mary Frances send food. No need for Marcie to be over a stove."

"I can help. Can I go, too?"

"Son, if Mr. Clay will keep his eye on you, you can."

As the big old wagon jostled away downhill, Billy turned and flashed a grin. Skipjack turned to Marcie and searched her eyes.

"Hard to believe?"

"Even the sky is grumbling," Skipjack said when he sat beside Marcie.

"We need the rain, honey. Don't be mad at me, Jack, but with what you're fixing to do, you best watch the drinking."

"I'll be fine; you know me."

"Jack, it's not every day you're called to kill your brother."

"True enough."

"You know if there was another way, I would be begging you take it."

"A big part wishes you could," Skipjack replied.

"So we could get riled up, you saying there's no choice and stomping around?"

"No point, is there?"

Marcie touched Skipjack's hand, then stroked his cheek and neck.

"I thank God for your touch, Marcie. This stuff gnaws; makes me feel sick and empty."

"He brought this on himself. What part did you invite?"

"No part. I never run him off, though I would have done worse had I known."

"You can't blame yourself for not knowing. Can you stop the storm that's brewing?"

"Not in a million years."

"We got good folks on our side, Jack. We're doing what needs to be."

"Sick about it."

"Who could love you if you weren't? Wickedness is poison, Jack. When the time comes, you'll feel different. Don't forget there's a lot at stake," Marcie added, patting her belly.

———————

A bit later, Marcie slipped out onto the front porch to retrieve Skipjack's glass when she spotted a strange little man parting brush on the creek side of the woods downhill. He parted tall grass, crouched like a wild creature surveying the layout. His eyes roved over her but did not linger; their cold indifference made her shudder. Without looking again, she picked up her husband's glass and tiptoed back inside.

"Jack, someone's here," she hissed, unaware that Jack was standing right beside her staring at the same man. He put his hand on her shoulder. Marcie, startled by his comforting gesture, twitched and splashed the drink full in his face. He chuckled, as she trembled and faced him.

"That's Trapper. He's one of us. Don't worry."

Marcie buried her face in Skipjack's chest. He watched Trapper slink up the slope through tall amber grasses and late summer weeds. "Everything's all right, believe me. Everything's fine."

Suddenly Trapper ducked and peered down the lane. Skipjack grabbed Marcie's rifle, stepped onto the porch and called out to

Trapper as Brawl's wagon pulled clear of the woods and began the ascent into the yard.

"Trapper. Trapper, it's all right. Come on."

The sweet aroma of apple-smoked pork wafted across the porch the same instant Van Nutt's foot hit the first step. His utter lack of personal hygiene contributed to the afternoon's pungency and left Skipjack with no choice but to throw back his head and laugh aloud.

"Yes, sir, I'm here all right, yes, sir! Just like I said. I'm here at five o'clock, sure 'nuff."

"Trapper, you are indeed," Skipjack exclaimed. He waved at Brawl, then at Green, whose team was hauling him and three other men up the hill. Skipjack's skin tingled head to toe. The sight of Bill with his clenched fist upraised and the strong faces of men looking down from the wagon, Trapper's 'yes sirs,' even the jangle of harness and the approaching thunder filled him to overflowing. When he squeezed Marcie to him, he meant it from the bottom of his soul. Everyone present witnessed that, and when all eyes met, something of value was unmistakably added.

"Let's eat," Billy hollered. "Momma, I made the potatoes."

Lightning flashed and a few seconds later, the sky crackled menacingly. At least, that's the way Billy heard it, so he corrected himself.

"All except for putting them in and taking them out; Mary Frances wouldn't let me go near the oven."

"Come on let's eat 'fore it gets cold," Skipjack said.

"Nothing's getting cold in this heat, honey," Marcie said.

"Well then, let's eat before it gets wet. Appears we're going to have some rain."

———

Trapper stayed to the side, but all the other men crowded the middle of the front porch. The only other exception was Green, who had followed the food inside. He handed Skipjack a jug and suggested he pour out a few shots.

"You have to try it, if I do say so myself."

Skipjack nodded, then asked Billy where Mary Frances was. He handed Green two glasses, then turned his full attention to the boy.

"She said she's swamped with supper. She said Andy and her would be up after a while."

Skipjack wanted both of them there right then but didn't want to signal that. Instead, he studied the boy's earnest face, put his hand on his head, and asked, "So you made the potatoes?"

"I even used the knife this time and she taught me to sharpen it, too."

"They smell great, son," Skipjack said as Green handed him a glass of whiskey and grinned.

"Try that and you'll know why I'm the number-one purveyor. There's none better."

"Jack, get some beer for the men and hand down those plates, if you please."

A bolt of lightning smacked into a tree up the hill and its blue/white light seared the room. Billy jumped, Green slurped down his whiskey and Skipjack placed his drink on the table and did what he was told.

"Ain't you going to take a sip?"

"More than that, after this is over. Come on, Green, help me here."

"I'm trying, dad burn it."

"Then spread out these plates so Marcie can load 'em, while I go out back and fetch us some beer."

Green frowned but did what he was told right after he took another nip.

———————

By eight o'clock, they were all of a mind to tear sunset out of the sky. There had been a downpour with thunder and lightning, but then sun blazed through, trailing purple clouds and coaxing steamy air out of sodden ground, humidity spiraling like smoke. There were hours to fill before time to strike.

Marcie lit pitch pots to repel mosquitoes. Skipjack told stories to drive away drinks. He knew as well as Marcie did that too much booze would lead to disaster. The plan was loose but forming. Trapper was already snooping the creek. Bandits often swooped out to prowl after dusk, so Trapper had set out just before. He was to report back in a few hours. Privately, he told Skipjack that about a half dozen runaway hunters were eager to wipe out these double-dealing river pirates. Skipjack had inquired if they were available this evening. Trapper didn't know, but he knew they were in the area and vowed to find out. If he found them in time, he told Skipjack, he would plant them on the opposite side of the creek.

"Hates each other, yes, sir. Robbing the same nest, same nest. Only ones these bastards won't kill is slaves, yes, sir."

"If you can find those bastards, Trapper, plant 'em downstream or I'm liable to shoot 'em myself," Skipjack said. "I can't abide those folks."

"At least they don't steal chickens and hogs or butcher beef in the field. No sir, at least, not that."

Trapper planned to be back within two hours. The idea was to attack between one and two. A deep purple sky was rumbling. Heat lightning scoured the horizon. The air was still heavy as damp wool, but surprisingly, the men's spirits were upbeat. They loaded Clay's cannon into the small wagon beside Brawl's nail keg surprises. Strong hot breezes swirled as the men settled down on the porch. The stone-cutters produced a bottle of wine and, with Brawl's help, attempted to teach Tom to say hello, thank you, and good-bye in Italian.

With Marcie's help, Skipjack scurried a reluctant Billy to bed. Prepared to offer the moon for sleep, he was pleasantly surprised when the boy sighed into his pillow. Marcie coaxed her man with languorous glances and a gentle touch up to their bedroom. She peered into his eyes, then seemed to float back toward the bed.

"Don't rush it, honey. Bide your time," she whispered.

"Are you all right? You know I'm with you?"

Marcie brushed Skipjack's lips with hers. He remarked that he hadn't shaved yet. She nodded and squeezed his hand, "God be with you."

"I'll be back."

"We're counting on that."

"Mary Frances and Andy will be here directly. You won't be alone."

"Be careful."

"I'll come back up before we set out. They'll be gone by morning time."

———

Skipjack's pocket watch showed twelve thirty; Trapper had still not returned. A steady rain fell; thunder boomed north and south, but only hollow crackling echoed overhead. Brawl announced something was coming up the road. Lightning jiggled glistening space for an instant, but long enough for Green to declare, "It's your man, that trapper fellow."

"We're set, we're set up on the other side," Trapper said. "Don't be firing across the creek. Crossfire. Crossfire." Trapper emphasized his words, nodding, his eyes bulging.

"You know what's happening at their camp?" Green asked.

"There's some there, but most of 'em out. Out messing the river. Gotta be careful; they mess land, too."

"Not where we are. Too damn steep. When you think they'll join up?"

"Hard to say, can't say exactly. Normal, come back a few hours before light. I'd give it two hours 'fore I climbed. Course, nobody could say. They smoking something stinks like hell."

"Where across the creek you gonna be?" Skipjack asked.

"Downstream half a stretch. I end up there. See, I paddle down like usual. Just like usual and you hear me singing to God Almighty. You hear me singing, you know it's time. Say, Mr. Maddox, you got a shot a whiskey handy? My pipes is raw, sir."

Skipjack sent Trapper off with a bottle of whiskey, which seemed to make everyone else a little thirsty, too. He cracked out another and passed it around. The whiskey was Green's and Green bragged on it until Skipjack wished he'd kept it in the cupboard. With almost two hours to go before they rolled, he was worried his crew might be wobbly. Spirits seemed high among the men, so he wondered if it was only him wrestling dread and nausea.

As soon as Mary Frances and Andy arrived, Skipjack led her to the first curve at the crest of the hill. She would watch the front. Andy was up behind the house. No one was getting in. Still, no matter how he looked at it—the right and wrong, or even the obvious need—there was nothing in the damned mess he wanted. He needed Brother gone. That was fact. Did he want to kill him? In place of an answer, his bowels wrenched. He could find no wisdom to make it right, and here he sat, missing the punchline of some dumb joke Green had told, that even Italians apparently seemed to understand.

Finally, he raised his hand and excused himself. Clay shook his head and placed his forefinger on his lips. All eyes turned to him. Clay sat stone still. When Skipjack's footsteps could be heard nearing the stair top outside the bedroom door, Clay leaned forward and whispered, "It's a family thing."

The Italian stonemasons did not fully understand, until Brawl translated quietly behind a cupped hand and hugged Tom Thurston. Then everyone nodded, and lantern light flickered on shut eyelids and bowed foreheads moving slowly side to side.

"But they've tried to kill us," young Tom said in a voice sharp with anger.

Everyone nodded, but no one answered. Eventually Tom stared silently into the lantern glowing, puzzled by moths fascinated by flame. But there was nothing more to be said and Tom began to know that as Brawl rested a soft heavy palm on his knee.

———

Skipjack tiptoed into the room and sat quietly on the overstuffed armchair beside the washstand. He needed some quiet; Marcie's steady breathing and the gentle rain sounds seemed to slow things. He took out a cigar, chewed on it, and then leaned back into the hard steel of Marcie's rifle.

"Jack," Marcie said softly. "Why don't you sit here? You know I'm not asleep."

Skipjack moved beside her and placed his hand on her shoulder.

"I know what you're thinking, honey, and yes, we can handle this."

"How can we do this?" Skipjack whispered hoarsely.

"Putting a stop to it, Jack. That's what you're doing. Don't lose sight."

"No other way, is there?"

A thunderbolt exploded right overhead. Their eyes locked in the cold electric flash, then their fingers adjusted toward comfort as trailers of thunder roiled through pitch-dark sky.

"Stay here with me," Marcie whispered.

"Guess I better get back to the men."

"Mary Frances and Andy here?"

"She's downhill; he's up above."

"Come get me when it's time. I'll be ready; just need to rest."

"Me, too," Skipjack said, wishing he hadn't.

"Of course, you do. God knows you deserve it."

"I'll be back after a while," he said as they gently unlaced their fingers.

"Watch the booze, Jack. Sounds like the men are getting rowdy."

Skipjack heard Green bellowing and Brawl's infectious laughter imitating the rumbling heavens. "I'll keep an eye on 'em," he said, pulling the door shut. At the bottom of the stairs, Billy sat with his shotgun across his knees, looking over his shoulder.

"What you doing, boy?"

"Can't sleep."

"Too noisy? I'll tell the men to hold it down."

"It's not that. It's everything. Not one thing."

Skipjack sat on the step beside the boy and didn't say a word. He hunched there and tried to focus on rain. Shadows from the lantern danced on walls.

"Billy, I need your help and I'm counting on it."

"I want to go uphill, too," the boy implored.

"I need you here to look after Mother. Don't let any harm come, understand?"

After a moment's hesitation, Billy looked Skipjack square in the eye and nodded.

"Try to rest. I've got to see to our men."

CHAPTER 10

TRAPPER'S SCREECHING SONG OF PRAISE

efore setting out, Skipjack had Billy take jars of water to both Mary Frances and Andy. He chained Gracie to her hook in the stable and half seriously asked her to keep an eye on things. Rain showers arrived in waves, some noisy and some not. Jessie was hitched to the small wagon that would haul Clay's cannon and Brawl's nail barrel surprises. That part worried Skipjack. The damn wagon was squeaky, and the trail was slick. As sure-footed and calm as Jessie was, Skipjack wasn't comfortable. They needed stealth. They didn't need squawk and rattle.

But it worked out fine. Maybe the booze even helped a bit. Slowly, carefully, they ascended the ridge. The lantern glow at the front and back of the house dissolved into darkness as the sounds the men made seemed to blend into rain and rolling grumble. Skipjack led the way. Green strode right beside him, quietly coaxing Jessie. Brawl and Tom walked at her flanks. Two stone carvers and Clay brought up the rear. Illumination was flickering lightning.

Near the top of the ridge, still several hundred yards from their destination, the rim of the rear wagon wheel hub jammed in a limestone outcropping. With a tap and a nudge, the wagon lurched forward, and the stone carvers grinned. Along the ridge, they moved at a snail's pace. The storm noise provided cover. Though the leaves sheltered them from much of the downpour, they were drenched to the bone. Lightning and thunder drove them the last hundred yards, and then right at the top of the cliff overlooking the smudge of coals in the fire pit below, the storm abruptly ceased and was no louder than raindrops pattering leaf to leaf. Skipjack quickly removed Jessie's harness. He snatched a rope out of the wagon, led the mule away, and tied her to a sapling. He stroked her soft muzzle, then rubbed her with his forehead.

The Italians blocked the wagon wheels with stone, then helped unload the cannon. Brawl and Tom rolled barrel surprises to the edge of the drop-off. The moonlight that revealed these nearly silent movements was scant and not steady; clouds swirled, broke, then gathered.

At least ground is soft, Skipjack thought and suddenly realized that they had no real plan. Clay was busy on an outcrop toying with his cannon, and ten paces over, Brawl and Tom positioned barrels not all that quietly. Green tapped Skipjack on the shoulder and he flinched. Green motioned with his head and a slight hiss. Skipjack followed him until they stood next to Jessie.

"I know this must be a terrible strain," Green whispered, "but hold tight, old man. They won't know what hit 'em."

"But how's it going to work?"

"All you got to do is shoot, Skipjack. The dagos are doing the lion's share. Good chunks of rock are coming down that cliff. They're setting charges now. Brawl and Tom are the introduction. Clay and then Trapper across the way will provide the grand finale. There won't be nothing left. Just relax."

"Where have I been, Green? When did you work this out?"

"Didn't exactly. Be calm. We got waiting ahead."

Andy was thinking about freedom. The word roused him, but as he stared through shimmering greenery into diffused light from the cabin, he was positively baffled. He knew he wanted no boss. He wanted Lacy. He wanted to stand tall and say put this here, put this there. He knew that much. But how could he be like Brawl or Mr. Maddox, for that matter? It was confusing. Here he was protecting a man's place, a man who for a handful of days and dollars owned him, due to some arrangement with a man of his own damn color who had bought and sold him. And he wanted to be like that? He wanted to run a human livery stable? Not likely; but how to avoid it?

Should he work for Skipjack Maddox? Should he try to figure some deal with Brawl? Was there something he was missing?

His skin chilled. Something was moving, or was it?

———

Loneliness didn't often occur to Mary Frances. Work and husband kept her plenty in company. She had vowed until death do us part and meant it but had never imagined the life this vow would lead her to. "Long-suffering" was the way she was seen. She knew Skipjack and Marcie saw it that way. Tonight, darkness she stared into at least held promise of excitement. Chanting, droning insects and intermittent dripping leaves were at least neutral. They were what they were without accusation or bitter insinuation. Miserable in the damp, she was somehow performing an appreciated function. If she lived and Skipjack lived, there would be some small reward. The rustling she heard that raised the hair on her neck could be potentially settled, what she had to face every night at home could not. She only wondered how long it would be before she could sit and drink a cool glass of beer and maybe even smoke a cigar without the necessary compliance to her poor man's tyrannical helplessness.

"Billy, it's important to keep low and not tarry in front of windows. Don't you shoot at anything unless you see close and clear."

Marcie extinguished all lamps. Two candles were lit: one in the front room, one in the kitchen.

"Billy, did you hear what I told you?"

"Yes, ma'am."

Billy was sulking. Marcie understood. He felt he should be on the hill with the men. Nothing to do about that. What she feared most was a stray bullet. She lit one of her husband's stubbed cigars. Billy gave a funny look.

"You smoking? Why are you smoking, Momma?"

"To calm myself. I'm nervous is why. Are you?"

"Just a little," Billy admitted. "But ain't there some other way?"

"Maybe so. Want to try?" The boy nodded. "Come sit yourself on the sofa and I'll put this thing out. Maybe sitting still with you beside will ease me some."

"Well, we can try, Momma. I sure don't like to see smoke coming out of your mouth. Makes you scary."

Marcie laid the cigar in the ashtray and patted the sofa cushion. The boy walked over and sat. Marcie pointed to the shotgun the boy cradled, then pointed at the floor. She placed her rifle at her feet.

"We know where if we need them."

The boy nodded and gently lowered his gun. His eyes studied hers, until he nestled back.

"Do you feel better now, Momma?"

"A little. Do you?"

"I'm not so sure yet. Just don't smoke no more. You don't look like yourself."

"Anymore, Billy. Don't smoke anymore."

The boy nodded.

"You think we're going to be all right, don't you?"

"I believe we're fixed to be. Somehow, I feel a little calmer, thanks to you."

The boy leaned closer.

"If I'm helping, I don't know how."

"Just breathe easy. Don't know why, but it helps."

"I'll be right here."

Rain clattered the roof and windowpanes. Suddenly it seemed almost peaceful. Breezy bursts provided innocuous sound cover; however, that worked both ways. Marcie crossed her fingers. She thought a silent prayer. Embarrassed, she uncrossed her fingers and then almost knocked on wood before she snatched the cigar back out of the ashtray. Marcie took a deep breath, then put the cigar back. She stubbed it out and watched smoke thinly snake and swirl in the candle's pale light.

Staying dry was not an option. As night deepened, intermittent showers strengthened. On the bluff, there wasn't much to think about. Water either poured through leaves or dripped. The sting of autumn pierced damp clothing as the breeze shifted and blew straight south.

Skipjack signaled Green, then walked to the wagon. He struck a match and checked his timepiece. He allowed himself a few puffs off his stogie. It was close to two. Skipjack reached beneath the seat of the wagon, lifted out a jug, and lugged it back to the hunkered-down men.

He drank first, then passed. Only Tom refused. Green made the jug gurgle. Suppressed laughter was masked by whispering leaves. Smiles looked more like grimaces. Skipjack nodded and made a thumbs-up sign.

"Holy Father, Father of all creation, precious Savior of my salvation . . ."

"Jesus Christ above, whatever is that?" Clay whispered.

Skipjack raised both hands and grinned as he motioned for the men to lean in closer.

"Oh yes, Gawd in great gloree! Hung on a tree for meee!"

Some of the men were holding their ears, so that Skipjack found himself waving his hands up and down and shaking his head.

"Listen to me," he hissed, "that's Trapper. That's our signal. They're just about here. Now be easy and take your places."

From below in darkness, a discordant chorus competed with Trapper's screeching song of praise. Obscene responses were swallowed by the elements and barely dinged Trapper's sharp-edged falsetto. His amen was so intensely spine tingling it seemed to lance thunder applauding a damn close lightning strike.

"Keep your heads," Skipjack said. Two Italians disappeared over the hill. Clay was a shimmering blur down ridge, hunched low. Tom was crouched a few yards closer. Suddenly Green and Brawl were on either side of him, holding his elbows. They eased him down. Skipjack didn't resist.

"Stay back," Green whispered as Brawl kept firm pressure on Skipjack's elbow. "Ease back now. All you got to do is shoot. We got this covered."

Skipjack nodded, but his mind was near blank.

"Step back, sir, and sit tight," Brawl said. "Mr. Green will give the word."

As Brawl led Skipjack to the wagon, the discordant chorus below raucously strained into the rain, as Trapper's voice pierced everything. He was now sawing away at "Rock of Ages." Brawl pushed Skipjack down.

"Stay put. I'll tell you when," Brawl said.

Skipjack discovered he was wobbly. The fingers that clutched his rifle were almost numb. He found it helpful to close one eye to articulate shapes folding and stretching down his sightline. Trapper howled "Cleft for meee!" and that gave way to cursing and yelps from below the cliff. Leaves reflecting bonfire light went from yellow green to smudgy orange as Trapper launched into "Amazing Grace." The first bit was almost near drowned out by the melee below, but then his voice sliced through like sleet through rain: "That saved a wretch like meee. Aaahh once was lost but now am found, was blind, but now aaahh seeee!"

Instead of holding his ears, Skipjack shook the cobwebs out of his head. It must have been a spell, he thought as Trapper's voice stopped without echo. The clamoring men below seemed to momentarily respect newfound silence, but then within seconds, one of the men farted loudly and either he or a compatriot hurled a foul oath. There were a few preliminary chuckles, and then, accompanying a heavenly rumble, a guttural thump shook the cliff side. Brawl was waving to stay down, as another concussion rolled the ground. To Skipjack, it was slow motion as he saw trees arc across his line of sight and fall forward with the solid masses that had held them. The ground trembled. He stooped low, moved forward, and heard crashing and splintering like muted thunder and then two thuds, and beside him high-pitched laughter almost like screaming. Off to his right, he heard a grunt, then a sound like loud rain, then saw sparkle of fuse sputtering, then flashing and another burst of rain. He realized the rain sounds were buckets of rocks pelting down. He heard the sound of shooting spark across the creek; then saw a flash of fire and felt a convulsive explosion, followed by a blast of smoky heat and blinding light on the near bank. To his left, he saw a fuse lit, then another. Both lights disappeared. There was one explosion, not especially loud. Brawl cursed as Skipjack knelt beside him.

Skipjack fired at a glimmering shape running past the flaming skiff. A bullet ricocheted off a rock directly beneath his feet, and Skipjack fired at a spot where he had seen a quick flash, but it was impossible to see clearly. There were intermittent popping sounds downstream. The skiff was ablaze. One large boulder had crashed the fire pit, throwing sparks, smoke, and fire. There was stunned silence; no human sounds above or below.

Nothing but stench and acrid smoke. The men stood where the huge boulders had been, looking down, but there was nothing to see, nothing to hear. Eyes were burning, throats raw with thirst. Rain marched in with vengeance. Silently, they reloaded the hot slippery cannon into the wagon. The men who weren't riding held on. Jessie was the sure-footed one that knew the way home.

None could know what, if anything, had been accomplished. Boulders had been blown loose and crashed down; Tom Thurston's rocks surely had hit something. One of Brawl's nail kegs had exploded and the other may have hit someone. Clay had destroyed the skiff. They had all got off a few rounds, but no one had seen anyone fall. Storm and smoke had shrouded it all. Plodding home, no one felt especially safe or exhilarated. They all had listened for survivors, in fact, continued to do so, but nothing was audible except strained wagon complaints, muffled by the rain.

Before the incline down, Skipjack took control, braked the rig, and everyone climbed out. He wasn't about to let Jessie bear the brunt on slippery uneven ground. He walked at her head, relieved when Andy stood and said, "No problems here, sir." Skipjack gently punched Andy's shoulder and sighed as he saw the faint glow in the windowpanes downhill.

———

At the back door, Marcie jumped at Skipjack's neck and kissed him again and again. Then shed him and hollered for Mary Frances.

"Don't you want to open the front door, Marcie?"

"I sure do. Oh, I'm so glad you're safe. Mary Frances? Mary Frances?"

"Just open the door, Marcie, and then call out," Skipjack said.

But before she could, all the men and Mary Frances walked in.

"Damn, you people got no thought for nobody," she said. "Crank up the heat and pour out some brandy."

Marcie stoked the cook stove and Skipjack lit a fire in the fireplace. Soon ham was sizzling, lanterns were glowing, and brandy, wine, whiskey, and hot coffee were being joyously consumed. All were more than a little glad to be out of the weather. Rain drummed the roof.

"This keeps up, whatever is left will be washed to the river," Green said.

"Long as they're gone."

"You think they are?" Marcie asked.

"Hard to say."

Everybody nodded.

"Could anybody see anything at all?" Skipjack asked.

"I'm damn sure I saw one man fall," Clay said.

"I heard a woman scream," Tom said.

"I thought I did, too," Clay said, "but couldn't tell you what it meant. Sounded like a curse more than anything."

"Couldn't see a dern thing, Miss Marcie; bound to have got some."

"We'll know more when it's light," Skipjack said.

One of the stonemasons was asleep by the hearth and the other, who was seated beside him, was pointing at him and laughing. Skipjack offered him a bottle of wine. The man grinned from ear to ear.

"Where's Billy, Marcie?"

"He's in his room. Went there as soon as you all pulled up; he wanted to be up the hill."

"Did he stay right with you?"

Marcie nodded. "He was a comfort, too."

Skipjack glanced at the men, then went down the short hall to Billy's door and knocked. He was sitting on his bed with his shotgun across his knees. He looked up expectantly, then slumped away.

Skipjack sat beside the boy but didn't touch him and listened to the rain with no idea what to say. Mary Frances was laughing, insisting she could beat eggs about as good as anybody. Brawl chortled. Skipjack looked at his timepiece. It was four o'clock in the morning.

"Son, I want to thank you for taking care of your mother."

"All I did was sit on the sofa."

"Well, all I did was stand in the rain. You did what was needed. That's what counts."

Skipjack could see tears on the boy's cheeks.

"Your job was as important as anybody's and I mean it. I honestly didn't know if they were going to hit us here again or not. You were probably in more danger than you know. I am proud of you and grateful."

The boy looked up, then looked quickly down and started to wipe his cheek with his sleeve.

"Give a hug, boy. I need a hug."

Skipjack pulled the boy's face into the front of his shirt. He pressed on the back of Billy's head so that when he led him back there would be no trace of tears.

"Bring your shotgun if you want but come out and eat."

"I don't want to."

"Why not, Billy? You're one of us, aren't you?"

The boy thought for a moment, then nodded.

"Well, come on then. Second thought: stash that gun. We've had enough guns."

"Can I put it under the bed?"

"It's your gun, ain't it?"

The boy knelt down, shuffled some things around under the bed, then gently placed the shotgun, still cocked, on the floor, stood and smiled.

"What else you got under there, young man?"

"Just stuff, nothing much; my shotgun is the main thing, I guess."

———

Rain fell hard until first light, then slacked off. Green had wanted to head home, but Brawl, Clay, and Skipjack dissuaded him. It wasn't fear of surviving thieves that had stopped him, though that was one argument; rather he had been convinced that his good judgment and marksmanship would be vital when the camp was surveyed in morning light. That and a full glass of un-watered whiskey had sealed the deal; soon after Green dozed off. He and the stonemason had alternated entertaining snorts and snores.

When sun broke through, Marcie and Mary Frances were pouring coffee, slicing bacon, mixing up corn bread, cracking eggs. Men were straggling back and forth from the outhouse. Billy let Gracie out the front door and she tore down the hill barking like crazy.

"Someone's coming up," he shouted.

Clay picked up a rifle and pulled the boy back inside. He peered through the window beside the door.

"That's the trapper fellow, don't you think so, Brawl?"

Tom had a look.

"That's him and he looks to be bleeding."

A few moments later, Trapper was inside. Turns out one of his own had shot his earlobe off. The bullet had grazed his cheek as well.

"Damn lucky, I say damn lucky. No two ways about it, no, sir. I'm lucky!"

Skipjack had to laugh to look at the man, so full of pluck and looking like hell. He wasn't only bloody; he was soaked and muddy. But his eyes sparkled, and in his own foul unkempt way, he stood there noble and proud.

"What have you got to report, my friend?"

"God knows for sure, I don't. We fired into 'em, but who could see anything? Rain and smoke. Smokey mess, yes, sir. I'm telling you what. Nothing living, nobody, nothing living come by us. No, sir."

"So you couldn't see anything?" Skipjack asked.

"Saw the skiff blow to blazes, then nothing. After your blasted cannon. After that," Trapper said, "I was most all alone. That blast changed my side considerable. Folks scattered like mice. Yes, sir, sure did."

"Saw nobody come downstream?" Green asked.

"Nothing, not even dead. No, sir."

"Come have some coffee," Skipjack suggested. "Maybe you will join us when we go have a look."

"Do I smell fatback?"

"Trapper, would you take a spot of whiskey?"

"Only if you is."

———————

Curiosity drew them forward. Although they were armed, none of them expected to encounter anyone. Skipjack had left Marcie in the care of Andy and Mary Frances. Until they reached the easy path down to creek bottomland, Billy was allowed to lead. Once they started down the incline, which sloped gently at this point, Skipjack, using the back of his hand, passed Billy back so that he was soon between Green and Brawl. Tom Thurston was flanked by the two Italians. Clay brought up the rear.

As they approached the camp, sunshine glinted off leaves and the air was already warming. Skipjack crouched. He wiggled his finger, and everyone drew near.

"Step softly. Careful now."

He winked at Brawl. Billy found himself restrained by the stone carvers. Tom stopped as Clay flashed a grin at him. Clay then moved forward so that Tom hovered over them all. One of the Italians relieved Billy of his shotgun and then turned, joined Tom, and faced the rear.

As Skipjack and the rest of the crew stalked and slid down the bank of slick dark mud, a smudge of dank smoke tickled their lungs, yet no one coughed. Billy watched them disappear into undergrowth and smoke, only then did he realize both of his hands were empty.

"Come on down," Skipjack called out.

Billy shrugged forward. The two men restrained him. Then both Green and Skipjack repeated this directive simultaneously. Billy found himself barely touching ground as the stone carvers floated him downhill.

Sunlight was erasing deep shadow. Billy could see Skipjack beside a boulder at least twice his height, signaling to Clay, who was on the creek bank slicing a hemp rope still cleated to what remained of the skiff. The creek was rolling out. When Clay cut the taut line through, the shattered bow was sucked into the torrent then spun downstream.

Billy saw caramel-colored water lapping at the banks. Skipjack, Clay, and Green were probing undergrowth. Brawl sauntered over to one giant boulder that had smoke seeping around it, bent down for a close look, then turned and hollered at Skipjack.

"We got one at least."

"Here's one, yes, sir. There's one right here hugging this sycamore, sure is," Trapper called out. "Could be a runaway, black as pitch."

"This one sure ain't your brother," Brawl said, as he bent down and studied the mud and ash beside one of the dislodged boulders. "All I see is a hand. But this hand's done worked. It ain't your brother, for certain."

The sky grumbled and then once again, rain poured down, slightly diminishing the rank smell that made Billy's eyes crinkle. He couldn't understand what they were doing down here. He knew one thing for sure, he wanted to get home. There was nothing but stench and rocks, broken stuff and mud. He looked up the cliff right above the two places that looked raw and different; he thought he saw something duck behind a tree. But wasn't sure, so he looked side to side and then at the creek slashing past. Skipjack was on the bank pointing at something he wanted Clay to see. Billy happened to look back up and saw a man aiming a rifle.

"Get down!" he screamed and pulled with such conviction the two stone carvers sank with him.

Cottonwood bark erupted right above Skipjack's head. The slap of the slug seemed louder than the rifle that delivered it. Billy pointed up at the spot where he had seen the man, but there was nothing, only wisps of smoke.

"Get next to the cliff, Billy."

When the boy hesitated, Skipjack sloshed over and pointed at the base of the cliff. His face looked fierce, but then he winked.

"We best get back to the house," Clay said.

"Hard to tell what we did," Green said.

"No telling, no telling."

"Found my damn barrel that didn't explode. The thing busted to pieces."

Tom laughed. "But one blew up; there's nails all over the place."

"We better get home," Skipjack said. "Got a couple."

———————

As they wound their way up to high ground, Billy looked back to see puddles forming where he had stood, then saw those puddles grow larger and pool to become a stream glazing everything. He was now carrying his own gun again, careful to keep it pointed down. But part of him was confused, part disappointed. He had hoped to fire at something but now wasn't so sure. Everything seemed bleary and stupid. He was cold, but the air was sort of warm. He was shivering but knew he was sweating.

Careful not to snap branches back, Skipjack slogged the path that hugged through shack-sized chunks of limestone that seemed randomly placed on the steep incline. When they finally reached the crest-view trail, he looked down on swirling water, and realized he had hoped for more than what they had found. All he could report to Marcie was that the squatters weren't there. But where they were was anyone's guess and that thought was far from comforting.

Rain was now slashing straight down and the path at their feet turned into a small gushing creek. Visibility was so poor that Skipjack contemplated firing a couple of rounds to alert Andy that they were near. But then, two shots rang out from downhill; small-bore pistol shots, which sounded like flat sticks slapping. Without urging, everyone hurried along.

They found Andy face down across the path. Skipjack took one look at him, and sure that he was dead, urged Brawl to check and charged to his house. Clay and Tom followed halfway.

"Keep your eye on the hill," Clay admonished as he watched Skipjack pound on the door. He seemed to pound forever, the sound muffled by downpour. Then the door opened, and Marcie stood there.

"Get here now!"

Everybody started slipping and sliding down the trail. Green and one of the Italians dragged poor Andy, who groaned when they banged his head against the corner of the springhouse. It was such a welcome sound that they all rediscovered laughter as they neared the back stoop—soaked, muddy, bloody, but joyous. Nobody knew how badly Andy was hurt. But no one was dead. They knew that.

Skipjack ran out front and called for Mary Frances. It took three loud shouts before she appeared, walking uphill slowly like rain was nothing.

"You all right?" she asked.

He nodded. "Are you?"

"I got one," she said.

"Didn't hear shooting down this way."

"I sliced him."

"You what?"

"Sucker ducked in to watch but forgot to look where he ducked. Was this damn close," she said, as she raised her hands to the width of her shoulders. "There's more out there, I'm afraid."

"Where is he?"

"Right where you left me. I ain't no undertaker. He was a young un. All he had was this."

Skipjack had to laugh. It was the kind of pistol some dandy might choose. Its best feature was the pearl handle.

"Sort of felt sorry I done him when I seen this thing; only a shaver, but he was up to no good. He was aimed this way."

Skipjack hugged Mary Frances. She squinted and grinned.

"How did you come out?"

"Fair, I suppose. Andy's hurt. But how the hell did you do it?"

"Poke greens grow to have big broad leaves that ain't fit to eat; some say they poison. If you hide in 'em, I say they're deadly."

———

One ball had removed a nice chunk of scalp. The other was lodged beneath the skin of his right arm. Brawl and Green were holding Andy's arm steady. Tom held his legs, while Marcie opened the wound, dug in, and popped the thing. It rolled across the floor and stopped at Billy's feet. Gracie licked at it. Andy grimaced and moaned.

"Knew you were a hard head first time I seen you," Brawl chuckled. "Anybody else, we'd be planning a funeral."

Andy rolled his eyes and made a poor attempt at a grin.

"You'll be all right, Andy," Marcie said. "Hold him steady while I wash this out."

While Andy tried unsuccessfully not to struggle, Tom winked at Brawl.

"Damn good thing this table's sturdy."

"Hold the man," Brawl said. "No lip. Understand?"

Billy attempted to catch Tom's eyes, but they were closed, so he looked down at the dull chunk of metal at his feet. Skipjack placed his hand on Billy's shoulder and pulled him close.

———

Sun came out mid-afternoon, and so did the sheriff. Green, Brawl, and the stone carvers had left. Skipjack and Tom were discussing finishing touches for the front walk when Tom motioned with his head and Skipjack saw the lawman and one of his low-life deputies.

"Now, Tom, don't let the man trick you. No matter what they ask, don't say a thing. Get around back and tell Andy the same. Just shake your head. Don't say nothing, understand?"

Tom nodded, and Skipjack grimaced as Tom slunk toward the back just as the sheriff and his deputy were reining in.

"Been having a fine day, Maddox?" asked the sheriff.

"So far so good, and you?"

"Heard there was some disturbance. You look tired."

"Funny you should say, because I am right tired. Hardly slept a wink."

"Now, why might that be? Something I should know?"

"Not unless you like being bored. What brings you?"

"Nothing you will offer willingly, I suppose."

Skipjack scratched his head and peered at the deputy.

"Why won't you try? What do you need?"

"Mind if I have a look around?"

"Depends on where you want to look," Skipjack said with a grin

The deputy nodded vigorously. The sheriff blew out a deep sigh.

"I want to walk up behind your house and want to check the bottomland, too."

"You want me to hold your horses?"

"Who's inside the house?"

"My wife and my son."

"Who else?"

"You're amusing me, sheriff. Why not look? I give permission."

"Awful kind of you but, I don't need to ask."

"Then do your worst. The place is yours."

"What you got up your sleeve?"

"Tell me what you're after, sheriff. You'll make my job a little easier."

The sheriff and his deputy wandered up the hill muttering; then less than an hour later, they scuffled down the path again.

"Did you have good luck?"

The deputy scowled, and the sheriff sneered.

"You know you ain't right," the sheriff said. "I'm going to put my finger on it."

"So, what you aiming to put your finger on?"

"Every inch you standing on. This whole damn country's crazy. Mark my words."

"What you looking for, sheriff?"

"You know what you done."

"I do?"

"Don't push me, Maddox."

"Hard to push a man when you're holding his horse," Skipjack said.

CHAPTER 11

THE DIFFERENCE BETWEEN A THIMBLE AND A JIGGER

Marcie became prone to nightmares and at first, Skipjack had attempted to laugh her out from under them, but then he began to have them himself. Billy cried out one night and Skipjack slipped quietly downstairs to comfort him. Halfway down, stepping softly, he realized that he had forgotten his pistol. Then he opened his eyes and saw it was morning. Skipjack listened intently. All he heard was Marcie's breathing. He slipped out of bed and tiptoed to the stairway, listened again, realized he was soaked with sweat, and that he was still in bed. In the pitch dark, Skipjack reached for his pistol and placed the palm of his hand over the grip, then tucked the weapon beneath his pillow and summoned sleep. Morning's faint glow was welcome and so was Clay.

Clay stayed on for a few more days and Skipjack was grateful for his company. After dinner the night before he left, Skipjack offered to help re-crate the cannon. Clay chuckled and said there was no need.

"Least I could do."

"Two of my people are coming to pick me up; they'll do it."

"Don't tell me they're slaves?"

"I can't tell you they're not, but if you insist, I will," Clay replied.

"At least not mine, though under my yoke and I suppose my protection, too."

"I ain't clear. Shoot straight, Mr. Clay."

"Skipjack, I freed the ones that I personally owned about three years past. I had inherited them from my family. Some are with us still. I am the guardian of the estate; the few that remain are legally bound in a trust agreement to my family members, drawn up in Father's will. I can neither sell nor free them."

"That hardly makes sense."

"They are property, Skipjack. The law is the law. I am the trustee for a future generation. Unless God intervenes, they will inherit this nightmare."

"You're saying your hands are tied, but you're against it?"

"You know I am, but it has to be done right. Some of them are old; some are young. Some would maybe do all right. But at least I can feed them and give shelter. I can't afford to do that though unless they're productive."

"The cure is hard to figure. Makes you want to look the other way."

Clay nodded solemnly. "That's why it's called 'the peculiar institution.'"

"Sickening, ain't it?"

"We're hanging by threads, Skipjack. I pray Lincoln will prove a force for reason."

"You don't sound settled."

"Only the Almighty knows outcomes."

"Think there might be war?"

"I dread and fear it. I hate this business with my whole heart."

Skipjack studied Clay's face for some sign of hope. He saw courage, resignation, and pain. Clay's gaze was steady. Skipjack extended his hand. Clay clasped it with both of his.

"I know what you're about to say. There is no need to."

Skipjack hesitated before responding. "Let's have a taste before we lay it down."

"You'll fare all right, Skipjack," Clay said as they strolled into the kitchen.

"What do you mean?"

"You're on the border. If war breaks out, both sides will likely curry your favor. You may even prosper, my friend."

Skipjack turned suddenly and the strain he harbored sculpted his features. Clay stepped back a pace. Skipjack was surprised to feel his jaw tense. His eyes focused icily on Clay, who had both hands outstretched. Skipjack turned and poured two more shots of whiskey. He took a deep breath before he faced Clay.

"Skipjack, believe me, I intended no offense. It was an insensitive remark born of my concern for Marcie, yourself, Billy, and your unborn child. I simply meant that you and yours, including all of your crew, Mary Frances, Andy, and all, might have a good chance of making it through. God knows, that is all I meant."

Skipjack pushed the glass across the table, until it touched Clay's outstretched fingers.

"Hard to know what anything means. Could be asleep and dreaming for all I know."

Clay raised the glass and their eyes met above its rim. The two men tapped their glasses together.

"I suppose I missed your drift," Skipjack said.

"Maybe so, but I believe you thought I missed yours. I assure you, I did not."

They had to try to get life back to normal. The next morning, early, Skipjack dressed and was almost out the door to the tavern, when Marcie asked him if he had heard that Billy's new teacher was a Roman Catholic.

"Can the man teach sums? Can he read?"

"Some of the women are worried. I'm not. Don't you want your coffee?"

"Not right now. I need to check some things. I'll be back for lunch."

Marcie put her hand on his elbow.

"Billy's school starts in the morning and I've arranged for Lacy to come help me with some sewing. They say she's a good seamstress."

Skipjack's brow knitted. "What on earth does that have to do with anything?"

He knew he should have kept his mouth shut. Before he could step out onto the porch, Marcie grabbed his sleeve. He turned, looked into eyes dark with fury.

"I don't see the damn connection, that's all. School, sewing?"

"It's all about you, isn't it, mister? Well, it hasn't been easy for anybody around here. You think I don't want to run away?"

"Who's running away, Marcie? I'm going to the tavern."

Marcie repeated his words verbatim and poked out her belly as she uttered them. Skipjack was genuinely startled. He reached out for her shoulder as much to steady himself as to somehow reassure her. She took a step backward.

"Don't you put a hand on me! Have you forgotten we're having a baby?"

Her eyes were full of soulful rage, tears spilled over, and streamed down her cheeks. Skipjack didn't know what to do with his hands, so he spread them and tried to smile.

"You think it's funny? Just go when and where you want," she hissed. "You don't see the connection? Bodies buried all over the place and I get to make baby things. You think I want to make baby things? You know I hate to sew. Just go where you want."

"But—"

"Don't you 'but' me. I been nursing, cooking, and God knows what else. I'm fat, ugly, worn out, and tired. Don't look at me all concerned. You tell me how Billy's going to get to school tomorrow. Walk through the woods? Who's going to make baby clothes, Yankee Doodle Dandy?"

"You want me to help sew?" Skipjack asked with an earnest expression that didn't fit.

"Ha! Just go to your tavern," she said with a laugh. "You sew? You don't know the difference between a thimble and a jigger."

"Well, that is true, Marcie, I don't."

Marcie's expression softened as she clasped her belly, canted her head, and listened intently.

"Oh, now I've stirred everything up. I hear Billy clomping around and the baby's kicking," she paused and gazed into Skipjack's eyes. "What's going to happen to us, Jack?"

Skipjack stepped forward, gently placed his hands on her arms and coaxed Marcie against his chest. Marcie trembled against him.

"I don't know, Jack. Some things I know, but this I don't."

Billy glanced furtively into the room. Skipjack had seen the boy's shotgun first.

"Is everything all right?" he asked.

"Nothing to worry about, Billy," Skipjack said. "Put your gun up and never let it lead you into a room."

"Why not?"

"Some fool might grab it, that's why. Put it up."

As Marcie dried her eyes on his shirt, Skipjack allowed as how he would have some coffee after all. Within half an hour, he and Bill were frying bacon, while Marcie made a list of things she would need and then hung a blue ribbon bow on the back door. Pretending not to notice, Skipjack lit a cigar.

Bill said, "So you keep your gun close?"

"Close and at the ready. You can point quick enough when you see what you see."

———

Mary Frances chewed him out. She got so outspoken and rambunctiously loud that Skipjack ran to his office holding his ears. Fumbling with the lock, he was not scared, but neither was Mary Frances silenced by his oft-repeated entreaties. It was midday. He was attempting to avoid a scene that he feared would upset customers. Mary Frances was inflamed and didn't give a damn.

"How the hell can you be so blockheaded? Damn, if you were my husband, God help you!"

Skipjack shoved the door open and put fingers to his lips, but Mary Frances slammed the heavy door and kept on coming, until she had him backed up against his desk and towered over him, voice booming.

"You have no earthly idea what that woman is going through."

"I had coffee and bacon," Skipjack said, trying to figure a way to slip off to the side.

"Listen to me. That woman is ten of you. You couldn't give her everything she needs if you were ten men. And you bragging about coffee? You understand, you might be on the right side of some stuff, but God almighty, you sure missing some basics."

"Okay, what?"

"Don't look fierce at me, little brother," she said. "I ain't gonna use this knife, but I could. I could filet you like a channel cat. You listen to me. I am your friend."

Skipjack chuckled and nodded.

"Think it's funny? Fine, but Marcie needs you now like the moon needs the sun. She can't be her old self, 'cause she ain't her old self. Can you get that? Her whole blooming world is upside down and backwards, and all that was before your damn brother strolls in. Throw in the sheriff and a half dozen others to stitch and fool with, and you got the nerve to ask what connects sewing to schooling? What the hell kind of fool you fooling to be? What damn difference does it make how it connects? Connects to what? Your Marcie is torn this way and that. If you can't see that, I quit."

"You can't quit now. I need you."

"Marcie needs you more than this place. I can run this nightmare my own damn self."

"I thank you. You know we couldn't have done without you."

"I don't want no bonus, Skipjack, or none of your sweet talk either. What I want is that you go back home and show Marcie you will never leave her. Then you bring her back down, so I can fix her dinner. Send Andy up to guard the place. Make her feel special; she needs to smile."

"So, you say just drop everything?"

Mary Frances stepped back.

"No. I say get home to your wife."

―――――――――

Jessie blinked when Skipjack approached and climbed on muttering and out of sorts. Mary damn Frances! The whole damn crazy morning. Then a voice in his head quietly asked him how Billy was going to get to school. How do I know? The voice asked again. I'll take him then. Good, then who will be there with Marcie? Skipjack frowned. On such a beautiful September morning, his frown suddenly felt foolish. Tom and Lacy, will they look after Marcie? Can you begin to see the connection? Before Skipjack could think up an answer, he looked up to see Green rolling his way.

"What are you doing here?"

Green pulled up his team and laughed.

"You seen the sheriff?"

"Yesterday; he sniffed all around."

"He's a nervous son of a bitch, ain't he?"

"Truthfully, Green, I hardly noticed."

"He's convinced, or so he says, that you are a slave runner, river pirate, and livestock thief. He asked me if I would like to press charges. After I said yes, I laughed in his face. Didn't make him happy."

"Suppose not. Why you heading here?"

"Late breakfast."

"Well, I've been sent home by Mary Frances. Can you believe that?"

"Maddox, that's the place to be."

"What do you know?"

"Sheriff thinks he knows something."

"You think he does?"

"I believe he knows your brother's alive. I think he's fearful of a firestorm. Afraid someone might talk. Face it, your brother's a thorn in his side now."

"Why do you think?"

"We hurt 'em, that's why. The way he's steamed, he knows it, too. He's been on the take. Now he's got both of you mad. You better duck."

"What did he say, Green?"

"It ain't what he said, but what he didn't. His eyes are jittery. Send for me if you need me."

Skipjack winked. "Tell Mary Frances you saw me on my way home."

"I will and please tell your Marcie that Green is solid on her side."

"You know she knows that."

"This is bad business, my friend. I don't believe anyone knows anything."

"I've got it about tomorrow," Skipjack said, "but today we'll have a picnic."

"What about tomorrow?" Marcie asked.

"I'll take him and pick him up, that's what."

"So, what's this picnic?"

"Let's go fishing, all right?"

"Aren't you forgetting something?"

"What might that be?"

"What's wrong, Momma," Billy asked.

"Marcie, I'll have Andy stand guard tomorrow when we're off to school. Is that better?"

"Yes, or else Andy can go and you stay."

"Whatever suits. Now let's all get out on the water for a while. We can get some food down at the tavern and then we'll fish."

Skipjack hoped that fresh air would do Marcie some good. While Billy trolled, Skipjack rowed and noticed Marcie sat there as self-contained as some of the women he had carried across. He pointed out the white glinting seagulls swooping overhead. She looked up and nodded, then she looked down. He shrugged and dug in with the oars.

"I've got one!" Billy shouted, then his line broke. Skipjack realized he hadn't thought to bring the tackle box. He tried to make a joke about it, but before he could hand Billy his rig to use, Marcie had given him hers.

"Don't you want to fish, honey?"

"Jack, please, I know you mean well, but I don't. You all fish."

"You don't feel well, Momma?"

Marcie closed her eyes and took a deep breath.

"No," she whispered.

Skipjack knew better than to ask why or if there was anything he could do, but Billy did not. Marcie stared into Skipjack's eyes as the boy probed her with questions.

"Hush up, son," Skipjack said. "We're heading back. No more talk."

"You're scared aren't you, Momma?"

Marcie raised her hand before Skipjack could speak. She grabbed Billy by the shoulder and fixed him in her gaze.

"You heard your father, and no, I ain't afraid."

The boy looked stunned. His eyes widened, and then he grinned. "You said 'ain't,' Momma. You said 'ain't.'"

Marcie shook her head and started laughing. She stroked her son's head and pulled him close. With her free hand, she pointed to the shore.

Skipjack pulled on the oars. Marcie said thank you without uttering a sound.

"I can't believe you said 'ain't.'"

"Maybe you were hearing things."

"No, I heard you say it. You said 'ain't' plain as day."

"Can you forgive me? We both know 'ain't' is wrong."

Billy nodded. Marcie pressed him into her breast.

———

Marcie and Billy had their picnic in the office. Marcie fidgeted through Mary Frances's entries in the ledger book, and Skipjack, after bolting down his pork sandwich, excused himself and strolled outside. The air was cool and refreshing. He inhaled deeply, then lit a cigar.

A side-wheeler was plowing upstream and a sternwheeler was sliding down. He closed his eyes for a moment and tried to remember another time, a time when everything seemed smoothly under control. A fingertip tapped his shoulder. He sighed and turned. Trapper's glittering eyes confronted him.

"Bend down, down."

Skipjack complied and tilted his head.

"Believe they're holed up upriver, Indiana side. Fourteen Mile Creek. Heard that, ain't seen them, but good source let me in."

"At least they ain't here," Skipjack said.

"Not likely to be for a while at least. Not for a while."

"Make yourself clear. What're you saying, Trapper?"

"They're pretty tore up, no foolin'. But be careful if you plan to row across. They waiting."

"Where'd you get this?"

"Cousin of mine, deputy. Deputy in with the sheriff."

"So why did this cousin tell?"

"He didn't. Didn't tell me nothing. Overheard bragging. Bragging full of drink."

"What're you saying?"

Trapper grinned, crooked his finger and winked. Skipjack leaned closer.

"Said they was gonna nab you stealin' slaves, what he said. Thought it was right funny. Said the sheriff let on there was a big reward."

Skipjack shook his head and laughed out loud.

"You think I'm a thief, Trapper?"

"How's it matter what I think?" Trapper asked. "Be watchful. Yes, sir, fixin' to nail you."

"What're you talking about?"

"One claims he was stole. Claim you stole him, yes sir. Cousin thought it funny as upside-down turkey. Wish we'd killed all. Killed them all. Yes, sir."

"Where'd you hear this?"

"Family reunion!" Trapper said, standing straight. "We Van Nutts sticks together, unlike some folks."

"It's hard to believe, Trapper."

"Cousin claims he's gonna spin a wheel a fortune. They all in. Don't be rowing across."

―――――

"Say I don't care about the money, but you know I do," Marcie said.

Skipjack pulled off his shirt and nodded. Marcie fixed him in her gaze and smiled.

"Are you even listening, Jack? I'm not saying Mary Frances isn't valuable."

"No, I hear you. You're saying she ain't a good record keeper."

"Isn't."

Skipjack sat on the bed's edge and began to tug off his trousers. In the windowpanes, Marcie's reflection froze. Her head tilted. He couldn't clearly see her eyes but felt them burning his back. He raised one hand and then the other.

"Can we go out on the front porch and talk?" he asked.

"There's a chill in the air, Jack."

"No worse than in—"

"What?"

Skipjack said nothing, stood, stepped back into his pants, motioned toward the door. He was most surprised when Marcie followed without a word. In the kitchen, he poured a drink for himself and a glass of sherry for her.

He looked up at the half moon and took a breath. Marcie stood a step behind him still holding the door.

"Please bring me my cigar, Marcie. There's something you need to hear."

Skipjack sat and asked Marcie to bring him his pistol as well.

"Sit down," he said. "We got two choices."

"What are you saying?" Marcie asked.

"One is ours and one is theirs."

"You're making me nervous."

"Maybe that's good. Unless we're together, we're in a bad way."

"I love you, Jack Maddox, and that's no lie."

"Marcie, they're trying to pry us apart. Your life and Billy's, and mine too. We need our lives knit together; they aim to rip us apart."

"What are you talking about?"

"What if someone called me a thief?"

"You, a thief? I would laugh. You're more likely to give stuff away. That's what I'm mad about."

"I'm not talking about Mary Frances and her books. I'm talking the sheriff."

"What have you been stealing?" Marcie asked.

"Nothing. But some are saying I'm stealing slaves."

Marcie drew in her breath and then exhaled.

"For goodness sakes, who could think that? The sheriff?"

"I don't know who's thinking what. I know what I heard. Some are trying to frame me, and you know there are some trying to kill us. Please believe me, this is no time for you and me to be fighting."

"Who said it was? We're in this together."

"Afraid you might hear some awful stuff."

"Doesn't make it true," Marcie said as she stroked his wrist. Skipjack settled back, acutely aware of the pistol beside him.

"Just breathe, Jack, that's the main thing. We'll be all right. Try to relax. Breathe."

"I am breathing. That's the problem."

"No, you're wound tight and holding your breath. Look, you even let your cigar go out."

CHAPTER 12

A SCARY MONSTER CALLED FRANKENSTEIN

By the time Skipjack walked down to the kitchen, Marcie was frying eggs. Billy handed him a mug of coffee. The eager sparkle of the boy's expression surprised him. Skipjack couldn't remember ever being excited by the first day of school, but Billy sure was.

As he opened the door on his way to the privy, Marcie told him that Billy wanted to ride to school with him. She added that she felt safe with Tom and Andy there, so Skipjack nodded and stepped into the cool September air. Heavy dew sparkled the grass. Everything looked so peaceful; if not for the necessary pistol in his hand, he might have felt at ease as well.

Before the mare had drawn the buggy twenty feet, Billy said, "You shoot better than anybody."

"Just keep your eyes open," Skipjack replied. "Spot what ain't supposed to be and look out for what is. That's all there is to it. The rest is mechanical: aim and fire."

"But when we shoot," Billy said, "you hit so many times it makes me sick."

"You do fine, son. Nothing but practice will get you there."

"What if I haven't practiced enough?"

"See that you do. That will solve the problem, sure enough."

"I'm glad you're taking me."

"You think Andy couldn't?"

"No, he could, but I'd rather have you."

Skipjack pulled the mare to a halt.

"What're you saying, Billy?"

"Andy is Andy and Andy is good, but you look after Momma, Mary Frances, Andy, Tom, and everyone else. I'm glad you're looking after me, too."

"What the hell else can I do?" Skipjack asked.

"I don't know," Billy answered.

"Keep a sharp eye."

———

Mr. Paganini's long sharp beak greeted them; bony fingers poking out of black sleeves scooted Billy into the small schoolhouse. Skipjack saw an undertaker, not a schoolmaster. The concerned glance Billy tossed back over his shoulder confirmed he shared this impression.

Skipjack asked this skeletal being if he was armed. The man fluttered pale fingers in front of his bespectacled face and stated quite firmly that the Lord would provide.

"Be that as it may," Skipjack said, "until you are informed otherwise, no one will have any say with that child but me. I will bring him; I will take him back home. Understand?"

"Mr. Maddox, this is a place of learning," Mr. Paganini insisted with a long-toothed grin, "but I do have a shotgun, a rifle, and this." He pulled a muzzleloader out of his britches. "And this," he added as he brandished a stiletto; he waved it discreetly at waist level. His eyes narrowed, and his teeth gleamed. "I think your boy is quite safe."

"He's a good shot," Skipjack said.

"I am sure you have taught him well," Mr. Paganini said. "Now he is my challenge."

———————

For the first few days, nothing short of militia would have calmed anyone. Andy did double duty and so did Tom, but then Tom's stonework trickled down to fine-tuning and Andy started to be a hang-around. One evening, Brawl rolled up and announced that he needed Tom for a day or so. There was no anger.

Marcie was pleased that her boy was reading. The teacher had him excited about Socrates, Shakespeare, and Mary Shelley's *Frankenstein*. All the way home Skipjack heard questions: Could you really make a man out of animal parts? What if your mother killed your father?

"Answers lead to questions, one after another," Billy said.

The weather turned gentle. It was what they called Indian summer. Days were warm, yet there were hours of coolness, and the evening sky was clear and full of stars. Early morning air was so crisp that there was a crunch beneath every footfall, but in late afternoon, there was softness in grass bending underfoot and folks dreamed of a warm hearth but didn't need one.

"I heard geese fly over," Marcie said. "Why don't you build us a fire?"

"Pretty warm for a fire, don't you think?"

"'Tis the season; thought you might want to snuggle."

"I'm still reading," Billy said.

Skipjack and Marcie shared a glance.

"What are you reading, son?" Skipjack asked.

"Did you know some folks said the world revolves around the stars?"

"Some folks will say just about anything."

"I know. That's what I'm finding out."

———

New routines began to form. Each morning, Andy reported business was good down at the tavern. By midday, Lacy and Marcie busied themselves sewing baby things, then reading lessons took a part of afternoon and both seemed to enjoy these projects wholeheartedly. Skipjack fidgeted. After a few days, Marcie began to regain her sense of humor and urged him to go check the tavern. He did and since revenues were up, he gave Mary Frances a pay raise.

"Hell, the place is better with me home," Skipjack said. "Got to give credit where credit is due."

Mary Frances nodded and pointed with her forehead. Skipjack turned as the sheriff sauntered into the bar. The sheriff looked relaxed, more like his old self. He smiled steadily at Skipjack when he stated quietly that things seemed to be calming down.

"Happy to hear that. Tell me, have you got leads on the where-abouts of my brother and his outfit?"

"Skipjack, perhaps some things are best left behind."

Mary Frances gave Skipjack a hard look and excused herself. The sheriff ordered a whiskey. Skipjack seconded the motion, then they moved to a corner table. When Louis brought the drinks over, Skipjack waved him away, but Louis stood stock still, until cash was stuffed into his hand. Marcie's new rules. All three men shook their heads and smiled.

"What were you about to say?"

"We have nothing on your brother that could stand. That's a fact. You might think you know something. I might agree, but that don't make evidence. We both know he's slick and he's kept bad company, but you can't convict a man with that."

"You don't want to know where he is?"

"Do you?"

"I know what I've heard."

"Let me take a wild guess. He's out of my jurisdiction across the river, holed up on Fourteen Mile Creek."

Skipjack nodded.

"I will further venture the man who whispered this is a man known as Trapper; his mother's a Beasley. Would you happen to know how many times Trapper paddles over to work that creek?"

"No, I sure don't, sheriff."

"He doesn't. He got his damn information from a jackass deputized for one honorary function involving our mayor. His job was to take up space in front of the podium. Was supposed to stand up straight and couldn't even do that. He was a one-night deal, but also a hard-core drinker and apparently, an all-night blowhard, a know-it-all who knows every path leading to a wild goose chase. Trapper wasn't the only one he blabbered at. I have my ear to the ground. Trapper ain't as quiet and to himself as you might believe. Just how the hell do you think I learned of this?"

"I wouldn't know."

"Well, let me tell you something, and they are words to the wise: Walls have ears. You live by the sword, you die by the sword. And don't take the law into your own hands. I have checked this rumor about Timothy's whereabouts with my Indiana counterpart, and to the best of our knowledge, there is no substance. But let me add this—rumors are gathering about some of your personal activities. Between you and me, in respect for our long and cordial association, I have so far managed to reduce these allegations to the same kind of idle hearsay." The sheriff swallowed his whiskey and stood. "I trust I make myself clear."

"I believe I understand your position."

"I hope, because there's only so much that I can do."

"Good to have you on my side, sheriff," Skipjack said, as he raised his glass.

"Maddox, hear me for all time. I'm on the side of the law, sworn to uphold it, so help me God."

Skipjack stood on the riverbank for about an hour after his conversation with the sheriff, and though his eyes were vaguely aware of the water sloshing on the shore, he actually registered nothing. Riverboats churned up and downstream, but they were blurred shapes at best. He breathed in slowly and exhaled still more slowly. His enforced stillness was an attempt to stave off an internal undertow. Fragile balance impelled by a slight breeze led him up the bank step by step in the direction of his bar, where he promptly ordered a glass of whiskey, which he refused to pay for, stalked to his office, then slammed the heavy oak door.

His office chair, the familiar gouges and scars of the old desktop, the smooth curling cigar smoke—none of these could erase his observation of unease behind the sheriff's eyes. Skipjack had peered into many different souls: fancy ladies deceiving, glittering, and their dandies' flashing shallow wealth; gamblers stalking phantoms; brute thugs with blades much sharper than wits. Legions of drowning self-assured beings had masqueraded before him, but somehow it had always seemed that these masks and costumes would at some point be removed. The sheriff's glinting orbs hinted at something menacingly durable hidden within.

The sheriff's countenance—pugnacious, defiant, fearful, doomed, and assertive, all at once—burned into his forehead. There was no lost quality, no reckless foolish innocence. Skipjack saw pulsing motive without hope of redemption, a fierce spirit not yet dead. Skipjack sloshed down his whiskey.

"Goddamn it!" he croaked into his cupped hand as there was a knock on his door. "Come in."

He expected Mary Frances, enforcing Marcie's cash-on-the-barrel-head rule, but it was Andy.

Skipjack waved him in. With one swirling pass of his hand, he instructed him to close and lock the door, which Andy seemed to do all in one graceful motion. Once seated, Andy glanced at Skipjack, then stared at the floor. Neither man spoke. Skipjack drew on his cigar, took a sip of whiskey, then shut his eyes, and with three fingertips, kneaded his forehead.

bride-to-be."

"Business is business. You know that."

"You want to hire Andy?" Skipjack asked with a slowly forming grin. "He's free at the end of the week."

Green poked out his chin, shut both eyes, drew in a breath, and then forcefully exhaled.

"Andy claims he wants to stay," Skipjack said. "But he's resourceful and love being what it is, it's hard for me to guarantee they'll stick around."

"Cut to the point. I paid good money for that girl's mother. What will you give me for her?"

"Shhh! Now you hold down your voice. We can work it out. I'm as good as my word. You know it. How about Christmas, New Year's, and two dates of your choosing, and I give you eighteen hundred?"

"You are worse than your brother," Green exclaimed, red-faced.

"What has he offered?" Skipjack asked.

"You know this girl is worth plenty."

"Yes, and you know you want her to be with Andy, so she'll stick around."

"I'm entitled to something," Green said, defiantly.

"Satisfaction," Skipjack said as he poured whiskey into both of their glasses. "Think about it. What if you don't let the girl go? How will that feel? I'm sure you could sell her for more somewhere else. Why come to me?"

Green looked down, then stared directly into Skipjack's eyes. His gaze did not waver.

"You're a hard man, Maddox."

"No, that's not true and you're not either. That's why you're here. You're a regular Cupid, that's what you are. Act hard all you want. You don't like this game any more than I do. I'll give eighteen five and that's it."

"Give me a couple more days of option time. We entertain quite a bit you know."

"Am I invited, Green?"

"Well, of course you are. My place is yours, you know that."

"Then we have a deal, so long as you don't raise the price of whiskey for two years more than 10 percent of what I boost the price of corn."

"You snake," Green said. He grimaced, then smiled. "How about we keep the prices on your menu at current levels for the same duration?"

"Done," Skipjack said.

"Let's have a toast then," Green said. "A hard man. But you have a reasonable side."

"Shh," Skipjack said and winked. Green winked back, then they clinked glasses and drained them.

"This here's my whiskey?"

"I've been intending to bring that up, Green. Perhaps a good cigar might help smooth it."

"A cigar might be welcome, but I was meaning to ask you about your corn. I'm not altogether convinced I'm satisfied," Green replied.

FINE PRINT: DEVIL'S IN THE DETAILS

"Don't you think we should ask Andy first?" Marcie asked.

Billy was in bed. Skipjack, full of hooch, was planning a party in celebration of Andy's freedom and presumed betrothal to Lacy. Skipjack wanted a surprise. Marcie strongly disagreed.

"Jack," she said stroking her belly. "Some things are so personal you might not want to share them with the whole wide world."

"I ain't talking the whole world. I'm talking Green. I'm thinking Mary Frances, Brawl, Tom—"

"I'll tell you what you're thinking. You're thinking of stirring a pot of trouble."

"No, Marcie, it's a celebration. Can't you see?"

Marcie turned from the stove and faced him square. From the look in her eyes, Skipjack knew he must be tipsy and off the mark. He started to say something to defend himself, but Marcie's raised spatula set him to sputtering.

"Now you're making sense. Let me pour you a stiff one, prospector, and maybe you'll hit gold."

"Hit gold? Woman, what you talking about?"

"You're dreaming, Jack. For one thing it sounds to me like the deal you struck with Green isn't so much about freedom as it is a deal that in the long run appears to benefit us. I can't argue with that, husband, but I will caution you not to draw too much attention."

"Ten years. What's ten years for a house?"

"Do you want to build a new house for Mary Frances?"

"No, but she doesn't need a house."

"That's most likely your opinion, not hers. But suppose Brawl comes up with another Andy he sees has promise. Are you supposed to throw a house and land into the deal?"

"This is a one-time thing, Marcie."

"My point exactly, Jack. Keep it quiet."

Skipjack slumped forward in his chair and stroked his chin.

"Hold the drink."

"Why do you say that, angel?" Marcie said, as she filled his glass.

"I must be crazy. I just got through telling Andy himself to keep all under wraps."

"Honey, I knew you were fine. You're not crazy, you're drunk."

"So that explains it." Skipjack yawned. "Maybe a little bit tired, too."

"I'll talk to Lacy and see what she thinks. She sews real well, you know."

"Well, that's sure good to hear," Skipjack said as he laid his head on the table.

"We're going to keep this quiet," Skipjack said as he greeted Andy.

"That's fine with me, sir. It's eleven o'clock, like we said and time to be quiet."

"Who's talking about being quiet?"

"Well, you were, sir."

"So I was."

"Are you all right, sir?"

"Close to it," Skipjack said as he stepped onto the porch. "Listen, I'm three-fourths drunk and halfway asleep, but I know one thing and the other pretty close. Don't breathe a word of our deal to a soul, or else it will cause trouble. I know that certain."

Andy nodded.

"The other, I gotta ask solemnly. Are you sure you and your Lacy are willing to stay on here and work at least ten years?"

Andy looked confused. His eyes clamped shut and when they opened, a fire burned inside that Skipjack never had seen before. He motioned for Andy to speak.

Andy sighed and said firmly, "Mr. Maddox, I can say yes only for myself, sir. Lacy is the property of the Green family. If you make it that we can marry, and Lacy is my wife, even then I could not speak for the Greens."

Skipjack nodded and placed his hand on Andy's shoulder.

"God help us all, Andy."

"Yes, sir."

"Andy, give your word and I'll take care of the rest."

Andy leaned forward and his eyes narrowed.

"What you mean, take care of the rest, sir?"

"Andy, I've talked to Green. I beg you not to tell Lacy or anyone. You give me your promise, I'll set her free."

"Lord have mercy! Bless you, sir."

"And bless Green, but it ain't done yet. Do I have your promise?"

"You know you do."

"Don't breathe a word. Marcie doesn't know, and like I say, it ain't done. But I tell you this—if Green changes his mind, I'll kill him."

"Oh, no, sir."

"Don't worry, Andy. He's a man of his word. He won't change his mind."

"Thank you, sir."

"You're welcome, but by the way, between guarding us and working the tavern, when the hell do you sleep?"

"Sleep? Sleep? I suppose that's something free folks do."

"Well, this free man's turning in. Please keep an eye on things. See you in the morning."

"Yes, sir. Don't worry about a thing."

"Only three more days."

"Yes, sir and hopefully ten years at least."

"Amen."

———

Morning came quickly. Skipjack's head felt two sizes too big when he lifted off the pillow. The sunlight glinting through windowpanes pinched his eyes. His throat was raw. He tried to swallow and shaking his head didn't help one bit.

He scooped clothes, slipped out of the room, then dressed on the landing. Gracie barked at him from the base of the stairs and he hushed her with a hiss. After he tied up his laces, he tiptoed down, and as quietly as he could, made coffee.

Andy was on the front porch steps. Skipjack handed him a steaming cup, then lit a cigar.

"You hear anything?"

"Thought I did but reckon I didn't."

"What do you think you heard?"

"Down there where that boy was shot, I thought I heard some rustling around, but then nothing."

"There's a breeze blowing."

"Sure is. Most likely was the breeze or a critter."

"Andy, I sure appreciate what you're doing."

"Sir, I've been sitting up all night thinking the same. What you're doing for us, that is."

"I'll take the boy to school this morning. On the way back, I'm stopping by Green's to get this done. Then sending out for the surveyor. Got your word, don't I?"

Andy nodded. Skipjack nodded back.

"Could you hitch up the mare? You can pick Billy up this afternoon."

A hint of frying bacon began to tingle the morning air. Skipjack looked puzzled. The kitchen had been empty a moment before.

"Dad, you want two eggs or three?" Billy asked from the doorway. "You want some, Andy?"

Andy shook his head no but smiled.

"Of course, he does, son. Good of you to think."

"I'm making corn cakes, all except for momma; she always wants a fritter and I'm frying her two."

"Ain't you the rascal chef? I thought you were still asleep."

"Something woke me up and I couldn't get back to sleep."

"You know what it was?"

"Breathing or whispering, but maybe dreaming."

"The sun's up now."

"Yeah, better check my bacon."

"A good young man," Andy said.

"Seems to be coming along."

"Stronger than I was at his age for sure," Andy said.

Skipjack let the morning silence speak before he did. Then he asked Andy if all went as they hoped, would he mind if there was a small celebration in honor of his freedom, or as Skipjack put it, "Your ass in the sling with the rest of us."

Andy laughed and tried to muffle it with his fist.

"That ain't necessary. The sun coming up and freedom papers will be sufficient."

"Please don't tell Marcie I asked you this. I want it small; only a few folks, Green, Brawl, one or two others. Of course, you could invite one or two."

Andy nodded and looked down before he spoke.

"Yes, sir. Well, what if I invited my father?"

"Hell, yeah. Where's he?"

"He's with Mr. Green, sir."

"He works for Green? I never knew that. Where's your mother?"

"We don't know. Been a long time, sir."

Skipjack closed his eyes.

"Maybe it's not such a good idea, after all. What's your father do for Green?"

"He works the house, sir. He's the one greets you at the door."

"You telling me Johnson is your daddy?" Skipjack laughed.

"He is for sure."

"Hell, he's old enough to be my grandfather."

"No, sir," Andy smiled. "Maybe your father, but Daddy's still spry. I ain't the youngest."

"Well, God bless him. Of course, he's welcome. I'll talk to Green.

"Don't think Mr. Green will change his mind, do you?"

"Can you smell that bacon, Andy?"

"I sure can."

"Trust your nose."

Green's private drive, more than a mile, snaked up the hillside above the river-bordered bottomland. There were gnarly locust trees but also stout oaks and maples with silver trunks. Near the summit of the hill, there were stands of white pine and hemlock that completely obscured the house. A visitor looking over his shoulder across the fields below and out to the river would see most of the Creekside community.

Skipjack rested the mare, lit a cigar, and turned in his seat. He couldn't see his own house, nestled into the same ridge at a lower elevation, but could see the tavern and, through cottonwoods on the riverbank, saw steamboats billowing dark gray smoke and flatboats that looked like slivers stacked with boxes tended by colorful ants.

He took a nip from his pocket flask and a draw from his cigar. The day was clear, and the air crisp, rich with tang of burning oak and hickory. Traces of smoke trailed nearly everywhere, up or downriver. Skipjack found the smell, the promised warmth, comforting. Then the breeze delivered a sweet-sour taste that caused Skipjack to grin. Green's private stills were cooking full bore. He clucked at the mare and the buggy lurched.

He trusted Green but wasn't totally at ease. Mrs. Green had to agree. Despite what he had said to Green about Christmas and so forth, he was prepared to promise Lacy a few days a year but would rather not. He was angling for a straightforward buyout. After all, free was free, and he had assured Andy that Lacy would be free. He wasn't too concerned about Green, but Mrs. Green was a puzzle he had never had to confront.

Skipjack crossed his fingers and prayed as the circular entrance drive of the Green family compound appeared. He saw six tall brick chimneys, a roof of black slate, long paned windows reflecting the cloudless morning sky. There was a porch, expansive enough to hold two carriages, if they somehow could have been driven up lengthy limestone steps. These steps were flanked by dark green boxwood bushes as large as carriages themselves. The bushes seemed to anchor fluted columns that stood like sentinels out in front of double doors that buttressed two regal arched stained-glass panels above. As Skipjack drew closer, the mystique diminished. Sure, the place was large, but not out of scale. He pulled up front and set the brake.

From the top step, Johnson beckoned and though dressed in black livery, there was nothing formal about his gesture. He waved as if leading a joyous charge. Johnson does look spry, Skipjack thought, as he climbed the steps, trying to ignore a sudden unpleasant hitch in his right knee.

"Get on up here, Mr. Maddox. Mr. Green's expecting you, sir."

"How is that possible, Johnson? He didn't even know I was

coming."

"Maybe not, but I alerted him to that fact, and when I seen you close, I verified it, sir."

"You're a mystery, Johnson. You always have been, you old rascal."

"Yes, sir. Step on in," Johnson replied as he swung open the door. "There's a little mystery in all, sir."

Skipjack attempted to search Johnson's heavily lidded eyes. He could read nothing. Johnson blinked and signaled him to enter. Skipjack stepped into the vast hall, which stretched from the entrance straight through to identical double doors at the back of the house. The door shut behind him as softly as a curtain closing, but the key in the lock sounded as certain as jail.

———

Skipjack was shown to a bench embroidered with pastel sheep and shepherdesses placed across the hall from Green's sturdy chestnut door. When the door opened a few moments later, a short florid man stormed out.

"May your dreams come true, sir," the man said with a scowl. Johnson stepped forward calmly and escorted the visitor to the front door.

Green appeared in his office doorway and motioned Skipjack in; he pointed to a leather armchair in front of the large walnut table that served as his desk, poured two tiny shots of whiskey, smiled, and sat down.

"To your health," he said and took a sip. "I trust our business will go smoothly. Nothing has changed, has it?"

"Not on this end, Green. How about yours?"

"No, not at all. Do you realize how rare that is nowadays?"

"You been dealing with back-biters and slippery arrangers?"

"Up until the last minute," Green said, amused.

"That man didn't look happy."

"Nor should he. He can eat corn and turn to whiskey his own self."

Within ten minutes, Lacy was transferred to Skipjack. Money changed hands and Green's secretary, Mr. Leggit, witnessed the transaction: Maddox to assume possession of Lacy Green, free and clear.

As Skipjack was leaving, he offered that the girl would most likely be available on special occasions if Mrs. Green needed extra help.

"No, let's not complicate things."

"Fair enough," Skipjack said. "But how about if I invite you to a small party celebrating Andy's freedom on Saturday night, just a toast or two?"

Green's face pinched toward his nostrils.

"That doesn't sit well. You don't want to go too far, do you? I know there's a fondness for Andy, but it don't pass."

"Seems like that's what Marcie's saying. I don't see what's offensive. Everything's on the up and up."

"Keep it that way. We start celebrating, no telling where gossip will go. Listen to Marcie. You got a good heart, but that there's a bad idea."

"Strange when freedom bought, paid for, and well deserved can't be celebrated."

"You're preaching to the choir, but have you any idea how many men there are who would cut nuts for such a thought?"

Before Skipjack could answer, Green continued. "We're rich, you and me, compared to most. Do you realize the contempt we're held in? You surely know they're gunning. Don't know much about rumors but damn well know plenty lowlifes don't share your vision. Keep this quiet. But you breathe a word, don't call me when they call on you."

"All right, I'm convinced," Skipjack said and stood.

Green stood as well, extended his big hand, and smiled.

"Keep your eyes open. Things are changing."

Johnson gently pulled the huge front door open as soon as

Skipjack's heels stepped off the carpet runner and clattered on the chestnut parquet of the foyer. Johnson bowed, smiled broadly, said, "Good evening, sir."

Skipjack stopped and chuckled.

"Johnson, it ain't even full morning yet." He looked into the old man's eyes and saw milky clouds settled there.

"Of course, you're correct, sir. Most times is evening to me, sir."

Skipjack wished he had kept his mouth shut.

"Thank you," he said as he passed through the doorway.

"God bless you, sir," Johnson said.

CHAPTER 13

THE DOG PIT

O
n the way downtown, it started to drizzle and by the time Skipjack tied up in front of Woods & Johanson, he was soaked. Miss Betty, the secretary, informed him the appraisal, complete with a certified plat, would be completed and filed the next day.

"Thank your stars that times are slow, Mr. Maddox," she said as she scribbled him into her ledger.

So, the whole thing was nearly done. Skipjack pointed the mare toward home, but then hunger and the steady rain turned him around. Though he had partaken of Billy's breakfast, he found himself headed for a Galt House brunch. Yet as soon as he walked into the lush hotel dining room, he spotted the sheriff and wished he hadn't. He was about to leave when the sheriff, who was seated with the mayor, motioned him over. Skipjack smiled. There was no good way out. He sat, ordered a shot of whiskey with a raw egg and a cup of coffee.

"If you don't have the crepes, you're missing something," the sheriff said.

"And crepes with sausage and bacon on the side," Skipjack added.

Both the sheriff and the mayor winked. The waiter pursed thin lips and scampered off.

"I'm hungry," Skipjack said.

"Sheriff tells me you know more than most about thieving in these parts, Mr. Maddox."

"Reckon the sheriff knows whereof he speaks, Mr. Mayor."

"I simply stated that a band of them was camped out right near you," the sheriff said.

"Were twice; flood washed them out once," Skipjack said.

"Once? What happened next?"

"Mr. Mayor, this river is full of thieves. I wouldn't dare outguess an expert."

"Skipjack, guesswork has nothing to do with it," the sheriff exclaimed.

"That's what I'm trying to tell his honor. Due to your expertise, you are inclined to know more about thievery than anyone."

"Seriously, Mr. Maddox," the mayor said, "we do have a dreadful bunch working these parts. Whatever you might be able to reveal would be appreciated."

"Mayor, I assume the honorable sheriff has informed you that my own brother, Timothy, is likely one of the leaders, if not the leader of this gang."

The mayor wiped his mouth with his napkin, which he then held steady as he tilted his head toward the sheriff, who said, "I told the mayor no more than anyone else knows who's mindful."

"Now that's a good point, sheriff. Who is more likely than you to be mindful of the situation?"

"Those close," the sheriff muttered, leaning in.

"I suppose that's how you separate the wheat from the chaff, being close, that is?"

"Meaning exactly what, Maddox?"

"Your honor, I am first going to stress that I have no inkling of this gang's inner workings, their whereabouts, plans, or leadership, despite anything this elected official might have implied. However, I must say that if the gentleman can pass judgment on who knows what, then it stands to reason that he is in a position to know. Would you not agree?"

The mayor chewed and nodded vigorously.

"Then it follows, if you catch my drift, that perhaps you might ask him to reveal his sources, before he attempts to discover mine or if I even have any. Surely, you understand if he can pass judgment on what I say, then he already knows the answers, sir. Why not ask him?"

"Nice try, Maddox. Deny they were on your property. Deny your own blood." The sheriff snorted.

"You must admit, mayor, that he does sound informed."

The waiter placed the whiskey and egg in front of Skipjack, who chugged it down in one quick gulp and had a mess of sausage, egg, and crepes working between his jaws before his companions released their grimaces. He nodded and pointed at the mayor with a greasy fork.

"Well, I don't know," the mayor said.

"Of course not, otherwise you wouldn't be asking."

"He knows more than he's letting on, mayor. Don't let him fool you. He's slick."

"Once again, mayor, the sheriff makes my point for me. If he knows so much, why won't he take action against these scoundrels? I promise you from the bottom of my heart that nothing would please me more."

"But after all," the mayor said, "Timothy Maddox is your brother."

"Unfortunately, that I cannot deny, but I know nothing of his business. Believe me, the gentleman to your left by his own assertions knows more."

The mayor leaned back and chuckled. His jowls shook, his eyes narrowed and sparkled.

"Well, well, well. Time will tell, won't it now? You two squabble like brothers yourselves."

The sheriff smirked as Skipjack stabbed a hunk of sausage. The mayor summoned the waiter, ordered a round of drinks, and put it on his tab.

"On the record, I know nothing about any of this and I've got work to do. One more and I would stiff-leg out of here. I don't need that. Gentlemen, have a good day," Skipjack said.

———

Sheets of rain swirled as the mare slogged past the shacks that bordered River Road. Water poured off the brim of his hat and found its way down his back, but he had to laugh. Hadn't the sheriff grown into his role as a full-fledged politician? There was no longer an honest bone in him. The sheriff reminded Skipjack of a child stretching truth to see how far it would stretch; and the mayor, sturdy round pillar of virtue, was a melodic clown.

In the early morning, Orin Johanson would draw up the boundaries of Andy's place, the guardhouse, which would be built at the bottom of Maddox hill. That would be a good thing. The sheriff and the mayor could screw themselves for all Skipjack cared. In some way, they made him sad, but in spite of himself, he burst out laughing, clucked at the mare, and continued to smile as he recalled how foolish they looked sitting side by side, ignoring everything that was real.

Perhaps the rhythm of the downpour, the steady tingling thrum, relaxed him. Tears mingled freely with rain; there was no one there to see. There had to be a way out of this. This sheriff, this mayor, Timothy—were they not temporary? Who would want to bet on their success?

The yellow- and orange-dabbed trees above his house glowed against dank gray smudge. Where can anyone hide forever? Eventually light will march through every nook and cranny.

Though the rain had picked up two notches, Skipjack was laughing as he stabled the mare. What the hell did it matter what any of them thought? What difference did it make what the mayor and sheriff considered to be important as long as he could keep his own people safe?

Skipjack stomped three times on the flagstone at the base of the steps. On the porch, he sat in a chair and removed his boots before entering the house. Through the steamed glass of his front window, he saw Marcie's form troubling something in a pot on top of the stove.

With his shoulder, he scrunched the door open and the way Marcie spun to greet him, Skipjack nearly pulled his pistol from his belt.

"It's you," she said and smiled.

"Everything all right?"

"Everything's all right now."

"Something I need to know?"

Her eyes brightened, she smiled, and said, "I feel better now you're here."

Skipjack kissed her neck. Marcie raised her shoulders and sighed.

"Husband, you want me to give you a shave?"

"Would be a good day for a bath and such, wouldn't it?'

"If you'll haul in the water, it might be," Marcie said and winked.

"Damn, woman, I just took my boots off."

"Well, if it's too much trouble . . ."

"I'll slip 'em back on." Skipjack felt a flash of warmth in his groin.

"What do you mean there's nothing better than my chicken soup, Jack?" Marcie said.

"You keep flirting like that, you better figure out we ain't got much time before Bill and Andy's here."

"Oh well." Marcie sighed. "If you continue to insist I make nothing better, I might supply evidence to the contrary, if your salt still has its savor."

"Now, Marcie, that's hardly fair. You know what I mean."

"You know what I meant," Marcie said and licked her lips.

"Well, your soup is God-blessed good." Skipjack laughed.

"You think it might have been the seasoning or the meat that give things such a kick?"

"Honey," Skipjack rasped, "we only got ten minutes on the outside."

Marcie stood and beckoned with her forefinger.

"Then we only got seven minutes on the inside. Are you able?"

Skipjack clattered his spoon back into the bowl and stood.

"Are you willing?" he asked.

"Are you kidding?" Marcie replied.

Skipjack began to undress as Marcie strode to the stairs.

"Hurry," Marcie cried. "They're close."

They kissed.

"Believe I might hear something, Jack."

"Damn, my stuff's on the stairs," he whispered as he stretched up and dashed to the doorway. The front door opened as he grabbed up his shirt and pants. It was Bill. Andy stood stock-still behind.

"Just had a bath," Skipjack said.

"We on in the morning, Mr. Maddox?" Andy asked.

"Where's the tub at?" Bill wondered. "You didn't take a bath in the cold rain, did you?"

"Poured it out, son."

"Why ain't you dressed?"

The boy crinkled his nose, but Andy smiled broadly.

"We're on, Andy. Right after you take Bill to school, they'll be down there."

"You want me here, too?"

"Damn right, I do."

Andy saluted and backed away.

"Why's your pistol on the table? Why ain't you wearing no clothes?"

"Any clothes, Billy," Marcie insisted, as she slipped past Skipjack. "How was school? Would you care for some soup?"

———

Orin Johanson must have been ten minutes early. His starched white shirt glinted against the shadowy woods, and before the shirt began to wilt, Mr. Johanson's maple tripod was fully assembled. He was ready to proceed the minute Skipjack sauntered up. The two men shook hands perfunctorily and then the surveyor opened his palms.

"So where do you suggest?" he demanded more than asked.

"I want to build a small home here, slightly off the road, maybe a little further up the hill, for as you can see, down here will flood from time to time."

Johanson picked up his outfit and hauled it up the hill.

"You tell me when and I will stop," he said.

"Stop," Skipjack said.

"You want it here?"

"Mr. Johanson, I want about two acres. I don't want the building site to flood. I want the slope to be as gentle as possible, because I don't want building problems."

Andy rolled up the hill in the buggy and saw the two men staring at one another.

"I am no architect; I am a surveyor. Maybe I can't make you so happy. This land is a mess. I cannot see ten feet in. How do I know what is beyond these weeds?"

"Maybe we should walk it off together," Skipjack suggested. "Just to get an idea."

Andy edged the mare up.

"Can I help?" he asked.

Skipjack smiled.

"If this boy is yours, maybe he can tramp down weeds, so I can see what I am looking at."

Skipjack pulled a flask from his pocket, unscrewed the top, and took a sip. After sighing, he extended the flask to Johanson and suggested he have a nip.

"You want a good job or what?" Johanson said.

"I want you to calm down and survey a plot. Apparently, you're short-handed today. Maybe a drink will help make up for it."

Johanson reached for the flask, took a quick slug, then passed it back.

"Can your boy help me? My damn son's locked up for fighting. I apologize; too old to be stomping through brush and setting stakes.

Hard to be in two places at once anyway."

"Andy and I are glad to help you, sir. Just point us."

"Be more comfortable pointing the boy; you don't scramble much better than me."

"Got a damn sore toe, Johanson. Let's get this job done. Andy, set the brake and help, if you please."

The whole thing took no more than an hour. The lot was shaped more like a trapezoid than a square. Buffered from the road by twenty yards of slope and edged on the downtown side by an outcrop of limestone, it was staked into the hillside with about a fifty-foot easement to connect with the main drive uphill to Skipjack's.

At the end, Andy was beaming ear to ear, and Johanson's mood had improved not at all.

"Mr. Maddox, I have two questions," Johanson said as he slid the tripod onto his wagon. "One, will you pay now in cash or do you wish a bill, and also, why is this darkie so happy? He smiles like the promised land."

Skipjack took out his wallet and counted the necessary bills, winked at Andy, and held out the cash.

"Thanks, Mr. Johanson. It's been a pleasure," Skipjack said.

After the surveyor departed, Skipjack and Andy climbed into the buggy.

"Get Brawl to draw up some sensible plans."

"Yes, sir," Andy said. "You feeling all right, sir?"

"Hard to answer; must say I have felt better."

That afternoon, Mary Frances handed Skipjack a small stack of mail. On top was a letter in bold script from Clay. It was a thank-you note, but in it, he jokingly threatened to return. He had heard that, in Cincinnati, locals were on the lookout for Timothy and that it was rumored a gang was holed up right below Newport.

Rumor after rumor and nothing definitive. Skipjack thought that life was puzzling enough without all this doubt and confusion. He hated to admit it, but if he could contract the slaughter of Brother and his ilk, he would do so in a heartbeat.

Business was good. Mary Frances had everything on track and what she couldn't get done, Andy could. Skipjack had it made, except for one thing. Upriver, downriver? What difference did it make? As long as these demons breathed air, he knew his family would never be safe and he couldn't figure what the hell to do. For far too long, hours had felt like days and some weeks had felt like months.

Tom Thurston was through with the stonework. It wasn't feasible to have Andy pull double time forever, but Marcie wasn't safe alone and he couldn't stay on guard at all times. Then there was the baby coming; he could hire a nurse, but where could he hire one who could shoot and drive off intruders? His gut told him, Brother, crazy as he had become or maybe always had been, would return.

At his desk, he stared at the stone wall, then bowed his head, but it wasn't prayer that overtook him. He expelled a sigh and felt utterly defeated yet knew there must be some way. There always had been and as his forehead ground into his hands, Skipjack knew he should head home but loathed going empty-handed with the same utter confusion. On impulse, he determined he had to do something immediately.

A dive about two miles toward town drew much of the tough crowd on this part of the riverbank. Part of him wanted to go there, sit in dingy squalor with his hat pulled down, and eavesdrop. Maybe he would overhear some gossip, so that at least when he walked into his house, he had something to say. Then he realized whiskey and tarted-up whores were unlikely to offer him more than innuendo and squeamishness. He fought his urge, stalked to his own bar, and ordered one. Louis sat the drink down and then motioned with his fingers.

"Two men were in earlier talking about a gambling man."

Skipjack nodded.

"A dealer both had lost to. Didn't like him. One told the other that he seen the man shooting dice in a joint. Said the man had lost his thumb. Thought it was funny and both of 'em busted out laughing."

"So why you telling me this, Louis?" Skipjack asked. Louis narrowed his eyes and grinned. He wiped the bar with his towel.

"Believe they were referring to your brother," he whispered.

"Where and when was this?"

"The Dog Pit. Joint down the way. Few nights ago, I was led to believe."

"Why would you conclude they were talking about Brother?"

"You know how he talks worldly wise. The way they acted out, it sounded just like him."

"Those men still here?"

"No sir, unless they moved outside and switched drinks. One was drinking port and the other brandy. I ain't had no orders like that for at least an hour, so I reckon they left."

Skipjack clenched his teeth and breathed out. Remembering Marcie's new rule, he counted out money, plus a generous tip, and laid it on the bar.

"Any idea where they might have gone?"

"Wouldn't know," Louis said, "but they say leopards don't change their spots."

"The Pit?"

"Wouldn't doubt it."

Skipjack walked outside and stared over flat gray water. There was a cool front slowly sliding in. Moisture-bearing clouds stretched overhead and released misty droplets. Mary Frances walked out of the kitchen and stood beside him.

"Aleeta was here a minute ago."

"She gone?"

"She's got three. Wants to bring them tonight."

"She's already gone?"

Mary Frances shook her head.

"That ain't right," Skipjack said. "She just run in and out?"

Mary Frances said, "I know. She whispered in my ear when I was in the back pantry, then out the back door like an alley cat."

"Except it's broad daylight."

"No one in the kitchen saw her, but she was acting strange, I admit."

"She shows up later, you know where to put 'em, unless you know some way to stop it."

"Not without calling attention."

"I'll try to get back. That's all I can promise."

THE UNDERBELLY

Skipjack was past damp when he entrusted Jessie to the Pit's liveryman. He said he wouldn't be long and tossed him a coin. The man's pasty expression remained blank as he led Jessie away.

The sky was still gray, which meant it was early to be frequenting this joint, but Skipjack tugged down the brim of his hat and entered anyway. He walked straight toward the bar. Out of the corner of his eye, he saw candles flickering on small tables. It was so dark in the place he bumped into a woman, or else she bumped into him. She tried to kiss his mouth. He felt for his wallet. It was still there. Skipjack wiped his mouth and ordered a first-rate Green. The bartender poured a small shot and slid it over.

Before he had even tasted the whiskey, Skipjack knew he had made a mistake. The dog-fighting ring in the middle of the room was empty, but he didn't like dog fighting anyway. There was no one at the bar, except an old passed-out relic and the cadaverous bartender. He still hadn't tasted his drink when some young girl no more than fifteen asked the barkeep for change for a dollar. She bragged that it was her second john for the day. When she asked if Skipjack would like to be her third, he declined and took a slug of whiskey that was obviously not Green's. The face he made when he tasted the whiskey frightened the girl, even in that dark room.

"Hey," she said. "How would I know you don't like it? Jesus Christ!"

"No, honey," Skipjack tried to say, but she had stepped off the bar rail by then and mingled among the smoky tables, voice elevated and high-pitched.

"Don't belong here. You believe he turned my sugar down?"

Skipjack turned his back to the room and asked for a glass of the best they had. The bartender leaned in closely.

"Know you from somewhere," he said softly. He poured a shot from another bottle that looked exactly the same.

Skipjack imagined hair on the baldhead, a mustache on his face, then a beard, yet still couldn't place him. He took a sip and smiled.

"No, I think not, but this is sure a big improvement over the last."

"It's your voice," the bartender said.

"You ever work for me?"

"No, sir, it's something I can't quite figure."

Skipjack grabbed his glass, which almost sloshed over, then grappled with it and before taking a sip, winked and snorted. "Hell, I ain't dealing aces. Excuse me, I seem to be all thumbs. Pissed that young one off and everything."

"You from around here?"

"Where you think I sound like I'm from? New Orleans?"

"You work boats?" the bartender asked.

"In a manner of speaking, I suppose."

"I swear to God there's something familiar. You have a brother owns property here?"

"I've got a world of cousins—first, second, and third—if you get my drift."

The bartender squeezed out a wheezy snicker.

"Why do you ask?"

"Well, I notice things," the bartender said. "I wasn't always a barkeep, you know?"

"Reason for everything, isn't there?"

"Well, I suppose there is," the bartender agreed. "I could see something the minute you come in."

"You're all over it, aren't you?" Skipjack asked.

"Once had a place wouldn't use this dump as an outhouse. I was a lawyer, too."

"You were on your way up."

"One of your cousins is missing a thumb, ain't he? No need to hide."

"So, you know a little bit? Best keep it quiet."

The bartender reached in and poured a small splash.

"Mister, I know the rules."

"That's good," Skipjack said and looked into the smoky bar.

"Can hardly wait till first of the year. Know what I mean?" he whispered.

Skipjack nodded as if he couldn't care less. The bartender cleared his throat and scrubbed the bar top. He coughed and when Skipjack lifted a cigar to his lips, he extended a lit match. Skipjack studied a young girl waving a handkerchief before he acknowledged the flame, puffed, and nodded. The girl bent over and raised her skirt.

"She ain't nothing to what's planned, believe me."

Skipjack stared forward as the crowd around the girl tightened.

"Mister, if that's your taste, hold your horses."

Skipjack grinned over his shoulder.

"We're not talking small time," the bartender insisted. "I shouldn't say, but I will. Your cousin wouldn't even notice that trash. Where you from? He told me there would be all kinds. Let me guess: Cairo?"

Skipjack spun around and looked the man in the eye. "Where you building? This land here is low, isn't it?"

"Well, of course I know that. You can't fool. I been warned. He done got the land. You're one of the speculators and I personally don't blame you. But here's the thing, this cousin, if he is indeed your cousin, has got the whole kit and caboodle."

"Higher ground's that way," Skipjack exclaimed sweeping his arm upstream toward the tavern.

"Never said it wasn't," the bartender said softly.

"You say all parcels upstream are bought up. Damn, you sure he's got 'em all? I tell you upfront that's hard to believe. He can't have 'em all."

The bartender leaned in so close that his nose touched Skipjack's ear hairs.

"Never have known the man to lie, I'll tell you that, and I've watched him clean many a table."

"Backs it up, does he?"

"Wouldn't bet against him. Damn waste."

"You must be close?"

"Near enough."

"Maybe I should throw in then. I got cash. You think he might want it?"

"I wouldn't know, but all ventures need capital. This thing is big, I tell you."

"I reckon I need to talk to old Cuz. He'll remember me. When you see him last?"

"He's around time to time, but I can't speak for him. I could mention something, I suppose."

"I don't want to miss the boat."

"We're talking serious money here. You understand that?" the bartender said.

"I haven't been asleep the last twenty years. Hell, I don't want to haggle. Maybe I could play a small part, and I can keep my mouth shut; can you?"

"Why you think I'm here?"

"Well, pour me a splash for the road. When should I check back?"

The bartender closed his eyes.

"Where you staying at, if you don't mind."

"When can we meet?" Skipjack answered.

"What's your name?" the bartender asked, "so I can pass it on."

"What's your name, barkeep?"

"They call me Nelson."

"Now, ain't that a coincidence?" Skipjack replied. "My mother was a Nelson from down in Breckinridge County. My father was a Hardy. You tell cousin that Nelson Hardy dropped by."

"It's a small world, ain't it?" the bartender said.

"I'll check back."

"Won't promise anything."

"I wouldn't expect you to, Nelson, but you will talk to him, won't you?" Skipjack laid generous folding money on the bar.

"If not, won't be for lack of trying, sir."

———

Jessie was the sure-footed mule if ever there was one and a good thing, too. Skipjack had more trouble than he should have mounting, then after that, simply dropped the reins, slumped forward, and left the rest to Jessie and God. His brother was still around, or was he? Skipjack, dazed and bleary, leaned into Jessie's coarse mane. He was way past tired.

With one eye squinted shut and the other clouded, straining hard to remain open, he watched familiar roadside slip past. He was nearing Green's turnoff as he tried to fight dull weight that filled his head and coursed through his body until feet like anchors hung. Dimly saw a light approach. Tried asking for help but so dry he couldn't make his tongue move. His open eye locked shut. Within this darkness, he began to slide. He lacked strength and as soon as he hit mud, hands were upon him. Head hung as arms were yanked, wrenched back, and he was plowed this way and that over slush and dropped. A boot in the ribs sent him spinning down until he stopped.

He was inside all this and yet could do nothing. Not even see. Heard murmuring voices. Arched to keep mouth out of water, water, ditch. Tried to raise his arm to grab, then rag was stuffed in mouth, and when his eye flickered open, saw rope, raw and tight on one wrist, wrench the other. Voices above squawking and laughing. Both eyes open now, saw something shiny.

"Kill you quick."

What seemed hours later, heard boots sloshing. Knife still toying his throat. He was jerked upright and sloppily blindfolded, wrangled uphill, and hoisted onto the back of a wagon. Legs and arms were bound and the rag in his mouth supplemented with a cord pulled tight. Skipjack thought flesh would tear. Knifepoint pressed deeper. The wagon began to roll. A woman laughed softly. The knife was lifted from his throat and a hand rested gently on his thigh.

"Don't worry, Brother; you're headed home," Timothy said.

"Careful with that mule, Andre. Give the bitch her head."

"Brother, Brother, Brother," Timothy sighed. "It sure didn't have to come to this, did it?"

"Timmy, show some breeding," the female voice cooed. "No need to rub salt in a wound."

"Forgive me, Nan, for you are certainly right. Regrets born on judgment day are salty enough. Praise his name. I lost myself thinking on your dear Ashley so cruelly killed."

"By this one's hand, too. Torn from communion in a cowardly attack," the woman muttered. "Please, forgive me, Timothy, pain claws. I need medicine. Andre, my pipe. You best have some yourself, Tim. Blood is thick, loss is always. What difference, son or brother? Lord God!"

"Pass it when done, because you are correct. Blood is thick, and business rends souls."

Skipjack was as alert as he had ever been. Nelson had drugged him, sure as hell. Sour oily smoke wafted over, and he wondered if Louis was in on it, too. He tried to stretch, but was bound so tight, he could barely wriggle.

"Blow some in his face, Timmy, we don't want him restless."

Acrid smoke seemed all there was to breathe. Skipjack tried to growl, but all that came out was grating croak. Finally, trying to not breathe at all forced him into a desperate gasp that burned his nostrils and filled lungs with jagged crud, swirling his mind into velvety darkness infused with mocking laughter. With every ounce of his being, Skipjack struggled to focus on a diminishing pinpoint of light, but then vision swarmed to black; no wagon, no road, no anything.

Later, moon jiggling overhead; they crunched uphill. Skipjack recognized familiar trees. At first, comforted by known silhouettes, he tried to yawn but could not, then stared into the gaze of a crone peering down. He felt pistol barrel cold on his temple, heard Brother exhale, saw icy eyes through wisps of smoke, knew Brother's free hand rested just above his knee.

"Andre," Timothy whispered, "until we are certain, best go slow."

"No, there, by the stable. I see him."

"Andre's right. I see him as well," the woman rasped.

A man walked confidently toward the wagon, smiling in a broad-toothed, wholesome way. He made a motion like hammering and then twirled his hands, nodded with his lower lip extended.

"Boy's inside tied with momma. Slave's in the barn trussed by the mare; he'll bring a righteous price if you ask me."

"Well, nobody did," Timothy said.

"Now, don't kill incentive. Lord God, it's a challenge to keep a band together."

"I want him dead, Nan. Do I have to kill him myself?"

"You newborn jackass; you might have a big prick, but your brain, like your dealing thumb, is completely missing. If you are unaware of what that critter's worth, I am not."

Skipjack could see Timothy's face absorb this tirade, and in spite of himself, he nodded until the pistol under his jaw gritted his teeth.

"Of course, you're right. Can we discuss details later? This is much bigger than one darkie."

"Maybe so and maybe not. Gambling hall is a powerful dream, but I have this critter sold."

"You got to have papers," Timothy said.

"How the hell you think I placed him?" the woman hissed. "Jesus, Tim, keep a hold. I keep forgetting just what a neophyte you are."

CHAPTER 14

RENDER UNTO CAESAR, CHILD

G etting into the house wasn't easy. Bound tight as a mummy, Skipjack was leaned precariously beside the front door where Andre and another had deposited him. He could see Marcie knotted on the sofa and Bill's motionless feet sticking out behind on the floor.

Over the creaking sounds of the departing wagon, Skipjack suffered foolish jabber as Timothy insisted he wanted Andy dead and buried, and Nan, who in the light of flickering lanterns, appeared to be vocal sticks and rags, screeched that Andre knew where he would be as good as dead and worth a whole lot more.

"How do you know Frenchie's even coming back?" Timothy said through clenched teeth.

"Why wouldn't he? He's always paid."

"That sloppy bastard you sent with him. Do you trust him?"

"Just tell me, Timothy, what kind of fallen angel are you? Dragged slop wet out of Hell's own river. Have you forgotten you were anointed by me? What is special about you is mine. You are the king of my choosing."

"God knows, I am pleased to live and admit you saved me and also admit that fool's worth money, but I see no sense messing with small change. Sending them after Trapper's liable to draw attention."

The woman wagged a fine-boned face that still retained a hint of beauty.

"I thought you were a promised one," she said. "Damnation! We haven't a gambling hall as yet and that boy is pure money and Trapper is a fat liability thin as he is. One of them is worth something alive, the other dead."

Skipjack caught a flicker in Marcie's eye. She was bound as tightly as he was. Timothy and the hag scuffled and snarled. Skipjack did his level best to seem oblivious and was aided by the fact that only with great effort could he focus his eyes.

Brother and the debutante dragged him into the kitchen and lashed him to a chair. After Skipjack's legs were rebound, Timothy secured his chest and arms, freed his hands, then cinched him back taut at elbows and ankles. The whole time, Nan's pistol was just out of reach and aimed at his forehead, her eyes filmy as stagnant water.

Then Nan perched beside Marcie on the sofa and asked politely if she was comfortable. Marcie stared at the ceiling and when asked again, stomped her feet as best she could.

"Here to do business are we not, Timothy? I would propose Miss Marcie would be much more helpful if we loosen knots and bring her darling boy out from behind the sofa and sit him at table."

Marcie nodded.

"The girls understand, don't we, dear?"

At this Skipjack nodded as well.

With curses and a sharp knife, the lanky crone had young Bill standing, then seated and lashed to a chair. With mouths contorted by ropes, Skipjack, Marcie, and Billy exchanged wide-eyed expressions. The boy shook his head up and down until Nan registered concern.

"Do we need gags? No one's around."

So, one by one, deep welt marks were revealed. Marcie's eyes darkened and both Timothy and Nan noticed.

"We did the untying, not the tying. Remember that, dear," Nan said in a lilting voice.

"Your fiends did the tying," Marcie said.

Billy's eyes got big and Timothy told Marcie to shut her mouth.

"Damn it!" Marcie shouted. "They did what you told 'em."

"Little miss lady," Nan said as she put an icepick to Billy's throat, "you have a point. I have mine. Believe our menfolk have business to transact."

A tiny drop of blood descended from a puncture on the boy's neck. Nan reached into filthy black trousers, pulled out her long folding knife, and opened it. Her bloodshot eyes glinted above crimson lips as she stabbed the blade into the tabletop. Timothy sat at the table's end.

Nan confided, "This is not a negotiation. The reconciliation will be conceived this night, isn't it so, Timothy?"

Timothy rubbed the side of his face and smiled faintly.

"Justice will be done, angel."

Rain began to slap the front of the house, then thunder crashed, and rain poured straight down.

"Whoo-hoo!" Nan exclaimed as she extracted her pipe from an elaborately beaded pouch strung on rawhide tied around her neck. "I just love a thunderstorm."

When she sucked the small carved-stone pipe, all her features furrowed toward flame. For the first time, Timothy looked almost flustered. He cleared his throat, then asked Skipjack if he was thirsty and their eyes locked for a fleeting instant.

"Reckon we all are. I could use a whiskey, reckon Marcie could use wine, and the boy some water."

"I see no harm," Timothy said.

"He's stalling." The woman coughed a spray of spittle and smoke.

"Now, don't forget we're blood, Nan. I know my way."

"Sun up every morning, so what?"

"How can it hurt?"

"In and out."

"We're in, Nan, just like I said."

"Out." Nan spewed another cloud of smoke and grinned. "Now, it's out."

When Timothy rubbed the side of his face with his four-fingered hand, Skipjack noticed Brother was sweating. While Timothy fiddled with bottles and glassware, Nan closed her eyes as if she were communing with entities far removed. Skipjack took the opportunity to make eye contact with Marcie and Billy.

He attempted to project strength. Marcie blinked. Billy went jittery. Skipjack blew impatiently near to whistle.

"Now, Brother, surely you can appreciate it takes a minute."

Skipjack didn't answer but focused on Billy's hands still tightly bound as Tim turned to grin.

"You always were brave, weren't you, Timothy?"

"Still is, potbelly," Nan said.

"Are you afraid of a child's hands?"

"What you referring to, two-faced?" the woman asked

"No offense, but I was wondering how the boy was to drink water."

"Oh, goodness," Nan simpered. "His wrists are bound."

Timothy sat wine in front of Marcie and placed a whiskey in Skipjack's hand. When he put the water glass in front of Billy, the boy asked could he still do card tricks?

"This is just like Christmas," Timothy said, winking at Skipjack.

"This ain't near Christmas," Billy stated. "Uncle Timothy, can you still do the three kings like you showed?"

"Damnation! Tim, will you permit prattle to continue all night?"

Tim raised his hand before speaking.

"Nan, please respect the fact that, as this is a family meeting, we must follow protocol."

"You best start following, or I'll lead," Nan said as she cocked her pistol.

Timothy sat opposite Skipjack and leaned forward.

"I know where you keep papers, Brother, and I know where the deed is. Sure would be good if you cheerfully signed it over, but knowing you, I don't expect it to be quite that simple. I got a proposition to make."

"Quickly," Nan said between puffs.

"We could have worked together. I made overtures."

"Timothy," Skipjack said. "The will gave me this place and you run off a full five years before."

"Water over the dam," Nan said. "Get it."

"I don't even know you, lady, but you don't know the half."

She pointed her pistol at his forehead. "I could give a rat's ass."

"Nan, don't point that thing. First things first. Business, remember?"

"I remember plenty, Tim. You said this wouldn't take a smidgen.'"

"Hold your tongue. This is the path. We need papers signed."

Nan said nothing but started rocking slowly. She raised the pistol to her temple and hummed. Her wrinkled face attained sleepy childish softness. Skipjack thought he was the only one holding breath until he glanced around. Timothy raised his hands and leaned back in his chair.

Finally, she said, "Timothy," accentuating all three syllables. "I know when you play poker, you always know to keep your hand close. Something I'm missing?"

"No, sugar, I know the cards."

"Then play, shoot, or fold."

Thunder crashed directly overhead and the whole place rolled. Billy shuddered and announced that he had to pee. No one paid him any mind as the thunder rumbled for an impossibly long time and a drop of water splatted on the table.

"Roof's leaking," Timothy said, flashing a grin.

Nan lowered her pistol and gently placed it on the table.

"Now I got to go," she announced. "Might as well, if we're going to discuss upkeep. Where you crap here?"

"Privy's out back," Timothy said.

"Who's going out in this slop?"

"There's a pot in Billy's room," Marcie said.

The woman stood unsteadily, and Marcie signaled with a tilt of her head.

"Something about a storm. Thanks kindly, sugar."

When she swayed into Billy's room, Skipjack strained forward. "Timothy, I could give you a pile of money, but you can't get away with this."

With raggedy pants halfway to her knees, Nan reappeared in the doorway.

"Sweet damn, heard that coming. You have nothing." She farted, reentered Billy's room and demanded all discourse cease. "Hold your fire, Tim," she hollered. Timothy shook his head and rubbed the side of his nose.

"This is an unfortunate state of affairs," he offered after a moment.

"Don't know sorry from mother's arse," Nan hollered. "Don't even think about looking at my gun, Timothy. If you go soft on me, I'll cut it off and fish." A moment later she sneered and swayed back to her seat beside Marcie. "Proceed," she said as she clutched the pistol and pulled her knife out of the tabletop.

Timothy took a deep breath. Surprising everyone, Nan kept her mouth shut.

"I knew from an early age you were Dad's favorite. You were my hero."

Skipjack started to speak, but Marcie moved her head slightly, and he desisted.

"For as long as I can remember, it was you this and you that, and Timothy take the rear. So, Timothy took off to see the world and has seen the world. Oh, yes, has he ever. And you—with what you claim as wife and son—fatten yourselves on our homestead, willfully oblivious to the twisted legal logic that gave it to you because you were firstborn. You remain blind to the future that I, who have seen this world, could reveal, and sit frog-eyed and forget that I begged to share."

"I have to pee," Billy said, grimacing.

"Won't take much longer, son," Timothy said softly. "You're behind the times, Brother."

"He missed," Nan stated, eyes blazing.

"Now, Nan's right about that. You fail to accept the march of change. This country is dividing. Do you know where you stand? Don't get me wrong. I don't care where you stand on issues. I'm talking geography. I'm talking location. I could make you richer than Croesus and all you had to do was to sign a paper. Don't you see everything that goes north and south passes here? No way out of that, you blind mole who claims everything but good sense with your birthright."

"Somebody, everybody, I got to piss 'fore I pop."

"Now, son, this—"

"Ain't your son, Uncle Tim, but I'm going to die you don't let me pee."

"Hold your horses, little man."

"Are you daring to spare?" Nan asked.

"Please allow me to finish," Timothy said.

"Where are the damned papers?"

"I know," Timothy insisted, resting his palms on the table.

"Well, then damn your hide, get 'em signed."

"Almost there, Nan. Give me one minute."

"You're sparing, ain't you? My Ashley's pissing, Tim."

"Uncle Timothy, please! Me and Ashley both got to pee."

"Fine and dandy. Go get the papers. I'll let the boy drain before he drowns us."

Timothy leaned on his hand and stood. Nan busied herself with Billy's knots.

"Who tied this bastard?" she muttered. "Don't leak on me, sawed-off, or you'll wish you were a girl."

Billy wailed. "I got to."

"Go get those bloody papers. Cannot believe you fathered this squirmer."

"Can't even untie your own grunt's granny knot."

"Get papers signed, Mr. High and Mighty."

"She's not always like this," Timothy said apologetically. "Guess, I best get the papers. Still up under your bed, Brother?"

"Wouldn't answer the jackass," Nan slurred.

"Please hurry up," Billy whimpered as a blast of thunder rattled the windows.

"Get a hold, boy," Skipjack said. Billy met his gaze.

"I'm trying to," the boy cried.

"There," Nan said as she sliced the last cord binding the boy's feet. "Now, pee, damn you."

Billy scampered. Nan swayed upright and softly chuckled, while Timothy climbed stairs two at a time.

"Did you two ever think about having children?" she asked.

"I'm expecting now," Marcie said.

Nan patted Marcie's belly and lightly grazed her breast with the back of her hand.

"You know, I could tell. I'm different like that and knew the first time I saw you," she confided. "His this time?" she asked tilting her head. "Better luck next time, sugar."

"Here we go," Timothy exclaimed. "It's all here," he announced as he bounded down the stairs. "Now all we need is a pen and we're in business."

Timothy stood at the head of the table studying the papers.

"This is what we need. Darn, I think the pen's upstairs in Marcie's sewing room on the table, Nan."

"Render unto Caesar, child. Damn that boy's a cataract," Nan exclaimed before fixing Timothy in scornful glare. "Get it your own damn self, emperor."

"Keep an eye on them, then." Timothy remounted the stairs. Nan clucked her tongue and licked the long blade of her knife. She laid her pistol on the table and smiled conspiratorially at Marcie and Skipjack. She lowered the flat of her knife to Marcie's throat and grinned as Timothy's steps shook the staircase.

"Have to know how to milk him, you know," she confided. "But I will tell, in case you forgot, he ain't no soft man. I wouldn't train him if that was the case. I got to school this way time to time. It's a challenge. And sugar and spice so far works fine."

Timothy bounded back down the stairs.

He placed the heirloom inkwell respectfully between them. Skipjack saw Nan straighten and stare out at the glint of her blade point.

Brother Timothy said, "Now . . ." and Skipjack saw Billy's double-barrel poke into the room as Nan slowly began to turn. There was a blast, a thud, and Timothy was no longer beside him. Skipjack signaled Marcie to throw her body sideways and as his own chair tilted, he saw Nan's knife draw back. A second roaring concussion echoed as Skipjack's skull smacked the floor.

Warm liquid was dripping into his ear. He twisted and looked up at what remained of Nan's shoulder and arm, bloody fingers inches above his face.

"Aw, you pissing bastard."

"Reload, Billy. Marcie, Marcie!"

There was no reply. He scooted and wriggled until he could see Marcie's face. Her eyes were shut. Then as Billy tromped back into the room, snapping the barrel shut, her eyelids fluttered.

"Keep that gun level, son. Keep it on your uncle, too."

Billy didn't say anything.

"Billy? Talk to me."

Skipjack rocked furiously, trying to loosen his bonds, but struggled in vain. He noticed one of Marcie's eyes open slowly.

"Uncle Tim don't have no head. She's dead, too, or at least ain't breathing."

"Come cut me loose, so we can tend to Momma."

Billy laid the shotgun down on the floor beside Skipjack.

"Boy, cut the rope. Just one cord."

The boy sawed with what Skipjack figured was the dullest knife they owned, but when he looked into Billy's eyes, he kept his mouth shut. The stricken look he saw was beyond instruction.

"Going to be all right. Keep cutting."

"Trying," Billy said. "I swear I'm trying."

"You're doing it, too," Skipjack said, "then we're going to get your momma free."

"Should I do it now?"

"No, Billy," Marcie said. "Free your dad."

"Sure thing, Momma." The last strands broke. Billy handed the knife to Skipjack and shouted, "I need to get the paring knife. All that's good for is spreading butter."

Skipjack eased over, and when he freed his feet, picked up Billy's shotgun and surveyed the carnage. The room was sloshed with blood: the wall behind him, the table, the floor. Timothy— unrecognizable and crumpled against the wall—was missing everything from lower jaw up. The woman's arm dangled by tendons. Skipjack knelt down beside Billy and helped loosen Marcie's knots.

"We got to get out of here," Skipjack said.

Within minutes, they were headed downhill. The mare hitched up, Gracie and Ducky in back, and Jessie tethered behind. None of them noticed the cool damp breeze. Huddled together, they all leaned forward.

"I had to," Billy said in a quavering voice.

Skipjack shook his head, while Marcie stroked the boy's brow.

"You saved our lives."

"Son," Skipjack asked softly, "what if you hadn't?"

"We'd be dead," Billy said.

Rain drizzled lightly, and Skipjack patted the papers in his coat pocket to make sure they were tucked in out of the weather. His pocket was bulging, not only with the deed and stuff off his table, but also with a batch of paperwork that he had lifted out of Timothy's inner coat pocket.

"Marcie, I'm taking you to Green's."

"What about Andy?"

"Just keep steady."

"You think they're more?" Billy asked.

"Damn right. Be a fool not to think so. Keep steady, you hear?"

"Yes, sir."

———

A lantern glowed at the bottom of the hill. All Skipjack could see was jiggling light and jutting shapes. He handed the reins to Marcie as he pulled the brake.

"Stay here and look sharp," he said as he stepped from the buggy.

"Trapper here," said a voice emerging from shadow. "Trapper here, Trapper here, don't shoot."

Skipjack figured since he wasn't yet dead, he had nothing to fear.

"What is it?"

"Can't tell in a hurry, but once you hear, it ain't strange."

"For once, Trapper, you ain't jabbering and I still can't understand a word."

"What's it like for me? How you think I like it? I'm me," Trapper insisted.

Skipjack scanned every dark inch that surrounded them.

"Are we safe here, Trapper? Yes or no?"

"Pretty damn safe, yes, sir. The fox's in the cage. I reckon what I see, you have bagged the rest."

"God help me, Trapper."

"Oh, he will, Mr. Maddox. God will serve his servant. Yes, sir, he surely will."

"What happened down the way? What is that lantern?"

"It's a long story . . ."

"Trapper! Who is it, goddamn it?"

"Sheriff Winston, sir. But he come after. Yes, sir, I seen it."

"What all did you see, Trapper? It's raining, don't you know?"

"It sure is. Well, maybe I should begin at the beginning, just to set you straight."

"Trapper, can I walk down and not get shot? Can I leave my wife and son here while I do?"

"Well, sure, else I could guard 'em. Your Andy's safe and sound, so maybe he could come if you wanted."

"Andy's safe?" Billy asked.

"Bruises, nothing 'cept bruises. Just like the day he's born."

"Guard 'em with your life," Skipjack said and stomped down the hill toward the lantern.

As he neared men standing around an overturned wagon in the drainage ditch, Andy waved. Skipjack saw the sheriff looking down at a dray horse still in traces laid out half on the road. There was a flash-blast from a pistol and the horse kicked still.

Out from under the wagon, a clump of rags seemed to have crawled partly out of the ditch. But the shape did not move. Another nestled on the bank. Skipjack lowered his rifle, walked into lantern light and tried to catch the sheriff's eye, but the sheriff was whispering in a deputy's ear, who after a quick look at Skipjack, stepped back into shadow.

"What the hell is going on here, sheriff?"

"Saved your boy from getting stole. How 'bout that?"

Skipjack tugged the brim of his hat down.

"How the hell you happen on that opportunity?"

"Trapper got suspicious and sent word."

"Trapper sent word?"

"As you know, Trapper does surveying."

"No."

"Well, he claims he done work for your brother. As it turns out, he hasn't been paid. Trapper was to be paid here tonight. He found that so unusual he told my deputy, who told me."

"What had he surveyed?"

"According to him, three parcels of land. Said he was afraid the meeting was not really about pay."

"Who are these all quiet and dead?" Skipjack asked, pointing.

"That's the odd thing," the sheriff said. "Just as we rode up, there was gunfire and the wagon went over into the ditch. Your boy, Andy, flew in head first and if it ain't been for Josh, who was here a minute ago, would still be in the ditch, drowned and wouldn't be worth nothing. Can you beat that?"

Skipjack pulled the pistol out of his belt, handed it to Andy, and asked him to run up the hill and drive Miss Marcie and young Bill down.

"I do thank you, sheriff, for protecting my property, and I'm sure Andy thanks you, too. But are you in the habit of protecting the likes of Trapper who fear they might not get paid?"

"I do what I can, Maddox."

"So, who are these?" Skipjack asked again, pointing to the crumpled bodies. The dead horse expelled a long fart. Skipjack chuckled and asked. "Is that your answer?"

"Your old-time humor is not all that amusing." The sheriff swelled. "But I believe these men may be in your brother's employ."

"Well, how do you know? Who killed them, sheriff?"

"Killed them?" The sheriff grinned and glowed like he was laying down aces. "If I were you, I would ask your bushwhacker friend, Trapper. I believe he was first on the scene."

"Is that's so? How do you know who they are?"

"Skipjack, please." The sheriff smiled indulgently. "You excel at your business, I'm good at mine."

"You saying Trapper killed 'em?" Skipjack said harshly.

"Not at all. We haven't searched the thicket. There were several shots fired. The investigation has just begun. Wouldn't be surprised to find a body or two, would you?"

"Damn it, Ballard Winston. Have you questioned the man?"

"Are you referring to your friend Trapper?"

"You're damn right I am."

The sheriff chuckled as his handkerchief daubed right beneath his hooded eyes.

"Surely you're joking. The man is a fool. Good with hooks and traps, that's all."

The buggy—with Marcie, Billy, Trapper, and Andy—rolled to a stop.

"Andy, come with us," Skipjack shouted. "You too, Trapper. You join us."

"Can I bring my mule?"

"Please do. Ride shotgun."

"Yes, sir. Dandy."

"We'll talk tomorrow sometime," the sheriff said as he lifted his lantern.

"Where's your deputy hiding, Winston?"

"He ain't hiding. Be assured."

"You might not like what he finds," Skipjack said.

"What would you know?" the sheriff replied. Andy clucked at the mare and the buggy lurched.

CHAPTER 15

SHERIFF'S GOOSE HAS TURNED TO CROW

"I want to check Mary Frances before we hit Green's. Turn in."

"Sir, my Lacy's helping Mary Frances in the kitchen tonight."

In the turnaround spot, Skipjack jumped off the buggy. Ran straight to the kitchen. Mary Frances was already shutting down. Took her aside. Her face was intense even before the first word tumbled out of his mouth.

"Lock up. I want Lacy out of here. Where is she?"

"Clearing glassware."

"Send that girl out front. Andy's there. Where's Louis?"

"You didn't see him when you came through the bar?" Mary Frances asked.

"Forgot to look. Thank God you're all right."

Mary Frances looked puzzled, then held a finger to her lips. She walked to the opening that led into the bar. She called out to Lacy. Asked her where Louis was.

"He came outside, sent me to clean the bar, and went toward the water."

"Go to Andy out front, now!"

"How many are here?" Skipjack asked.

"Dining room has about four river ramblers into us for a good sum. Outdoor tables all clear."

"Grab the money. I'll deal with the dining room."

Mary Frances wanted to ask what was going on but didn't. She trusted the man, and within five minutes, most doors were locked.

In the dining room, Skipjack said with a forced grin, "The drinks, the dinners, are all on me, but get back to your boats now. We're closed."

"Don't suppose he's aware who he deals with, is he?" a sporty fellow offered.

"Sir, no offense intended. I want your business, but tonight if you don't leave peacefully, I swear to heaven above, you will leave the other way."

"Who are you to be threatening, sir?" a jowly gentleman slurred, while his compatriots knocked noggins and chuckled.

Before Skipjack drew his pistol, Mary Frances strode in with butcher knife raised and said, "Boys, I grant he looks a bloody sight, but Mr. Maddox here is the owner." Then she gripped the tablecloth and yanked the thing with such a snap that most of the dishes and glassware settled in place as the tablecloth fluttered at her feet.

"What is the meaning of this?" one blustered.

"We're closed. Head your hams downriver."

"Seriously, gentleman, the dinner's on us," Skipjack said.

"They don't hear sweet talk, Skipjack. Get the hell out of here," Mary Frances shouted.

"I'll walk beside, sir," Andy said. "So will Lacy."

"Me, too," Billy piped in.

"Hop in, Mary Frances. We got plenty room here," Skipjack said.

"I could ride the mule," she offered.

"Andy, you and Lacy ride Jessie," Skipjack said.

"Then Willy can sit in my lap, can't he, Marcie?" Mary Frances asked.

So that's the way they rode to Green's—guns bristling in each and every direction—through drizzle beneath a gauzy moon.

"What's happened?" Mary Frances asked.

"Wait till we get off the road," Marcie answered.

"It's not good, no sir. Not good," Trapper exclaimed as he trotted up ahead. He turned and waved them forward. Skipjack saw a wagon shape up ahead. Instinctively, he slowed the struggling mare in spite of Trapper's positive signal.

"Come on with it. Come on," Trapper called out from up the hill. "Brawl Thurston. It's Brawl."

"Marcie, what's happened?" Mary Frances whispered. Marcie shook her head.

"Billy saved our lives."

"Uncle Tim's dead," Billy said.

Mary Frances hugged the boy and looked sideways at Marcie. Marcie nodded.

"Billy done what had to be done," Skipjack said.

———————

Flickering torchlight silhouetted Brawl and Green against the white brick of the mansion. Skipjack slipped the reins to Marcie, jumped down, and hurried to where the two men stood. Neither looked surprised. Green shook his head. Brawl just stared with his jaw set.

"Green, I need help. Can you put us up?"

"Thank God, you're alive," Green said. "Don't have to ask."

"They need a place to stay," Skipjack near shouted as he swept his arm to encompass his entourage. "The boy shot them both," he said huskily. "Saved our lives. Got to go back before what's left burn the place down."

"Not tonight they won't," Green said. "Tom Thurston and three of mine, plus two Italians took out over the ridge trail about half hour ago. Brawl heard shooting when he was on his way here."

"Still need to get back. Got to clean the place. Two dead devils. Brother with his head blown off."

"Johnson," Green called and before the mare had stopped breathing hard, Johnson was leading everyone except Andy, Trapper, and Brawl to a guesthouse. The mare, buggy, and mule were led off by two young boys, one coaxing Gracie, the other cradling Ducky as if she were a squirming infant. Green said something behind his hand to a giant dark-skinned man and then motioned all inside.

"Skipjack, before we go anyplace, you're going to have a drink."

In the mudroom off the kitchen, an old woman lit lanterns, while a young woman hoisted a tray laden with glasses, whiskey, and beer. Green motioned to the chairs surrounding a long, rough-hewn worktable. He urged everyone to be seated. Andy sat after Skipjack did, but Trapper grinned and looked confused.

"You got trouble sitting down to table, Trapper?" Brawl said flatly. Green motioned and Trapper sat.

At Green's urging, Skipjack spilled the story from Louis to Nelson, bartender at the Pit, the mugging, and all the stuff that happened after that, including the sheriff down the hill and Andy's rescue. He then insisted he had to get home.

"Not all by yourself you don't."

"Mr. Maddox," Brawl said, "Mr. Green and I have sent six men to guard your house. We all know you eager. But let us try to understand the lay of the land."

"Like what the hell were you doing there, Trapper?" Green asked.

"Sheriff said he killed the men that were hauling Andy off," Skipjack said.

"Andy," Brawl said. "What do you say?"

"Seemed like the shooting came from lots of directions," Andy replied.

Without knowing why, Skipjack reached into his coat pocket and slipped out the papers he had stashed. One by one, he unfolded them on the table as Trapper stuttered, and the room grew tense. The first sheath was his own deed. The second was an old surveying map, but the other bundle was the batch he had plucked out of Brother's pocket. He spread them out, some speckled with blood.

"I heard things, two things," Trapper said. "First thing was that I weren't getting paid unless I helped sell Andy. I had nothing against him; you mark my words and deeds. I survey, knowing this land, knowing it plain as my hand, yes, sir. Hired way back before any of this got started, by what I took to be a landowner, Tim Maddox, your brother.

"I drew chains and drafted maps, accurate maps, not like some," he said. "I did what I was hired to perform and never did get paid one dollar. Not yet ever."

"Wait a minute," Skipjack said. "This you here?" He thrust papers under Trapper's nose.

"Yes, sir, that's exactly it. That's what I done. They asked, but no way never paid."

Skipjack shakily laid the papers in front of Green.

"That's my place," Skipjack said. "Look, it's divided into three plots."

"Who hired you?" Green asked.

Before Trapper answered, Skipjack offered up another document edged with blood.

"This explains a lot," he said.

Green took it in pudgy fingers and slowly worked his lower jaw side to side, then smiled and chuckled.

"You're a lucky man, Trapper," Green smiled.

"I sure am, sir. Sure am at that," Trapper replied, fumbling for his missing earlobe.

"Thank God above your name ain't on this."

"It's a partnership, ain't it?" Skipjack asked.

"Bancroft Maddox Winston Development Company, est. 1859."

"Can you believe it?" Skipjack said and lowered his head to the table. Brawl rested a hand on his shoulder.

"Parcel one: the river section (site of casino?), blah de dah, plus three hundred yards of creek front. Parcel two: entire bottomland and creek to existing road. Parcel three: hillside and creek property, including meadow, until Ballard fork and large boulder bordered by sycamore thirty-two feet in circumference."

"You remember who Bancroft was, don't you, Andy?" Skipjack asked. "You all remember? He's the one my brother disappeared with. The man turned up a floater with his balls cut off. Sheriff made like he was all steamed and was going to bring Brother to justice, remember?"

"You went there to get paid, did you, Trapper?" Green asked.

"Not exactly that way at all. No, sir."

"Exactly what way?" Brawl pushed himself up in his chair.

"Other morning 'fore light, I come up from the creek. Man's standing by my mule. He ask, do I want my surveying money. Other voice in the dark ask if I want a piece of nigger. Yes, sir, he said that. I asked what? God help me, sir. First voice guarantees money if I show up at the bottom of Maddox Road tonight. I get paid, yes, sir. I agree."

"Did you know it was Andy he was talking about?" Skipjack asked.

"Didn't know nothing, but the time, the time he said to be there."

"Who was this man?" Green asked.

"Couldn't hardly see; big though. Talk French-like. Other man say, 'Money' and 'survey' in funny English. But that man I never see, stuck behind the first."

"When was that?"

"Night before. Didn't feel right. Tonight, I slip up near two hours early and slid in under branches and got soaked. Warn't long before I hear a rustling'. I froze; sure did. Two men pass by within a hand, then hunker four paces downhill."

"Same ones you talked to?" Green asked.

"Not likely," Trapper said. "These ones talk proper."

"Green, I got to check on family and house," Skipjack said. Brawl laid his hand on his shoulder and pushed down. Skipjack grimaced but sat.

"Didn't dare breathe. They discussing money, yes, sir. Laughing how this was Skipjack's lucky day. Started quarreling how they was to split cash. First, they was joking. Then one said to the other, 'What do you know?' The other said, 'So what you know?'"

"What's your point, Trapper? What happened?

"Yes, sir. Well, turned out all was on the take. One hauling Andy was trying to cut a deal. Must 'a told the wrong man, 'cause these found out. Figured they'd profit, too. Yes, sir. I didn't draw a breath. You know how a mink can lay low. It was hard. I hate to say my bowels was trembling. Then a wagon come uphill. Them two gets excited and then it weren't long 'fore another come down.

"'Go,' the one fella says and the other jumps and goes crashing forward. The one talking stands, takes dead aim, and fires. The wagon lurches toward the ditch. Running man grabs at the harness, but the kit and caboodle's falling right on top him, and he jumps barely clear. I make out some other horses riding up. I figured I couldn't hold breath no longer, so I jump forward; my knife bites 'fore the man can reload. Turns out, it was the sheriff that done rode up. When I come out of the woods, that's when I help pull Andy out of the ditch. I got no idea what come of the other fella. If he didn't run off, he's crazy."

"Who were those two, Trapper?" Green asked as he leaned his heft across the table.

"Don't know names; they prowl nameless. Nigger snatchers, sir."

"You never were paid?"

"No sir. 'Bout got kilt, that's what."

"You weren't a go-between then," Green said.

"Hard to go between you don't know what's what."

"I believe the man, don't you?" Brawl asked.

Skipjack nodded slowly. Trapper nodded eagerly.

"Hard to figure the sheriff's name on something like this," Green said.

"Brother was persuasive. You can make book the sheriff will say he never knew."

"His signature, Skipjack? The man's goose is cooked." Green said.

"Got to check Marcie and Billy. Then maybe someone will ride over to the house with me."

"Hell, we'll all go. Won't we?" Green offered.

———

Billy was still seated in a shallow hammered copper tub in the middle of the guesthouse floor. He was attended by Lacy, Mary Frances, and his mother. Skipjack saw Marcie throw back a slug of wine and Mary Frances drizzled steaming water out of a kettle. As far as he could tell, the boy was being well cared for. Before he could say a word, Marcie caught his eye and hugged him.

Billy looked steadily into Skipjack's eyes and nodded. Skipjack quietly said he would return shortly. Marcie walked him to the door and stepped outside.

"We're riding over to the house. The sheriff's in on it."

"Damn it, Jack, be careful. A man in a trap is dangerous."

"A man just freed should not be underestimated."

"You need a bath, too, you ornery fool," she said and then hugged him hard.

"You'll be safe. Keep the doors locked. I'm not alone."

———

They called it the ridge road, but it was actually an old deer trail. Not wide enough for a buggy and much too rugged for an easy ride. Skipjack rode Jessie. Trapper shared his mule with Andy. Green rode his favorite horse, a huge chestnut stallion, who snorted and complained of poor footing throughout the journey. Skipjack and Trapper gave their beasts free rein and they stepped surefootedly. Bred to run, Green's horse, Big Boy, was spooked and skittish. Brawl, on his mule, Blackfish, brought up the rear.

Skipjack had to pass the shortcut, knowing full well Green couldn't make it.

"Think it's better we approach from the back," he said.

"Andy and I could slip down this way," Trapper offered.

"Let's stick together."

"Better call out we're coming down," Green said.

"If Tom and your men ain't heard us by now, they're dead asleep."

"They heard us," Brawl said and at that moment, Tom Thurston spoke up out of the brush right beside Brawl.

"I got your lantern, Mr. Maddox. I'll run up ahead and lead you all in."

"You'll make a fine target with a lantern," Skipjack said.

"Ain't nobody here."

———

Before Skipjack had even stepped on his porch, Brawl and Green had tried to talk him out of going inside. One of the Italians stood beside a trail of blood, shaking his head. Brawl promised he would have the house cleaned before noon.

"We got the place guarded. Nothing coming in; nothing getting out," Green said. "Let it be, Skipjack."

Skipjack wrenched free. Both men stepped back and shrugged. Tom whispered, "No one in there." But Skipjack either didn't hear or didn't care; he punched the front door with his shoulder and entered. A lantern burned inside, and his shadow staggered on the interior walls.

"Lord have mercy," Brawl muttered.

"Where did they go?" Skipjack roared from inside. "Bastards."

Skipjack stumbled out the front door and leaned against the jamb. His hollow eyes shifted. "Where the hell are they? What have you done?" He charged at Tom Thurston. Green and Brawl caught him in midair as he dove off the porch and they laid him out in the mud. Brawl placed his hand on Skipjack's back. Tom walked over to the edge of the woods and stayed there until Skipjack was propped against a step, flat-out sobbing.

Green motioned Tom over. Andy led him gently by the elbow. Skipjack looked up out of fiery red eyes.

"Nobody in there? You saw nothing?"

"Answer the man," Brawl said.

"No, sir, nobody."

"There's blood over here," Trapper called out. "Yes, sir. Here's where they loaded."

"You got some brandy in there, Skipjack?" Green asked.

"What the bloody hell?" Skipjack nodded.

Green went inside and, a few minutes later, came out with several glasses and a bottle of brandy. Thunder rolled across the southern sky and light rain rode the breeze. At first, no one sought shelter under the porch, but no one refused the brandy.

Moments later, they were huddled inside. Rain thrummed and slapped the windows. They passed brandy until it disappeared. When rain slackened, all but Tom, Andy, and one of the Italians headed back to Green's place.

"How'd you get Andy, a man good as Andy?" Trapper asked.

"Better ask Brawl," Skipjack answered.

"Or Mr. Green," Brawl said.

Heading down to River Road, they passed the overturned wagon. The horse was stone stiff in the road, but the two bodies were gone.

"Where you think they are, Green?"

"There's not much point in thinking."

"But why would they do that?"

"Who you talking about?" Green asked.

"Sheriff Winston, damn it!"

"You don't know that," Green said.

"We don't know anything," Brawl added.

"I don't believe you people," Skipjack said.

"Just keep steady now, Mr. Skipper; we be home soon," Trapper said.

"We got you covered, Skipjack."

"Mr. Green, you sure got that right," Brawl said.

Big Boy, with Green astride, led the way. Skipjack hustled up to Trapper as they ascended Green's hill.

"You never knew of the sheriff's involvement? Is that what I am supposed to take away?"

"Yes, sir. Your brother seemed natural. Never knew none of it."

"You never knew?"

"No, sir, not hardly. Just trying to do peoples' bidding. Yours too, I was led to understand."

"Yet you never told me," Skipjack said harshly.

"Skipjack . . ." Green said over his shoulder.

"Yes, sir. Told to keep secret. Secret you would deny."

"Forgive me, Trapper," Skipjack said. For a few moments, the group climbed the hill in silence, then Skipjack encouraged his mount to sidle up to Green's.

"What do you think?"

Green took his time answering. When he spoke, his words fell slowly.

"I know less than you and you know nothing. You're fishing blind."

"Can you blame me?"

"No, but I can't help. Who has any earthly idea what these fools planned?"

"Will you help me with the sheriff and all?"

"I swear I will, but there may be no answer. You must calm down. Marcie needs you. Your son needs you more than you could know. Believe me on this."

"We're here for you, sir," Brawl said.

"That's right," Trapper said. "Yes, that's right."

"Sheriff's goose has turned to crow," Green said aside to Skipjack. "Now it's time for him to eat."

"Forgive me," Skipjack said softly.

"Come on, let's get a nightcap. Your family's safe. We can discuss this in the morning."

Without joy, booze was glue. Brawl, Andy, and Trapper were persuaded to guard the back door by sleeping on cots in the mudroom off the kitchen. Skipjack sluffed across the backyard to the guesthouse, where he found Marcie and Mary Frances rocking in front of the fireplace. Lacy was stretched out next to Billy.

One look at Skipjack told both women that it was past time for rest, and soon Marcie had Jack squatting in bathwater Bill had just vacated. She bathed him as gently as a child. His soiled, muddy garments hung from pegs on the wall, but there was nothing to be done about that. He shook his head as she kneaded his shoulders, and she looked into eyes that seemed stunned with both innocence and unwelcome knowledge. When she pulled his head into her breast, the child seemed to shift in her belly.

Skipjack blinked and whispered, "I'll never understand this, will I?"

"Jack, there's no way to say. Please trust: this too shall pass."

Billy jumped up and Lacy put her hand to his forehead and eased him down.

The lantern light went out and Mary Frances heard Marcie chide Skipjack as she toweled him off. She stared into darkness through her candle-flickered window and heard them creak across the plank floor and settle into bed in the adjoining room. She couldn't hear what was said, but was comforted by the timbre of their voices

Mary Frances pinched the candle's wick and her room went dark.

She prayed for her husband, crippled and alone. She prayed for Billy, Marcie, and Skipjack, too. She closed her eyes and rested her hand on her knife.

In the other room, Marcie stroked Skipjack's head as he dug deeper into the pillows. She whispered his name, but he never answered. After a good while, she tiptoed in to check on Billy. She bent over to listen to his breathing and Lacy touched her cheek with the back of her hand. In a voice so low that Marcie was never quite sure she really heard it, Lacy said all was well.

Mary Frances, always a light sleeper, awakened with a foggy notion something was amiss. The hollow feeling steadily filled with certainty. If it was true, she felt sick about it.

Had Miss Aleeta brought three local runaways and had she, Mary Frances, locked them up in the whiskey shed and promised food and water they didn't get? When Skipjack burst in, had she forgotten all about them? She shook her head, but it wasn't a dream. She clenched her fists. There was nothing to be done now. Still she couldn't sleep for worrying and she slipped onto the front porch with her pipe.

She had barely inhaled the first puff when the door opened behind her, and Skipjack, wrapped in a blanket, quietly floated up beside her.

"Got a light?" he whispered.

She drew on her pipe and handed it to him. He lit a cigar stub off the hot core. When he handed the pipe back, she had to draw heavily and in the faint glow motioned him to lean closer. "We got three in the whiskey house. Didn't think to tell before."

Skipjack sighed, then sucked on his cigar.

"Barely got 'em in. She brung 'em a little early. Nobody saw, but don't ask how."

"Dawn in an hour."

"I'll get 'em fixed after a while."

Before Skipjack could reply, the door opened, and Marcie stepped out.

"Jack, is everything all right?"

"Sure is, I suppose. Couldn't sleep."

"Must've woke him, Miss Marcie. I couldn't sleep for anything."

"Wish you both would get back to bed. Whatever it is can keep."
Skipjack stubbed his cigar.

"Come on, Mary Frances, Marcie's right, morning comes quickly."

"You go on in. Morning's nudging the hilltop."

———————

Green's fine front porch crowned the valley through which the silvery Ohio River snaked. On the porch, two tables were spread with platters of ham, bacon, eggs, corn fritters, grits, and biscuits. Johnson poured coffee and a young woman poured water. Lacy and Andy stood to the side and nobody seemed to notice until Green insisted they sit down.

"This is no time for that; now sit," he said with a voice like a lash.

Trapper, who was already seated at the end of one table with two empty seats on each side of him, stood and offered his seat to Andy, so that he and Lacy could sit side by side. Green chuckled loudly and waved his hand.

"No time for that either. Sit down, Trapper, Andy, Lacy. Just sit."

"I was just, I was trying—"

"Trapper, I believe everyone present appreciates what you were trying to do. Hold your fire." Green was still smiling as he bowed his head. "Dear God of our fathers, we thank you for deliverance from evil and praise you with all humbleness and gratitude for the bounty spread before us. May we partake of this blessing full of your grace, truth, and loving spirit. Please guide us to fulfill your purpose and may we abide with you forever and ever. In Christ's name we ask. Amen."

"Amen," said Mary Frances, then everyone else said amen as well.

"So, let's eat," Green said with a mischievous grin. Andy and Lacy quickly glanced at each other. Skipjack placed his hand on Andy's shoulder, and when he did, Marcie patted Billy's knee and bumped Lacy gently with her shoulder.

"Thornton, there is no way to thank you for this. 'Unprecedented' is a big word for me, but I heard Clay use it a number of times, so I think I will try it out. This hospitality and helpfulness is unprecedented in all of my lifetime, and I want you to understand that me and mine will never forget. Will we, son? Will we, wife? Will we, Andy and Lacy?"

"What about Brawl and Mr. Trapper?" Billy asked.

Brawl burst out laughing and raised his coffee mug as if making a toast. Trapper grinned toothlessly.

"Eat before it gets cold," Green said.

"Son, Brawl and Trapper know what I'm talking about. Praise God, so do you, apparently."

"Amen, Skipjack," Brawl said. Trapper, sparkling, chewed and grinned.

From down on the river, a calliope screeched into tune and proceeded to prance through a spirited jig, then another with a slightly less sour pitch edged into the melody and, with somewhat more volume, soon smothered the first, though the weak sister could still be heard needling below.

"Must be a boat race," Green chuckled. "Bet you another enters the fray."

No sooner had he said that, then a much louder calliope overrode the two of them and left them wheezing behind. Green dug into his plate with knife and fork.

"We hear it all up here," he said.

CHAPTER 16

ARE YOU SURE IT'S LUCK?

After breakfast, Green offered Skipjack a taste of whiskey in his office. Skipjack declined at first and then changed his mind.

"I'll hold on to those documents and stash 'em in my safe. You don't need to be carrying them around."

"How the hell you think they planned to get away with it?" Skipjack asked. "Did they suppose they could convince folks I would just pick up and run?"

"Who knows? Dead folk don't talk."

"Guess I always knew he was rotten. Someway I wouldn't let myself believe it."

"You were looking after your little brother."

"I covered his ass for years."

"Not so hard to figure. But would you ever guess the boy could do what he did?" Green said softly.

"No, not really."

"No way to predict."

Skipjack reached into his coat pocket and extracted the sheath of papers. He handed them to Green, picked up his glass, took a slug.

"Can you call the sheriff off with that?"

Green rocked back in his chair, closed his eyes.

"I will bet you the sheriff is long past that. He knows he stepped in it. If he ain't headed west yet, I guarantee he will. These papers are safe, but I doubt we need them. Bet you a dollar the mayor drops by for lunch."

"You think he was part of it?"

"How would I know?"

"Why would he drop in?"

"Wouldn't be surprised if he was hungry, and if I were you, I wouldn't know much."

"Well, I don't, as it turns out," Skipjack said.

"More?" Green asked, lifting the bottle.

"Suppose I've had enough," Skipjack said.

"You have had your share, old friend. No need to talk now, is there?"

———

One of Green's men had been sent to summon the sheriff. When he returned, he reported that the sheriff was investigating a homicide and would be tied up most all day.

"I hate being wrong," Green said to Skipjack as they sipped whiskey at the tavern. "I tell you something told me the mayor would show."

"Why'd you think he would?"

"Maybe try to smooth things over. I wouldn't think he was directly involved. But the fact he ain't here makes me wonder. Like you said, you met with them both."

"But looking back, I feel more like Sheriff Winston was simply trying to discredit me. It was an accidental meeting to begin with, and I never did get the idea the mayor knew what was going on. He seemed thick if you know what I mean."

"I'll grant you that, but I wouldn't doubt there is some collusion."

"Could be," Skipjack said. "I wouldn't know."

"Well, will you look over there? Hot damn! I knew it. Just look distraught and don't say anything."

"I am distraught," Skipjack said under his breath. He looked up and watched the mayor approach.

The mayor, flanked by two aides, stopped in front of the table and nodded solemnly.

"May I join you gentlemen?"

When Green nodded, the mayor dismissed his aides and settled in a chair as Skipjack focused his gaze on the tan milky river and snipped a cigar. Both Green and Skipjack remained silent. Finally, Green opened his palm.

"Something's not right. I want you to know something's not adding up," the mayor said softly as he leaned forward, watery eyes focused on both men, but neither responded.

"I do not control the county. My job is the city. My chief is a decent man. You both know that. Duties overlap, and you know that, too. The sheriff's department covers the entire county and a small part of this county is mine. I like to think I run a clean operation."

"Who says you don't?" Skipjack asked.

"Mr. Maddox, if lawlessness was localized and would stay put, it would make things one hell of a lot easier. When we had our visit at the Galt House with the sheriff, I was attempting to learn as much as I could about a gang that did not respect boundaries. I had been told by the sheriff that they were on your property, and he had also informed me that you claimed that your own brother might have been the gang's leader."

"Mr. Mayor, I hope you also recall that I encouraged you to pay attention to the sheriff, because he was much better informed than I."

"I do remember, sir," the mayor said with a smile. "That is precisely why I am here. You made your point. You stated that if the sheriff could dispute your rendering of facts, then it stood to reason he was better informed. Is that not what you said?"

"Pretty damn close."

"Yes, I was impressed by your passion as much as by your reasoning. You suggested I query the sheriff."

"True."

"Well, I'm here to tell the dumb bastard has shit his nest," the mayor whispered.

"Whiskey all right?" Skipjack asked. The mayor nodded. Skipjack circled his head with his forefinger.

"I donated to get you elected and may again if you tell me what's going on," Green said.

"Well, Mr. Green, I appreciate your support and candor. Truth is, Ballard Winston and I have been butting heads since boyhood. We grew up in the same end of town, and I suppose for a while, we seemed to share pretty good values. I believe mine have evolved, and I hope they've grown stronger. Hate to say, but it would seem Ballard Winston's have regressed.

"Power can be a wonderful incentive. We both sought it. We fought and won. Ballard Winston desired the best for this community; only trouble is, I'm afraid, he'd do anything necessary to stay atop. He always wants to be baddest dog, so he sucks up to big dreams."

The mayor accepted his drink and reached for his wallet. Skipjack waved Julie off with a wink.

"To cut to the chase," the mayor continued, "after delving into Ballard Winston's dealings, we discovered that he aspired to build a gambling enterprise that would stretch from where we sit most all the way downtown."

Green and Skipjack burst out laughing. People at nearby tables turned and stared. The mayor took a sip and leaned in closer.

"It's true," he said. "If we had known how consumed he was by this, by this ambition, we may have done things differently. But we didn't know about your brother. That's where Sheriff Winston screwed up. Some folks out of New Orleans were scouting. That's how we first heard rumors. Then Bancroft turned up dead. That didn't smell right. He didn't fit in with the bunch we knew of. Then seemed to me it was unusual that the sheriff was so set on maligning Skipjack and implicating him as the center of a crime ring and runaway slave runner. Then by chance, we met and that wasn't my impression of Mr. Maddox at all.

"So, we dug a little deeper and found out about the killings in the jail and that scoundrel who ended up down here driving Bancroft's buggy. The façade started crumbling, but I guess not fast enough. Two men dead on your road last night, trying to steal a slave, Mr. Maddox?"

Skipjack and Thornton Green peered into each other's eyes. They both laughed reservedly.

"What? Have I said something wrong?" the mayor asked.

"Drink up, mayor," Green said, signaling for another round.

"Did you hear about the two who . . ." Skipjack trailed off and lowered his head.

Green said, "Two others—a man and a woman up to no good—were killed in Skipjack's house last night."

"What are you talking about?" the mayor said.

"I'm talking killers," Skipjack said. Green coaxed him back into his seat. "Killers! My brother and whatever she was. Did you hear about them?"

The mayor's face slackened. He shook his head in quick short motions. Nobody said anything and when the next round of drinks arrived, they adjourned to Skipjack's office.

OPAQUE

As soon as the door was shut and locked, Skipjack sat behind his desk.

"Key's in the door, Mr. Mayor, you can leave at any time, but you may want to listen. Ain't that right, Green?"

"At this point, it can't hurt."

"No one knows," Skipjack whispered and engaged the mayor's eyes.

The mayor settled into the armchair across from Skipjack.

"It don't matter what you do or don't know. Let's let that sink in, Mr. Mayor."

Green slid his chair near the wall and leaned back until he was up on his tiptoes.

"You should take heed," Green said.

"Your name does not appear on the documents that we possess. Do you know what I am referencing, sir?"

"I surely don't," the mayor said.

"Well, then, you are lucky."

"I don't understand, sir."

"You'll never have to." Skipjack smiled. "We'll keep everything safely locked away and you'll never have to explain anything."

"I wish you would make yourself more clear, sir."

"If you know nothing at all, there is no less or more."

"What are you driving at, Mr. Maddox?" the mayor asked.

"Opaque."

"Opaque?"

"You know what it means, don't you, Green?"

Green nodded and smiled.

"What exactly do you know about Bancroft, Winston, and Maddox?"

"Nothing, I swear to the Almighty," the mayor said, hand flat on his breast.

"So, it is opaque to you, is it?"

"Skipjack Maddox, I swear I have no earthly idea what you're talking about."

"Would you prefer it remained opaque, mayor?"

"You can be the judge," the mayor replied. "What do I know?"

"You didn't know there were two dead bodies in my house last night, did you?"

"Would just as soon not."

"Perhaps you might prefer certain information remains unknown," Skipjack said.

"Something to consider, mayor," Green said. "I could keep the documents secure until such time as they may be needed."

"Opaque," Skipjack said. "Dark as this office at midnight; no light escapes these walls."

"I have no idea what you're talking about, gentlemen," the mayor said as he stood, "but I must be on my way. My chief constable's sleuthing skills leave much to be desired, and I have already told you the sheriff has damaged his own reputation. I am certainly not aligned with him in any way. I hesitate to say more. Guard your documents, whatever they may be. Be assured I know nothing."

"Opaque, Mr. Mayor," Skipjack said. "I am certain you can handle the key and let yourself out. I would stand, but I have indigestion."

"Good afternoon," Green said, as the mayor turned the key and let himself out.

As soon as the door shut, Green and Skipjack slumped back and smiled. Both lit cigars and smoke curlicued through shafts of afternoon light. Neither spoke. Skipjack drained his whiskey and noticed that the mayor's glass sat across the desk untouched. He poured half into his glass and half into Green's without even asking,

"So, what did you think?"

Green picked up his libation and heaved with amusement.

"Mr. Mayor was on a fishing trip. Where'd you learn to talk like that, is what I want to know."

"Now, Green, you always knew Marcie was a reader."

"What's she read?"

"You ever hear of the Holy Bible?"

"Of course, I've heard of the Holy Bible."

"You ever heard of *Pilgrim's Progress*?"

"Who do you think I am?" Green said.

"What about *Gulliver's Travels*?"

"I think you stuck me there."

"She reads a bunch. I suppose stuff rubs off."

———

Before riding home, Skipjack checked on Mary Frances, who was barking orders. He winked at Lacy and she pointed at Mary Frances whose back was turned; Mary Frances spun, hoisting her carving knife. Skipjack grinned and motioned her aside.

"They're watered and fed," she whispered, then signaled a cook searing a pork chop. She turned back to Skipjack. "You best get home. That boy needs you. I'll take care here."

"On my way. God bless you," Skipjack said. Mary Frances shook her head dismissively. Skipjack saw Lacy purse her lips and try to look busy, but when their eyes briefly met, she gave him a thankful glance.

"Go see to your boy," Mary Frances reiterated. "Marcie, too." As she nudged him toward the door, she said, "Suppose the mayor told you Louis is dead."

"What are you saying?"

"I just heard a while ago. Found hung downtown. Say the sheriff's calling it a suicide."

"My ass."

"Take that ass home. Your family needs you."

———

Mules are sturdy, steady, and often intelligent. If Skipjack had succeeded in urging Jessie out the drive as fast as he intended, he might never have run into Brawl. The damn mule would not be hurried, until finally Skipjack aligned his pulse with Jessie's stubborn certain pace.

As they turned onto River Road, Brawl rolled up. Skipjack didn't rein in because Jessie had already come to a full stop and seemed more interested in wiggling ears than walking. Brawl halted his team and raised his right hand.

"They're falling apart, Skipper," he said.

"What you say?"

"I run into a deputy I know who's beating it out of the county."

"What are you telling me?"

"It's hard to keep a lid on a boiling pot."

"What boiling? You talking about Louis?" Skipjack asked.

"You know something?" Brawl asked slowly.

"Mary Frances told me that the sheriff was calling Louis's hanging a suicide," Skipjack said.

"Before evening's out, they'll know the sheriff up and down. I'm telling you the whole damn bunch is scurrying. That deputy sure didn't mind telling me he had nothing to do with any of it. Way he carried on, sheriff will be standing alone by morning."

"They were all in on it, you think?"

"No, but some might know more than is healthy."

"Makes you sick, don't it?"

"Yes, sir. You don't see her, till she's slinking away."

"Any idea where the bodies went?"

"No sir, but we cleaned best we could."

"Marcie up there?"

Brawl nodded.

"You might want to remember Tom some way. That was nasty business."

"He still there?" Skipjack asked.

"He'll stay the night if you want. I think you should ask him to. You need rest."

"You haven't heard anything about Brother's body?"

"Where you hope to put him if you find him?"

"Jesus, Brawl, I don't know."

"Hard to say, but where you think he planned to put you?"

"That's not something I want to think."

"Go home," Brawl said. "We got you covered."

"How can I ever thank you for what you've done?"

Brawl broke into a broad grin and said, "It'll come, Mr. Maddox. You'll think of something."

Skipjack stared into Brawl's squinted eyes.

"I can't believe this," he said.

"Who can? Get home. This here's a crown of thorns."

AFTERMATH

A cool shiver shimmied through Skipjack's shoulders and spine as he rode uphill. He blew out and sagged. How could it come to this? His teeth struggled to find alignment, so he could tighten his jaws. Then Jessie laid her ears back and came to a full halt. Skipjack stared deep into the undergrowth on either side of the drive. He clucked his tongue and Jessie strode forward, and as she did, he seemed to catch his breath.

"Easy," he said aloud.

As soon as Skipjack espied the slant of his roof, Billy and Tom Thurston stepped out from behind a huge maple tree. Tom froze with his rifle forty-five degrees into the sky. Billy paced onto the roadway with his shotgun pointed down. His eyes bored into Skipjack, who tried to fetch an expression that would complement the one that carved Billy's face.

Skipjack dismounted and handed the reins to Billy and was about to ask the boy to please put Jessie up. He was planning to say he was tired, but then he reached for the boy and hugged him to his chest.

He held the boy close, while he tamped down whatever was about to leap from his chest. God only knew what was right to say. Tom stood rock steady. Skipjack realized he might have squeezed too hard and relaxed his grip.

"You all right?"

"Yeah, I suppose I am, son. How's your momma?"

"She seems bossy, you ask me," Billy said conspiratorially.

"What's she doing?"

"Scrubbing everything with boiling water and lye."

"Why aren't you helping?"

"She bossed us out. She won't let us help."

"Well, son, you boys put Jessie up. Give her oats. I'll see if I can't settle Momma."

Tom nodded when Skipjack thanked him for his help. Skipjack sucked in as much fresh air as he possibly could, then planted his foot on his front porch step, crossed his fingers, and knocked on wood before opening the door.

───────

All furniture was piled in the middle of the room. Marcie was scrubbing the floor. She would not be deterred, but after a while, she slowed some. He knew not to rush her. When he offered to help, she gave him such a look that he froze. What she was scrubbing was invisible, but he knew that was the wrong thing to say, so he said nothing.

"We don't have to stay tonight, Marcie. You know we could stay at Thornton Green's."

He watched her scour between chestnut planks with the edge of her brush and somehow block out ugliness. Skipjack felt helpless, useless, and sick all at once.

"For the love of God, I need a hug," he said, taking what he felt to be his last best chance.

Marcie glanced fiercely, eyes ablaze, turned away, and scrubbed.

"We almost lost it all last night," Skipjack said softly. "Please, love, let's not lose it now."

Marcie thrust her brush into the bucket, stirred it around, then gazed into Skipjack's eyes. He saw a mask as dreadfully empty as living death, a desolation he never had seen before. Her eyes were condemnation of all humankind. Then, eyes closed, she threw her arms around his waist and moaned. Both of them shook together until she stood leaning against him, swaying, and sobbing.

"Please, woman, hold me close," Skipjack said.

Skipjack kneaded Marcie's shoulders and buried his face in her hair.

"We'll get through this, if we stick tight."

"I'm worried about Billy," Marcie said.

"We got to take a step at a time."

"Make it disappear. That's what I'm after, isn't it?"

"Marcie, that won't work."

"Why did this happen?"

"If you couldn't ask, it would be worse."

"You sure? Feel I'm the cause."

Skipjack laughed and hugged tighter.

"Don't flatter yourself. Are you in charge of wickedness? Tell me what part. Better grab hold you want to survive."

"I'm so stirred around," she whispered, as a shudder passed through.

"Somewhat confused myself," Skipjack drawled. "Perhaps you can help set me straight. Think I should have a talk with Billy?"

"Yes, I do."

"Then, please pour me a drink and come out to the porch."

"What about this?" Marcie said with a sweep of her arm.

"I need your help. Perfect can wait."

Billy was sitting on the lowest step of the front porch. Downhill, Tom Thurston leaned against a hackberry. Skipjack sat beside the boy and placed his pistol down between them but said nothing. The first strong chill of the season was in the air. The boy stared downhill to where Tom stood guard, exhaled, and Skipjack saw two smoky pink plumes dissolve. Skipjack felt the need to speak quickly, but Billy beat him.

"Tom said to mind myself. Momma told me to stick with Tom. I feel like nobody wants me around."

"Andy's uphill, ain't he?" Skipjack asked.

"Ain't seen him leave," Billy said.

"You won't either. You know why not?" Skipjack asked.

"No, sir."

"Because he's a true son of a bitch; a good man, like you are, son."

"A son of a bitch?" Bill protested and squirmed to face Skipjack.

"Careful with that gun, boy, and forget the 'son of a bitch' part. You think about the good man, the good man. I'll never forget what you've done my whole life. You stepped up, saved yourself, and your mother and me. You did right. Very few would have had the sense or the guts to do what you did, and I want—"

"But I blowed Uncle Timothy's head off. Am I going to hell?" he asked, biting his lower lip.

"What do you think?" Skipjack said.

"What else could I do?"

Skipjack put his hand on Billy's shoulder and pulled him close.

"Maybe you could have asked him real nice to shut up."

"They were going to kill us all," the boy exclaimed in a voice infused with disbelief. Tom looked toward them. Skipjack tugged Billy near and stroked his head.

"No one but you. You did what had to be. That's hard and ugly sometimes."

"Closed my eye when I pulled the trigger," Billy confessed.

"Opened enough to see the knife, didn't you?"

"That time I didn't think."

"Thank God."

Marcie walked out and handed Skipjack a glass of whiskey and Billy a glass of cider.

"Thank you, sweetheart, but what about you?"

"I don't know," Marcie said.

"How about some port? That might brace you."

Skipjack went into the kitchen, poured Marcie a glass of port, then called uphill for Andy to come down. His glass was a bit light, so he spiked it. There were no cooking smells in the kitchen and the stove was smoldering low. He stoked it with a few chunks of hickory to fend off chill. When Andy appeared at the back door, Skipjack motioned him in.

"Getting cool out there?"

"There's a sting," Andy said.

Skipjack slipped Andy some cash and handed him a glass of whiskey. Andy assumed a determined look. Skipjack nodded, "Please hitch the mare and fetch some dinner, enough for all. I'll make it up, I promise."

"What happens if Mary Frances has a side of beef?" Andy conjectured.

"Bring it on and everything else you can load."

"This might be a long night, mightn't it?"

"What do you know?"

"Nothing, sir, except a feeling," Andy grinned.

"You need rum, don't you?"

"Don't have to put it like that, sir."

"And two bottles of rum and a cobbler of some kind, if she's fixed one. Please hurry," Skipjack added, as he stuffed some more money into Andy's outstretched hand. "Be careful. Don't stop for nothing or nobody."

"I'll fly like the devil and be right back."

————

Skipjack was bone tired and as Andy strolled to the stable, Skipjack settled in his chair. He didn't want to talk about anything, nor did he want to go anywhere, but stretched in certain knowledge he would have to do both.

"Where's Andy off to?" Billy asked.

"Tavern for food. You're hungry, aren't you?"

"Can I go?"

"No, I need you here."

"You think we're all right, don't you, Jack?"

"Marcie, they won't be back. They're running."

"I could cook something," Marcie said.

"So could I," Billy said.

"Please indulge me," Skipjack said quietly. "There's also another reason I'm sending Andy."

"Why?" Billy asked.

"All you need to know is dinner's coming," Skipjack answered as he waved at Andy.

"If everything's all right, why can't I go?"

"Listen to your father," Marcie said.

Skipjack covered Marcie's hand gently. They both leaned closer and clinked glasses, then leaned closer still until their lips brushed lightly. Billy watched as if they were insects. He asked why nobody ever tapped glasses with him.

"Don't be in such a hurry, honey," Marcie said as she tapped his cider mug with her glass.

"You'll get your share," Skipjack said.

Billy smiled, and then looked puzzled.

"Do you think Uncle Timothy and that woman's gone to hell?"

Both Skipjack and Marcie leaned back, then studied each other. Billy scraped his mug across the planks of the porch and looked up earnestly. First Skipjack closed his eyes, then as Marcie shut hers, her smile became a thin taut line. Neither spoke.

"They're dead. Did I send them to hell? And where would we go if they killed us?"

"Please, honey," Marcie whispered. "Don't talk so loud."

"Don't you think I should know?"

"Damn right, you need to know," Skipjack said gruffly. Billy sat up straight and Marcie fidgeted. Skipjack raised his hand. "We all hanker to know, yet none does. Who knows where anyone goes? Do you know for sure where Andy's gone?"

"Down to the tavern."

"God knows, I hope so, but although I sent him and gave him money, I sure can't guarantee he'll bring dinner. Surely you will grant me that, won't you?"

"He won't run off, do you think?"

"Why not," Skipjack asked. "He's got money. He could have that, the buggy, the mare, and the dinner besides—all to himself. Why wouldn't he?"

"Andy's not like that. If he was, you wouldn't send him."

"But you will admit it's his choice? To come back or not, that is?"

"Sure, but he'll be back."

"But not because of me?" Skipjack said.

"No, he'll be back because Andy's Andy."

"So, it's him doing it. Not me bringing dinner, but him."

"But you told him."

"Your daddy asked him to," Marcie interjected.

"I can't make anybody go anywhere, Billy," Skipjack said as Marcie lifted his drained glass. "Neither can you. I can't send a man to heaven. I can't send a man to hell. I can ask a man to go to the tavern, but I can't make him. I hope he returns with our dinner, God knows."

"But he will, won't he? I sure am hungry," Billy said.

Marcie hollered from the kitchen for Billy to bring his mug if he wanted cider. Billy stood up and shook his head.

"Maybe you should have had Momma send him. He wouldn't do her wrong, I don't think."

"Billy, come in here now," Marcie called from the kitchen.

"Better check on your mother," Skipjack said, as he peered down the drive at Tom in the skyward pink wash of gathering mist.

NOT FOR LOVE OR MONEY

With each step creakier than last and a moon too bright to suit, Skipjack made his way slowly downstairs, one gentle footfall after another. He knew Andy was at the back stoop and that Tom was on the front porch, but the way his too-full stomach was rumbling, he half expected Gracie, Billy, and all to interrogate him at the bottom of the staircase.

In the kitchen beneath the bedroom, where he had left Marcie lightly snoring, he knotted his boot laces, then slipped out the back and lifted a finger as Andy stood, features puzzling in pale moonlight. Skipjack leaned forward, whispered so softly that he had to try twice before he was understood.

"Tell Tom that Jessie and I will be right back."

After Andy acknowledged, Skipjack walked to the stable and was soon riding quietly. His shadow fell upon silvery glistened grasses. Jessie seemed excited. Her ears twitched, and Skipjack stroked her neck to keep her calm. She farted loudly. Skipjack heard Tom Thurston snicker. He clucked, and Jessie lengthened her stride and stepped into deep shade of thicket that lined the drive.

Once on River Road, Jessie turned toward the tavern. Skipjack unleashed one of his dinner's contributions. Jessie complemented him with a more vigorous stride and another sputtering report. The only light was that of the moon, damn bright, and hardly a cloud. His advantage was that only a fool would try to sneak anything across river on a night clear as this.

The squat stone beige of the tavern against the green mass of cottonwoods on the bank and the metallic glint of the river beyond were comforting sights. He perked up and blanked out all unpleasant intrusive stuff. At the tavern, he tied Jessie to a post beside the stable and took a stroll.

Down on the shore, as he checked the skiff, a large cloud blotted the moon. Skipjack prayed for dozens more, but it appeared that his prayer would likely go unanswered. The sky was clear and full of stars. The raucous sounds of a boat party were hushed and smoothed by waves rhythmically sloshing. Then a calliope, commandeered by a drunkard, screeched and gleefully butchered "Yankee Doodle Dandy." Skipjack gritted his teeth, observed that the skiff was dry enough, turned, and strode toward the whiskey house. The discordant calliope squalled horribly, then abruptly stopped and faint tittering laughter gave birth to eerie silence.

Skipjack slunk in shadow until he stood atop the thick limestone slab in front of the door. He turned his big key, jiggled, and shoved the heavy oak door open.

"Come on," he said. "It's time. Move quick. Keep quiet. Stay with me."

Had he spoken into an empty room? A spider's breathing would make more noise.

"Time to go," Skipjack whispered toward murmur and scuffle. "Hurry, now. No time to waste."

As the man, a good head taller than he, stepped into the shaft of moonlight, Skipjack motioned with his head toward the river. Skipjack sensed commotion in the corner of the room; a baby whimpered, a voice shushed.

"Quiet that child and please hurry."

The man reached behind into the dark and soon two women, one almost a child, and the other, older, wrapped in a shawl, holding a tiny infant, stood beside him.

"Whatever you do, keep everyone quiet."

The man whose face was dark as Bible leather nodded. The baby fussed.

"You keep that child quiet or we ain't going. Choice is yours. Stay close."

As soon as Skipjack locked the door, they traipsed and ducked between trees. On the river, downstream voices mingled with light-hearted laughter.

Channel traffic? Next to none.

Most boats settled in.

Damn moon too damn bright.

"Climb aboard."

"Where you want us, sir?" the man asked.

"If you can shoot a rifle, you're in the bow," Skipjack whispered.

"Sure can."

"Make 'em stay low. Fire at nothing unless I say." He handed the man the rifle.

Skipjack shoved off and pulled into the river. Within several tugs, he was contending with current. To his relief, the calliope launched into a rousing martial tune and then before he had taken twenty strokes, eased into a lullaby. The baby whimpered once, then latched onto mother's tit. The calliope diddled inane melodies as Skipjack dug in, pointed the skiff upstream, and reminded himself he had done this before.

With each stroke, he asked himself why. It sure wasn't money. His nagging muscles concurred. Was it love? No. The oars grew heavy as tree trunks. Skipjack felt grateful it was October and cool. For a moment, he lifted and let the skiff drift. A chill breeze touched the nape of his neck and seemed to wash his face. Then Skipjack pulled again and again and did not stop until the skiff's bow scratched through pebbles that littered the Indiana shore.

"All right, hurry. Climb the hill. You'll find a church of friends up yonder. Maybe a light will shine your way. Maybe not. I don't know. God bless you, but please, shove me off."

"Thank you," the man said.

"Welcome." Skipjack reclaimed his rifle.

LUCK?

Skipjack was so weary he sloughed through dead water, allowing himself to drift a hundred yards before he dipped oars. Still upstream, he pivoted and rowed at a spot above the creek mouth, then allowed himself to coast the last quarter mile.

When he hit sandy bank, a northerly breeze chilled. One glance at the moon's halo and stars stretched out forever quickened his pace toward the tavern. But then, an internal voice insisted, *Down now!*

He dove into damp, dew-laden grass, crushing fall's first crackling leaves, then *blam!* He smelled dark river-bottom soil and bits of bark pattered his head, neck, and back. There was a flash across the creek and another echoing roar. Skipjack heard the guttural outcry of a man tasting something much too hot, then a rasping gasp, followed by unnerving silence. He lay still as a corpse and listened.

Riverbank darkened as cloud occluded the moon. Skipjack belly-crawled a few feet, and when motion drew no fire, stood and loped bent low. Part of him wanted to discover what had just happened, but instead, he prayed that Jessie was still there to get him home. He wove his way through shadows and was grateful to find Jessie tethered.

———

Without urging, Jessie broke into a full trot with Skipjack low on her neck. No thought crossed his mind until they were on the lane through the woods. The next thought was so simple it made him laugh. Goddamn! Don't want to get shot by my own. He reined Jessie in and hoarsely called out it was him. He called Tom Thurston and Andy by name, until Tom responded, "Ride on up, sir."

It wasn't until then that Skipjack tried to piece it together. Didn't try hard; his throat was so dry he could have drunk a pitcher of water. He craved whiskey and a strong cigar.

"You all right, sir?" Tom asked as he stepped into the road.

Skipjack nodded and then said, "Yes, if you'll take Jessie that would help. Thank you."

"You ain't been hit, sir?"

"No. Everything fine here?"

Tom nodded.

"Hurry. I'll watch the front till you get back. Give her extra oats. Make sure she's watered."

He expected to see Marcie in the kitchen, but though a candle was burning, it appeared everyone was asleep. Skipjack poured down some water and then teased that same glass with whiskey, grabbed a cigar, then walked back to the porch. Within a minute or two, Tom hurried over and asked if there was anything special he should do.

"Please, just take your place. I'll take care of you in the morning, Tom, and I thank you."

Skipjack found Andy up by the springhouse.

"A bite in the air," Andy said.

"Maybe, I should fetch you a dram."

"Glad you're not hurt, sir."

"You heard?"

"Two shots. Didn't know what."

"Still don't, Andy. Somebody shot at me. Don't know who. I cleared out, fearing worse."

"Nothing here."

Skipjack exhaled deeply, then remembered to light his cigar. Andy's face—made visible by match glow—twisted into concern.

"What?" Skipjack asked.

"You're bleeding, sir. Your forehead's bleeding," Andy said.

"It's nothing, believe me. Need you to go with me to the tavern right before first light."

"Yes, sir."

"I'll stand guard a minute. Go fix what you need. Be quiet and quick about it."

"You sure?"

"Take this glass and pour me a shot."

———

The branches, the stars above, everything was spinning. Andy sidled back through the door and handed Skipjack his replenished drink. Rich tobacco smoke and the sweet bite of whiskey seemed to calm Skipjack's nerves. He stared over the tree line at stars gauzed by a flurry of clouds. Skipjack laughed under his breath. Lord, I sure could have used those critters earlier. He laughed aloud, then coughed himself into silence. Not to be complaining.

What had happened? He didn't know. Did he duck every time he heard "down"? Had he actually heard "get down" or was it something he felt, or knew he had to do? Did someone get shot or was it a rotten tree limb falling? He was tired and needed to go to bed.

"You say what, sir?" Andy asked as he walked back out with his rifle, plate of food, and a full glass of rum.

"You heard me thinking, Andy?"

"Must have, elsewise, you're questioning out loud."

"Damn, I must be tired."

"You got a right."

"See you first light. I'm turning in."

"You're covered, Mr. Maddox. Don't worry 'bout a thing."
Skipjack slipped in the back door and tiptoed to bed.

———

He left the candle burning in the kitchen. Andy let it burn, until it was guttering just before dawn. How the devil was he to awaken him? Andy puzzled in the kitchen with hot wax between thumb and forefinger. The floor squeaked overhead and then a stair strained. Andy let himself out. A moment later, Skipjack joined him.

"Damn house smells like smoke," Skipjack muttered as he wrestled into his boots.

"Everything fine out here," Andy replied. "Just chilly."

"Fall's coming. You snuffed the candle, didn't you?"

"Yes, sir. I did that while I was figuring how to wake you."

"Strange world, ain't it, Andy?"

"Most peculiar. Yes, sir, it is."

"Getting light. You ready?"

"Let's go," Andy said.

———

"Nothing here," Andy said, scuffing with his boot.

"You can see where I was," Skipjack said, pointing down at bark fragments. "Here's the bullet hole right here." He slapped busted bark. Andy walked down closer to the river and snooped behind the largest sycamore.

"Might be there was someone here," he said, as he crouched.

Skipjack knelt, then walked over to the river's edge and studied the sand.

"Something dragged here, don't you think?"

"I reckon. Is this where you heard a thump?"

"Hell, I don't know, Andy. It happened fast."

"I heard two shots, but nothing here to tell."

"We best head back," Skipjack said.

"It's daylight now. Tom's all right. Appears you might have friends you don't even know."

"Enemies, too, but something sure told me to get down."

"Good thing you paid heed."

"Did you ever tally the times you have, Andy?"

"Starting my tally from here."

"Pays to listen, don't it?"

———

At the top of the hill, Skipjack and Andy could see Tom and Billy jawing on the front porch.

"Damn, I'm weary."

"What're you going to tell missus about where we was?"

"Maybe she's asleep."

"No, sir, I smell bacon."

"Can I explain what I don't understand?"

"Well, I plan to stay out of it," Andy said.

"For right now, I'll say I couldn't sleep. Think that's best."

"Twice in one night?" Andy queried.

"Stay out of it."

"Yes, sir."

"Best you do."

———

It was so chilly by midmorning, they laid a fire. To Skipjack's surprise, Marcie didn't ask anything and neither did Billy. Skipjack had snuggled back into bed with Marcie and somehow had slowed his heart and dozed off to wake up by himself in space large enough for stretching. Andy had been wrong. Billy had fried bacon, but when Skipjack finally descended the stairs, that bacon had been eaten and a slab of pork was frying in its grease. Marcie offered him a mug of coffee and her smile concealed no insinuations. He tried not to look taken aback.

"It's a hard time, Jack, but we can make it, if we have a mind."

Skipjack asked, "Are you all right?"

"Come over here and feel my belly, Jack."

"Is it—?"

"Just come feel."

Skipjack placed his hand low and Marcie guided it up the globe of her abdomen and smiled.

"Can you not feel?"

Beneath his hand a pressure punched, then slid slowly, creating new contours. Marcie's eyes sparkled.

"How can a man be so lucky?" he said barely above a whisper.

"Are you sure it's luck?" she asked.

———

Later.

"Even if Green's right and sheriff's run off, don't I need to check on Brother's body?"

"Lay still, honey."

"What about Billy?" Skipjack asked. "There's something I know I need to do."

"Close your eyes and dream moving pictures," Marcie said, placing her hand gently over his brow.

"I thought maybe to take him fishing."

"Relax. You're late. Brawl and Tom already have."

"Woman," Skipjack whispered, "there's bound to be something."

"Well, there's nothing you can do for Mary Frances and Lacy."

"Why not?" Skipjack asked with both eyes flickering.

"Because they're already cooking the wedding dinner you ordered up."

"I ordered up a wedding dinner?" Skipjack said, betraying a hint of smile.

"Yes. Close your eyes and don't ask the rest."

"Rest of what?"

"About how to make me comfortable in the short time we have."

"That's all you worry about?" Skipjack smiled.

"Isn't that enough for now?" Marcie whispered.

"Yes, it seems to be."

ABOUT THE AUTHOR

Ed Middleton was born in Louisville, Kentucky, and with the exception of exploratory years, has mostly always been blessed to live there. Aside from publishing poems and short fiction in mostly forgotten rags, he has worked in many capacities to pursue his quest to be forever learning and studying about and from the timeless world that surrounds us and the courageous ones who bear witness.

ACKNOWLEDGMENTS

The author would like to thank Susan Lindsey of
Savvy Communication LLC for her tireless and astute editing.
Further, Shellee Marie Jones deserves praise for
thoughtful and sensitive design work.

www.ingramcontent.com/pod-product-compliance
Lightning Source LLC
Chambersburg PA
CBHW071156250626
47159CB00001B/109